NIGHTWEBS

A Collection of Stories by

CORNELL WOOLRICH

NIGHTWEBS

edited by Francis M. Nevins, Jr.

1817

HARPER & ROW, PUBLISHERS
New York, Evanston, San Francisco, London

ACKNOWLEDGMENTS

Grateful acknowledgment is hereby made for permission to reprint the following stories by Cornell Woolrich:
"Graves for the Living." Originally published in *Dime Mystery*. Copyright
1937 by Popular Publications, Inc. Reprinted by permission of Popular Publications, Inc.
"The Red Tide." Originally published in *Street & Smith's Detective Story
Magazine*. Copyright 1940 by Street & Smith Publications, Inc. Copyright
renewed © 1968 by The Condé Nast Publications Inc. Reprinted by permission
of The Condé Nast Publications Inc.
"The Corpse Next Door." Originally published in *Detective Fiction Weekly*.
Copyright 1937 by Popular Publications, Inc. Reprinted by permission of Popu-
lar Publications, Inc.
"You'll Never See Me Again." Originally published in *Street & Smith's Detec-
tive Story Magazine*. Copyright 1939 by Street & Smith Publications, Inc.
Copyright renewed © 1967 by The Condé Nast Publications Inc. Reprinted by
permission of the agents for the Estate of Cornell Woolrich, Scott Meredith
Literary Agency, Inc.
"Dusk to Dawn." Originally published in *Black Mask*. Copyright 1937 by
Popular Publications, Inc. Reprinted by permission of Popular Publications, Inc.
"Murder at the Automat." Originally published in *Dime Detective*. Copyright
1937 by Popular Publications, Inc. Reprinted by permission of Popular Publica-
tions, Inc.
"Death in the Air." Originally published in *Detective Fiction Weekly*. Copy-
right 1936 by Popular Publications, Inc. Reprinted by permission of Popular
Publications, Inc.
"Mamie 'n' Me." Originally published in *All-American Fiction*. Copyright
1938 by Popular Publications, Inc. Reprinted by permission of Popular Publications, Inc.

(*Continued on the next page*)

FIRST EDITION

STANDARD BOOK NUMBER: 06-013173-X

LIBRARY OF CONGRESS CATALOG CARD NUMBER: 70-144199

"The Screaming Laugh." Originally published in *Clues Detective Stories.* Copyright 1938 by Street & Smith Publications, Inc. Copyright renewed © 1966 by The Condé Nast Publications Inc. Reprinted by permission of the agents for the Estate of Cornell Woolrich, Scott Meredith Literary Agency, Inc.

"Dead on Her Feet." Originally published in *Dime Detective.* Copyright 1935 by Popular Publications, Inc. Reprinted by permission of Popular Publications, Inc.

"One Night in Barcelona." Originally published in *Mystery Book Magazine.* Copyright 1947 by Best Publications Inc. Reprinted by permission of the agents for the Estate of Cornell Woolrich, Scott Meredith Literary Agency, Inc.

"The Penny-a-Worder." Originally published in *Ellery Queen's Mystery Magazine.* Copyright © 1958 by Davis Publications Inc. Reprinted by permission of the agents for the Estate of Cornell Woolrich, Scott Meredith Literary Agency, Inc.

"The Number's Up." Originally published in *Beyond the Night.* Copyright © 1959 by Cornell Woolrich. Reprinted by permission of the agents for the Estate of Cornell Woolrich, Scott Meredith Literary Agency, Inc.

"Too Nice a Day to Die." Originally published in *The Dark Side of Love.* Copyright © 1965 by Cornell Woolrich. Reprinted by permission of the agents for the Estate of Cornell Woolrich, Scott Meredith Literary Agency, Inc.

Grateful acknowledgment is also made to Allen J. Hubin for permission to reprint the following editorial and bibliographic material:

"Cornell Woolrich: Part I," by Francis M. Nevins, Jr. Originally published in *The Armchair Detective.* Copyright © 1968 by Allen J. Hubin.

"Cornell Woolrich: Part II," by Francis M. Nevins, Jr. Originally published in *The Armchair Detective.* Copyright © 1969 by Allen J. Hubin.

"Cornell Woolrich: Part III," by Francis M. Nevins, Jr. Originally published in *The Armchair Detective.* Copyright © 1969 by Allen J. Hubin.

"Cornell Woolrich: A Bibliography," by Harold Knott, Francis M. Nevins, Jr. and William Thailing. Originally published in *The Armchair Detective.* Copyright © 1969 by Allen J. Hubin.

The quotation by Edna St. Vincent Millay on page 358 is from *Collected Poems* by Edna St. Vincent Millay. Copyright 1923 by Edna St. Vincent Millay. Copyright renewed © 1951 by Norma Millay Ellis. Reprinted with the permission of Norma Millay Ellis.

I was only trying to cheat death. I was only trying to surmount for a little while the darkness that all my life I surely knew was going to come rolling in on me some day and obliterate me. I was only trying to stay alive a little brief while longer, after I was already gone. To stay in the light, to be with the living a little while past my time.

—CORNELL WOOLRICH

Contents

Contents

Introduction

It was an old sneaker that started it, an old soft-soled canvas gym shoe. It rubbed his heel raw, the heel became infected and the doctor made him keep his foot elevated for six weeks. When he began to walk again, he had completed the first draft of a novel. The beginning was that simple. Except that in his unfinished autobiography he said that it was jaundice, not a heel infection, that kept him immobilized, and that he recovered long before that first draft was finished. Which is truth, which a trick of memory? Nothing is that simple.

Cornell George Hopley-Woolrich was born in New York on December 4, 1903, and spent much of his childhood traveling

in Latin America with his father, a civil engineer. During the
Mexican revolutions prior to World War I, he collected spent
rifle cartridges—an apt hobby in view of his later career. He
seems to have been shunted back and forth between parents,
living with his socially prominent mother in New York during
the school year but traveling with his father during vacation
periods. It was not the healthiest way to go through adoles-
cence, and it left marks on his life and his work.

In the early 1920's he entered Columbia College, and one of
his contemporaries there came to attain the same eminence as
a historian of ideas that Woolrich was to achieve as a writer.
Jacques Barzun attended with Woolrich both a course in creative writing and one on the novel. (The latter course was taught
by Harrison R. Steeves, who himself wrote a memorable crime
novel, *Good Night, Sheriff,* 1941.) Barzun remembers Woolrich
as shy and introspective and mother-dominated even then, and
as keenly interested in literature. Woolrich would have gradu-
ated with the Class of 1925, but while he was an undergraduate
the incident took place that started him writing, and he left
school to write full time.

Very few photographs of Woolrich exist, but an interesting
verbal portrait appears in Chapter 5 of *I Wake Up Screaming*
(Dodd Mead, 1941), a novel by Steve Fisher who was a pulp-
writer contemporary of Woolrich. "He had red hair and thin
white skin and red eyebrows and blue eyes. He looked sick. He
looked like a corpse. His clothes didn't fit him. . . . He was frail,
grey-faced and bitter. He was possessed with a macabre humor.
His voice was nasal. You'd think he was crying. He might have
had T.B. He looked like he couldn't stand up in a wind." The
character's name is Cornell.

Woolrich's first novel, *Cover Charge,* was published by Boni
& Liveright in 1926, and even in its opening paragraph the
distinctive Woolrich style is already present: "Luminaires were
lit upon the walls, and from an orange dish a pencil-line of azure
hung breathlessly above an expiring cigarette." His next novel,

Children of the Ritz (1927), won first prize of $10,000 in a contest conducted jointly by *College Humor* and First National Pictures, which filmed the book in 1929. Woolrich was invited to Hollywood to help with the adaptation. It is to be noted that one of the dialogue-and-title writers working for First National around this time was a gentleman named William Irish.[1] While in Hollywood, Woolrich fell in love with and married a producer's daughter who left him after a few weeks and later had the marriage annulled. Woolrich returned to New York and his mother. Four more of his novels were published: *Times Square* (1929), the partially autobiographical *A Young Man's Heart* (1930), *The Time of Her Life* (1931), and *Manhattan Love Song* (1932). All of the early novels were heavily indebted to Scott Fitzgerald (who remained to the end one of Woolrich's favorite authors), but are at the same time authentically Woolrichian: love is the leitmotif, and the prose approaches poetry. "Blair heard the snap of the electric light, and the lining of his flickering eyelids turned vermilion," *A Young Man's Heart* begins.

In addition to the six novels, Woolrich between 1926 and 1932 published a number of short stories, two articles and a serial in such magazines as *College Humor, College Life, Illustrated Love, McClure's,* and *Smart Set.* But during 1933 not a single word appeared under his byline: the Depression had caught up to him. He did write another novel that year, called it *I Love You, Paris,* but was unable to sell it and finally threw it into the garbage, although at the end of his life he insisted that someone in Hollywood had read the manuscript while it was making the rounds and had without authorization based a movie on it.[2] In

1. Irish's name appears in the credits of three First National films of 1928–29, all directed by Benjamin Christensen: *Haunted House, Seven Footprints to Satan,* and *House of Horror.* He is not known to have worked on any other films.
2. Woolrich did not identify the movie he had in mind, but from his description it was probably *Bolero* (Paramount, 1934), directed by Wesley Ruggles, starring Carole Lombard and George Raft. According to the credits, the screenplay was by Horace Jackson from a story by Carey Wilson and Kubec Glasmon. It is impossible to tell whether Woolrich's suspicions were justified, since the alleged source novel was destroyed.

any event, Woolrich grew to dislike all of his work up to the middle Thirties. "It would have been a lot better if everything I'd done until then had been written in invisible ink and the reagent had been thrown away," he commented in his autobiography.

His second chance came to him about halfway through 1934, when he turned to a new market and a new kind of story. His first mystery, "Death Sits in the Dentist's Chair," appeared in *Detective Fiction Weekly* for August 4, 1934.

There was another patient ahead of me in the waiting room. He was sitting there quietly, humbly, with all the terrible resignation of the very poor.

With these words a new creative life began; and just as Woolrich's style was fully his own even in the first chapter of his first novel, so the motifs of his first mystery were uniquely Woolrichian. The evocation of New York City during the worst of the Depression, the integration of the Depression (in this case its effect on the dental profession) into the story structure, the *outré* method of murder (here cyanide in a temporary filling) —we will see them again and again in his work.

Woolrich's two other mystery stories of 1934 are equally characteristic. "Walls That Hear You" (*Detective Fiction Weekly*, 8/18/34) opens with the invasion of the demonic into the protagonist's workaday existence, turning his life into sudden nightmare as he finds his younger brother with all ten fingers cut off and his tongue severed at the roots. "Preview of Death" (*Dime Detective*, 11/15/34) is distinguished by its movie-making background (films being a recurrent element in Woolrich) and another unusual mode of murder (setting fire to an actress in a flammable Civil War hoopskirt).

The ten crime stories Woolrich published in 1935 were of uneven quality but incredible variety; together they expressed almost all of the motifs and beliefs and devices that form the nucleus of Woolrich's fiction. "Murder in Wax" (*Dime Detective*,

3/1/35) is his earliest attempt at first-person narrative from the viewpoint of a woman. "The Body Upstairs" (*Dime Detective*, 4/1/35) is a straight detective story marked by casual police brutality and by intuition passing for reasoning in the solution. "Kiss of the Cobra" (*Dime Detective*, 5/1/35) is another tale of the demonic invading ordinary life, ridiculous in conception (the narrator's widowed father-in-law brings home as his new wife a Hindu snake-priestess complete with instant Dr. Grimesby Roylott kit), but with a climactic scene involving the smoking of poisoned cigarettes that is pure Woolrich. "Red Liberty" (*Dime Detective*, 7/1/35) comes close to the police procedural story in its simplicity of plot and to cinematic immediacy in its vividly realized setting inside the Statue of Liberty—the same setting that Alfred Hitchcock, so close to Woolrich in world-view and technique, would use seven years later in *Saboteur*. "Dark Melody of Madness" (*Dime Mystery*, 7/35), better known under its later title "Papa Benjamin," deals with the fate of a jazz composer and bandleader who learns too much about a New Orleans voodoo cult, and marks the first appearance of a presence that will soon dominate the stage of Woolrich's imagination: the evil power whose prey is man. "The Corpse and the Kid" (*Dime Detective*, 9/35), Woolrich's best-known 1935 story (under its later title "Boy with Body") and for me his best tale of that year, concerns a young man who finds that his father has killed his tramp stepmother, and desperately tries to conceal the crime by carrying the body out of the New Jersey seaside town where the family lived and over to the roadhouse rendezvous where the woman's current lover is waiting for her. The account of the boy's journey with the body wrapped in a rug is the first of those magnificent set-pieces of pure nail-biting suspense that only Woolrich can do so stunningly well, and the psychological overtones of the story (in effect the son is carrying the mother in his womb and is struggling to place her dead in her lover's bed) suggest something of the horrors in the author's relations with his parents. "Dead on

Her Feet" (*Dime Detective*, 12/35) is a classic of bitter ironic suspense that will be discussed at greater length in my afterword to the story later in this book. In "The Death of Me" (*Detective Fiction Weekly*, 12/7/35) Woolrich adapts for the first time a motif from James M. Cain on which he would ring dozens of changes over the years: the guy who gets away with the crime he committed but gets nailed for the one he didn't. "The Showboat Murders" (*Detective Fiction Weekly*, 12/14/35) is the first of Woolrich's fast-action whizbangs, with the thinnest of plots but a whirlwind pace and an attention to precise details of physical movement, even in the midst of a running gun battle, that reflects Woolrich's youthful desire to be a dancer. And his final story of the year, "Hot Water" (*Argosy*, 12/28/35), is no great shakes as a story but, dealing as it does with a Hollywood star and her bodyguard, gives further evidence of the influence of films on the author.

By the end of 1935 Woolrich was a professional, and between 1936 and 1939 he published at least 105 stories (of every length from the short-short to the novella, but the majority of them long short stories) as well as two book-length magazine serials. By the end of 1939 his name had become a commonplace on all the top-quality mystery pulps—*Argosy, Black Mask, Detective Fiction Weekly, Dime Detective*—and had also appeared on the covers of low-grade cheapies like *Black Book Detective* and *Thrilling Mystery*, not to mention his tales in such a high-quality general fiction magazine as Whit Burnett's *Story*. These hundred-odd stories are astonishing in their unity—hardly a single one lacks Woolrich's unique mood, tone and preoccupations—no less than in their variety. They include straight historical adventure ("Black Cargo," "Holocaust"), attempts at Runyonesque humor ("Oft in the Silly Night," the central section of "Change of Murder"), morally terrifying cop stories ("Detective William Brown"), blistering tales of pure whizbang action and violence ("Double Feature," "Murder on the Night Boat," "You Pays Your Nickel"), nightmares of ghoulish panic

("The Living Lie Down with the Dead"), mordant tales of biter-
bit irony ("Post Mortem," the final section of "Change of Murder"), simple little stories where the smart dick proves that the
apparent accident or suicide was murder ("U, As in Murder,"
"The Woman's Touch," "Short Order Kill"), tales of crime and
punishment with intimations of realities beyond the experienced world ("Mystery in Room 913"), heart-pounding
clock races packed with unbearable tension ("Johnny on the
Spot," "Three O'Clock," "Men Must Die" which is better
known as "Guillotine"), and chaotic tragedies of suspense and
horror presided over by powers whose plaything is man ("I
Wouldn't Be in Your Shoes").

By the turn of the decade Woolrich had made uniquely his
own certain settings—the seedy hotel, the cheap dance hall, the
precinct station back room, the inside of a rundown movie
theater—and certain motifs: the clock race, the corrosion of
love and trust, the little guy trapped by powers beyond his
control. These malign powers that shatter people's lives take a
variety of forms. They may be personal, as in the stories about
the self-appointed avenging angel who in punishing crimes
beyond the law often destroys the innocent either along with
or instead of the guilty ("Somebody on the Phone," "After-
Dinner Story"). They may be socioeconomic, as in the stories of
little people driven over the edge by the Depression ("The
Night I Died," "Goodbye, New York"). Or they may be meta-
physical, as in that most terrifying situation that arises in what
I call the quintessential Woolrich story: only two resolutions are
conceivable but neither is consistent with the known facts and
each causes the destruction of innocent lives ("I Wouldn't Be in
Your Shoes"). Whatever form the malign powers take, they
destroy.

Reading the reminiscences of Woolrich's fellow writers (I am
thinking especially of the late Frank Gruber's invaluable 1967
memoir *The Pulp Jungle*), one can obtain an indirect picture of
the man's life and of the powers that were eating away at him.

We get the impression of a terrifyingly introverted man, living alone with his mother in a hotel, never going out except when it was absolutely necessary, his entire external life dominated by the overpowering figure of Claire Attalie Woolrich and his inner life, his work, reflecting in tortured and horrific patterns the repressions and frustrations in which he was suffocating.

In 1940 Woolrich published his first mystery novel, *The Bride Wore Black,* which quickly became and today remains a classic in the literature of suspense. Its central theme is the avenging angel: Julie Killeen's husband was killed on the church steps and the novel follows her as she slowly tracks down and kills, one by one, the drunk driver and his four cronies whom she holds responsible for her husband's death. Eventually a homicide cop named Lew Wanger picks up the trail and begins to stalk the huntress through the years. Their paths finally converge at a lonely country estate and both stalkers suddenly find themselves in the presence of Woolrich's malign powers. *Bride* was followed by five other novels over the next eight years, each including the word "black" in its title: *The Black Curtain* (1941), *Black Alibi* (1942), *The Black Angel* (1943), *The Black Path of Fear* (1944), and finally *Rendezvous in Black* (1948), which deals with the same themes as Woolrich's first suspense novel, thus bringing the series around full circle to its beginning.

Woolrich's short stories and novellas were somewhat reduced in number during the early Forties—fourteen were published in 1940, eleven in 1941, six in 1942, ten in 1943—but these included such classics as "All at Once, No Alice," "Finger of Doom," "One Last Night," "Three Kills for One," and "Marihuana." At least some of the energy that during the Thirties had gone into stories for the pulps was now diverted into a new form: the radio play. Many of Woolrich's stories were "naturals" for adaptation and broadcasting on such series as *Suspense,* and at times Woolrich wrote the radio versions himself. Judging from the transcriptions I have heard, in his own adaptations he succeeded in maintaining something of the unique Woolrich mood, despite the inherent limitations of the radio-drama form.

As if all this were not enough, Woolrich continued to write other novels—too many for publication under a single byline. Woolrich showed the manuscript of one of these novels to Whit Burnett, who had published some of his shorter fiction in *Story*, and Burnett showed it to the editors at J. B. Lippincott, who agreed to publish it. Since Simon & Schuster, then publishing the *Black* books, had exclusive right to use the name Cornell Woolrich, a pseudonym was needed; and together Woolrich and Burnett came up with one. The name they hit upon was William Irish. Had Woolrich met that obscure First National title writer thirteen years before, perhaps at a Hollywood party, and had he been carrying the man's name around in the back of his mind ever since? If so, his conscious mind must have forgotten it completely, for the existence of a "real" William Irish remained virtually unknown until recently.

The novel that Lippincott published under the Irish byline was, of course, the classic *Phantom Lady* (1942), the supreme masterwork on the theme of the race against the clock to save the innocent but convicted man from execution. The next Irish novel, *Deadline at Dawn* (1944), is structurally irritating—most of the book is a series of blind alleys—but magnificently evokes New York City after dark, the quiet despair of those who walk its deserted streets, and a clock race not against the executioner but against the city and the sunrise. In *Night Has a Thousand Eyes* (1945), published under the final Woolrich pseudonym of George Hopley, the sustained evocation of gibbering nightmare chaos rises to a literally unbearable pitch as the tale unfolds of a simple-minded recluse with uncanny powers who predicts the imminent death of a millionaire by the jaws of a lion, and of the frantic efforts of the doomed man's daughter and the police to avert a destiny which, they suspect and come to hope, was conceived by a merely human power. *Waltz into Darkness* (1947), set in the New Orleans of 1880, is a poor novel (the male lead is such a goop and the female such a black-hearted bitch that they both seem more laughable than tragic) but contains some haunting evocations of love and loneliness. And the final Irish novel of the Forties, *I Married a Dead Man* (1948), is, like "I Wouldn't Be in Your Shoes," a quintessential Woolrich story: a woman with nothing to live for, fleeing from her sadistic husband, is injured in a train wreck, is mistaken for another woman with everything to live for who was killed in the wreck, grasps this heaven-sent chance to start a new life with a new identity, falls in love again, and is destroyed along with the man she loves. The novel culminates in that most terrifying Woolrichian paradox where only two resolutions are logically possible, neither makes sense, and each destroys people's lives. "I don't know what the game was. . . . I only know we must have played it wrong, somewhere along the way. . . . We've lost. That's all I know. We've lost. And now the game is through."

The popular and critical success of the novels led to publication of several collections of Woolrich's shorter work in a series of hard-cover volumes from Lippincott and in a number of paperback originals which today are collector's items. His stories appeared regularly in the endless stream of mystery anthologies published in the Forties. And in addition to the many radio plays adapted from his work by himself and others, fifteen movies were made from Woolrich material between 1942 and 1950 alone, including *Phantom Lady* (Robert Siodmak, 1944), *Deadline at Dawn* (Harold Clurman, 1946, with screenplay by Clifford Odets), and *Night Has a Thousand Eyes* (John Farrow, 1948); but almost all of them badly mauled their sources, and one can find little in them of the authentic Woolrich.

After 1948 Woolrich published little: a novel apiece under each of his three bylines in 1950–51, and one novella late in 1952. That he was remembered at all during the early Fifties is due largely to Ellery Queen, who reprinted in his magazine a host of Woolrich's early pulp stories, and to Alfred Hitchcock, whose *Rear Window* (1954) gave some idea of Woolrich's cinematic potential even though little distinctively Woolrichian is left in the finished film.[3] Woolrich's silence in the Fifties was probably connected with the prolonged illness of his mother: having spent most of his life trapped in an intense, almost pathological love-hate relationship with her, he was unable to function during the last years of her life. Indeed on several occasions he passed off slightly updated old stories as new work, fooling both book and magazine publishers as well as the public. Thus the jackets on *Nightmare* and *Violence*, two collections of Woolrich's short fiction issued by Dodd Mead in 1956 and 1958, claimed that each book included two stories never published before, whereas in fact all the stories had appeared in magazines earlier; nevertheless these collections performed a great service in returning to print not only such fine stories as "I'll Take You Home, Kathleen" (originally titled "One Last Night") and "Don't Wait Up for Me Tonight" (originally entitled "Goodbye, New York") but also those supreme masterworks "Three O'Clock" and "Guillotine" ("Men Must Die").

Woolrich's mother died in 1957, and not long after her death came her son's first new book in seven years.

To
Claire Attalie Woolrich
1874–1957
In Memoriam
This Book: Our Book

Hotel Room (1958) is a collection of largely noncriminous stories set in a New York City hotel at different periods of its history from its early years of sumptuous fashionableness to the last days before its demolition. The Hotel St. Anselm was appar-

3. In 1957 Hitchcock directed for the television series *Suspicion* a one-hour version of Woolrich's "Three O'Clock" (unaccountably retitled *Four O'Clock*) which is not only completely faithful to the story but also one of the greatest films of soul-pounding suspense ever made—pure Hitchcock and pure Woolrich, the finest adaptation of Woolrich in any form, and already virtually forgotten.

ently an amalgam of all the desiccated Victorian residential hotels in which Woolrich and his mother had lived, and the stories set in the hotel mark the beginning of Woolrich's last period, which consists of a mere handful of stories, most of them near-shapeless, hyperemotional "tales of love and despair" (to cite the subtitle of a collection Woolrich was putting together at his death). Woolrich's best story of the Fifties, though originally conceived as a chapter in *Hotel Room,* was excised at the last minute and appeared separately in *Ellery Queen's Mystery Magazine* as "The Penny-a-Worder." It is included in this book, and further comment will follow the story itself.

In 1959 Avon published *Beyond the Night,* a paperback collection mainly devoted to Woolrich's excursions into the preternatural. The credit page states that three of its six stories were never before published, but in fact both "My Lips Destroy" and "The Lamp of Memory" were already over twenty years old. The only totally new story in the book was "The Number's Up," a bitter little tale that is among Woolrich's best late stories and is included in this book. The year 1959 also saw publication of Woolrich's last new novel and his worst, *Death Is My Dancing Partner,* in which he reworked motifs from "I Wouldn't Be in Your Shoes" and "Papa Benjamin" and *Waltz into Darkness* but buried them in gobs of mawkish sentimentality. The book deals with Mari, a dancer in the temple of the death goddess Kali, and Maxwell Jones, a third-rate bandleader who sees her dance as his key to that room at the top, despite the legend that at each performance of the death dance Kali claims a victim. In effect, Woolrich in his last novel came around full circle to the sentimental novels he wrote during and just after his college days.[4]

And so the sad, last years wore on. Woolrich had become a diabetic and an alcoholic, he was obsessed with the fear that he

4. One later novel appeared, *The Doom Stone* (1960), but this was merely the book version of Woolrich's 1939 *Argosy* serial "The Eye of Doom," with the original Part Four removed and replaced by a new last section.

was homosexual, he had lost touch with most of the few acquaintances he had ever had. His fellow writers Michael Avallone and Robert L. Fish, his editors Frederic Dannay and Hans Stefan Santesson, one academic (Prof. Donald A. Yates of Michigan State), and a few business people; no others. He had never believed in God; he had ached all his life to believe in love but nothing had worked right for him; now he no longer believed even in himself. He would sometimes come to a party, bringing his own bottle of cheap wine in a paper bag, and would stand alone in a corner the whole evening. Someone would be introduced to him, and would tell him how much he admired Woolrich's work, and Woolrich would growl, "You don't mean that," and find himself another corner. A tiny rivulet of new stories appeared every so often in *EQMM* or *Saint Mystery Magazine,* each eagerly awaited and discussed by those who loved his work, none equal in power to those great novels and stories of the Thirties and Forties, most of them full of agony, bitterness, and self-contempt.

In 1965 two more collections of his short fiction were published. *The Ten Faces of Cornell Woolrich,* edited by Ellery Queen, was of high quality, but seven of its ten stories came straight out of earlier collections. *The Dark Side of Love* brought together eight stories from the author's last period, including three, unsaleable to magazines, that appeared for the first time in the collection itself. The hypnotic power of his own self-disgust and his longing for just a little love permeate these stories and make them hard to forget, objectively poor though most of them are. And there are two good stories in the book: "The Clean Fight," a sloppy but nightmarish evocation of the NYPD as Gestapo, and "Too Nice a Day to Die," a bitter ironic little gem on the randomness and gross injustice we call the world.

There were no more books published in his lifetime and less than half-a-dozen further stories, and his condition continued to deteriorate. He developed gangrene in his leg and did nothing about it; when the doctors reached it, it was too far gone to do anything but amputate. He must have thought he was going to die, for he told the story of his life to the hospital chaplain and said that he wanted to return to the Catholic faith in which he had been baptized. Whether this was a true conversion or a reflex of fright is not clear; those who knew him best do not seem to remember any change in his beliefs after he left the hospital. In any case, he remained in lonely isolation, confined in a wheelchair, unable to learn how to walk on an artificial leg, probably unable to write anything.[5] He died of a stroke a few months later, on September 25, 1968, leaving no survivors. His estate of close to a million dollars he left in a trust fund to Columbia University, for scholarships to go to students of creative writing. The fund is named after his mother.

II

Why is Woolrich not only one of the greatest suspense writers in the history of crime fiction but also a literary artist that some people think the equal of Poe? Perhaps we can begin to suggest answers to these questions by sketching the forces at the heart of Woolrich's world.

Ideally, at the end of a detective novel of the formal-deductive-problem type, all the intellectual perplexity that we have experienced as the plot developed has been dissolved, every fragment of the story has been given its *raison d'être,* and we can step back and view the entire array of fragments as a rationally harmonious mosaic. Likewise, at the end of an orthodox suspense novel all the howling panic we have experienced while reading has been dissolved, the demons have been scattered and the world is again without abysses. Akira Kurosawa in his great film *Rashomon* (1950) reversed the convention of the formal problem, telling a murder story and then showing that no rational explanation is possible. This is exactly what

5. Details of the books left unfinished at Woolrich's death are given in the afterword to the last story in this volume and in Section II of the Bibliography.

Woolrich had done several times, beginning at least a dozen years before Kurosawa's film, and reversing the convention not only of the detective story but also, and even more characteristically, of the suspense story. Woolrichian suspense stories typically end not with the dissolution of terror but with its omnipresence. For Woolrich's world is controlled by powers that delight in destroying us. They are not reachable by human goodness, their ways are not our ways, and against them we are helpless.

The nature of the god of Woolrich's world is the subject of many of his stories. In *Night Has a Thousand Eyes* (1945) we see that nature directly in all its power and hideous malignancy; more often, however, we see it only as reflected in the nature of the universe itself—chaotic, irrational, abandoned to the demonic, as in "I Wouldn't Be in Your Shoes" and *I Married a Dead Man*. A graphic portrait of the Woolrichian god is sketched in "The Light in the Window" (*Mystery Book Magazine*, 4/46), in which a mentally disturbed soldier returns from World War II to his home city. While standing in the darkness across the street from his girl's apartment, wondering how to tell her he is home, he is brought up against a barrage of circumstantial evidence whose inevitable cumulative effect in his mind is an overpowering conviction that she has been sleeping with another man. In a scene faintly suggestive of *Othello,* he strangles the girl, then walks out of her apartment as if in a trance. Almost at once his shellshock returns, and the night streets are transformed for him into a battleground. He tries to dig a foxhole in the sidewalk with bare and bloody hands. He mistakes a solicitous passerby for a lieutenant and salutes him. Finally taken to a hospital, he comes out little more than a vegetable, with nothing left but the wait for the merciful release of death. "You had to wait for it, what else could you do? It was an order, from a lieutenant. A different one, you never saw. But He'd given it just the same; you had to obey." Now both the soldier and the reader learn that the girl had been faithful, that the cumulative evidence had all been "coincidence," and that the janitor of the girl's apartment building has just been executed for her murder. Less than half a page later we re-enter the soldier's thoughts: "You just had to be patient and wait, that was all. You couldn't question a lieutenant." In view of what Woolrich has shown us, it would not be unreasonable to conclude that once again no lieutenant is present—that, in short, the only god is chance—except for the inescapable fact that the pattern of events is so utterly dependent on multiple coincidence that something more than coincidence must underlie the events. Where the pattern is so complex and so directed to a single end, it cannot be attributed to chance: the old watchmaker argument, but used here to infer a god we would be much happier without. And the only possible response of the god's victims is that of Helen in *I Married a Dead Man:* "We've lost. That's all I know. We've lost, we've lost."

The workaday naturalistic world is no more comforting in Woolrich's vision than the powers beyond, for the dominant reality in that world is the Depression. There is very little either in or out of the crime genre that can match Woolrich's evocations of a frightened little guy in a seedy apartment, with a hungry wife and children, no money, no job, and desperation eating him like a cancer. One can learn more about the anguish of the Thirties from "Dusk to Dawn" and "Borrowed Crime" and "Goodbye, New York" and other Woolrich stories than from volumes of social history. And yet these stories are not primarily naturalistic reportage; the Depression functions for Woolrich not so much as brute social fact but rather as a part of his own malignant universe.

If both the preternatural powers above us and the socioeconomic forces of the Depression have us as their target, so too do the police. Individual policemen and the police system as such appear in dozens of Woolrich's stories, sometimes as the central motif, at other times peripherally. The overall impression Woolrich creates is of a human power just as brutal and malignant as the dark powers above, indeed their earthly counterpart.

The characteristic means of evoking this impression is by por-
traying incredible police brutality and its casual acceptance as
completely natural by everyone, including the victims. In "The
Body Upstairs" (*Dime Detective*, 4/1/35) a woman is murdered
and the police stick lighted cigarettes into her husband's arm-
pits until, though innocent, he is on the brink of confessing—
at which point the homicide dick who is the protagonist chews
out the husband for being a weakling who can't take it! In
"Graves for the Living" (*Dime Mystery*, 6/37) the police, purely
on the basis of an incredible (though, as it turns out, true) story
told them by a complete stranger, take one of their own people
into an all-night drugstore, kick the proprietor out, and pour
acid on the cop until he confirms the story. "Murder at the
Automat," "Dead on Her Feet," and the unbearably terrifying
"Three Kills for One" all deal in one way or another with police
brutality; and the nature of the system as a whole is the central
concern of "Detective William Brown" (*Detective Fiction
Weekly*, 9/10/38), which on the surface seems to reflect a Nix-
onian law-and-order viewpoint but which beneath the surface
is one of the most subtly disturbing of Woolrich's police stories.
Brown is a conscienceless opportunist who rises through the
ranks by a combination of courage and ruthlessness, as when he
shoots at and, by skill mixed with luck, kills a felon fleeing
through a crowd of schoolchildren—both the product and the
vigorous exponent of the good old American principle that only
results count and that the ends justify the means. Those who
remain on the story's surface will conclude that Brown is ultimately revealed as a bad cop, as a traitor to the force; those who
go deeper will see that Brown's philosophy is the philosophy of
the system itself. There is a scene where the police "interro-
gate" a murder suspect that chillingly reflects the views of
Brown. "They kicked the chair out from under him again and
again, they tortured him by holding glasses of water before his
swollen, bleeding lips, then slowly emptying them out on the
floor as he strained forward to drink." Brown himself takes part

in the questioning until his "knuckles are all swollen." At the climax Brown dies a heroic death in a gunfight with a wanted gangster, and his buddy, the dedicated but plodding cop Greeley, decides to suppress his knowledge that Brown's career had been based on framing an innocent man for murder and then shooting him "while resisting arrest." So we see how the filth embedded in the system begins to eat into people like Greeley, the system's best men.

Woolrich never changed his mind about the police. In one of his last stories, "The Clean Fight," a team of New York City detectives, acting out of reverence for their dying squad commander, tracks down and shoots in cold blood an ex-cop who was very remotely responsible for the death of the commander's son. The relation between the dying commander and his men is portrayed quite explicitly in terms of racial mysticism and of Hitler's *Führerprinzip*. There is nothing that the young, the black, the poor, and the dissenting have learned about the police that Woolrich did not know long ago (except the political function of repression, for Woolrich was apolitical; his concentration was on relationships not power politics).

So this is the world into which we are thrown, and nothing can be done about it, Woolrich says, except to try to create a few tiny islands of love and trust which can perhaps, for a few moments, make us forget what kind of world we live in. All his life Woolrich wanted to love and be loved, just a little love, as a dying man in a desert longs for just a few drops of cool water; but it never worked out for him. That fact probably explains how and why he evoked the power of love, its joys and risks and heartbreaks, so often and with such matchless poignant artistry.

But love is so fragile, so momentary, and there is so little of it. There is a haunting moment in Chapter 2 of *Phantom Lady* when the morgue men are removing the body of Marcella Henderson.

The bedroom door had opened again. There was awkward, commingled motion in it. Henderson's eyes dilated, they slowly coursed the short distance from door to arched opening, leading out into the foyer. This time he gained his feet fully, in a spasmodic jolt. "No, not like *that!* Look what they're doing! Like a sack of potatoes— And all her lovely hair along the floor—she was so careful of it—!"

Hands riveted to him, holding him there. The outer door closed muffledly. A little sachet came drifting out of the empty bedroom, seeming to whisper: "Remember? Remember when I was your love? Remember?"

This time he sank down suddenly, buried his face within his two gouging, kneading hands. You could hear his breath. The tempo was all shot to pieces. He said to them in helpless surprise, after his hands had dropped again, "I thought guys didn't cry—and now I just have."

And in the last chapter of his unfinished novel *The Loser* (published as an independent short story "The Release") there is a similar moment when the protagonist—probably an autobiographical figure—speaks to his dead wife: "I just want your voice in my ear. Just want to hear your voice in my ear. Just say my name, just say Cleve, like you used to say Cleve. Just say it once, that'll be my forever, that'll be my all-time, my eternity. I don't want God. This isn't a triangle. There's no room for outsiders in my love for you. Just say it one time more. If you can't say it whole, then say it broken. If you can't say it full, then say it whispered. Cleve."

This may not be art as art commonly goes; the lack of discipline, of control, would seem to rule it out of that category. And yet Woolrich's lack of control over emotions is a crucial element in his work, not only because it intensifies the fragility and momentariness of love but also because it tears away the comfortable belief, evident in some of the greatest works of the human imagination such as *Oedipus Rex,* that nobility in the face of nothingness is possible. And if Woolrich's work is not art as commonly understood, there is an art beyond art, whose

form is not the novel or story but the scream; and of this art
Woolrich is beyond doubt a master.

The process of love's dying was as central to Woolrich as love
itself, and he is at his most powerful when he evokes the slow
corrosion of doubt eating away at the fragile foundations of love
and trust between persons. We have already seen the corrosion
motif in "The Light in the Window" and it recurs in "I Wouldn't
Be in Your Shoes," "The Red Tide" and its revision "Last
Night," "Two Fellows in a Furnished Room," "Charlie Won't
Be Home Tonight" and in many other stories. In most of the
corrosion stories there is a very close relationship between the
two central characters: lovers, husband and wife, father and
son, roommates. A murder or similar act is committed, and a
slowly but inexorably mounting body of evidence compels or
comes within an inch of compelling one of the two to believe
that the other is guilty. The suspense stems from the slow unfolding of the damning evidence, the oscillation between trust
and doubt, and our own unawareness of the truth. For in some
of these stories the suspected person turns out to be innocent
and the damning evidence to be the result of wild coincidence
or a frame-up; in other stories the suspect is in fact guilty; and
in still others neither the people involved nor the reader ever
learns what the truth is.

The dark side of love, the perversions that rise from love,
were always close to Woolrich, and he evoked them with the
same white-hot intensity and poignance he brought to the evocation of its daylight side. One thinks of Marie in "Mind Over
Murder," subjecting the man she loves to nightmare atrocities
in order to destroy his marriage; of the terrifying interplay
between the hallucinogen-crazed King Turner and his estranged wife in "Marihuana"; and of those most typical Woolrichian dark lovers, the avenging angels. For when one loves
another intensely, that love can beget a raging drive to redress
an atrocity against the beloved, which in turn begets new atrocities of its own. Thus in *The Bride Wore Black* an ice-cold

widow spends years tracking down and killing the four men she
wrongly blamed for killing her bridegroom on the church steps.
In *Rendezvous in Black* a grief-crazed young man, holding one
among a small group of people responsible for his fiancée's
death, devotes his life to entering the lives of each of that group
in turn, finding out whom each one most loves, and murdering
these loved ones, so that the person who killed his fiancée will
live the grief he lives. In "After-Dinner Story" an aristocratic
embittered father invites all the suspects in the murder of his
son to dinner, where he springs a lethal psychological trap
which (as Woolrich intends the reader to see) is senseless but
which nevertheless by pure chance kills the right man. The
stony unforgiving narrator of "I'll Never Play Detective Again"
forces his best friend, who is mentally unbalanced but apparently has yet committed no crime at all, to commit suicide. In
"Three Kills for One" and "The Clean Fight" avenging cops
track down and destroy someone they have come to hate because of what he did to someone or something they love.

"I got him! Call Mike at the hospital, and tell him I got him! Tell him
it was me, Cleary! Tell him I got him for him!
"I got him! . . .
"I got him for him! . . .
"I got him!"

III

It is a commonplace that in most significant works of the
imagination form and content are inseparable (except in the
critic's butchering mind). The proposition is true of the works
of Woolrich, and any discussion of how he achieved his effects
will overlap considerably with the substantive analysis of his
work. We shall focus here only on a few aspects of his procedure.

First of all we must consider the concept of *functional illogic.*
It is simply undeniable that Woolrich is the sloppiest plot crafts-

man among all the giants of the genre. Many even of his best
stories abound in incredible coincidences, contradictions, and
implausibilities, so that Ellery Queen, one of his staunchest
defenders, has remarked that a Woolrich tale often contains
holes big enough to drive a truck through. The Appraiser in
"Orphan Ice" steals a blotter from the desk of a police officer
sitting opposite him and takes it out of the station completely
undetected. At the climax of "Post Mortem" the detective
blows the fuse in the basement at the exact split second that the
murderer upstairs is flinging a hot water heater into a woman's
bathtub. Bailey in "One Last Night" starts literally from nothing, piles up one eye-poppingly ludicrous "deduction" on top of
another, and winds up with a complete (and, as it turns out,
completely accurate) psychological portrait of a murderer.
Then there are the ridiculous alibi of Colin Hughes in "What
the Well-Dressed Corpse Will Wear," and the inane motivation
for the frame-up of Scott Henderson in *Phantom Lady*, and
dozens of other examples which any alert reader of Woolrich
can recall. And yet all this sloppiness is a precondition to one
of Woolrich's greatest strengths: his ability, in his best work, to
make coincidence and contradiction and implausibility functional to his black vision. A careful craftsman could not have
conceived of "I Wouldn't Be in Your Shoes" and *I Married a
Dead Man*, where we are confronted with the fact that no
possible explanation can account for all of the events, and
thereby with the irreducible senselessness of the universe. No
rational plot maker could have revealed the features of his
world's god by creating the string of interlocking coincidences
which led the soldier of "The Light in the Window" to believe
that his girl had been sleeping with another man. No invariably
competent storyteller could have evoked Eric Rogers' fanatical
hunger for justice in "Three Kills for One" by anti-naturalisti-
cally having him pursue his crusade for three years with no
means of support, as if his rage for justice were all the food and
drink he needed. The playwrights of the Absurd have made it

a commonplace that a senseless story may best reflect a senseless universe, but Woolrich knew and acted on the same principle long before they became prominent.

The next facet of his technique we shall consider is his *feverish emotionalism*. Woolrich sometimes assumed the public mask of a tough little banty-rooster, but in reality he was living at the edge of his nerves his life long. No man but one of abnormal sensitiveness could have projected himself so completely into women like Bricky in *Deadline at Dawn* and Lizzie Aintree in "Death Escapes the Eye" and Helen in *I Married a Dead Man*. No man who was not himself unbearably lonely and afraid could have evoked loneliness and despair and fright so powerfully, as in Bricky's famous prayer to a clock in the 4:27 chapter of *Deadline at Dawn:* "Oh, Clock on the Paramount, that I can't see from here, the night is nearly over and the bus has nearly gone. Let me go home tonight." Or as in this passage from the same chapter.

She turned and walked down the musty, dimly-lighted corridor, along a strip of carpeting that still clung together only out of sheer stubbornness of skeletal weave. Doors, dark, oblivious, inscrutable, sidling by; enough to give you the creeps just to look at them. All hope gone from them, and from those who passed in and out through them. Just one more row of stopped-up orifices in this giant honeycomb that was the city. Human beings shouldn't have to enter such doors, shouldn't have to stay behind them. No moon ever entered there, no stars, no anything at all. They were worse than the grave, for in the grave is absence of consciousness. And God, she reflected, ordered the grave, for all of us; but God didn't order such burrows in a third-class New York City hotel.

Woolrich was far more than a victim of his darker emotions; he understood them, and, at his best, understood how to transform them into art.

The characteristic emotional feverishness which imparts such driving nightmarish urgency to many of Woolrich's greatest works has its physical counterpart in that most Woolrichian device, *the race against time and death.* By entitling Chapter 1 of *Phantom Lady* "The Hundred and Fiftieth Day Before the Execution," he begins, even before Marcella Henderson is strangled, the countdown of days before her innocent husband is to be electrocuted. By using clock faces instead of chapter titles or numbers in *Deadline at Dawn,* he makes us feel in our bones, like Quinn and Bricky, the inevitable approach of the dreaded sunrise. In "Johnny on the Spot," "Three O'Clock," "Men Must Die," and the other clock-race stories, he uses the ticking away of the seconds before the protagonist is to be destroyed to create an atmosphere that becomes almost unbearable.

There are some haunting lines at the beginning of *Waltz into Darkness:*

And suddenly, one day, the cumulative loneliness of fifteen years, held back until now, overwhelmed him, all at one time, inundated him, and he turned this way and that, almost in panic.

Any love, from anywhere, on any terms. Quick, before it was too late! Only not to be alone any longer.

That man is Woolrich and it is we, and that concept is what transforms the clock race from a brilliant device to keep us on the edge of our seats into an organic part of Woolrich's universe.

Characterization and viewpoint are the final points of procedure we have to consider. The way Woolrich portrays the people trapped in these nightmarish situations is a part of the terror of the situations themselves, and yet at the same time the situations in which his people are trapped are vital to his portrayal of the people. For in one sense there are very few villains in Woolrich: if one loves or needs love, and has lost it, or if one is at the brink of death or destruction, Woolrich is with that person, indeed becomes that person, no matter what else the person has done. Even in an incredibly silly story like "The Mystery of the Blue Spot" (*Detective Fiction Weekly,* 4/4/36), on the

exposure of the truth Woolrich suddenly shifts viewpoints from
the investigator to the murderess, who killed because she had
lost her love, and who now kills herself. But also in his most
powerful work he makes us empathize with all sorts of morally
mixed people. He makes us sit, bound and gagged, and paralyzed, with Paul Stapp in his own basement, while the time
bomb which Stapp himself has set but now cannot reach ticks
closer and closer to "Three O'Clock." He makes us count the
minutes with the murderer Robert Lamont in "Men Must Die"
while the executioner, unwittingly poisoned but still function-
ing, approaches closer and closer to the prison to cut off Lamont's head. He puts us inside the skins of the dope-crazed
King Turner in "Marihuana" and the Depression-crazed Richard Paine in "Murder Always Gathers Momentum" and the
grief-crazed Johnny Marr in *Rendezvous in Black*. He makes us
share the last moments of the murderer Gates in "Three Kills
for One," when the cold steel hood falls over his head, and he
says in a tired voice, "Helen, I love you," just before the current
fries him: one of the most haunting scenes in Woolrich, and one
of the best keys to the man, his world, his way of creating his
world, and to how much he longed to love.

Alfred Hitchcock filmed a story by Woolrich in 1954 and another in 1957. Then in 1960 he made *Psycho,* transforming a
good but by no means great novel into one of the most compas-
sionate, savage, and compelling films ever made, a literally inex-
haustible work that can be seen over and over with fuller understanding each time. It is worthwhile in closing to consider
some of the ties that bind Woolrich to that most disturbed and
disturbing of Hitchcock's creations, the Norman Bates of *Psycho.*[6] Both men were dominated by their mothers throughout
their lives and long after the mother's death; both were trapped

6. I speak of Hitchcock's creation, not Robert Bloch's; for Bloch knew nothing
of Woolrich when he wrote his novel and his Norman is a fat repulsive toad not
even in the same universe with Hitchcock's Norman, who is complex and fully
human.

by accident of birth, through no fault of their own, in the most wretched psychological conditions; each was gifted (cursed?) with an unobtrusive yet penetrating intelligence that made him deeply aware of his own and all men's trappedness. The difference between them is that Norman Bates was given no alternative but to translate his nightmares into reality; Woolrich on the other hand was endowed with the ability to take his decades alone and wretched in his personal hell and to shape them into a body of work that theologians must read to understand despair, philosophers to comprehend pessimism, social historians to grasp the Depression, and those concerned with the heart of man to experience through him what it means to be utterly alone. As for plain readers, they will be reading him long after our grandchildren are dust, because he will move and haunt our descendants as he did us and our forebears. He is dead, but he lives. He will outlive us all.

FRANCIS M. NEVINS, JR.

I

THE CLAWS OF NIGHT

Graves for the Living

"There he is," the grave-keeper whispered, parting the hedge so the two detectives could peer through. "That's the third one he's gone at since I phoned in to you fellows. I was afraid if I tried to jump on him single-handed he'd get away from me before you got out here. He's got a gun, see it lying there next to the grave?"

His feeling of inadequacy was understandable; he was not only elderly and scrawny, but trembling all over with nervousness. One of the plainclothesmen beside him unlimbered his gun, thumbed the guard off, held it half-poised for action. The one on the other side of him carefully maneuvered a manacle

3

from his waistband so that it wouldn't clash.

They exchanged a look across the keeper's crouched, quaking back, each to see if the other was ready for the spring. Both nodded imperceptibly. They motioned the frightened cemetery-watchman down out of the way. They reared suddenly, dashed through the opening in the hedge simultaneously, with a great crackling and hissing of leaves.

The figure knee-deep in the grave stopped clawing and burrowing, snaked out an arm toward the revolver lying along its lip. One of the detectives' huge size 12's came down flat on it, pinning it down. "Hold it," he said, and his own gun was inches away from the ghoul's face. A flashlight balanced on a little mound of freshly-excavated soil like a golf-tee threw a thin, ghostly light on the scene. Off to the left one of the other graves was disturbed, wavy with irregular furrows of earth instead of planed flat.

The manacle clashed around the prisoner's earth-clotted wrist, then the detective's. They hauled him up out of the shallow trough he had burrowed almost at full arm-length, like a piece of carrion.

"I thought you'd come," he said. "Where'd you put her? Where is she?"

They didn't answer, for one thing because they didn't understand. They weren't supposed to understand the gibberings of a maniac. They didn't ask him any questions, either. They seemed to feel that wasn't part of their job in this case. They'd come out to get him, they'd got him, and they were bringing him in—that was all they'd been sent to do.

One of them stooped for the gun, put it in his pocket; he picked up the torch too, clicked it off. The tableau suddenly went blue-black. They made their way out of the burial-ground with him, the watchman trailing behind them.

Outside the gate a prowl-car was standing waiting; they jammed him into it between them, told the watchman to appear at Headquarters in the morning without fail, shrieked off with him.

He only said one thing more, on the way. "You didn't have to hijack a patrolcar to impress me, I know better than to take you for detectives." They careened through the midnight city streets stonyfaced, one on each side of him, as though they hadn't heard him. "Fiends," he sobbed bitterly. "How can the Lord put things like you into human shape?"

He seemed vastly surprised at sight of the Headquarters building, with its green-globed entrance. When they stood him before a desk, with a uniformed lieutenant at it, his consternation was noticeable. He seemed unable to believe his eyes. Then when they led him into a back room, and a captain of detectives came in to question him, there could be no mistaking the fact that he was stunned. "You—you really are!" he breathed.

"What did you think we were?" one of the detectives wanted to know caustically. "CCC boys?"

He looked about uncomprehendingly. "I thought you were—*them.*"

The captain got down to business. "What were you after?" he said tersely.

"Her." He amended it, "My girl, my girl I was going to marry."

The captain sighed impatiently. "You expected to find her in the cemetery?"

"Oh, I know!" the man before him broke out bitterly. "I know, I'm insane, that's what you'll say! I came to you people for help, of my own accord, before it happened—and that's what you thought then, too. I spoke to Mercer, at the Poplar Street Station, only yesterday morning. He told me to go home and not worry." His laughter was horrid, harsh, deranged.

"Quit it, shut up!" The captain drew back uncontrollably, even with the width of his desk between them. He took up the thread of his questioning again. "You were arrested just now in the Cedars of Lebanon Cemetery, in the act of disturbing the graves. The watchman at the Sacred Heart Cemetery also phoned us, earlier tonight, that he had found some of the resting-places in there molested, when he made his rounds. Did you do that too?"

The man nodded vigorously, unashamed. "Yes! And I've also been in two others, since sundown, Cypress Hills, and a private graveyard out beyond the city limits toward Ellendale."

The captain shivered involuntarily. The two detectives in the background paled a little, exchanged a look. The captain let out his accumulated breath slowly.

"You need a doctor, young fellow," he sighed.

"No, I don't need a doctor!" The prisoner's voice rose to a scream. "I need help! If you'll only listen to me, believe me!"

"I'll listen to you," the captain said, without committing himself on the other two pleas. "I think I understand how it is. Engaged to her, you say. Very much in love with her, of course. The shock of losing her—too much for you; temporarily unbalanced your mind. Judging by your clothes—what I can see of them under that accumulation of mold and caked earth, and the fact that you left a car parked near the main entrance of Cedars of Lebanon—robbery wasn't your motive. My men here tell me you were carrying seven-hundred-odd dollars when they caught up with you. Crazed by grief, didn't know what you were doing, so you set out on your own to try and find her, is that it?"

The man acted tormented, distracted. "Don't tell me things I know already!" he pleaded hoarsely.

"But how is it," the captain went on equably, "you didn't know where she was buried in the first place?"

"Because it was done without a permit—secretly!"

"If you can prove that—!" The captain sat up a little straighter. This was getting back on his own ground again. "When was she buried, any idea?"

"Some time after sundown this evening—that's over six hours

ago now! And all this time we're standing here—"

"When'd she die?"

The man clenched his two fists, raised them agonizedly above his head. *"She—didn't—die!* Don't you understand what I'm trying to tell you! She's lying somewhere, under the ground, in this very city, at this very minute—still breathing!"

There was a choking stillness as though the room had suddenly been crammed full of cotton-batting. It was a little hard to breathe in there; the three police-officials seemed to find it so. You could hear the effort they put into it.

The captain said, brushing his hand slowly across his mouth to clear it of some unseen impediment, "Hold him up." Then he said to the man they were supporting between them: "I'm listening."

✤

To understand about me, you must go back fifteen years, to 1922, to when I was ten years old. And even then, perhaps you'll wonder why a thing like that, horrible as it was, should poison my whole life. . . .

My father was a war veteran. He had been badly shell-shocked in the Argonne, and for a long time in the base hospital behind the lines they thought they weren't going to be able to pull him through.

But they did, and he was finally sent home to us, my mother and me. I knew he wasn't well, and that I mustn't be too noisy around him, that was all. The others, my mother and the doctors, knew that his nerve-centers had been shattered irreparably; but that slow paralysis was creeping on him, they didn't dream. There were no signs of it, no warning. Then suddenly, in a flash, it struck. The nerve-centers ceased to function all over his body. "Death," they called it, in ghastly error.

I wasn't frightened of death—yet. If it had only been that, it would have been all right; a month later I would have been over it. But as it was. . . .

His government pension had been all we'd had to live on since he'd come back. It had been out of the question for him to work, after what that howitzer-shell exploding a few yards away had done to him. Mother hadn't been able to work either; there wouldn't have been anyone to look after him all day. So there was no money to speak of.

Mother had to take any undertaker she could get, was glad to get anybody at all for the pittance that was all she could afford. The fly-by-night swindler that she finally secured, turned up his nose at first at the sum offered, she had to plead with him to take charge of the body. Meanwhile the overworked medical examiner had made a hasty, routine examination, given the cause as a blood-clot on the brain due to his injuries, and made out the death-certificate in proper order.

But he was never prepared for burial in the proper way. He couldn't have been or it wouldn't have happened. Those ghoulish undertakers must have put him aside while they attended to other, more remunerative cases, until they discovered there was no time left to do what they were supposed to. And, cold-bloodedly figuring no one would ever know the difference anyway, simply contented themselves with hastily composing his posture, putting on his best suit, and perhaps giving his face a hurried, last-minute shave. Then they put him in the coffin, untouched, just as he was.

We would never have known, perhaps, but mother was unable to meet even the first monthly payment on the plot, and the cemetery officials heartlessly gave orders to disinter the coffin and remove it elsewhere. Whether something about it excited their suspicions, or it was of such flimsy construction that it accidentally broke open when they tried to remove it, I don't know. At any rate, they made a hideous discovery, and my mother was hastily summoned to come out there. Word was also sent to the police.

Thinking it still had to do with the money due them, she frantically borrowed it from a loan-shark, one of the early forerunners of that racket, and in an evil hour allowed me to go with her out there to the cemetery-grounds.

We found the opened coffin above ground, lying in full view, with a number of police-officials grouped around it. They drew her aside and began to question her, out of earshot. But I didn't need to overhear, I had the evidence of my own eyes there before me.

The eyes were open and staring; not just blankly as they had been the first time, but dilated with horror, stretched to their uttermost width. Eyes that had tried vainly to pierce the stygian darkness that he found about him. His arms, no longer flat at his sides, were curved clawlike up over his head, nails almost torn off with futile tearing and scratching at the wood that hemmed him in. There were dried brown spots all about the white quilting that lined the lower half of the coffin, that had been blood-spots flung about from his flailing, gashed fingertips. Splinters of wood from the underside of the lid clung to each of them like porcupine-quills. And on the inside of the lid were even more tell-tale signs. A criss-cross of gashes, some of them almost shallow troughs, against which his bleeding nails had worn themselves off. But it had held fast, had only split now, when it was being taken up, weeks later.

The voice of one of the police-officials penetrated my numbed senses, seeming to come from far away. "This man—your husband—" he was saying to my mother—"was buried alive, and slowly suffocated to death—the way you see him—in his coffin. Will you tell us, if you can—"

But she dropped at their feet in a dead faint without uttering a sound. Her agony was short, merciful. I, who was to be the far greater sufferer of the two, stood there frozen, stunned, without a whimper, without even crying. I must have seemed to them too stupid or too young to fully understand the implications of what we were looking at. If they thought so, it was the greatest mistake of their lives.

I accompanied them, and my mother, back to the house without a word. They looked at me curiously once or twice, and I overheard one of them say in a low voice: "He didn't get it. Good thing, too. Enough to frighten the growth out of a kid that age."

I didn't get it! I was frozen all over, they didn't understand that; in a straight-jacket of icy horror that was crushing the shape out of me.

Mother recovered consciousness presently and—for just a little while, before the long twilight closed in on her—her reason, sanity. They checked with the coroner, the death-certificate was sent for and examined, they decided that neither she nor he was to blame in any way. She gave them the name of the undertaker who had been in charge of the burial preparations, and word was sent out to arrest him and his assistants.

Fate was kind to her, her ordeal was made short. That same night she went hopelessly, incurably out of her mind, and within the week had been committed to an institution. Nature had found the simplest way out for her.

I didn't get off so easily. There was a brief preliminary stage, more or less to be expected, of childish terror, nightmares, fear of the dark, but that soon wore itself out. Then for a year or two I seemed actually to have gotten over the awful thing; at least, it faded a little, I didn't think of it incessantly night and day. But the subconscious doesn't, couldn't, forget a thing like that. Only another, second shock of equal severity and having to do with the same thing, would heal it. Fighting fire with fire, so to speak.

It came back in my middle teens, and from then on never again left me, grew steadily worse if anything as time went on. It was not a fear of death, you must understand; it was a fear of *not* dying and of being buried for dead. In other words, of the same thing happening to me some day that happened to him. It was stronger than just a fear, it grew to be an obsession, a phobia. It happened to me over and over again in my dreams, and I woke up shivering, sweating at the thought. Burial alive! The most horrible death imaginable became easy, preferable, compared to that.

Attracted by the very thing I dreaded, I frequently visited cemeteries, wandered among the headstones, reading the inscriptions, shuddering to myself each time: "But was he—or she —really dead? How often has this thing happened before?"

Sometimes I would unexpectedly come upon burial services being conducted in this or that corner of the grounds. Cringing, yet drawing involuntarily nearer to watch and listen, that unforgotten scene at my father's grave would flash before my mind in all its pristine vividness and horror, and I would turn and run as though I felt myself in danger then and there of being drawn alive into that waiting grave I had just seen.

But one day, instead of running away, it had an opposite effect on me. I was irresistibly drawn forward to create a scene, a scandal, in their solemn midst. Or at least an unwelcome interruption.

The coffin, covered with flowers, was just about to be lowered; the mourners were standing reverently about. Almost without realizing what I was doing, I jostled my way through them until I stood on the very lip of the trench, cried out warningly: "Wait! Make sure, for God's sake, make sure he's dead!"

There was a stunned silence, they all drew back in fright, stared at me incredulously. The reading of the service stopped short, the officiating clergyman stood there book in hand blinking at me through his spectacles. Even the lowering of the coffin had been arrested, it swayed there on an uneven keel, partly in and partly out. Some of the flowers slipped off the top of it and fell in.

Realizing belatedly what a holy show I had made of myself, I turned and stumbled away as abruptly as I had come. No one made a move to detain me. Out of sight of them, I sat down on a stone bench behind a laurel hedge, and tormentedly held my head in my hands. Was I going crazy or what, to do such a thing?

About half an hour went by. I heard the sound of motors starting up one after the other on the driveway outside the grounds, and thought they had all gone away. A minute later there was a light step on the gravel path before me, and I looked up to meet the curious gaze of a young girl. She wore black, but there was something radiantly alive about her that looked strangely out of place in those surroundings. She was beautiful; I could read compassion in her forthright blue eyes. She had evidently been present at the services I had so outrageously interrupted, and had purposely stayed behind to talk to me.

"Do you mind if I sit here?" she murmured. I suddenly found myself wanting to talk to her. I felt strangely drawn to her. Youth is youth, even if its first meeting-place is a cemetery, and outside of this one phobia of mine, I was no different from any young fellow my age.

"Who was that?" I asked abruptly.

"A distant relative of mine," she said. "Why did you do it?" she added. "I could tell you weren't drunk or anything. I felt you must have a reason, so I asked them not to complain to the guards."

"It happened once to my father," I told her. "I've never quite gotten over it."

"I can see that," she said with quiet understanding. "But you shouldn't dwell on it. It's not natural at our age. Take me for instance. I had every respect for this relative we lost. I'm anything but a hard-hearted person. But it was all they could do to get me to come here today. They had to bribe me by telling me how well I looked in black." She smiled shyly, "I'm glad I did come, though."

"I am too," I said, and I meant it.

"My name is Joan Blaine," she told me as we walked toward the entrance. The sunlight fell across her face and seemed to light it, as we left the city of the dead and came out into the city of the living.

"I'm Bud Ingram," I told her.

"You're too nice a guy to be hanging around graveyards, Bud," she told me. "I'll have to take you in hand, try to get rid of this morbid streak in you."

She was as good as her word in the months that followed. Not that she was a bossy, dictatorial sort of girl, but—well, she liked me, just as I liked her, and she wanted to help me. We went to shows and dances together, took long drives in my car with the wind humming in our ears, lolled on the starlit beach while she strummed a guitar and the surf came whispering in—did all the things that make life so worth living, so hard to give up. Death and its long grasping shadows seemed very far away when I was with her; her golden laughter kept them at a distance. But when I was alone, slowly they came creeping back.

I didn't let her know about that. I loved her now, and like a fool I was afraid if I told her it was still with me, she'd give me up as hopeless. I should have known her better. I never again mentioned the subject of my father, or my fears; I let her think she had conquered them. It was my own undoing.

I was driving along a seldom-used road out in the open country late one Sunday afternoon. She hadn't been able to come with me that afternoon, but I was due back at her house for supper, and we were going to the movies afterward. I had taken a detour off the main highway that I thought might be a short-cut, get me there quicker. Then I saw this small, well-cared-for burial-ground to my left as I skimmed along. I braked and sat looking at it, what I could see of it. It was obviously private. A twelve-foot fence of iron palings, gilt-tipped, bordered it. Inside there were clumps of graceful poplars rustling in the breeze, ornamental stone urns, trim white-pebbled paths twisting in and out. Only an occasional, inconspicuous slab showed what it really was.

I drove on again, past the main entrance. It was chained and locked, and there was no sign of either a gatekeeper or a lodge to accommodate one. It evidently was the property of some one family or group of people, I told myself. I put my foot back on the accelerator and went on my way. Joan wouldn't have approved my even slowing down to look at the place, I knew; but I hadn't been able to help myself.

Then sharp eyes betrayed me. Even traveling at the rate I was, I caught sight of a place in the paling where one of the uprights had fallen out of its socket in the lower transverse that held them all; it was leaning over at an angle from the rest, causing a little tent-shaped gap. My good resolutions were all shattered at the sight. I threw in the clutch, got out to look, and before I knew it, had wriggled through and was standing on the inside—where I had no right to be.

"I'll just look around a minute," I said to myself, "then get out again before I get in trouble."

I followed one of the winding paths, and all the old familiar fears came back again as I did so. The sun was rapidly going down and the poplars threw long blue shadows across the ground. I turned aside to look at one of the freshly-erected headstones. There was an utter absence of floral wreaths or offerings, such as are to be found even in the poorest cemeteries, although nearly all the slabs looked fairly recent.

I was about to move on, when something caught my eye close up against the base of the slab. A small curved projection, like a tiny gutter to carry off rainwater. Then just under that, protected by it, so to speak, and almost indiscernible, a round opening, a hole, peering through the carefully-trimmed grass. It was too well-rounded to be an accidental gap or pit in the turf. And it was right where the raised grave met the tombstone. But that curling lip over it! Who had ever heard of a headstone provided with a gutter?

I glanced around to make sure I was unobserved, then squatted down over it, all but treading on the grave itself. I hooked one finger into the orifice and explored it carefully. Something smooth, hard, lined it, like a metal inner-tube. It was *not* a hole in the ground. It was a pipe leading up through the ground.

I had a penknife with me, and I got it out and scraped away the turf around the opening. A half-inch of gleaming, untarnished pipe, either chromium or brass, protruded when I got through. Stranger still, it had a tiny sieve or filter fitted into it, of fine wire-mesh, like a strainer to keep out the dust.

I was growing strangely excited, more excited every minute. This seemed to be a partial solution to what had haunted me for so long. If it was what I thought it was, it could take a little of the edge off the terror of burial—even for me, who dreaded it so.

I snapped my penknife shut, straightened up, moved on to the next marker. It wasn't close by, I had to look a little to find it, in the deepening violet of the twilight. But when I had, there was the same concealed orifice at its base, diminutive rain-shed, strainer, and all.

As I roamed about there in the dusk, I counted ten of them. Some bizarre cult or secret society, I wondered uneasily? For the first time I began to regret butting into the place; formless fears, vague premonitions of peril, that had nothing to do with that other inner fear of mine began to creep over me.

The sun had gone down long ago, and macabre mists were beginning to blur the outlines of the trees and foliage around me. I turned and started to beat my way back toward that place in the fence by which I had gained admittance, and which I had left a considerable distance behind me by now.

As I came abreast of the entrance gates—the real ones and not the gap through which I had come in—I saw the orange flash of a lantern on the outside of them, through the twilight murk. Chains clanged loosely, and the double gates ground inward, with a horrid groaning sound. Instinctively I jumped back behind a massive stone urn on a pedestal, with creepers spilling out of the top of it.

The gates clanged shut again, lessening my chances of getting out that way, which was the nearer of the two. I peered cautiously out around the narrowed stem of the urn, to see who it was.

A typical cemetery-watchman, no different from any of the rest of his kind, was crunching slowly along the nearest path, lantern in hand. Its rays splashed upward, tinged his face, and downward around the ground at his feet, but left the middle of his body in darkness. It created a ghastly effect, that of a lurid head without any body floating along above the ground. I quailed a little.

He passed by close enough for me to touch him, and I shifted tremblingly around to the other side of the urn, keeping it between us. He stopped at the nearest grave, only a short distance away, set his lantern close up against the headstone, and turned up the oil-wick a bit higher. I could see everything he was doing clearly in the increased radiance now. Could see, but couldn't understand at first.

He squatted down on his haunches just as I had—this, fortunately, wasn't the one I had disturbed with my penknife—and I saw him holding something in his hand that at first sight I mistook for a flower, a single flower or bloom, that he was about to plant. It had a long almost invisible stalk and ended in a little puff or cluster of fuzz, like a pussywillow. But then when I saw him insert it into the little orifice at the base of the slab, move it busily around, that gave me the clue to what it really was. It was simply a wirehandled brush, such as housewives use for cleaning the spouts of kettles. He was removing the day's accumulated dust and grit from the little mesh-strainer in the pipe, to keep it from clogging. I saw him take the brush out again, put his face down nearly to the ground, and blow his breath into it to help the process along. I heard the sound that made distinctly—*"Phoo!"* Even as I watched, he got up again, picked up his lantern, and trudged on to the next grave, and repeated the chore.

A chill slowly went down my spine. Why must those orifices be kept unclogged, free of choking dust, like that? Was there something living, breathing, that needed air, buried below each of those headstones?

I had to grip the pedestal before me with both hands, to hold myself up, to keep from turning and scampering blindly away then and there—and betraying my presence there in the process.

I waited until he had moved on out of sight, and some shrubbery blotted out the core of his lantern, if not its outermost rays;
then I turned and darted away, frightened sick.

I beat my way along the inside of the fence, trying to find that
unrepaired gap; and maddeningly it seemed to elude me. Then
just when I was about ready to lose my head and yell out in
panic, I glimpsed my car standing there in the darkness on the
other side, and a few steps further on brought me to the place.
Arms shaking palsiedly, I held up the loosened paling and
slipped through. I stopped a minute there beside the car, wiping off my damp forehead on the back of my sleeve. Then with
a deep breath of relief, I reached out, opened the car-door. I
slipped in, turned the key. . . . Nothing happened. The ignition
wire had been cut in my absence.

Before the full implication of the discovery had time to register on my mind, a man's head and shoulders rose silently, as out
of the ground, just beyond the opposite door, on the outside of
the road. He must have been crouched down out of sight,
watching me the whole time.

He was well-dressed, no highwayman or robber. His face, or
what I could see of it in the dark, had a solemn ascetic cast to
it. There was a slight smile to his mouth, but not of friendliness.

His voice, when he spoke, was utterly toneless. It held neither
reproach, nor threat, nor anger. "Did you—" His stony eyes
flickered just once past the cemetery-barrier—"have business
in there?"

What was there I could say? "No. I simply went in, to—to rest
awhile, and think."

"There was rather a severe wind—and rainstorm up here a
week ago," he let me know. "It may have uprooted the sign we
had standing at the entrance to this roadway. Thoroughfare is
prohibited, it runs through private grounds."

"I saw no sign," I told him truthfully.

"But if you went in just to rest and think, how is it you were
so agitated when you left just now? I saw you when you came
out. What had you done in there to frighten you so?" And then,

very slowly, spacing each word, "What—had—you—seen?"

But I'd had about enough. "Are you in charge of these grounds? Well, whether you are or not, I resent being questioned like this! You've damaged my car, with deliberation. I've a good mind to—"

"Step out and come with me," he said, and here was suddenly the thin, ugly muzzle of a Lüger resting across the doorstep, trained at me. His face remained cold, expressionless.

I pulled the catch out, stepped down beside him. "This is kidnaping," I said grimly.

"No," he said, "you'd have a hard time proving that. You're guilty of trespassing. We have a perfect right to detain you—until you've explained clearly, to our satisfaction, what you saw in there to frighten you so."

Or in other words, I said to myself, just how much I've found out—about something I'm not supposed to know. Something kept warning me: No matter what turns up, don't admit you noticed those vents above the graves in there. *Don't let on you saw them!* I didn't know why I shouldn't, but it kept pounding at me relentlessly.

"Walk up the road ahead of me," he directed. "If you try to bolt off into the darkness, I'll shoot you without compunction."

I turned and walked slowly back along the middle of the road, hands helplessly at my sides. The scrape and grate of his footsteps followed behind me. He knew enough not to close in and give me a chance to wrest the gun from him. I may have been afraid of burial alive, but I wasn't particularly afraid of bullets.

We came abreast of the cemetery-gate just as the watchman was letting himself out.

He threw up his head in surprise, picked up his lantern and came over.

"This man was in there just now. Walk along parallel to him, but not too close, and keep your lantern on him."

"Yes, Brother." At the time I thought it was just slangy informality on the caretaker's part; the respectful way he said it should have told me different. As he took up his position off to one side of me I heard him hiss vengefully, "Dirty snooper!"

We were now following a narrow brick footpath, which I had missed seeing altogether from the car that afternoon, indian file, myself in the middle. It brought us, in about five minutes, to a substantial-looking country house, entirely surrounded by such a thick growth of trees that it must have been completely invisible from both roads even in the broad daylight. The lower story was of stone, the upper of stucco. It was obviously not abandoned or in disrepair, but gave no sign of life. All the windows, upper as well as lower, had been boarded up.

The three of us stepped up on the empty porch, whose floorboards glistened with new varnish. The man with the lantern thrust a key into the seemingly boarded-up door, turned it, and swung the entire dummy-facing back intact. Behind it stood the real door, thick oak with an insert of bevelled glass, veiled on the inside by a curtain through which an electric light glimmered dully.

He unlocked that, too, and we were in a warm, well-furnished hall. The watchman took up his lantern and went toward the back of this, with a murmured "I'll be right in." My original captor turned me aside into a room furnished like a study, came in after me, at last pocketed the Lüger that had persuaded me so well.

A man was sitting behind a large desk, with a reading lamp trained on it, going over some papers. He looked up, paled momentarily, then recovered himself. I'd seen that however; it showed that all the fear was not on my side of the fence. The same silent, warning voice kept pegging away at me: Don't admit you saw those vents, watch your step!

The man who had brought me in said, "I found his car parked beside the cemetery-rail—where lightning struck and loosened that upright the other night. I waited, until he came out. I thought you'd like to talk to him, Brother." Again that "Brother."

"You were right, Brother," the man behind the desk nodded. He said to me, "What were you doing in there?"

The door behind me opened and the man who had played the part of caretaker came in. He had on a business-suit now just like the other two, in place of the dungarees and greasy sweater. I took a good look at his hands; they were not calloused, but had been recently blistered. I could see the circular threads of skin remaining where the blisters had opened. He was an amateur—and not a professional—gravedigger.

"Did he tamper with anything?" the man behind the desk asked him in that cool, detached voice.

"He certainly did. Jerome's was disturbed. The sod—around *it*—had been scraped away, just enough to lay *it* bare." He accented that pronoun, to give it special meaning.

My original captor went through my pockets deftly and swiftly, brought to light the penknife, snapped it open, showed them the grass-stains on the steel blade.

The beat of Death's dark wings was close in the air above my head.

"I'm sorry. Take him out in back of the house with you," the one behind the desk said flatly. As though those words were my death-warrant.

The whole thing was too incredible, too fantastic, I couldn't quite force myself to believe I was in danger of being put to death then and there like a mad dog. But I saw the one next to me slowly reach toward the pocket where the Lüger bulged.

"I'll have to go out there and dig again, after I got all cleaned up," the one who had played the part of watchman sighed regretfully, and glanced ruefully at his blistered hands.

I looked from one to the other, still not fully aware of what it all portended. Then on an impulse—an impulse that saved my life—I blurted out: "You see, it wasn't just idle curiosity on my part. All my life, since I was ten, I've dreaded the thought of burial alive—"

Before I knew it I had told them the whole story, about my

father and the lasting impression it had made.

After I had finished, the man at the desk said, slowly, "What year was this—and where?"

"In New Orleans," I said, "in 1922."

His eyes flicked to the man on my left. "Get New Orleans on long distance," he said quietly. "Find out if an undertaker was brought to trial for burying a paralyzed war-veteran named Donald Ingram alive in All-Saints Cemetery in September 1922."

"The 14th," I said, shutting my eyes briefly.

"You are a lawyer," he instructed, "doing it at the behest of the man's son, because of some litigation that is pending, if they ask you." The door closed after him; I stayed there with the other two.

The envoy came back, silently handed a written sheet of paper to the one at the desk. He read it through. "Your mother?" he said.

"She died insane in 1929. I had her cremated, to avoid—"

He crumpled the sheet of paper, threw it from him. "Would you care to join us?" he said, his eyes sparkling shrewdly.

"Who—are you?" I hedged.

He didn't answer that. "We can cure you, heal you. We can do more for you than any doctor, any mental specialist in the world. Would you not like to have this dread, this curse, lifted from you, never to return?"

I would, I said; which was true any way you looked at it.

"You have been particularly afflicted, because of the circumstances of your father's death," he went on. "However, don't think you're alone in your fear of death. There are scores, hundreds of others, who feel as you do, even if not quite so strongly. From them we draw our membership; we give them new hope and new life, rob death of all its terrors for them. The sense of mortality that has been crippling them ends, the world is theirs to conquer, nothing can stop them. They become like the immortal gods. Wealth, fame, all the world's goods, are theirs for the taking, for their frightened fellow-men, fearful of dying, defeated before they have even begun to live, cannot compete with them. Is not this a priceless gift? And we are offering it to you because you need it so badly, so very much more badly than anyone who has ever come to us before." He was anything but cold and icy now. He was glowing, fervent, fanatic, the typical proselyte seeking a new convert.

"I'm not rich," I said cagily, to find out where the catch was. And that's where it was—right there.

"Not now," he said, "because this blight has hampered your efforts, clipped your wings, so to speak. Few are who come to us. We ask nothing material from you now. Later, when we have helped you, and you are one of the world's fortunate ones, you may repay us, to assist us to carry on our good work."

Which might be just a very fancy way of saying future black-mail.

"And now—your decision?"

"I accept—your kind offer," I said thoughtfully, and immediately amended it mentally: "At least until I can get out of here and back to town."

But he immediately scotched that, as though he'd read my mind. "There is no revoking your decision once you've made it. That brings instant death. Slow suffocation is the manner of their going, those who break faith with us. Burial while still in full possession of their faculties, is the penalty."

The one doom that was a shade more awful than what had happened to my father; the only one. He at least had not come to until after it had been done. And it had not lasted long with him, it couldn't have.

"Those vents you saw can prolong it, for whole days," he went on. "They can be turned on or off at will."

"I said I'd join you," I shuddered, resisting an impulse to clap both hands to my ears.

"Good." He stretched forth his right hand to me and much against my inclination I took it. Then he clasped my wrist with his left, and had me do likewise with mine. I had to repeat this double grip with each of the others in turn. "You are now one of us."

The cemetery watchman left the room and returned with a tray holding three small skulls and a large one. I could feel the short hairs on the back of my neck standing up of their own accord. None of them were real though; they were wood or celluloid imitations. They all had flaps that opened at the top; one was a jug and the other three steins.

The man behind the desk named the toast. "To our Friend!" I thought he meant myself at first; he meant that shadowy enemy of all mankind, the Grim Reaper.

"We are called The Friends of Death," he explained to me when the grisly containers had been emptied. "To outline our creed and purpose briefly, it is this: That death is life, and life is death. We have mastered death, and no member of the Friends of Death need ever fear it. They 'die,' it is true, but after death they are buried in special graves in our private cemetery —graves having air vents, such as you discovered. Also, our graves are equipped with electric signals, so that after the bodies of our buried members begin to respond to the secret treatment our scientists have given them before internment, we are warned. Then we come and release them—and they live again. Moreover, they are released, freed of their thralldom; from then on death is an old familiar friend instead of an enemy. They no longer fear it. Do you not see what a wonderful boon this would be in your case, Brother Bud; you who have suffered so from that fear?"

I thought to myself, "They're insane! They must be!" I forced myself to speak calmly. "And the penalty you spoke of—that you inflict on those who betray or disobey you?"

"Ah!" he inhaled zestfully, "You are buried before death— without benefit of the attention of our experts. The breathing-tube is slowly, infinitesimally, shut off from above a notch at a time, by means of a valve—until it is completely sealed. It is," he concluded, "highly unpleasant while it lasts." Which was the most glaring case of understatement I had ever yet encountered.

There wasn't much more to this stage of my preliminary initiation. A ponderous ebony-bound ledger was brought out, with the inevitable skull on its cover in ivory. I was made to draw blood from my wrist and sign my name, with that, in it. The taking of the oath of secrecy followed.

"You will receive word of when your formal initiation is to be," I was told. "Return to your home and hold yourself ready until you hear from us. Members are not supposed to be known to one another, with the exception of us three, so you are required to attend the rites in a specially-constructed skull-mask which will be given to you. We are the Book-keeper (man behind the desk), the Messenger (man with the Lüger), and the Grave-digger. We have chapters in most of the large cities. If business or anything should require you to move your residence elsewhere, don't fail to notify us and we will transfer you to our branch in the city to which you are going."

"Like hell I will!" I thought.

"All members in good faith are required to be present at each of the meetings; failure to do so invokes the Penalty."

The grinning ghoul had the nerve to sling his arm around my shoulder in a friendly way as he led me toward the door, like a hospitable host speeding a parting guest. It was all I could do to keep from squirming at the feel of it. I wanted to part his teeth with my right fist then and there, but the Messenger, with the Lüger on him, was a few steps behind me. I was getting out, and that was all that seemed to matter at the time. That was all I wanted—out, and a lungful of fresh air, and a good stiff jolt of whiskey to get the bad taste out of my mouth.

They unlocked the two doors for me, and even flashed on the porch-light so I could see my way down the steps. "You can get a city bus over on the State Highway. We'll have your car fixed for you and standing in front of your door first thing in the morning."

But at the very end a hint of warning again showed itself through all their friendliness. "Be sure to come when you're sent for. We have eyes and ears everywhere, where you'd least expect it. No warning is given, no second chances are ever allowed!"

Again that double grip, three times repeated, and it was over. The two doors were closed and locked, the porch-light snuffed out, and I was groping my way down the brick footpath—alone. Behind me not a chink of light showed from the boarded-up house. It had all been as fleeting, as unreal, as unbelievable, as a bad dream.

I shivered all the way back to the city in the heated bus; the other passengers must have thought I had the grippe. Joan Blaine found me at midnight in a bar around the corner from where I lived, stewed to the gills, so drunk I could hardly stand up straight—but still shivering. "Take him home, miss," she told me afterwards the bartender whispered to her. "He's been standing there like that three solid hours, staring like he sees ghosts, frightening my other customers off into corners!"

I woke up fully dressed on top of my bed next morning, with just a blanket over me. "That was just a dream, the whole thing!" I kept snarling to myself defensively.

I heard Joan's knock at the door, and the first thing she said when I let her in was: "Something happen to your car last night? I saw a mechanic drive up to the door with it just now, as I was coming in. He got out, walked off, and left it standing there!"

There went my just-a-dream defense. She saw me rear back a little, but didn't ask why. I went over to the window and looked down at it. It was waiting there without anyone in or near it.

"Were you in a smash-up?" she demanded. "Is that why you stood me up? Is that why you were shaking so when I found you?"

I grabbed at the out eagerly. "Yeah, that's it! Bad one, too; came within an inch of winding up behind the eight-ball. Gave me the jitters for hours afterwards."

She looked at me, said quietly: "Funny kind of a smash-up, to make you say 'Little pipes coming up through the ground.' That's all you said over and over. Not a scratch on you, either. No report of any smack-up involving a car with your license-number, when I checked with the police after you'd been three hours overdue at my house." She gave me an angry look, at least it tried to be. "All right, I'm a woman and therefore a fibber. But I sewed you up pretty this time. I asked that grease-monkey what it was just now, and he said only a cut ignition-wire!"

Her face softened and she came over to me. "What're you keeping from me, honey? Tell Joan. She's for you, don't you know that by now?"

No, it was just a dream, I wasn't going to tell her. And even if it wasn't a dream, I'd be damned if I'd tell her! Worry her? I should say not! "All right, there wasn't any smash-up and there wasn't anything else either. I'm just a heel, I got stiff and stood you up, that's all."

I could tell she didn't believe me; she left looking unconvinced. I'd just about closed the door after her when my phone rang.

"You're to be complimented, Brother," an anonymous voice said. "We're glad to see that you're to be relied on," and then the connection broke.

Eyes everywhere, ears everywhere. I stood there white in the face, and calling it a dream wouldn't work any more.

The summons to attend came three weeks later to the day. A large white card such as formal invitations are printed on, inside an envelope with my name on it. Only the card itself was blank. I couldn't make head or tail of it at first, didn't even connect it with them. Then down in the lower corner I made out the faintly-pencilled word "Heat."

I went and held it over the steam radiator. A death's head slowly started to come through, first faint yellow, then brown, then black. And under it a few lines of writing, in hideous travesty of a normal social invitation.

Your Presence Is Requested
Friday, 9 P. M.
You Will Be Called For

F. O. D.

"Call away, but I won't be here!" was my first explosive reaction. "This goblin stuff has gone far enough. The keepers ought
to be out after that whole outfit with butterfly-nets!"

Then presently, faint stirrings of curiosity began to prompt
me: "What have you got to lose? Why not see what it's like,
anyway? What can they do to you after all? Pack a gun with you,
that's all."

When I left the office late that afternoon I made straight for
a pawnshop over on the seamy side of town, barged in through
the saloon-like half-doors. I already had had a license for some
time back, so there was not likely to be any difficulty about
getting what I wanted.

While the owner was in the back getting some out to show
me, a down-and-outer came in with a mangy overcoat he
wanted to peddle. The clerk took it up front to examine it more
closely, and for a moment the two of us were left standing alone
on the customer's side of the counter. I swear there was not a
gun in sight on the case in front of me. Nothing to indicate what
I had come in for.

An almost inaudible murmur sounded from somewhere beside me: "I wouldn't, Brother, if I were you. You'll get in trouble
if you do."

I looked around sharply. The seedy derelict seemed unaware
of my existence, was staring dejectedly down at the glass case
under him. Yet if he hadn't spoken who had?

He was turned down, took back the coat, and shuffled dis-
heartedly out into the street again, without a glance at me as
he went by. The doors flapped loosely behind him. A prickling
sensation ran up my spine. That had been a warning from *them*.

"Sorry," I said abruptly, when the owner came back with
some revolvers to show me, "I've changed my mind!" I went

out hurriedly, looked up and down the street. The derelict had vanished. Yet the pawnshop was in the middle of the block, about equally distant from each corner. He couldn't have possibly—! I even asked a janitor, setting out ashcans a few steps away. "Did you see an old guy carrying a coat come out of here just now?"

"Mister," he said to me, "nobody's come out of there since you went in yourself two minutes ago."

"I suppose he was an optical illusion," I said to myself. "Like hell he was!"

So I went without a gun.

A not only embarrassing but highly dangerous *contretemps* was waiting for me when I got back to my place a few minutes later. Joan was in the apartment waiting for me, had had the landlady, who knew her quite well, let her in. Tonight of all nights, when they were calling for me! I not only had to stay here, but I had to get her out of the way before they showed up.

The first thing my eye fell on as I came in was that damned invitation, too. It was lying about where I'd left it, but I could have sworn I'd put it back in its envelope, and now it was on the outside, skull staring up from it as big as life. Had she seen it? If so, she gave no sign. I sidled around in front of it and pushed it out of sight in a drawer with my hands behind my back.

"Take a lady to supper," she said.

But I couldn't, there wouldn't be time enough to get back there again if I did; they were due in about a quarter of an hour, I figured. It was an hour's ride out there.

"Damn! I just ate," I lied. "Why didn't you let me know—"

"How's for the movies then?" She was unusually persistent tonight, almost as though she'd found out something and wanted to force me to break down and admit it.

I mumbled something about a headache, going to bed early, my eyes fixed frantically on the clock. Ten minutes now.

"I seem popular tonight," she shrugged. But she made no move to go, sat there watching me curiously, intently.

Sweat was beading my forehead. Seven minutes to go. If I let her stay any longer, I was endangering her. But how could I get rid of her without hurting her, making her suspicious—if she wasn't already?

"You seem very tense tonight," she murmured. "I never saw you watch a clock so closely." Five minutes were left.

They helped me out. Eyes everywhere, ears everywhere. The phone rang. Again that anonymous voice, as three weeks before.

"Better get that young woman out of the way, Brother. The car's at the corner, waiting to come up to your door. You'll be late."

"Yes," I said, and hung up.

"Competition?" she asked playfully when I went back.

"Joan," I said hoarsely, "you run along. I've got to go out. There's something I can't tell you about. You've got to trust me. You do, don't you?" I pleaded.

She only said one thing, sadly, apprehensively, as she got up and walked toward the door. "I do. But you don't seem to trust —me." She turned impulsively, her hands crept pleadingly up my lapels. "Oh, why can't you tell me!"

"You don't know what you're asking!" I groaned.

She turned and ran swiftly down the stairs, I could hear her sobbing gently as she went. I never heard the street-door close after her, though.

Moments later my call-bell rang, I grabbed my hat and ran down. A touring-car was standing in front of the house, rear door invitingly open. I got in and found myself seated next to the Messenger. "All right, Brother," he said to the driver. All I could see of the latter was the back of his head; the mirror had been removed from the front of the car.

"Let me caution you," the Messenger said, as we started off. "You went into a pawnshop this afternoon to buy a gun. Don't try that, if you know what's good for you. And after this, see to it that the young lady isn't admitted to your room in your absence. She might have read the summons we sent."

"I destroyed it," I lied.

He handed me something done up in paper. "Your mask," he said. "Don't put it on until we get past the city-limits."

It was a frightening-looking thing when I did so. It was not a mask but a hood for the entire head, canvas and cardboard, chalk-white to simulate a skull, with deep black hollows for the eyes and grinning teeth for the mouth.

The private highway, as we neared the house, was lined on both sides with parked cars. I counted fifteen of them as we flashed by; and there must have been as many more ahead, in the other direction.

We drew up and he and I got out. I glanced in cautiously over my shoulder at the driver as we went by, to see if I could see his face, but he too had donned one of the death-masks.

"Never do that," the Messenger warned me in a low voice. "Never try to penetrate any other member's disguise."

The house was as silent and lifeless as the last time—on the outside. Within it was a horrid, crawling charnel-house alive with skull-headed figures, their bodies encased in business-suits, tuxedos, and evening dresses. The lights were all dyed a ghastly green or ghostly blue, by means of colored tissue-paper sheathed around them. A group of masked musicians kept playing the Funeral March over and over, with brief pauses in between. A coffin stood in the center of the main living-room.

I was drenched with sweat under my own mask and sick almost to death, even this early in the game.

At last the Book-keeper, unmasked, appeared in their midst. Behind him came the Messenger. The dead-head guests all applauded enthusiastically, gathered around them in a ring. Those in other rooms came in. The musicians stopped the Death March.

The Book-keeper bowed, smiled graciously. "Good evening, fellow corpses," was his chill greeting. "We are gathered to-

gether to witness the induction of our newest member." There
was an electric tension. "Brother Bud!" His voice rang out like
a clarion in the silence. "Step forward."

My heart burst into little pieces in my chest. I could feel my
legs getting ready to go down under me. That roaring in my
ears was my own crazed thoughts. And I knew with a terrible
certainty that this was no initiation—this was to be "the punishment." For I was of no value to them—having no money.

Before I had time to tear off my mask, fight and claw my way
out, I was seized by half-a-dozen of them, thrust forward into
the center of the circle. I was forced to my knees and held in
that position, writhing and twisting. My coat, vest and shirt
were stripped off and my mask was removed. A linen shroud,
with neck-and-arm holes, was pulled over my head. My hands
were caught, pulled behind my back, and lashed tight with
leather straps. I kicked out at them with my legs and squirmed
about on the floor like a maniac—I, who was the only sane one
of all of them! I rasped strangled imprecations at them. The
corpse was unwilling.

They caught my threshing legs finally, strapped those together at the ankles and the knees, then carefully drew the
shroud the rest of the way down. I was lifted bodily like a log,
a long twisting white thing in its shroud, and fitted neatly into
the quilted coffin. Agonizedly I tried to rear. I was forced down
flat and strapped in place across the waist and across the chest.
All I could make now were inchoate animal-noises, gurglings
and keenings. My face was a steaming cauldron of sweat.

I could still see the tops of their masked heads from where I
was, bending down around me in a circle. Gloating, grinning,
merciless death's heads. One seemed to be staring at me in fixed
intensity; they were all staring, of course, but I saw him briefly
hold a pair of glasses to the eyeholes of his mask, as though—
almost as though I was known to him, from that other world
outside. A moment later he beckoned the Book-keeper to him
and they withdrew together out of my line of vision, as though
conferring about something.

The face of the Grave-digger had appeared above the rim of my coffin meanwhile, as though he had just come in from outside.

"Is it ready?" the Messenger asked him.

"Ready—and six feet deep," was the blood-curdling answer.

I saw them up-end the lid of the coffin, to close it over me. One was holding a hammer and a number of long nails in his hand, in readiness. Down came the lid, flat, smothering my squall of unutterable woe, and the blue-green light that had been bearing down on me until now went velvety black.

Then, immediately afterwards, it was partially displaced again and the head of the Book-keeper was bending down close to mine. I could feel his warm breath on my forehead. His whisper was meant for me alone. "Is it true you are betrothed to a young lady of considerable means, a Miss Joan Blaine?"

I nodded, so far gone with terror I was only half-aware what I was doing.

"Is it her uncle, Rufus Blaine, who is the well-known manufacturer?"

I nodded again, groaned weakly. His face suddenly whisked away, but instead of the lid being fitted back into place as I momentarily expected, it was taken away altogether.

Arms reached in, undid the body-straps that held me, and I was helped to a sitting-position. A moment later the shroud had been drawn off me like a long white stocking, and my hands and legs were freed. I was lifted out.

I was too spent to do anything but tumble to the floor and lie there inert at the feet of all of them, conscious but unable to move. I heard and saw the rest of what went on from that position.

The Book-keeper held up his hand. "Fellow corpses!" he proclaimed, "Brother Bud's punishment is indefinitely postponed, for reasons best known to myself and the other heads of the chapter—"

But the vile assemblage of masked fiends didn't like that at all; they were being cheated of their prey. "No! No!" they gibbered, and raised their arms threateningly toward him. "The coffin cries for an occupant! The grave yearns for an inmate!"

"It shall have one!" he promised. "You shall witness your internment. You shall not be deprived of your funeral joys, of the wake you are entitled to!" He made a surreptitious sign to the Messenger, and the skull-crested ledger was handed to him. He opened it, hastily turned its pages, consulted the entries, while an ominous, expectant silence reigned. He pointed to something in the book, his eyes beaded maliciously. Then once more he held up his hand. "You shall witness a penalty, an irrevocable burial with the vents closed!"

Crooning cries of delight sounded on all sides.

"I find here," he went on, "the name of a member who has accepted all our benefits, yet steadily defaulted on the contributions due us. Who has means, yet who had tried to cheat us by signing over his wealth to others, hiding it in safe-deposit boxes under false names, and so on. I hereby condemn Brother Anselm to be penalized!"

A mad scream sounded from their midst, and one of the masked figures tried to dash frightenedly toward the door. He was seized, dragged back, and the ordeal I had just been through was repeated. I couldn't help noticing, with chill forebodings, that the Book-keeper made a point of having me stood up on my feet and held erect to watch the whole damnable thing. In other words, by being a witness and a participant, I was now as guilty as any of them. A fact which they were not likely to let me forget if I balked later on at meeting their blackmail-demands. Demands which they expected me to fulfill with the help of Joan's money—her uncle's, rather—once I was married to her. It was the mention of her name, I realized, that had saved me. I was more use to them alive than dead, for the present, that was all.

Meanwhile, to the accompaniment of one last wail of despair that rang in my ears for days afterward, the coffin lid had been nailed down fast on top of the pulsing, throbbing contents the box held. It was lifted by four designated pall-bearers, carried outside to a waiting hearse lurking amidst the trees, while the musicians struck up the Death March. The rest of the murderous crew followed, myself included, held fast by the Messenger on one side, the Book-keeper on the other. They forced me into a limousine between them, and off we glided after the hearse, the other cars following us.

We all got out again at a lonely glen in the woods, where a grave had been prepared. No need to dwell on the scene that followed. Only one thing need be told. As the box was being lowered into it, in complete silence, sounds of frenzied motion could distinctly be heard within it, as of something rolling desperately from side to side. I watched as through a film of delirium, restraining hands on my wrists compelling me to look on.

When at last it was over, when at last the hole in the ground was gone, and the earth had been stamped down flat again on top of it, I found myself once more in the car that had originally called for me, alone this time with just the driver, being taken back to the city. I deliberately threw my own mask out of the side of the car, in token of burning my bridges behind me.

When he veered in toward the curb in front of my house, I jumped down and whirled, intending to grab him by the throat and drag him out after me. The damnable machine was already just a tail-light whirring away from me; he hadn't braked at all.

I chased upstairs, pulled down the shades so no one could see in, hauled out my valise, and began pitching things into it from full-height, my lower jaw trembling. Then I went to the phone, hesitated briefly, called Joan's number. Eyes everywhere, ears everywhere! But I had to take the chance. Her peril, now, was as great as mine.

Somebody else answered in her place. "Joan can't talk to anyone right now. The doctor's ordered her to bed, he had to give her a sedative to quiet her nerves, she came in awhile ago in a hysterical condition. We don't know what happened to her, we can't get her to tell us!"

I hung up, mystified. I thought: "I did that to her, by asking her to leave tonight. I hurt her, and she must have brooded about it—" I kicked my valise back under the bed. Friends of Death or no Friends of Death, I couldn't go until I'd seen her.

I didn't sleep all that night. By nine the next morning I'd made up my mind. I put the invitation to the meeting in my inside pocket and went around to the nearest precinct-house. I regretted now having thrown my mask away the night before, that would have been more evidence to show them.

I asked, tight-lipped, to see the captain in charge. He listened patiently, scanned the invitation, tapped his lower teeth thoughtfully with his thumbnail. It slowly dawned on me that he considered me slightly cracked, a crank; my story must have sounded too fantastic to be altogether credible. Then when I'd given him the key to my falling in with them in the first place —my graveyard obsession—I saw him narrow his eyes shrewdly at me and nod to himself as though that explained everything.

He summoned one of the detectives, half-heartedly instructed him: "Investigate this man's story, Crow. See what you can find out about this—ahem—country-house and mysterious graveyard out toward Ellendale. Report back to me." And then hurriedly went on to me, as though he couldn't wait to get rid of me, felt I really ought to be under observation at one of the psychopathic wards, "We'll take care of you, Mr. Ingram. You go on home now and don't let it worry you." He flipped the death's-head invitation carelessly against the edge of his desk once or twice. "You're sure this isn't just a high-pressure circular from some life-insurance concern or other?"

I locked my jaw grimly and walked out of there without answering. A lot of good they were going to be to me, I could see that. All but telling me to my face I was screwy.

Crow, the detective, came down the steps behind me leisurely buttoning his topcoat. He said, "An interstate bus'll leave me off close by there." It would, but I wondered how he knew that.

He threw up his arm as one approached and signalled it to

stop. It swerved in and the door folded back automatically. His eyes bored through mine, through and through like gimlets, for just a second before he swung aboard. "See you later, Brother," he said. "You've earned the Penalty if anyone ever did. You're going down—without an air-pipe." Then he and the bus were gone—out toward Ellendale.

The sidewalk sort of swayed all around me, like jelly. It threatened to come up and hit me flat across the face, but I grabbed hold of a bus-stop stanchion and held onto it until the vertigo had passed. One of them right on the plainclothes squad! What was the sense of going back in there again? If I hadn't been believed the first time, what chance had I of being believed now? And the way he'd gone off and left me just now showed how safe he felt on that score. The fact that he hadn't tried to hijack me, force me to go out there with him, showed how certain they felt of laying hands on me when they were ready.

Well they hadn't yet! And they weren't going to, not if I had anything to say about it. Since I couldn't get help, flight was all that remained then. Flight it would be. They couldn't be everywhere, omnipotent; there must be places where I'd be safe from them—if only for a little while.

I drew my money out of the bank, I phoned in to the office that they could find somebody else for my job, I wasn't coming in any more. I went and got my car out of the garage where I habitually bedded it, and had it serviced, filled and checked for a long trip. I drove around to where I lived, paid up, put my valise in the back. I drove over to Joan's.

She looked pale, as though she'd been through something the night before, but she was up and around. My arms went around her. I said, "I've got to get out of town—now, before the hour's out—but I love you, and I'll get word to you where I am the minute I'm able to."

She answered quietly, looking up into my face: "What need is there of that, when I'll be right there with you—wherever it is?"

"But you don't know what I'm up against—and I can't tell you why, I'll only involve you!"

"I don't want to know. I'm coming. We can get married there, wherever it's to be—" She turned and ran out, was back again in no time, dragging a coat after her with one hand, hugging a jewelcase and an overnight-bag to her with the other, hat perched rakishly on the back of her head. We neither of us laughed, this was no time for laughter.

"I'm ready—" She saw by my face that something had happened, even in the brief time she'd been gone. "What is it?" She dropped the things; a string of pearls rolled out of the case.

I led her to the window and silently pointed down to my car below. I'd had the tires pumped up just now at the garage; all four rims rested flatly on the asphalt now, all the air let out. "Probably emptied the tank, cut the ignition, crippled it irreparably, while they were at it," I said in a flat voice, "We're being watched every minute! Damn it, I shouldn't have come here, I'm dragging you to your grave!"

"Bud," she said, "if that's where I've got to go to be with you —even that's all right with me."

"Well, we're not there yet!" I muttered doggedly. "Train, then."

She nodded eagerly. "Where to?"

"New York. And if we're not safe even there, we can hop a boat to England—that surely ought to be out of their reach."

"Who are they?" she wanted to know.

"As long as I don't tell you, you've still got a chance. I'm not dooming you if I can help it!"

She didn't press the point, almost—it occurred to me later— almost as though she already knew all there was to know. "I'll call the station, find out when the next one leaves—"

I heard her go out in the hall, jiggle the phone-hook for a connection. I squatted down, stuck the pearls back in the case for her. I raised my eyes, and her feet were there on the carpet before me again.

She didn't whimper and she didn't break; just looked through me and beyond as I straightened up. "They mean business," she breathed. "The phone's gone dead."

She moved back to the window, stood there looking out. "There's a man been standing across the way reading a newspaper the whole time we've been talking in here. He seems to be waiting for a bus, but three have gone by and he's still there. We'll never make it." Then suddenly her face brightened. "Wait, I have it!" But her enthusiasm seemed spurious, premeditated, to me. "Instead of leaving here together to try to get through to the station, suppose we separate—and meet later on the train. I think that's safer."

"What! Leave you behind alone in this place? Nothing doing."

"I'll go first, without taking anything with me, just as though I were going shopping. I won't go near the station. I can take an ordinary city-bus to Hamlin, that's the first train-stop on the way to New York. You give me a head-start, show yourself plentifully at the window in case he's one of their plants, then slip out the back way, get your ticket and get aboard. I'll be waiting for you on the station-platform at Hamlin, you can whisk me aboard with you; they only stop there a minute."

The way she told it, it sounded reasonable, I would be running most of the risk, getting from here to the station. I agreed. "Stay in the thick of the crowd the whole way," I warned her. "Don't take any chances. If anyone so much as looks at you cross-eyed, holler blue murder, pull down the whole police-force on top of them."

"I'll handle it," she said competently. She came close, our lips met briefly. Her eyes misted over. "Bud darling," she murmured low, "a long life and happy one to you!" Before it had dawned on me what a strange thing to say that was, she had flitted out and the door had closed after her.

I watched narrowly from the window, ready to dash out if the man with the paper so much as made a move toward her. To get the downtown bus she had to cross to where he was and wait beside him. He took no notice of her, never raised his eyes from his paper—a paper whose pages he hadn't turned in a full ten minutes. She stood there facing one way, he the other. They could, of course, have exchanged remarks without my being aware of it. The bus flashed by and I tensed. A minute later I relaxed again. She was gone; he was still there reading that never-ending paper.

I decided to give her a half-hour's start. That way, the train being faster than the bus, we'd both get to Hamlin about simultaneously. I didn't want her to have to wait there alone on the station-platform too long if it could be avoided. Meanwhile I kept returning to the window, to let the watcher see that I was still about the premises. I—Joan too for that matter—had long ago decided that he was a lookout, a plant, and then about twenty minutes after she'd gone, my whole theory collapsed like a house of cards. A girl, whom he must have been waiting for the whole time, came hurrying up to him and I could see her making excuses. He flung down his paper, looked at his wristwatch, took her roughly by the arm and they stalked off, arguing violently.

My relief was only momentary. The cut phone-wires, my crippled car, were evidence enough that unseen eyes had been, and still were watching me the whole time. Only they did it more skillfully than by means of a blatant look-out on a street-corner. At least with him I had thought I knew where I was at; now I was in the dark again.

Thirty-five minutes after Joan had gone I slipped out through the back door, leaving my car still out there in front (as if that would do any good), leaving my hat perched on the top of an easy-chair with its back toward the window (as if that would, either). I followed the service-alley between the houses until I'd come out on the nearest sidestreet, around the corner from Joan's. It was now one in the afternoon. There wasn't a soul in sight at the moment, in this quiet residential district, and it seemed humanly impossible that I had been sighted.

I followed a circuitous zig-zag route, down one street, across another, in the general direction of the station, taking time out at frequent intervals to scan my surroundings with the help of some polished show-case that reflected them like a mirror. For all the signs of danger that I could notice, the Friends of Death seemed very far-away, non-existent.

I slipped into the station finally through the baggage-entrance on the side, and worked my way from there toward the front, keeping my eyes open as I neared the ticket-windows. The place was a beehive of activity as usual, which made it both safer and at the same time more dangerous for me. I was safer from sudden seizure with all these people around me, but it was harder to tell whether I was being watched or not.

"Two to New York," I said guardedly to the agent. And pocketing the tickets with a wary look around me, "When's the next one leave?"

"Half-an-hour."

I spent the time by keeping on the move. I didn't like the looks of the waiting-room; there were too many in it. I finally decided a telephone-booth would be the likeliest bet. Its gloom would offer me a measure of concealment, and instead of having four directions to watch at once, I'd only have one. Then, too, they were located conveniently near to the gates leading outside to the tracks. Passengers, however, were not being allowed through the latter yet.

I took a last comprehensive look around, then went straight at a booth as though I had a call to make. The two on each side of it were definitely empty; I saw that as I stepped in. I gave the bulb over me a couple of turns so it wouldn't flash on, left the slide open on a crack so I could catch the starter's announcement when it came, and leaned back watchfully against the far partition, eyes on the glass in front of me.

Twenty minutes went by and nothing happened. An amplifier suddenly came to life outside, and the starter's voice thundered through it. "New York Express. Track Four. Leaving in ten minutes. First stop Hamlin—"

And then, with a shock like high-voltage coursing through me, the phone beside me started pealing thinly.

I just stood there and stared at it, blood draining from my
face. A call to a tollbooth? It must, it *must* be a wrong number,
somebody wanted the Information Booth or—! It must have
been audible outside, with all I had the slide partly closed. One
of the redcaps passing by turned, looked over, then started
coming across toward where I was. To get rid of him I picked
up the receiver, put it to my ear.

"You'd better come out now, time's up," a flat, deadly voice
said. "They're calling your train, but you're not getting on that
one—or any other."

"Wh—where are talking from?"

"The next booth to yours," the voice jeered. "You forgot the
glass inserts only reach halfway down."

The connection broke and a man's looming figure was shad-
owing the glass in front of my eyes, before I could even get the
receiver back on the hook. I dropped it full-length, tensed my
right arm to pound it through his face as soon as I shoved the
glass aside. He had a revolver-bore for a top vest-button, trained
on me. Two more had shown up behind him, from which direction I hadn't noticed. It was very dark in the booth now, their
collective silhouettes shut out all the daylight. The station and
all its friendly bustle was blotted out, had receded into the far
background, a thousand miles away for all the help it could give
me. I slapped the glass wearily aside, came slowly out.

One of them flashed a badge—maybe Crow had loaned him
his for the occasion. "You're being arrested for putting slugs in
that phone. It won't do any good to raise your voice and shriek
for help, try to tell people different. But suit yourself."

I knew that as well as he; heads turned to stare after us by the
dozens as they started with me in their midst through the station's main-level. But not one in all that crowd would have
dared interfere with what they mistook for a legitimate arrest
in the line of duty. The one with the badge kept it conspicuously
tilted in his upturned palm, at sight of which the frozen onlookers slowly parted, made way for us through their midst. I was
being led to my doom in full view of scores of people.

I tried twice to dig my feet in when we came to ridges in the level of the terraced marble floor, but the point of the gun at the base of my spine removed the impediment each time, I was so used to not wanting to die. Then slowly this determination came to me: "I'm going to force them to shoot me, before they get me into the car or whatever it is they're taking me to. It's my only way out, cheat death by death. I'm to be buried agonizingly alive, anyway; I'll compel them to end it here instead, by that gun. That clean, friendly gun. But not just shoot me, shoot me dead, otherwise—" A violent wrench backwards would do it, compressing the gun into its holder's body, discharging it automatically into me. "Poor Joan," I thought, "left waiting on the Hamlin station-platform—for all eternity." But that didn't alter my determination any.

The voice of the train-dispatcher, loudspeaker and all, was dwindling behind us. "New York Express, Track Four, leaves in five more min—"

Sunlight suddenly struck down at us from outside the station portico, between the huge two-story high columns, and down below at the distant bottom of the long terraced steps there was one of those black touring-cars standing waiting. "Now!" I thought, and tensed, ready to rear backward into the gun so that it would explode into my vitals.

A Western Union messenger in typical olive-green was running up the sloping steps straight toward my captors, arm extended. Not a boy though, a grown man. One of *them* disguised, I knew, even as I looked at him. "Urgent!" he panted, and thrust a message into the hand of the one with the badge. I let myself relax again in their hands, postponing for a moment the forcing of death into my own body, while I waited to see what this was.

He read it through once, then quickly whispered it aloud a second time to the other two—or part of it, anyway. "Penalty cancelled, give ex-Brother Bud safe-conduct to New York on promise never to return. Renewed oath of eternal silence on his part accepted. Interment ceremonies will take place as planned

—" He pointed with his finger to the rest without repeating it aloud, that's how I knew there was more.

The messenger had already hurried down again to where the car was, and darted behind it. A motorcycle suddenly shot out from the other side of it and racketed off, trailing little puff-balls of blue gas-smoke. A moment later the three with me, scattered like startled buzzards cheated of their prey, had followed him down, at different angles that converged toward the car. I found myself standing there alone at the top of the station-steps, a lone figure dwarfed by the monolithic columns.

I reeled, turned and started headlong through the long reaches of the station behind me, bent over like a marathon runner reaching for the guerdon. "'Board! 'Board!" was sounding faintly somewhere in the distance. I could see them pulling the adjustable exit-gates closed ahead of me. I held one arm straight up in the air, and they saw me coming and left a little opening for me, enough for one person to dive through.

The train was gathering speed when I lurched down to track-level, but I caught the handrail of the last vestibule of the last car just before it cleared the concrete runway beside the tracks. A conductor dragged me in bodily and I fell in a huddle at his feet.

"You last-minute passengers!" I heard him grumbling, "you'd think your life depended on it—"

I lay there heaving, flat on my back like a fish out of water, looking up at him. "It did," I managed to get out.

I was leaning far out from the bottom vestibule-step at nearly a 45-degree angle, holding on with one hand, when the Hamlin station-platform swept into sight forty minutes later. I could see the whole boat-shaped "pier" from end to end.

There was something wrong; she wasn't on it. Nobody was on it, only a pair of lounging darkies, backs against the station-wall. The big painted sign floated up, came to a halt almost before my eyes: "HAMLIN." She'd said Hamlin; what had happened, what had gone wrong? It *had* to be Hamlin; there wasn't any other stop until tomorrow morning, states away!

I jumped down, went skidding into the little stuffy two-by-four waiting-room. Nobody in it. I dashed for the ticket-window, grabbed the bars with both hands, all but shook them. "A girl—blue eyes, blonde hair, brown coat—where is she, where'd she go? Haven't you seen anyone like that around here?"

"Nope, nobody been around here all afternoon, ain't sold a ticket nor even had an inquiry—"

"The bus from the city—did it get here yet?"

"Ten full minutes ago. It's out there in back of the station right now."

I hurled through the opposite door like something demented. The locomotive-bell was tolling dismally, almost like a funeral knell. I collared the bus-driver despairingly.

"Nope, didn't bring any young women out at all on my last run. I'd know; I like young women."

"And no one like that got on, at the downtown city-terminal?"

"Nope, no blondes. I'd know, I like blondes."

The wheels were already starting to click warningly over the rail-intersections as the train glided into motion; I could hear them around on the other side of the station from where I was. Half-crazed, I ducked inside again. The agent belatedly remembered something, called me over as I stood there dazedly looking all around me. "Say, by the way, your name Ingram? Forgot to tell you, special messenger brought this out awhile back, asked me to deliver it to the New York train."

I snatched at it. It was in her handwriting! I tore it open, my head swivelled crazily from left to right as my eyes raced along the writing.

I didn't take the bus to Hamlin after all, but don't worry. Go on to New York and wait there for me instead. And think of me often, and pray for me sometimes, and above all keep your pledge of silence.

Joan

She'd found out! was the first thunderbolt that struck me. And the second was a dynamite-blast that split me from head to foot. She was in their hands! That gruesome message that had saved me at the station came back to me word for word, and I knew now what it meant and what the part was that they'd kept from me. "Penalty cancelled. Give Brother Bud safe-conduct. Renewed oath on his part accepted—" But I hadn't made one. She must have promised them that on my behalf. *"Interment will take place as planned—"* Substitute accepted!

And that substitute was Joan. She'd taken my place. She'd gone to them and made a bargain with them. Saved me, at the cost of her own life.

I don't remember how I got back to the city. Maybe I thrust all the money I had on me at someone and borrowed their car. Maybe I just stole one left unguarded on the street with the key in it. I don't remember where I got the gun either. I must have gone back to that same pawnshop I'd already been to once, as soon as I got in.

When things came back into focus, I was already on the porch of that boarded-up house at Ellendale, battering my body apart against the doorcasing. I broke in finally by jumping from a tree to the porch-shed and kicking in one of the upper-story windows, less stoutly boarded.

I was too late. The silence told me that as soon as I stood within the room, and the last tinklings of shattered glass had died down around me. They weren't here. They'd gone. There wasn't a soul in the place! But there were signs, when I crept down the stairs gun in hand, that they'd been there. The downstairs rooms were heavy with the thickly cloying scent of fresh flowers, ferns and bits of leaf were scattered about the floor. Folding campchairs were still arranged in orderly rows, as though a funeral service had been conducted. Facing them stood tapers thick as a man's wrist, barely cool at the top, the charred odor of their gutted wicks still clinging to them. And in a closet when I looked I found her coat—Joan's—her hat, her dress, her little pitiful strapped sandals standing empty side by side! I crushed them to me, dropped them, ran out of there crazed, and broke into the adjacent graveyard, but there were no signs that she'd been taken there. No freshly-filled in grave, no mound without its sprouting grass. I'd heard them say they had others. It had grown dark long ago, and it must be over by now. But how could I stop trying, even though it were too late?

Afterwards, along the state highway, I found a couple sleeping overnight in a trailer by the roadside who told me a hearse had passed them on its way to the city, followed by a number of limousines, *a full two hours earlier.* They'd thought it was a strange hour for a funeral. They'd also thought the procession was going faster than seemed decent. And after an empty gin-bottle had been tossed out of one of the cars, they were not likely to forget the incident.

I lost the trail at the city-limits, no one had seen them beyond there, the night and the darkness had swallowed them up. I've been looking ever since. I've already broken into two, and I was in the third one when you stopped me—but no sign of her. She's in some city graveyard at this very minute, still breathing, threshing her life away in smothering darkness, while you're holding me here, wasting precious time. Kill me, then, kill me and have it over with—or else help me find her, but don't let me suffer like this!

❖

The captain took his hand away from before his eyes, stopped pinching the bridge of his nose with it. A white mark was left there between his eyes. "This is awful," he breathed. "I almost wish I hadn't heard that story. How could it be anything else but true? It's too farfetched, too unbelievable."

Suddenly, like a wireless-set that comes to life, crackling, emitting blue sparks, he was sending out staccato orders. "For corroborating evidence we have her note to you sent to Hamlin station; we have her clothing at the Ellendale house, and undoubtedly that ledger of membership you first signed, along with God-knows what else! You two men get out there quick with a battery of police-photographers and take pictures of those campchairs, tapers, everything just as you find it. And don't forget the graveyard. I want every one of those graves broken open as fast as you can swing picks. I'll send the necessary exhumation-permits after you, but don't wait for them! Those grounds are full of living beings!"

"Joan—Joan—" Bud Ingram whimpered as the door crashed after them.

The captain nodded tersely, without even having time enough to be sympathetic. "Now we stop thinking like policemen and think like human beings for this once, departmental regulations to the contrary," he promised. He spoke quietly into his desk-phone. "Give me Mercer at Poplar Street. . . ." And then, "This man Crow of yours . . . He's off-duty right now, you say?"

"He's at the wake, he's beyond your reach," Ingram moaned. "He won't report back until—"

"Sh!" the captain silenced him. "He may be one of them, but he's a policeman along with it." He said to Mercer, "I want you to send out a short-wave, asking him to call in to you at his precinct-house at once. And when he does, I want you to keep him on the wire, I want that line kept open until his call has been traced! That man must not get off until I've found out where he's talking from and had a chance to get there, and I'll hold you responsible, Mercer. Is that clear? It's a matter of life and death. You can make whatever case he's on at present the excuse. I'll be waiting to start out from here the minute I hear from you." And then, into the desk-transmitter: "I want an emergency raiding-party made up at once, two cars, everyone you can spare. I want shovels, spades and picks, plenty of them. I want a third car, with an inhalator-squad, oxygen-tent and the whole works. Yeah, motorcycle escort—and give orders ahead: *No sirens, no lights.*"

Ingram said, "The short-wave mayn't reach him—Crow. And if it does, he may not answer it, pretend he didn't get it."

"He's got his car," the captain said, "and he's still a policeman, no matter what else he is." He held the door open. "There it goes out." A set outside in one of the other rooms throbbed: "Lawrence Crow, detective first grade. Lawrence Crow, detective first grade. Ring up Mercer at your precinct-house immediately. Ring up Mercer—"

Ingram leaned against the door in silent prayer. "May his sense of duty be stronger than his caution!"

The captain was buttoning on a coat, feeling for the revolver at his hip.

"It's no use, she's dead already," Ingram said. "It's one in the morning, seven hours have gone by—"

The desk-phone buzzed ominously, just once. "Hold him!" was all the captain rasped into it, and thrust Ingram out ahead of him. "He's calling in—get out there to the car!"

And as the car-door cracked shut after them outside the building, he gave a terse: "All-night drugstore, Main on the 700-block!" They started off like a procession of swift silent black shadows, the only sound of their going the muffled pounding of motorcycles around and ahead of them.

Crow's car was standing there outside the lighted place as they swept up, and he was still inside. Two of them jumped in, hurried him out between them. The captain stood facing him.

"Your badge," he said. "You're under arrest. Where was she taken, this girl, Joan Blaine? Where is she now?"

"I don't know who she is," he said.

The captain drew his gun. "Answer me or I'll shoot you where you stand!"

Ingram said hopelessly, "He's not afraid of death."

"No, I'm not," Crow answered quietly.

"He'll be afraid of pain, then!" the captain said. "Take him

back inside. You two come with me. The rest of you keep out,
understand?"

The glass door flashed open again after they'd gone in and the
drugstore nightclerk was thrust out on the sidewalk, looking
frightened. A full-length shade was suddenly drawn down behind him.

Ingram stayed in the car, head clasped in his arms, bowed
over his lap. A muffled scream sounded somewhere near at
hand in the utter stillness. The door suddenly flew open and the
captain came running out alone. He was stripping off a rubber
glove; the reek of some strong acid reached those in the car.
Through the open door behind him came the sound of a man
sobbing brokenly like a little child, a man in pain.

"Inhalator-squad follow my car," the captain snapped.
"Greenwood Park, main driveway. The rest of you go to a large
house standing in the middle of its own grounds over on the
South Side near Valley Road. Surround it and arrest every man
and woman you find in it."

They separated; the captain's and Ingram's car fled silently
westward along the nightbound boulevard toward the im-
mense public park on that side of the city.

Trees, lawns, meadows, black under the starlight, suddenly
swept around them, and to the left there was the faint corusca-
tion of a body of water. A bagpipe of brakes and a puff of
burnt-rubber stench and they had skidded to a halt.

"Lights!" ordered the captain, stumbling out. "Train the
heads after us—and bring those tools and the oxygen-tanks!"
The sward bleached vividly green as the two cars backed sideways into position. It was suddenly full of scattered, moiling
men, trampling about, heads down like bloodhounds.

The one farthest afield shouted: "Here's a patch without
grass!"

They came running from all directions, contracted into a knot
around him.

"That's it—see the oblong, see the darker color from the

freshly-upturned—!" Coats flew up into the air like waving banners, a shovel bit in, another, another. But Ingram was at it with his raw, bared hands again, like a mole, pleading, "Be careful! Oh be careful, men! This is my girl!"

"Now keep your heads," the captain warned. "Just a minute more. Keep him back, he's getting in their way."

A hollow sound, a *Phuff!* echoed from the inch of protruding pipe, and the man testing it, flat on his stomach, lifted his face, said, "It's partly open all the way down."

The earth parted like a wave across the top of it, and they were lifting it, and they were prying at the lid, gently, carefully, no blows. "Now, bring up the tanks—quick!" the captain said, and to no one in particular, "What a night!" They were still holding Ingram back by main force, and then suddenly as the lid came off, they didn't have to hold him any more.

She was in a bridal gown, and she was beautiful, even as still and as marble-white as she was, when they lifted the disarranged veil—when they gently drew aside the protecting arm she'd thrown before her eyes. Then she was hidden from Ingram by their backs.

Suddenly the police-doctor straightened up. "Take that tube away. This girl doesn't need oxygen—there's nothing the matter with her breathing, or her heart-action. She needs restoratives, she's in a dead faint from fright, that's all!"

Instantly they were all busy at once, chafing her hands and arms, clumsily yet gently slapping her face, holding ammonia to her nose. With the fluttering of her eyelids came a shriek of unutterable terror, as though it had been waiting in her throat all this time to be released.

"Lift her out of that thing, quick, before she sees it," the captain whispered.

Back raced the cars, with the girl that had come up out of her grave—and beside her, holding her close, a man who had been healed of all his fears, cured—even as the Friends of Death had promised.

"And each time I'd come to, I'd go right off again," she whispered huskily.

"That probably saved you," the doctor on the other side of her said, "lying still. You'll be all right, you've had a bad fright, that's all."

Bud Ingram held her close, her head upon his shoulder, eyes unafraid staring straight ahead now.

"I never knew there could be such a love in all this world," he murmured.

She smiled a feeble little smile. "Look in my heart sometime —and see," she said.

✤

There were sensational disclosures the next day, when the Friends of Death appeared in court. A number of leading citizens were among them—men and women whom the weird society was draining of their wealth. Others, there were, who claimed they had been brought back from the grave—and, indeed, there were doctor's certificates and burial permits to testify to the truth of this. Only later, at the trial of the leaders of the cult, did the whole story come to light. The people who had "died" and been buried were those chosen by the leaders for their reputations for honesty and reliability. They were then slowly poisoned by a member planted in their household by the society for this purpose—sometimes it was a servant, sometimes a member of the person's own family. But the poison was not fatal. It induced a state of partially suspended organic functions which a cursory medical examination might diagnose as death, the rest was handled by doctors and undertakers—even civil employees—who were members of the "Friends." Then the victim was resuscitated, persuaded he had been restored to life by the secret processes of the society, and initiated as a member. His testimony, after that, was responsible for gaining many new members, without the dangerous necessity of "killing" and reviving more than the first few. And the "penalties" inflicted upon recalcitrant members made those remaining, participants in capital crime—and made the society's hold on them absolute.

But the greatest hold of all—the one which made the vast majority of the members rejoice in their bondage, and turn into rabid fiends at the least suspicion of disloyalty in the organization—was the infinitely comforting knowledge that no longer need they fear death.

And, in the words of the state prosecutor, most of them had been punished sufficiently for their sins in the terrible awakening to the realization that they were not immortals—and that somewhere, sometime, their graves awaited them. . . .

The horror of being buried alive which seems to have obsessed Woolrich at times is central both to the above novella and to the equally nightmarish "The Living Lie Down with the Dead" (*Dime Detective*, 4/36). The treatment of this theme in "Graves for the Living" suggests that Woolrich may have connected it with his father, a civil engineer who spent much time on projects in Central and South America and who must have run the risk of burial alive in an explosion time and time again.

Woolrich's treatment of the police—especially their pouring acid on a man to make him confirm a story that on its face is absurd—will be matched by other horrors elsewhere in this book. Those whose work puts them in touch with the realities of station-house backrooms will find that Woolrich, tormented recluse that he was, knew those realities too.

The Red Tide

Young Mrs. Jacqueline Blaine opened a pair of gas-flame-blue eyes and looked wistfully up at the ceiling. Then she closed them again and nearly went back to sleep. There wasn't very much to get up for; the party was over.

The party was over, and they hadn't raised the twenty-five hundred dollars.

She rolled her head sidewise on the pillow and nestled it against the curve of one ivory shoulder, the way a pouting little girl does. Maybe it was that last thought made her do it, instinctively. Water was sizzling downward against tiling somewhere close by; then it broke off as cleanly as at the cut of a switch, and a lot of laggard, left-over drops went *tick, tick, tick* like a clock.

Jacqueline Blaine opened her eyes a second time, looked down her arm over the edge of the bed to the little diamond-splintered microcosm attached to the back of her wrist. It was about the size of one of her own elongated fingernails, and very hard to read numbers from. She raised her head slightly from the pillow, and still couldn't make out the time on the tiny watch.

It didn't matter; the party was over, they'd all gone—all but that old fossil, maybe. Gil had seemed to pin his hopes on him, had said he hoped he could get him alone. She could have told Gil right now the old bird was a hopeless case; Gil wouldn't be able to make a dent in him. She'd seen that when she tried to lay the groundwork for Gil the day before.

Well, if he'd stayed, let Leona look after him, get his breakfast. She sat up and yawned, and until you'd seen her yawn, you would have called a yawn an ungainly grimace. Not after, though. She propped her chin up with her knees and looked around. A silverish evening dress was lying where she last remembered squirming out of it, too tired to care. Gil's dress tie was coiled in a snake formation on the floor.

She could see a green tide rising and falling outside of the four windows, on two sides of the room. Not water, but trees swaying in the breeze. The upper halves of the panels were light-blue. The sun was somewhere straight overhead, she could tell that by the way it hardly came in past the sills. It wasn't a bad lookout, even after a party. "It would be fun living in it," she mourned to herself, "if the upkeep wasn't so tough; if I didn't have to be nice to eccentric old codgers, trying to get them to cough up. All to keep up appearances."

Gil came out of the shower alcove. He was partly dressed already—trousers and undershirt, but feet still bare—and mopping his hair with a towel. He threw it behind him onto the floor and came on in. Her eyes followed him halfway around the room with growing curiosity.

"Well, how'd you make out?" she asked finally.

He didn't answer. She glanced at the adjoining bed, but it was only rumpled on top, the covers hadn't been turned down. He must have just lain down on it without getting in.

She didn't speak again until she had come out of the shower in turn. He was all dressed now, standing looking out of the window, cigarette smoke working its way back around the bend of his neck. She snapped off her rubber bathing cap, remarked:

"I guess Leona thinks we died in our sleep."

She wriggled into a yellow jersey that shot ten years to pieces —and she'd looked about twenty to begin with.

"Is Burroughs still here," she asked wearily, "or did he decide to go back to town anyway, after I left you two last night?"

"He left," he said shortly. He didn't turn around. The smoke coming around the nape of his neck thickened almost to a fog, then thinned out again, as though he'd taken a whale of a drag just then.

"I was afraid of that," she said. But she didn't act particularly disturbed. "Took the eight-o'clock train, I suppose."

He turned around. "Eight o'clock, hell!" he said. "He took the milk train!"

She put down the comb and stopped what she was doing. "What?" Then she said. "How do you know?"

"I drove him to the station, that's how I know!" he snapped. His face was turned to her, but he wasn't looking at her. His eyes focused a little too far to one side, then shifted over a little too far to the other, trying to dodge hers.

"What got into him, to go at that unearthly hour? The milk train—that hits here at 4:30 a.m., doesn't it?"

He was looking down. "At 4:20," he said. He was already lighting another cigarette, and it was a live one judging by the way it danced around before he could get it to stand still between his cupped hands.

"Well, what were you doing up at that hour yourself?"

"I hadn't come up to bed yet at all. He decided to go, so I ran him in."

"You had a row with him," she stated positively. "Why else should he leave—"

"I did not!" He took a couple of quick steps toward the door, as though her barrage of questions was getting on his nerves, as though he wanted to escape from the room. Then he changed his mind, stayed in the new place, looking at her. "I got it out of him," he said quietly. That special quietness of voice that made her an accomplice in his financial difficulties. No, every wife should be that. That special tone that seemed to make her his shill in a confidence game. That special tone that she was beginning to hate.

"You don't act very happy about it," she remonstrated.

He took a wallet out of his pocket, split it lengthwise, showing a pleating of currency edges. And it was so empty, most of the time!

"Not the whole twenty-five hundred?"

"The works."

"You mean he carries that much in ready cash around with him, when he just comes for a week end in the country! Why . . . why, I saw him go in to cash a twenty-five-dollar check Saturday afternoon in the village. So he could hold up his end when he went out to the inn that night. I was embarrassed, because he asked me if I thought you could oblige him; I not only knew you couldn't, but I knew it was up to us as hosts to pay his way, and I didn't know what to say. Luckily you weren't around, so he couldn't ask you; he finally went in to get it cashed himself."

"I know," he said impatiently. "I met him out front and drove him in myself!"

"You?"

"I told him I was strapped, couldn't help him out. Then after he'd cashed it himself and was putting it away, he explained that he had twenty-five hundred on him, but it was a deposit earmarked for the bank Monday morning. He hadn't had time to put it in Friday afternoon before he came out here; our invitation had swept him off his feet so. He wanted this smaller amount just for expense money."

"But then he handed the twenty-five hundred over to you anyway?"

"No, he didn't," he said, goaded. "At least, not at first. He had his check book on him, and when I finally broke down his resistance after you'd gone to bed last night, he wrote me out a check. Or started to. I suggested as long as he happened to have that exact amount in cash, he make the loan in cash; that I was overdrawn at my own bank, and if I tried to put his check through there they'd put a nick in it and I needed every penny. He finally agreed; I gave him a receipt, and he gave me the cash."

"But then why did he leave at that ungodly hour?"

"Well, he did one of those slow burns, after it was all over and he'd come across. You know him when it comes to parting with money. It must have finally dawned on him that we'd only had him out here, among a lot of people so much younger than him, to put the bee on him. Anyway, he asked when the next train was, and I couldn't induce him to stay over; he insisted on leaving then and there. So I drove him in. In one way, I was afraid if he didn't go, he'd think it over and ask for his money back, so I didn't urge him *too* much."

"But you're sure you didn't have words over it?"

"He didn't say a thing. But I could tell by the sour look on his face what he was thinking."

"I suppose he's off me, too," she sighed.

"So what? You don't need an extra grandfather."

They had come out of the bedroom and started down the upper hall toward the stairs. She silenced him at sight of an open door ahead, with sunlight streaming out of it. "Don't say anything about it in front of Leona. She'll expect to get paid right away."

An angular Negress with a dust cloth in her hand looked out at them as they reached the open door. "Mawnin'. I about gib you two up. Coffee's been on and off 'bout three times. I can't drink no more of it myself; make me bilious. I done fix the old gentleman's room up while I was waitin'."

"Oh, you didn't have to bother," Jacqueline Blaine assured her happily, almost gayly; "we're not having any more guests for a while, thank—"

"He still here, ain't he?" asked Leona, peering surprisedly.

This time it was Gil who answered. "No. Why?"

"He done lef' his bag in there—one of 'em, anyway. He want it sent to the station after him?"

Jacqueline looked in surprise from the maid to her husband. The blinding sunlight flashing through the doorway made his face seem whiter than it actually was. It was hard on the eyes, too, made him shift about, as in their bedroom before.

"He must've overlooked it in his hurry, gone off without it," he murmured. "I didn't know how many he'd brought with him so I never noticed."

Jacqueline turned out the palms of her hands. "How could he do that, when he only brought two in the first place, and"—she glanced into the guest room—"this one's the larger of the two?"

"It was in the clothes closet; maybe he didn't see it himself," offered Leona, "and forgit he hab it with him. I slide it out just now." She hurried down the stairs to prepare their delayed breakfast.

Jacqueline lowered her voice, with a precautionary glance after her, and asked him: "You didn't get him drunk, did you? Is that how you got it out of him? He's liable to make trouble for us as soon as he—"

"He was cold sober," he growled. "Try to get him to drink!" So he had tried, she thought to herself, and hadn't succeeded.

"Well, then, I don't see how on earth anyone could go off and leave a bag that size, when they only brought one other one out with them in the first place."

He was obviously irritable, nerves on edge; anyone would have been after being up the greater part of the night. He cut the discussion short by taking an angry step over, grasping the doorknob, and pulling the door shut. Since he seemed to take such a trifling thing that seriously, she refrained from dwelling on it any longer just then. He'd feel better after he'd had some coffee.

They sat down in a sun-drenched porch, open glass on three sides. Leona brought in two glasses of orange juice, with the pulp shreds all settled at the bottom from standing too long.

"Wabble 'em around a little," she suggested cheerily; "dat makes it clear up."

Jackie Blaine believed in letting servants express their individualities. When you're a good deal behind on their wages, you can't very well object, anyway.

Gil's face looked even more drawn down here than it had in the lesser sunlight upstairs. Haggard. But his mood had cleared a little. "Before long, we'll sit breakfasting in the South American way—and will I be glad of a change of scene!"

"There won't be much left to travel on, if you take care of our debts."

"If," he said half audibly.

The phone rang.

"That must be Burroughs, asking us to forward his bag." Jackie Blaine got up and went in to answer it.

It wasn't Burroughs, it was his wife.

"Oh, hello," Jackie said cordially. "We were awfully sorry to hear you were laid up like that and couldn't come out with Mr. Burroughs. Feeling any better?"

Mrs. Burroughs' voice sounded cranky, put out. "I think it's awfully inconsiderate of Homer not to let me know he was staying over another day. He knew I wasn't well when he left! I think the least he might have done was phone me or send a wire if he wasn't coming, and you can tell him I said so."

Jackie Blaine tightened her hold on the telephone. "But, hold on, Mrs. Burroughs. He isn't here any more; he did leave, early this morning."

There was a startled stillness at the other end. Then: "Early this morning! Well, why hasn't he gotten here? What train did he take?"

Jackie swiveled toward her husband, telephone and all. She could see him sitting out there from where she was. "Didn't you say Mr. Burroughs took the milk train, Gil?"

She could see the gnarled lump of his Adam's apple go all the way up, then ebb down again. Something made him swallow, though why he should swallow at that particular point—his cup wasn't anywhere near his lips. Unless maybe there was some coffee left in his mouth from before, that he'd forgotten to swallow till now. He didn't move at all. Not even his lips. It was like a statue speaking—a statue of gleaming white marble. "Yes, that's right."

Somehow there wasn't very much color left in her own face. "What time would that bring him in, Gil?" She always used the car herself.

"Before eight." She relayed it.

"Well, where is he then?" The voice was beginning to fray a little around the edges.

"He may have gone direct to his office from the train, Mrs. Burroughs; he may have had something important to attend to before he went home."

Still more of the self-control in the other woman's voice unraveled. "But he didn't, I know he didn't! That's why I'm calling you; his office phoned a little while ago to ask me if I knew whether or not he'd be in today."

"Oh." The exclamation was soundless, a mental flash on Jackie's part.

The voice had degenerated to a pitiful plea for assistance, all social stiffness gone now. It was the frightened whimper of a pampered invalid wife who suddenly has the tables turned on her. "But what's become of him, Mrs. Blaine?"

Jackie said in a voice that sounded a little hollow in her own ears: "I'm sure there's nothing to worry about, Mrs. Burroughs;

I'm sure he's just unavoidably detained somewhere in town."
But somehow she caught herself swallowing in her turn now, as
Gil had before. It was such a straight line from here—or rather
from the station out here—to his home, how could anything
possibly happen to anyone traveling it?

"He was feeling all right when you saw him off, wasn't he,
Gil?"

He started up from his chair, moved over to one of the glass
panels, stood staring out, boiling smoke.

"Leave me out of it for two minutes, will you?" His voice
came back to her muffledly.

That "Leave me out of it" blurred the rest of the conversation
as far as she was concerned. The voice she was listening to
disintegrated into sobs and incoherent remarks. She heard herself saying vaguely: "Please don't worry. . . . I feel terrible.
. . . Will you call me back and let me know?" But what was there
she could do? And she knew, oh, she knew that she didn't want
to hear from this woman again.

She hung up. She was strangely unable to turn around and
look toward where Gil was standing. It was a physical in-
capacity. She felt almost rigid. She had remained standing during the entire conversation. She sat down now. She lighted a
cigarette, but it went right out again because she didn't keep
it going. She let her head fall slowly as of its own weight forward
into her upcurved hand, so that it was planted between her eyes
and partly shut them out.

She didn't want any more breakfast.

✦

She saw the man get out of the car and come up to the house.
She knew him by sight. He'd been here before. This was about
three that afternoon, that Monday afternoon, the day Burroughs had—gone. He had a cheap car. The sound of it driving
up and stopping was what had made her get up off the bed and
go over to the window to look. She'd stopped crying by then

anyway. You can't cry *all* day long; there isn't that much crying in you.

Then when she saw who it was—oh, that wasn't anything. This was such a minor matter—now. And of course it could be taken care of easily enough—now. She stayed there by the window, waiting to see him walk out to his car and drive off again, within five minutes at the most—with the money he'd come for. Because Gil was down there; he could attend to it and get rid of him for good—now. Then there'd be one fewer to hound the two of them.

But the five minutes were up, and the man didn't come right out again the way she'd expected him to. He seemed to be staying as long as those other times, when all he got was a drink and a lot of build-up. Angry voices filtered up to her—one angry voice, anyway, and one subdued, placative one.

She went outside to the head of the stairs and listened tautly. Not that this was new to her, but it had a new, a terrible significance now.

The angry voice, that of the man who had come in the car, was barking: "How long does this keep up, Blaine? You gimme that same run-around each time! You think all I gotta do is come out here? Look at this house you live in! Look at the front you put up! You mean you haven't got that much, a guy like you?"

And Gil's voice, whining plaintively: "I tell you I haven't got it this minute! What am I going to do, take it out of my blood? You're going to get it; just give me time."

The angry voice rose to a roar, but at least it shifted toward the front door. "I'm warning you for the last time, you better get it and no more of this funny business! My boss has been mighty patient with you! There are other ways of handling welshers, and don't forget it!"

The door slammed and the car outside racketed up and dwindled off in the distance.

Jackie Blaine crept down the stairs a step at a time toward where Gil was shakily pouring himself a drink. Her face was white, as white as his had been that noon when they first got up. But not because of what she had just heard. Still because of its implication.

"Who was it?" she said hoarsely.

"Verona's stooge. Still that same lousy personal loan he once made me."

"How much is it?"

"Six hundred odd."

She knew all these things; she wanted to hear it from him. She spoke in a frightened whisper: "Then why didn't you give it to him? You have twenty-five hundred on you."

He went ahead with his drink.

"Why? Gil, look at me. *Why?*"

He wouldn't answer.

She reeled over to him, like someone about to pass out; her head fell against his chest. "D'you love me?"

"That's the one thing in my life that's on the level."

"Then you've got to tell me. I've got to know. *Did you do anything to him last night?*"

She buried her face against him, waiting. Silence.

"I can take it. I'll stick with you. I'll string along. But I've got to know, one way or the other." She looked up. She began to shake him despairingly by the shoulders. "Gil, why don't you answer me? Don't stand there— That's why you didn't pay Verona's debt, isn't it? Because you're afraid to have it known now that you have money on you—after *he* was here."

"Yes, I am afraid," he breathed almost inaudibly.

"Then you—" She sagged against him; he had to catch her under the arms or she would have gone down.

"No, wait. Pull yourself together a minute. Here, swallow this. Now . . . steady, hold onto the table. Yes, I did do something. I know what you're thinking. No, not that. It's bad enough, though. I'm worried. Stick with me, Jackie. I don't want to get in trouble. I met him coming out of the house Saturday, wanting to cash that pin-money check, and I drove him in, like I told you.

The bank was closed for the half day, of course, and I suggested getting it cashed at the hotel. I told him they knew me and I could get it done easier than he could, so I took it in for him and he waited outside in the car.

"I didn't mean to put one over on him; it all came up sort of sudden. I knew I didn't have a chance at that hotel desk, not even if the check had been signed by a millionaire, and I didn't want him to come in with me and see them turn me down. Jack McGovern happened to come through the lobby just as I walked in, and on the spur of the moment I borrowed twenty-five from him as a personal loan without giving him the check. I didn't mean anything by it. It was just that I was embarrassed to let him know I couldn't even accommodate one of my own house guests for a measly twenty-five. You know how they talk around here. I went out and gave the twenty-five to Burroughs, and I kept the endorsed check in my pocket. I intended tearing it up, but I couldn't very well do it in front of him. Then later I forgot about it.

"I tackled him last night after you went to bed, and he didn't come through. He got crabby, caught on we'd just played him for a sucker, refused to finish out the visit, insisted on taking the next train back. I drove him in; I couldn't very well let him walk at that hour. He got out at the station and I came on back without waiting.

"I started to do a slow burn. There I was, not only no better off than before we asked him out, but even more in the red, on account of the expense of the big house party we threw to impress him. Naturally I was sore, after all the false hopes we'd raised, after the way you'd put yourself out to be nice to him. I couldn't sleep all night, stayed down here drinking and pacing back and forth, half nuts with worry. And then sometime after daylight I happened to stick my hand in my pocket for something and suddenly turned up his twenty-five-dollar endorsed check.

"It was a crazy thing to do, but I didn't stop to think. I lifted it, added two zips to the figures, got in the car then and there, and drove all the way in to town. I cashed it at his own bank the minute the doors opened at nine. I knew he had twenty times that much on tap at all times, so it wouldn't hurt him any."

"But, Gil, didn't you know what would happen, didn't you know what he could do to you?"

"Yeah, I did, but I guess I had a vague idea in the back of my mind that if it came to a showdown and he threatened to get nasty with me about it—well, there were a couple of times he got a little too affectionate with you; you told me so yourself— I could threaten to get just as nasty with him about that. You know how scared he is of that wife of his."

"Gil," was all she said, "Gil."

"Yeah, I'm pretty low."

"As long as it's not the other. But then what's become of him? Where did he go?"

"I don't know."

"Did you *see* him get on the train?"

"No, I just left him there at the station and turned around and drove back without waiting."

She hesitated a moment before speaking. Then she said slowly: "What I've just heard hasn't exactly been pleasant, but I told you I could take it, and I can, and I have. And I think— I know—I can stand the other, the worse thing, too, if you tell it to me *now*, right away, and get it over with. But now's the time. This is your last chance, Gil. Don't let me find out later, because later—it may be different, I may not still be able to feel the same way about it. You didn't *kill* Burroughs last night, did you?"

He breathed deeply. His eyes looked into hers. "I never killed anyone in my life. And now, are you with me?"

She raised her head defiantly. "To the bitter end."

"Bitter." He smiled ruefully. "I don't like that word."

✦

His name was Ward, he said. She wondered if that was customary on their parts, to give their names like that instead of their official standing. She wasn't familiar with their technique, had never been interviewed before. And of course, she would be alone in the house when he happened to drop in. Still, on second thought, that might be better. Gil might have given a —well, a misleading impression, been keyed up, on account of that check business. This was Tuesday, the day after Burroughs had last been seen.

Her caller spared her any of that business of flaunting a badge in front of Leona; that was another consoling thing. He must have just given his name to Leona, because Leona went right back to the kitchen instead of stalling around outside the room so she could hear. Just people that came to try to collect money didn't interest her any more; the novelty had worn off long ago.

Jackie Blaine said: "Sit down, Mr. Ward. My husband's gone in to town—"

"I know that." It came out as flat as a sheet of onion-skin paper, but for a minute it made her a little uneasy; it sounded as though they were already watching Gil's movements.

"If there's anything I can do—"

"There always is, don't you think?"

He didn't look so coarse, so hard-bitten, as she'd always imagined those men did. He looked—well, no different from any number of other young fellows they'd entertained out here, whom she'd danced with, golfed with, and almost invariably found herself putting in their places, in some dimly lighted corner, before the week-end was over. She knew how to handle the type well. But then she'd never parried life-and-death with them before. And maybe he just *looked* the type.

He said: "Mr. Homer Burroughs was here at your house from Friday until some time late Sunday night or early Monday morning." There wasn't the rising inflection of interrogation at the end of it.

"He was."

"When did you last see him?"

"My husband drove him to the station in time for—"

"That isn't what I asked you, Mrs. Blaine."

She didn't like that; he was trying to differentiate between Gil and herself. They were together in this, sink or swim. She answered it his way. "I said good night to Mr. Burroughs at ten to one Monday morning. My husband remained downstairs with him. My husband drove him—"

He didn't want that part of it. "Then 1 A.M. Monday was the last time you saw him. When you left him, who else was in the house with him besides your husband, anyone?"

"Just my husband."

"When you said good night, was it understood you weren't to see him in the morning? Did he say anything about leaving in the small hours of the night?"

That was a bad hurdle to get over. "It was left indefinite," she said. "We're . . . we're sort of casual out here about those things —formal good-byes and such."

"Even so, as his hostess, wouldn't it be up to him to at least drop some hint to let you know he was going, to thank you for your hospitality before taking his leave?"

She brought a gleam of her old prom-girl manner, of three or four years before, to the surface. Keep it light and off dangerous ground. It had worked to ward off boa-constrictor hugs; maybe it would work to keep your husband out of difficulties with the police. "You've read your Emily Post, I see. Won't you have a drink while you're doing this?"

He flattened her pitiful attempt like a locomotive running on a single track full steam ahead. "No, I won't! Did he drop the slightest remark to indicate that he wouldn't be here by the time you were up the following morning?"

He'd given her an opening there: her own and Gil's habitual late hour for rising any day in the week. "Well, we took that for granted. After all, he had to be back at the office by nine and—"

But it didn't work out so good. "But he didn't have to take the milk train to get back to the office by nine. Isn't it a little unusual that he should leave in the dead of night like that, a man of sixty-four, without getting his night's rest first?"

"Well, all right. Say it is!" she flared resentfully. "But we're not accountable for his eccentricities, why come to us about it? He left here, I assure you. Look under the carpet if you don't think so!" A second later she wished she hadn't said that; it seemed to put her ahead of him, so to speak. They got you all muddled, these professional detectives. Just think if it had been a case of out-and-out murder, instead of just trying to conceal that money business of Gil's!

Ward smiled wryly at her dig about the carpet. "Oh, I don't doubt he left the house, here."

She didn't like the slight emphasis he gave the word "house," as though implying something had happened to him right outside it, or not far away.

"Then what more have we got to do with it? Who's putting these ideas in your head, his wife?"

"I don't have ideas in my head, just instructions, Mrs. Blaine."

"Why don't you check at the other end, in the city? Why don't you find out what became of him there?"

He said very quietly, "Because he never got there, Mrs. Blaine."

Womanlike, she kept trying to retain the offensive, as the best defense. "How do you know for sure? Just because he didn't appear either at his home or his office? He may have been run over by a taxi. He may have been overcome by amnesia."

"To get to the city, he would have had to take the train first of all, wouldn't he, Mrs. Blaine? A man of sixty-four isn't likely to thumb a ride in along the highway at four in the morning, with week-end baggage in the bargain, is he?"

"He did take the train. He must have. My husb—"

"We happen to know he didn't. We've questioned the conductor on that train whose business it is to punch the passengers' tickets as they get on at each successive stop. No one got on the 4:20 train at all at your particular station out here. And that milk train is empty enough to make it easy to keep track. The ticket agent didn't sell anyone a ticket between the hours of one and six thirty that morning, and since you drove him out in the car yourself on Friday afternoon, it isn't likely he had the second half of a round-trip ticket in his possession; he would have had to buy a one-way one."

A cold chill ran down her spine; she tried not to be aware of it. "All I can say is, my husband drove him to the station and then came on back without watching him board the train. He may have strolled a little too far to the end of the platform while waiting and been waylaid by a footpad in the dark."

"Yes," he said reasonably enough. "But why should the footpad carry him off bodily with him into thin air? We've searched the immediate vicinity of the station pretty thoroughly, and now we're combing over the woods and fields along the way. His baggage has disappeared, too. How many pieces did he bring with him, Mrs. Blaine?"

That one was a son of a gun. Would it be better to say one and try to cover up the presence of the one he'd left behind? Suppose it came out later that he'd brought two—as it was bound to—and they identified the second one, upstairs, as his? On the other hand, if she admitted that he'd left one behind, wouldn't that only add to the strange circumstances surrounding his departure? She couldn't afford to pile that additional strangeness on top of the already overwhelming strangeness of the hour at which he'd gone; it made it look too bad for them, too much as though his leave-taking had been impromptu, conditioned by anger or a quarrel. And then in the wake of that would unfailingly come revelation of Gil's misdeed in regard to the check.

She took the plunge, answered the detective's question with a deliberate but not unqualified falsehood, after all this had gone through her mind. "I believe . . . one."

"You can't say for sure? You brought him out in the car with you, Mrs. Blaine."

"I've brought so many people out in the car. Sometimes I dream I'm a station-wagon driver."

Then, just as she felt she couldn't stand another minute of this cat-and-mouse play, just as she could feel the makings of a three-alarm scream gathering in her system, she recognized the sound of their own car outside and Gil was back at last. He sounded the horn once, briefly, as in a sort of questioning signal.

"Here's my husband now," she said, and jumped up and ran to the door before he could stop her.

"Hello, Gil," she said loudly. She wound an arm around his neck, kissed him on the side of the face, back toward the ear— or seemed to. "There's a detective in there," she breathed.

His own breath answered hers: "Wait a minute; stay like this, up against me." He said loudly down the back of her neck: "Hello, beautiful. Miss me?"

She could feel his hand fumbling between their bodies. He thrust something into her disengaged hand, the one that wasn't clasping the nape of his neck. Spongy paper, currency. "Better get rid of this. I don't think he'll search me, but bury it in your stocking or somewhere, till he goes." And then in a fullbodied voice: "Any calls for me?"

"No, but there's a gentleman inside waiting to see you now."

And under cover of that he'd gone on: "Go out and get in the car; take it away. Go down the village and . . . buy things. Anything. Keep buying, keep buying. Stay out. Phone here before you come back. Phone here first."

Then they had to break it up; they'd gotten away with m— Not that word! They'd gotten away with a lot, as it was.

She followed Gil's instructions now, but she did it her way. She couldn't fathom the motivation. But she couldn't just walk out the door, get in, and drive off; that would have been a dead give-away he'd cued her. She did it her way; it only took a minute longer. She went back into the living room after him, across it just to the opposite doorway, and called through to Leona in a war whoop: "Leona, need anything?" She didn't have to worry about getting the wrong answer; she knew how they'd be fixed.

"Sure do," said the uninhibited Leona, "all we got lef' after that bunch of cannibals is a lot of nothin'!"

"All right, I'll run down and bring you back a shot of everything." But as she passed the two men a second time, short as the delay had been—and necessary, she felt, for appearances' sake—Gil's face was almost agonized, as though he couldn't wait for her to do as he'd told her and get out. Maybe the other man couldn't notice it, but she could; she knew him so well. The detective, on the other hand, not only offered no objection to her going, but seemed to be deliberately holding his fire until she was out of the way, as though he preferred it that way, wanted to question Gil by himself.

She got in and drove off leisurely, and as she meshed gears, at the same time cached the wad of unlawful money under the elastic top of her stocking. Gil's motive for so badly wanting her to get in the car and get away from the house, and *stay* away until the fellow left, must be this money, of course. He wanted to avoid being caught in incriminating possession of it. That must be it; she couldn't figure out any other logical reason. Still, they couldn't keep on indefinitely running bases with it like this.

She'd stepped up speed now, was coursing the sleek turnpike to the village at her usual projectile clip. But not too fast to glimpse a group of men in the distance, widely separated and apparently wading around aimlessly in the fields. She had an idea what they were doing out there, though. And then a few minutes later, when that strip of woods, thick as the bristles of a hairbrush, closed in on both sides of the road, she could make out a few more of them under the trees. They were using pocket lights in there, although it wasn't quite dusk yet.

"What are they looking for him this far back for?" she thought impatiently. "If Gil says he let him off at the station platform—" Stupid police. That malicious Mrs. Burroughs, paying them back now because she'd sensed that the old fool had had a soft spot for Jackie. And then in conclusion: "How do they know he's dead, anyway?"

She braked outside the village grocery. She subtracted a twenty from the money first of all, tucked that in the pocket of her jumper. She hadn't brought any bag; he'd rushed her out so. Then she went in and started buying out the store.

By the time she was through, she had a knee-high carton filled with stuff. "Take it out and put it in the rumble for me, I'll take it right along with me. Let me use your phone a minute; I want to make sure I've got everything."

Gil answered her himself. "I just got rid of him this minute," he said, in a voice hoarse from long strain. "Whew!"

She said for the benefit of the storekeeper, "Do you need anything else while I'm out?"

"No, come on back now; it's all right." And then sharply: "Listen! If you run into *him*, don't stop for him, hear me? Don't even slow down; just drive past fast. He's got no authority to stop you; he's a city dick. He's done his questioning and he's through. Don't stop for *anyone* and don't let anyone get in the car with you."

The store manager called in to her just then from out front: "Mrs. Blaine, the rumble's locked. I can't get into it. Where'll I put this stuff?"

"The whole key rack's sticking in the dashboard; take it out yourself. You know the one, that broad flat one."

"That key ain't on it any more. I don't see it here with the rest."

"Wait a minute, I'll ask my husband. Gil, where's the key to the rumble? We can't find it."

"I lost it." She couldn't really hear him the first time; his voice choked up. Maybe he'd been taking a drink just then.

The storekeeper said: "Maybe it's just jammed. Should I try to pry it up for you?"

"No, you might spoil the paint job."

Gil was saying thickly in her ear: "Never mind about the rumble; let it alone. Get away from that store." Suddenly, incredibly, he was screaming at her over the wire! Literally screaming, like someone in pain. "Come on back, will ya! Come on back, I tell ya! *Come on back* with that car!"

"All right, for Heaven's sake; all right." Her eardrum tingled. That detective certainly had set his nerves on edge.

She drove back with the carton of stuff beside her on the seat. Gil was waiting for her all the way out in the middle of the roadway that passed their house.

"I'll put it to bed myself," he said gruffly, and drove the car into the garage, groceries and all, he was in such a hurry.

His face was all twinkling with perspiration when he turned to her after finishing locking the garage doors on it.

She woke up that night, sometime between two and three, and he wasn't in the room. She called, and he wasn't in the house at all. She got up and looked out the window, and the white garage doors showed a slight wedge of black between their two halves, so he'd taken the car out with him.

She wasn't really worried at first. Still, where could he have gone at this unearthly hour? Where was there for him to go—around here? And why slip out like that, without saying a word to her? She sat there in the dark for about thirty, forty minutes, sometimes on the edge of the bed, sometimes over by the window, watching the road for him.

Suddenly a black shape came along, blurring the highway's tape-like whiteness. But in almost absolute silence, hardly recognizable as a car, lights out. It was gliding along, practically coasting, the downward tilt of the road past the house helping it.

It was he, though. He took the car around, berthed it in the garage, and then she heard him come in downstairs. A glass clinked once or twice, and then he came up. She'd put the light on, so as not to throw a scare into him. His face was like putty; she'd never seen him look like this before.

"Matter, couldn't you sleep, Gil?" she said quietly.

"I took the car out for a run, and every time I'd stop and think I'd found a place where I was alone, I'd hear some other damn car somewhere in the distance or see its lights, or think I did, anyway. Judas, the whole country seemed awake—twigs snapping, stars peering down—"

"But why stop? Why should it annoy you if there were other cars in the distance? What were you trying to do, get rid of something, throw something away?"

"Yeah," he said, low.

For a minute she got badly frightened again, like Monday morning, until he, seeming to take fright from her fright in turn, quickly stammered:

"Uh-huh that other bag of his, that second bag he left behind. He's coming back, that guy, I know he is; he isn't through yet. I was on pins and needles the whole time he was here, this afternoon, thinking he was going to go looking around and find it up there." He let some sulphur matches trickle out of his pocket. "I was going to try to burn it, but I was afraid somebody'd see me, somebody was following me." He threw himself face down across the bed. Not crying or anything, just exhausted with spent emotion. "The bitter end," he panted, "the bitter end."

A minute later she stepped back into the room, astonishment written all over her face.

"But, Gil, you didn't even have it with you, do you realize that? It's right there in the guest-room closet, where it's been all along!"

He didn't turn his head. His voice came muffledly: "I'm going crazy, I guess. I don't even know what I'm doing any more. Maybe I took one of our own by mistake."

"Why did all this have to happen to us?" she sobbed dryly as she reached out to snap off the light.

✤

He was right, Ward came back. The next day, that was Wednesday, two days after It. He had a different air about him, a disarming, almost apologetic one, as though he were simply here to ask a favor.

"What, more questioning?" she greeted him caustically.

"I'm sorry you resent my interviewing you yesterday. It was just routine, but I tried to be as inoffensive as I could about it. No, so far as we're concerned, you people no longer figure in it—except of course as his last known jumping-off place into nothingness. We have a new theory we're working on."

"What is it?" she said, forgetting to be aloof.

"I'm sorry, I'm not at liberty to divulge it. However, a couple of interviews with Mrs. Burroughs were enough to give it an impetus. She's a hypochondriac if there ever was one."

"I think I know what you're driving at. You mean his disappearance was voluntary, to get away from the sickroom atmosphere in his home?"

His knowing expression told her she was right. And for a moment a great big sun came up and shone through the darkness she had been living in ever since Mrs. Burroughs' phone call Monday noon. How wonderful it would be if that should turn out to be the correct explanation, what a reprieve for herself and Gil! Why, it would automatically cover up the check matter as well. If the old man had been about to drop from sight, he certainly could have been expected to cash a check for that amount, to keep himself in funds; there wouldn't be any mystery about it, then.

Meanwhile, as to Ward: You could tell he wasn't here altogether on business. He was looking into her face a little too personally, she thought. Well, he was only a man after all. What could you do about it?

"The local chief out here, whom I'm co-operating with, can't put me up at his house; he's got three of our guys staying with him already. I was wondering if it would put you out if I . . . er . . . asked permission to make this my headquarters; you know, just sleep here while I'm detailed out here, so I wouldn't have to keep running back and forth, to the city and out again, every night?"

She nearly fell over. "But this is a private home, after all."

"Well, I wouldn't be in your way much. You can bill the department for it if you like."

"That isn't the point. There's a perfectly good hotel in the village."

"I already tried to get quarters there. They're all filled up. You're entitled to refuse if you want to. It'd just be a way of showing your good will and willingness to cooperate. After all, it's just as much to the interest of you and your husband as anyone else to have this matter cleared up."

By the time she got in to Gil, she was already beginning to see the humorous side of it. "It's Ward again. He wants to be our house guest; can you tie that? He hinted that now they think Burroughs disappeared voluntarily, to get away from that invalid wife of his."

His face was a white pucker of frightening suspicion. "He's lying! He's trying different tactics, that's all. He's trying to plant himself here in the house with us as a spy."

"But don't you think it'll look worse, if we seem to have anything to hide by not letting him in? Then they'll simply hang around watching us from the outside. If we let him in, we may be able to get rid of him for good in a day or two."

"He'll watch every move I make, he'll listen to every word that's said. It's been tough up to now; it'll be hell that way."

"Well, you go out and shoo him away then; you're the boss."

He took a quick step toward the door. Then his courage

seemed to ooze out of him. She saw him falter, come to a stop, rake his fingers through his hair.

"Maybe you're right," he said uncertainly, "maybe it'll look twice as bad if we turn him away, like we have something to hide. Tell him O. K." And he poured himself a drink the size of Lake Erie.

"He'll sleep on the davenport in the living room and like it," she said firmly. "I'm not running a lodging-house for homeless detectives."

It was the least she could do, she felt, meeting him along the road like that: ask him if he wanted a lift back to the house with her. After all, she had nothing against the man; he was just doing his job. And Gil's half-hysterical injunction, over the wire the day before, "Don't take anyone in the car with you!" was furthest from her thoughts, had no meaning at the moment. For that matter, it had had no meaning even at the time.

"Sure, don't mind if I do," he accepted. He slung himself up on the running board without obliging her to come to a complete stop, and dropped into the seat beside her without opening the door, displacing some parcels she'd had there.

"Why don't you put these in the rumble?" he asked, piling them on his lap for want of a better place.

She took one hand off the wheel, snapped her fingers. "That reminds me, I wanted to stop at a repair shop and have a new key made; we've lost the old one."

He was sitting sideways, face turned toward her, studying her profile. In one way it was annoying, in another way it was excessively flattering. She kept her eyes on the road ahead.

"Didn't the mister object to your coming out like this?"

She thought it was said kiddingly; it was one of those things should have been said kiddingly. But when she looked at him, his face was dead serious.

She eyed him in frank surprise. "How did you know? We had a little set-to about the car, that was all. I wanted it and he didn't want me to have it; wanted it himself, I guess. So I took it anyway, while he was shaving, and here I am." Then, afraid she had given him a misleading impression of their domestic relations, she tried to minimize it. "Oh, but that's nothing new with us, that's been going on ever since we've had a car." It wasn't true; it had never happened before—until tonight.

"Oh," he said. And an alertness that had momentarily come into his expression slowly left it again.

They came to the belt of woods that crossed and infolded the roadway, and she slowed to a laggard crawl. She fumbled for a cigarette and he put a match to it. Without their noticing it, the car had come to a full halt. The light wind, no longer in their faces, veered, changed direction. Suddenly she flung the cigarette away from her with a disgusted grimace.

They both became aware of it at the same time. She crinkled her nose, threw in the clutch.

"There must be something dead in these woods," she remarked. "Do you notice that odor? Every once in a while you get a whiff of it."

"There's something dead—somewhere around," he agreed cryptically.

As soon as they picked up speed again and came out between the open fields, it disappeared, left behind—apparently—under the dank trees. He didn't say a word from that time on. That only occurred to her later. He forgot to thank her when they drew up at the house. He forgot even to say good night. He was evidently lost in thought, thinking of something else entirely.

Gil's grip, as she entered their bedroom in the dark, fell on her shoulder like the jaws of a steel trap—and was just as merciless. He must have been standing unseen a little inside the doorway. His voice was an unrecognizable strangled sound.

"Didn't I tell you not to let anyone get in that car with you!"

"I just met him now, on my way back."

"Where'd you go with it? I've died every minute since you left!"

"I told you I wanted to see the new war picture."

The idea seemed to send him floundering back against the bedroom wall in the dark.

"You went to the *movies?*" he gasped. "And where was the car? What'd you do with it while you were in there?"

"What does anyone do with a car while they're in seeing a show? I left it parked around the corner from the theater."

This time he just gave a wordless gasp—the sort of sound that is wrenched from a person when something goes hurtling by and narrowly misses hitting him.

✦

She was in a half sleep when some sense of impending danger aroused her. It was neither a sound nor a motion, it was just the impalpable *presence* of some menace in itself. She started up. There was a late moon tonight, and the room was dark-blue and white, not black. Gil was crouched to one side of the window, peering down, his back to her. Not a muscle rippled, he was so still.

"Gil, what is it?" she breathed softly.

His silencing hiss came back even softer, no louder than a thread of steam escaping from a radiator valve.

She put her foot to the floor, crept up behind him. The sibilance came again:

"Get back, you fool. I don't want him to see me up here."

The sound of a stealthy tinkering came up from below, somewhere. A very small sound it was in the night stillness. She peered over his shoulder. Ward was standing down there at the garage doors, fumbling with them.

"If he gets them open and goes in there—"

Suddenly she foreshortened her glance, brought it down perpendicularly over Gil's shoulder, saw the gun for the first time, blue-black as a bottle fly in the moonlight. Steady, for all Gil's nerves; held so sure and steady there wasn't a waver in it. Centered remorselessly on the man outside the garage down there.

"Gil!" Her inhalation of terror seemed to fill the room with a sound like rushing wind.

He stiff-armed her behind him, never even turned his head, never even took his eyes off his objective. "Get back, I tell you. If he gets them open, I'm going to shoot."

But this would be murder, the very thing she'd dreaded so Monday, and that had missed them the first time by a hairbreadth. He must have the money hidden in there in the garage. She had to do something to stop him, to keep it from happening. She floundered across the room on her bare feet, found the opposite wall, groped along it.

"Gil, get back. I'm going to put on the lights."

She just gave him time enough to swerve aside, snapped the switch, and the room flared into noonday brilliance that cast a big warning yellow patch on the ground outside.

There was a single retreating footfall on the concrete runway down there, and the next time they looked, the space in front of the garage doors showed empty.

She crept out to the head of the stairs, listened, came back again.

"He's gone to bed," she said. "I heard the day bed creak."

The reaction had set in; the tension Gil had been under must have been terrific. He was shaking all over like someone attached to an electric reducing belt. "He'll only make another stab at it again tomorrow night. I can't stand it any more, I can't stand it any more! I'm getting out of here—now."

It was no use reasoning with him, she could see that at a glance. He was in a state bordering on frenzy. For a moment she was half tempted to say: "Oh, let's go downstairs to him now, the two of us, admit you raised the check, give him back the money, and get it over with! Anything's better than this nightmare!"

But she checked herself. How much did they get for doing what he'd done? Ten years? Twenty? Her courage failed her; she had no right to ask him to give up that much of his life.

Meanwhile he was whipping a necktie around his collar, shrugging on his jacket. She whispered: "Gil, let's stop and think before we cut ourselves off completely— Where can we go, at this hour?"

"I rented a furnished room in the city today, under an assumed name." He whispered an address. "We'll be safe there for a couple of days at least. As soon as I can get boat tickets— I have to get rid of that car, that's the main thing."

"But, Gil, don't you see we're convicting ourselves, by doing this?"

"Are you coming with me? Or are you doing to let me down just when I need you most, like women usually do? You're half in love with him already! I've seen the looks he's starting to give you. They all fall for you; why shouldn't he? All right, stay here with him then."

She silenced him by pressing her fingers to his mouth. "To the bitter end," she whispered, misty-eyed, "to the bitter end. If you want it this way, then this is the way it'll be."

He didn't even thank her: she didn't expect him to, anyway. "Go out there again and make sure he's sleeping."

She came back, said: "He's snoring; I can hear him all the way up here."

While she began to dress with frantic haste, Gil started down ahead.

"I'll take the brakes off, you take the wheel, and I'll push it out into the road so he won't hear us start."

Ward's snoring filled the house as she crept down the dark stairs after Gil moments later. "Why? Why?" she kept thinking distractedly. But she'd made her decision; she went ahead unfalteringly.

He had the garage doors open by the time she'd joined him. The place smelled terrible; a stray cat must have found its way in and died in there some place. She got in, guided the car out backward as he pushed at the hood. Then he shifted around to the rear. The incline of the concrete path helped carry them

down to the road. You could still hear Ward snoring inside the
house, from out where they were. Gil pushed it down the road
a considerable distance from the house, before he jumped in
and took over the wheel.

"Made it," he muttered hoarsely.

She wasn't a slow driver herself by any means, but she'd
never forced the car to such a speed as he got out of it now. The
gauge broke in new numbers on their dial. The wheels seemed
to churn air most of the time and just come down for contact
at intervals.

"Gil, take a little of the head off it." She shuddered. "You'll
kill the two of us!"

"Look back and see if there's anything in sight behind us."

There was, but far away. It had nothing to do with them. It
definitely wasn't Ward; he couldn't have gotten another car
that quickly. But it spurred Gil on to keep up that death-invit-
ing pace long after they'd lost sight of it. And then suddenly,
ahead—

The other car peered unexpectedly at them over a rise. There
was plenty of room for them both, at a normal rate of speed.
They wouldn't even have had to swerve; neither was hogging
the road. But Gil was going so fast, and in the attempt to shift
over farther, their rear wheels swept out of line with their front,
they started a long forward skid, and the other car nicked them
in passing. It wasn't anything; at an ordinary rate of speed it
would have just scraped the paint off their fender or something.
But it swept them against a tree growing close to the roadway,
and that in turn flung them back broadside on the asphalt again.
Miraculously they stayed right side up, but with a bad dent
toward their rear where they'd hit the tree. The rumble lid had
sprung up and that whole side of the chassis was flattened in.

The other car had stopped farther down the road; it hadn't
been going any too slow itself. She was on the floor, thrown
there in a coiled-rope formation, but unhurt. She heard Gil
swear icily under his breath, fling open the door, shoot out as
though pursued by devils.

She looked up into the rear-sight mirror and there was a face in it. The sunken, hideously grinning face of Homer Burroughs, peering up above the level of the forcibly opened rumble. She could see it so plain, swimming on the moonlit mirror; even the dark bruises mottling it under the silvery hair, even the heavy auto wrench riding his shoulder like an epaulette, thrown up out of the bottom of the rumble as his body had been thrown up—like a macabre jack-in-the-box. And the odor of the woods that she and Ward had noticed earlier was all around her in the night, though she was far from those particular woods now.

She acted quickly, by instinct alone. Almost before Gil had gotten back there, to flatten the rumble top down again, smother what it had inadvertently revealed before the occupants of the other car came up and saw it, she had opened the door on her side and jumped down. She began to run silently along the edge of the road, in the shadows cast by the overhanging trees. She didn't know where she was going. She only wanted to get away from this man. This man who had killed. This man who was no longer her husband, who spelled Fear and Horror to her now. She saw now that she had lied to him—and to herself—Monday, when she told him she could stand it even if he'd done this, so long as he only admitted it. If she'd seen Burroughs' battered corpse at the time, as she had now, the same thing would have happened then: she would have fled away from Gil like one demented. She couldn't stand cowardly murder.

He'd gotten the rumble down, and was standing there pressed slightly backward upon it, at bay, arms out at either side to hold it down. He either didn't see her scurry by along the edge of the trees, or was too preoccupied in facing the two men who were coming solicitously back toward him, to pay any attention. The half-formed idea in her churning mind was to get into that other, momentarily vacated car and get away from him. Anywhere, but get away!

She was halfway to it now. She could hear their voices, back there where she'd run from:

"Are you all right, brother? How badly did we hit you?"

"Gee, we banged up his rumble, Art."

And then Gil's sharp, dangerous: "Get away from it!"

The two shots came with sickening suddenness. Just *bam!* and then *bam!* again, and there were two huddled, loglike forms on the roadway in the moonlight up there by Gil's car.

Murder again. Murder trebled now. How far, how far away they'd stopped that other car! She'd never make it. She saw that now. He'd already called her name warningly once, he was already running toward her like a winged messenger of death. She was up to it at last, had one foot on the running board now. But he had a smoking gun in his hand that could reach out from where he was to where she was quicker than any car could get under way. And this one, too, like theirs, had brought up broadside to the road. Before she could back up for clearance, turn, and get away, he'd be upon her. In her frustrated panic, hand on the door catch, she was conscious of the caked dust spewed upon the sides of the car, thrown up by its wheel action. They'd driven it hard.

Instead of getting in, she ran around it to the opposite side, away from him, as though to take cover. Then she stood there staring at him over it. At last she rounded it once more at the rear and came back toward him, away from it. Met him a few paces before it.

He seized her relentlessly by the wrist. "So now you know," he heaved. "So you ran out on me."

"I lost my head for a minute; anyone would have."

"I watched you. You didn't go the other way. You started back toward *him,* the guy you love now."

He was dragging her toward their own car, swinging her from side to side like a primordial ape with a living victim.

"You're dangerous to me now, I can see that. I've just shot two men; I'm fighting for my life. And anything or anyone that might help to trap me, has got to be removed."

"Gil, you wouldn't do such a thing. I'm your wife!"

"Fugitives have no wives."

He half raised the gun toward her, lowered it again. He looked up the road, and down. The moonlight was crafty in his eyes.

"Get in, I'll give you one more chance."

She knew it was only a postponement. One thing at a time; he had to get to cover first. If he left her lying out here on the open road they'd know instantly who had done it. She could read her death warrant in his eyes, as they started off once more toward the city.

✦

It was inconceivable that he meant to go through with such a thing. Even the sight of the grimy tenement room, suggestive of crime and violence, failed to make it more plausible. "This isn't happening," she thought, "this isn't real; my husband hasn't brought me to this unspeakable room in the slums, intending to do away with me. I'm still asleep, at home, and I'm having a bad dream.

"Yet all these days he's known, and he hasn't told me. All these days I've been living with a murderer." She visualized again the way he'd shot those two men down in cold blood, without a qualm, without a moment's hesitation. Why wouldn't he be capable of doing the same to her? He was kill-crazy now, at bay. The red tide of murder had swept over him, effacing all love, trust, compassion, wiping away their very marriage itself. And he could kill this woman in the room with him, he could kill anyone on God's earth tonight.

She sat slumped on the edge of the creaky iron bedstead, fingers pressed to her temples. He'd locked the room door after they came in, pulled down the patched blue shade on the window. He stood listening for a moment by the door, to see if anyone had followed them up, then he turned to her. "I've got to get rid of that car first," he muttered to himself. Suddenly he'd come over, thrust her aside, was disheveling the bed, pull-

ing out the sheets from under the threadbare cotton blankets.
They squealed like pigs as he tore long strips down their
lengths.

She guessed what they were for. "No, Gil, don't!" she whimpered smotheredly. She ran for the door, pulled uselessly at the
knob. He swung her around back behind him.

"Don't do this to me!"

"I can't just leave you locked in here. You'd scream or break
a window. You sold out to him, and you're my enemy now."

He flung her face-down on the bed, caught her hands behind
her back, deftly tied them together with strips of sheeting.
Then her ankles in the same way. He sat her up, lashed her
already once-secured hands to the iron bed frame. Then he
wound a final length around her face, snuffing out her mouth.
Her eyes were wide with horror. It wasn't so much what was
being done to her, as whom it was being done by.

"Can you breathe?" He plucked it down a little from the tip
of her nose. "Breathe while you can." His eyes, flicking over to
the length of tubing connecting a wall jet with a one-burner gas
ring, then back again to her, betrayed his intended method
when the time came. He'd stun her first with a blow from his
gun butt, probably, then remove her bonds to make it look like
a suicide, disconnect the tube and let the gas take its course.
That happened so often in these cheap rooming houses; that
was the way out so many took.

He listened carefully at the door. Then he unlocked it, and
as he turned to go glanced back and said to her:

"Keep your eyes on this doorknob. And when you see it start
to turn, begin saying your prayers."

She heard him lock the door again on the other side, and the
faint creak of his step descending the warped stairs.

He would come back—in forty minutes, in an hour—and kill
her. But therein didn't lie the full horror of it. It was that this
man and she had danced by moonlight not so long ago, had
exchanged kisses and vows under the stars. It was that he had

brought her candy, and orchids to wear on her coat. It was that they had stood up together and sworn to cherish and cling to one another for the rest of their lives.

Yet she saw that it must have been in him from the beginning, this fatal flaw of character that had finally led him to murder. People didn't change that abruptly; they couldn't. There were some who could never be capable of murder, no matter what the circumstances. And others, like Gil, needed only a slight push in that direction to fall into it almost of their own accords. He'd been a potential murderer all along. He hadn't known it and she hadn't, so who was to blame?

She couldn't free her hands. She only succeeded in tightening the knots in the sheeting more inextricably when she strained against them; it was that kind of material. The bed had no casters, and one foot, caught in a crack in the floor, held it fast against her attempts to drag it after her.

He'd been gone a long time. Against her will she found herself eying the china knob on the inside of the door. When it started to turn, he'd said—

And suddenly the light, given back by its glossy surface, seemed to flash, to waver. It was moving, it was going slowly around! Without his having made a sound on the stairs outside. She could feel her temples begin to pound. But the key rattle didn't come. Instead the knob relapsed again to where it had been. With a slight rustling sound, so she knew she hadn't been mistaken, she had actually seen it move. She stared toward it till her eyes threatened to start from their sockets, but it didn't move again. Why didn't he come in and get it over with? Why this exquisite additional torture? Maybe he'd heard someone coming on the stairs.

There was another agonizing wait, during which she screamed silently against the gag. There, he was coming back again. Ths time she could hear the furtive tread on the oil-cloth-covered stairs. He must have gone down to the street again for a minute to make doubly sure no one was about.

The key hardly scraped at all, so deftly did he fit it in. And once again the china knob wheeled and sent out wavers of light. And this time the door opened—and let Death in. Death was a face she'd kissed a thousand times. Death was a hand that had stroked her hair. Death was a man whose name she had taken in place of her own.

He locked the door behind him, Death did. He said, tight-lipped: "I sent it into the river. It was misty and there was no one around to see. At last I'm rid of him, that damned old man! And by the time they fish him out again, if they ever do, I'll be far away. There's a tanker leaves for Venezuela at midday."

The rubber extension tube went *whup!* as he pulled off the nozzle of the jet. The key didn't make any sound as he turned it, and the gas didn't either, as it started coming in.

He dropped his eyes before hers. "Don't look at me like that; it's no use. I'm going through with it."

He drew his gun and gripped it down near the bore, and then he shifted his cuff back out of the way, as a man does when he doesn't want anything to hamper the swing of his arm. The last thing he said was "You won't feel anything, Jackie." That was Gil Blaine, dying inside the murderer.

Then he raised the gun butt high over his head, with a terrible intensity, so that his whole arm shook. Or maybe it was just the way she was looking at him, so that he had to use twice as much will power, to get it done.

It had gone up as high as it could; now it started to come down again. Her head seemed to be made of glass. It shattered, she could *hear* it shatter with the blow, and her skull seemed to rain all around her on the floor, and the blow itself exploded deafeningly in her own ears, like a shot. But without causing any pain.

Then as her eyes started spasmodically open again, it was *he* that was falling, his whole body, and not just his arm any more. She turned her head dazedly. The window shade was being held aside by an arm, and there was broken glass all over the floor, and Ward was out there looking into the room through a

sort of saw-toothed halo where the windowpane had been, lazy
smoke soft-focusing him. He reached up and did something to
the catch, raised the frame, climbed through across the sill.

When he'd turned off the gas jet and freed her, she hid her
face against him, still sitting there on the bedstead, and clung
like that for a long time. It was a funny thing to do, with a mere
detective, but still—who else had she?

"You weren't in line with the keyhole when I squinted
through it, or I would have shot the lock off then. I wasn't sure
that this was the right room, so I went through to the back yard
and climbed the fire escape from there. All I had to go by was
what you'd traced in the dust on the side of that car left standing
out there on the road: just my name and this address. And, gee,
Jackie, if you knew how close I came to never noticing it at all!"

"I didn't think it would be seen, but it was all I had time to
do. Anything could have happened. Someone's sleeve could
have brushed against it and erased it.

"He killed Burroughs early Monday morning. And he's had
him in our locked rumble seat ever since! That explains so many
things in his behavior the past few days I couldn't understand.
But, oh, you're so blind when you trust anyone! He finally
dumped him, car and all, into the river just now, before he came
back."

"We'll get it up. I was sure of him from the first, but without
a body or any trace of one, our hands were tied. And then you,
you pulled so much weight in his favor just by being in the
picture at all, so honest and so—We all knew you couldn't be
a party to a murder."

She lifted her head, but without trying to see past him into
the room. He seemed to understand what she was trying to ask,
and told her:

"He's dead. I wasn't very careful, I guess."

She wondered if he'd meant to do it that way. It was better
that way. Better even for Gil himself.

Ward stood her up and walked her out through the door,

leaning her against him so she wouldn't have to look at Gil lying
on the floor. Outside the night seemed clean and fresh again,
all evil gone from it, and the stars looked as new as though
they'd never been used before. She drew a deep breath, of
infinite pity but no regret.

"So this is how it ends."

Woolrich wrote this story in three versions, the first and to my mind
the best being the one you've just read. About two years later he
revised the tale into a radio play, broadcast on *Suspense* with the title
"Last Night," and marked by a complete reversal of the ending of the
original novella. A third version, more complex than the radio play but
still bearing in essence the play's ending, appeared in the first collection of Woolrich's short fiction, *I Wouldn't Be in Your Shoes* (1943), as
"Last Night."

It's interesting to compare the fate of this story with that of Alfred
Hitchcock's 1941 film *Suspicion*, another classic on the theme Is my
husband a murderer. As we know from François Truffaut's book and
other sources, Hitchcock intended the answer to be Yes but the busi-
nessmen holding the purse strings refused to allow that answer, since
the husband was being played by Cary Grant. The same shift in ending
—in fact the same forced, improvised tone to the climax—takes place
in the final version of Woolrich's story. Was Woolrich in 1942-43 hoping
to sell "Last Night" to the movies on the coattails of *Suspicion?* In any
case, Woolrich's original, unlike Hitchcock's, has survived (though un-
reprinted since 1940), and is as taut and nerve-jangling today as it was
thirty years ago.

The Corpse Next Door

Harlan's wife turned away quickly, trying to hide the can-opener in her hand. "What's the idea?" he asked. She hadn't expected him to look across the top of his morning paper just then. The can of evaporated milk she had been holding in her other hand slipped from her grasp in her excitement, hit the floor with a dull whack, and rolled over. She stooped quickly, snatched it up, but he had seen it.

"Looks like somebody swiped the milk from our door again last night," she said with a nervous little laugh. Harlan had a vicious temper. She hadn't wanted to tell him, but there had not been time to run out to the store and get another bottle.

"That's the fifth time in two weeks!" He rolled the paper into a tube and smacked it viciously against the table-leg. She could see him starting to work himself up, getting whiter by the minute even under his shaving talcum. "It's somebody right in the house!" he roared. "No outsider could get in past that locked street-door after twelve!" He bared his teeth in a deceptive grin. "I'd like to get my hands on the fellow!"

"I've notified the milkman and I've complained to the super-intendent, but there doesn't seem to be any way of stopping it," Mrs. Harlan sighed. She punched a hole in the top of the can, tilted it over his cup.

He pushed it aside disgustedly and stood up. "Oh, yes, there is," he gritted, "and I'm going to stop it!" A suburban com-muters' train whistled thinly in the distance. "Just lemme get hold of whoever—!" he muttered a second time with sup-pressed savagery as he grabbed his hat, bolted for the door. Mrs. Harlan shook her head with worried foreboding as it slammed behind him.

He came back at six bringing something in a paper-bag, which he stood on the kitchen-shelf. Mrs. Harlan looked in it and saw a quart of milk.

"We don't need that. I ordered a bottle this afternoon from the grocer," she told him.

"That's not for our use," he answered grimly. "It's a decoy."

At eleven, in bathrobe and slippers, she saw him carry it out to the front door and set it down. He looked up and down the hall, squatted down beside it, tied something invisible around its neck below the cardboard cap. Then he strewed something across the sill and closed the door.

"What on earth—?" said Mrs. Harlan apprehensively.

He held up his index-finger. A coil of strong black sewing-thread was plaited around it. It stood out clearly against the skin of his finger, but trailed off invisibly into space and under the door to connect with the bottle. "Get it?" he gloated vindic-tively. "You've got to look twice to see this stuff once, especially in a shadowy doorway. But it cuts the skin if it's pulled tight.

See? One tug should be enough to wake me up, and if I can only get out there in time—"

He left the rest of it unfinished. He didn't have to finish it, his wife knew just what he meant. She was beginning to wish he hadn't found out about the thefted milk. There'd only be a brawl outside their door in the middle of the night, with the neighbors looking on—

He paid out the thread across their living-room floor into the bedroom beyond, got into bed, and left the hand it was attached to outside the covers. Putting out the lights after him, she was tempted to clip the thread then and there, as the safest way out, even picked up a pair of scissors and tried to locate it in the dark. She knew if she did, he'd be sure to notice it in the morning and raise cain.

"Don't walk around in there so much," he called warningly. "You'll snarl it up."

Her courage failed her. She put the scissors down and went to bed. The menacing thread, like a powder-train leading to a high explosive, remained intact.

In the morning it was still there, and there were two bottles of milk at the door instead of one, the usual delivery and the decoy. Mrs. Harlan sighed with relief. It would have been very short-sighted of the guilty person to repeat the stunt two nights in succession; it had been happening at the rate of every third night so far. Maybe by the time it happened again, Harlan would cool down.

But Harlan was slow at cooling down. The very fact that the stunt wasn't repeated immediately only made him boil all the more. He wanted his satisfaction out of it. He caught himself thinking about it on the train riding to and from the city. Even at the office, when he should have been attending to his work. It started to fester and rankle. He was in a fair way to becoming hipped on the subject, when at last the thread paid off one night about four.

He was asleep when the warning tug came. Mrs. Harlan slept

soundly in the adjoining bed. He knew right away what had awakened him, jumped soundlessly out of bed with a bound, and tore through the darkened flat toward the front door.

He reached it with a pattering rush of bare feet and tore it open. It was sweet. It was perfect. He couldn't have asked for it any better! Harlan caught him red-handed, in the very act. The bottle of milk cradled in his arm, he froze there petrified and stared guiltily at the opening door. He'd evidently missed feeling the tug of the thread altogether—which wasn't surprising, because at his end the bottle had received it and not himself. And to make it even better than perfect, pluperfect, he was someone that by the looks of him Harlan could handle without much trouble. Not that he would have hung back even if he'd found himself outclassed. He was white-hot with thirty-six hours' pent-up combustion, and physical cowardice wasn't one of his failings, whatever else was.

He just stood there for a split second, motionless, to rub it in. "Nice work, buddy!" he hissed.

The hijacker cringed, bent lopsidedly to put the bottle on the floor without taking his terrified eyes off Harlan. He was a reedy sort of fellow in trousers and undershirt, a misleading tangle of hair showing on his chest.

"Gee, I've been so broke," he faltered apologetically. "Doctor-bills, an'—an' I'm outa work. I needed this stuff awfully bad, I ain't well—"

"You're in the pink of condish compared to what you're gonna be in just about a minute more!" rumbled Harlan. The fellow could have gotten down on his knees, paid for the milk ten times over, but it wouldn't have cut any ice with Harlan. He was going to get his satisfaction out of this the way he wanted it. That was the kind Harlan was.

He waited until the culprit straightened up again, then breathed a name at him fiercely and swung his arm like a shotputter.

Harlan's fist smashed the lighter man square in the mouth. He went over like a paper cut-out and lay just as flat as one. The empty hallway throbbed with his fall. He lay there and miraculously still showed life. Rolling his head dazedly from side to side, he reached up vaguely to find out where his mouth had gone. Those slight movements were like waving a red flag at a bull. Harlan snorted and flung himself down on the man. Knee to chest, he grabbed the fellow by the hair of the head, pulled it upward and crashed his skull down against the flagged floor.

When the dancing embers of his rage began to thin out so that he was able to see straight once more, the man wasn't rolling his head dazedly any more. He wasn't moving in the slightest. A thread of blood was trickling out of each ear-hollow, as though something had shattered inside.

Harlan stiff-armed himself against the floor and got up slowly like something leaving its kill. "All right, you brought it on yourself!" he growled. There was an undertone of fear in his voice. He prodded the silent form reluctantly. "Take the lousy milk," he said. "Only next time ask for it first!" He got up on his haunches, squatting there ape-like. "Hey! Hey, you!" He shook him again. "Matter with you? Going to lie there all night? I said you could take the—"

The hand trying to rouse the man stopped suddenly over his heart. It came away slowly, very slowly. The color drained out of Harlan's face. He sucked in a deep breath that quivered his lips. It stayed cold all the way down like menthol.

"Gone!" The hoarsely-muttered word jerked him to his feet. He started backing, backing a step at a time, toward the door he'd come out of. He could not take his eyes off the huddled, shrunken form lying there close beside the wall.

"Gee, I better get in!" was the first inchoate thought that came to him. He found the opening with his back, even retreated a step or two through it, before he realized the folly of what he was doing. Couldn't leave him lying there like that right outside his own door. They'd know right away who had— and they weren't going to if he could help it.

He glanced behind him into the darkened flat. His wife's peaceful, rhythmic breathing was clearly audible in the intense stillness. She'd slept through the whole thing. He stepped into the hall again, looked up and down. If she hadn't heard, with the door standing wide open, then surely nobody else had with theirs closed.

But one door was not closed! The next one down the line was open a crack, just about an inch, showing a thin line of white inner-frame. Harlan went cold all over for a minute, then sighed with relief. Why that was where the milk-thief came from. Sure, obviously. He'd been heading back in that direction when Harlan came out and caught him. It was the last door down that way. The hall, it was true, took a right-angle turn when it got past there, and there were still other flats around the other side, out of sight. That must be the place. Who else would leave their door off the latch like that at four in the morning, except this guy who had come out to prowl in the hallway?

This was one time when Mrs. Harlan would have come in handy. She would have known for sure whether the guy lived in there or not, or just where he did belong. He himself wasn't interested in their neighbors, didn't know one from the other, much less which flats they hung out in. But it was a cinch he wasn't going to wake her and drag her out here to look at a dead man, just to find out where to park him. One screech from her would put him behind the eight-ball before he knew it.

Then while he was hesitating, sudden, urgent danger made up his mind for him. A faint whirring sound started somewhere in the bowels of the building. Along with it the faceted glass knob beside the automatic elevator panel burned brightly red. Somebody was coming up!

He jumped for the prostrate form, got an under-arm grip on it, and started hauling it hastily toward that unlatched door. Legs splayed out behind it, the heels of the shoes ticked over the cracks between the flagstones like train-wheels on a track.

The elevator beat him to it, slow-moving though it was. He had the guy at the door, still in full view, when the triangular porthole in the elevator door-panel bloomed yellow with its arrival. He whirled, crouching defiantly over the body, like something at bay. He would be caught with the goods, just as he himself had caught this guy, if the party got out at this floor. But they didn't. The porthole darkened again as the car went on up.

He let out a long, whistling breath like a deflating tire, pushed the door carefully open. It gave a single rebellious click as the latch cleared the socket altogether. He listened, heart pounding. Might be sixteen kids in there for all he knew, a guy that stole milk like that.

"I'll drop him just inside," Harlan thought grimly. "Let them figure it out in the morning!"

He tugged the fellow across the sill with an unavoidable wooden thump of the heels, let him down, tensed, listened again, silhouetted there against the orange light from the hall —if anyone was inside looking out. But there was an absence of breathing-sounds from within. It seemed too good to be true. He felt his way forward, peering into the dark, ready to jump back and bolt for it at the first alarm.

Once he got past the closed-in foyer, the late moon cast enough light through the windows to show him that there was no one living in the place but the guy himself. It was a one-room flat and the bed, which was one of those that come down out of a closet, showed white and vacant.

"Swell!" said Harlan. "No one's gonna miss you right away!"

He hauled him in, put him on the bed, turned to soft-shoe out again when he got a better idea. Why not make it really tough to find him while he was about it? This way, the first person that stuck his head in was bound to spot the man. He tugged the sheet clear of the body lying on it and pulled it over him like a shroud. He tucked it in on both sides, so that it held him in a mild sort of grip.

He gripped the foot of the bed. It was hard to lift, but once he got it started the mechanism itself came to his aid. It began swinging upward of its own accord. He held onto it to keep it from banging. It went into the closet neatly enough but wouldn't stay put. The impediment between it and the wall pushed it down each time. But the door would probably hold it. He heard a rustle as something shifted, slipped further down in back of the bed. He didn't have to be told what that was.

He pushed the bed with one arm and caught the door with the other. Each time he took the supporting arm away, the bed tipped out and blocked the door. Finally at the sixth try he got it to stand still and swiftly slapped the door in place over it. That held it like glue and he had nothing further to worry about. It would have been even better if there'd been a key to lock it, take out, and throw away. There wasn't. This was good enough, this would hold—twenty-four hours, forty-eight, a week even, until the guy's rent came due and they searched the place. And by that time he could pull a quick change of address, back a van up to the door, and get out of the building. Wouldn't look so hot, of course, but who wanted to stay where there was a permanent corpse next door? They'd never be able to pin it on him anyway, never in a million years. Not a living soul, not a single human eye, had seen it happen. He was sure of that.

Harlan gave the closet door a swipe with the loose end of his pajama jacket, just for luck, up where his hand had pushed against it. He hadn't touched either knob.

He reconnoitered, stepped out, closed the flat up after him. The tumbler fell in the lock. It couldn't be opened from the outside now except by the super's passkey. Back where it had happened, he picked up the lethal bottle of milk and took it into his own flat. He went back a second time, got down close on hands and knees and gave the floor a careful inspection. There were just two spots of blood, the size of two-bit pieces, that must have dripped from the guy's ears before he picked him up. He looked down at his pajama coat. There were more than two spots on that, but that didn't worry him any.

He went into his bathroom, stripped off the jacket, soaked a handful of it under the hot water and slipped into the hall with it. The spots came up off the satiny flagstones at a touch without leaving a trace. He hurried down the corridor, opened a door, and stepped into a hot, steamy little whitewashed alcove provided with an incinerator chute. He balled the coat up, pulled down the flap of the chute, shoved the bundle in like a letter in a mail box and then sent the trousers down after it too, just to make sure. That way he wouldn't be stuck with any odd pair of trousers without their matching jacket. Who could swear there had ever been such a pair of pajamas now? A strong cindery odor came up the chute. The fire was going in the basement right now. He wouldn't even have to worry about the articles staying intact down there until morning. Talk about your quick service!

He slipped back to his own door the way he was without a stitch on him. He realized it would have been a bum joke if somebody had seen him like that, after the care he'd taken about all those little details. But they hadn't. So what?

He shut the door of his apartment, and put on another pair of pajamas. Slipping quietly into the bed next to the peacefully-slumbering Missis, he lit a cigarette. Then the let-down came. Not that he got jittery, but he saw that he wasn't going to sleep any more that night. Rather than lie there tossing and turning, he dressed and went out of the house to take a walk.

He would have liked a drink, but it was nearly five, way past closing-time for all the bars, so he had to be satisfied with a cup of coffee at the counter lunch. He tried to put it to his mouth a couple times, finally had to call the waiter back.

"Bring me a black one," he said. "Leave the milk out!" That way it went down easy enough.

The sun was already up when he got back, and he felt like he'd been pulled through a wringer. He found Mrs. Harlan in the kitchen, getting things started for his breakfast.

"Skip that," he told her irritably. "I don't want any—and shove that damn bottle out of sight, will you?"

He took time off during his lunch-hour to look at a flat in the city and paid a deposit for it. When he got home that night he told Mrs. Harlan abruptly, "Better get packed up, we're getting out of here the first thing in the morning."

"Wha-at?" she squawked. "Why we can't do that. We've got a lease! What's come over you?"

"Lease or no lease," he barked. "I can't stand it here any more. We're getting out after tonight, I tell you!"

They were in the living-room and his eyes flicked toward the wall that partitioned them off from the flat next door. He didn't want to do that, but he couldn't help himself. She didn't notice, but obediently started to pack. He called up a moving-van company.

In the middle of the night he woke up from a bad dream and ran smack into something even worse. He got up and went into the living-room. He didn't exactly know why. The moon was even brighter than the night before and washed that dividing wall with almost a luminous calsomine. Right in the middle of the wall there was a hideous black, blurred outline, like an X-ray showing through from the other side. Right about where that bed would be. Stiff and skinny the hazy figure was with legs and arms and even a sort of head on it. He pitched the back of his arm to his mouth just in time to douse the yell struggling to come out, went wet all over as though he were under a shower-bath. He managed to turn finally and saw the peculiar shape of one of Mrs. Harlan's modernistic lamps standing in the path of the moon, throwing its shadow upon the wall. He pulled down the shade and tottered back inside. He took his coffee black again next morning, looked terrible.

She rang him at the office just before closing-time. "You at the new place?" he asked eagerly.

"No," she said, "they wouldn't let me take the stuff out. I had a terrible time with the renting-agent. Ed, we'll just have to

make the best of it. He warned me that if we go, they're going
to garnishee your salary and get a judgment against you for the
whole two-years' rent. Ed, we can't afford to keep two places
going at once and your firm will fire you the minute they find
out. They won't stand for anything like that. You told me so
yourself. He told me any justified complaint we have will be
attended to, but we can't just walk out on our lease. You'd
better think twice about it. I don't know what's wrong with the
flat anyway."

He did, but he could not tell her. He saw that they had him
by the short hairs. If he went, it meant loss of his job, destitution;
even if he got another, they'd attach the wages of that too.
Attracting this much attention wasn't the best thing in the
world, either. When he got home, the agent came up to find out
what was the trouble, what his reasons were, he didn't know
what to answer, couldn't think of a legitimate kick he had coming. He was afraid now even to bring up about the chiseling of
the milk. It would have sounded picayune at that.

"I don't have to give you my reasons!" he said surlily. "I'm
sick o' the place, and that's that!"

Which he saw right away was a tactical error, not only because it might sow suspicion later, but because it antagonized
the agent now. "You can go just as soon as you've settled for the
balance of your lease. I'm not trying to hold you!" he fumed. "If
you try moving your things out without that, I'll call the police!"

Harlan slammed the door after him like a six-gun salute. He
had a hunch the agent wouldn't be strictly within his legal
rights in going quite that far, but he was in no position to force
a showdown and find out for sure. No cops, thanks.

He realized that his own blundering had raised such a stink
that it really didn't matter now any more whether he stayed or
went. They'd make it their business to trace his forwarding
address, and they'd have that on tap when disclosure came. So
the whole object of moving out would be defeated. The lesser
of two evils now was to stay, lie very low, hope the whole

incident would be half-forgotten by the time the real excitement broke. It may have been lesser, but it was still plenty evil.
He didn't see how he was going to stand it. Yet he had to.

He went out and came back with a bottle of rye, told his wife
he felt a cold coming on. That was so he wouldn't run into any
more hallucinations during the night like that phantom X-ray
on the wall. When he went to bed the bottle was empty. He
was still stony sober, but at least it put him through the night
somehow.

On his way across the hall toward the elevator that morning,
his head turned automatically to look up at that other door. He
couldn't seem to control it. When he came back that evening
the same thing happened. It was locked, just as it had been for
the past two nights and two days now. He thought, "I've got to
quit that. Somebody's liable to catch me at it and put two and
two together."

In those two days and two nights he changed almost beyond
recognition. He lost all his color; was losing weight almost by the
hour; shelves under his eyes you could have stacked books on;
appetite shot to smithereens. A backfire on the street made him
leave his shoes without unlacing them, and his office-work was
starting to go haywire. Hooch was putting him to sleep each
night, but he had to keep stepping it up. He was getting afraid
one of these times he'd spill the whole thing to his wife while
he was tanked without knowing it. She was beginning to notice
there was something the matter and mentioned his seeing a
doctor about himself once or twice. He snapped at her and shut
her up.

The third night, which was the thirty-first of the month, they
were sitting there in the living-room. She was sewing. He stared
glassy-eyed through the paper, pretending to read, whisky-
tumbler at his elbow, sweat all over his ashen forehead, when
she started sniffling.

"Got a cold?" he asked tonelessly.

"No," she said, "there's a peculiar musty odor in here, don't you get it? Sickly-sweet. I've been noticing it off and on all day, it's stronger in this room than in—"

"Shut up!" he rasped. The tumbler shook in his hand as he downed its contents, refilled it. He got up, opened the windows as far as they would go. He came back, killed the second shot, lit a cigarette unsteadily, deliberately blew the first thickly fragrant puff all around her head. "No, I don't notice anything," he said in an artificially steady voice. His face was almost green in the lamplight.

"I don't see how you can miss it," she said innocently. "It's getting worse every minute. I wonder if there's something wrong with the drains in this building?"

He didn't hear the rest of it. He was thinking: "It'll pay off, one way or the other, pretty soon—thank goodness for that! Tomorrow's the first, they'll be showing up for his rent, that'll be the finale."

He almost didn't care now which way it worked out—anything so long as it was over with, anything but this ghastly suspense. He couldn't hold out much longer. Let them suspect him even, if they wanted to; the complete lack of proof still held good. Any lawyer worth his fee could get him out of it with one hand tied behind his back.

But then when he snapped out of it and caught sight of her over at the inter-house phone, realized what she was about, he backed water in a hurry. All the bravado went out of him. "What're you doing?" he croaked.

"I'm going to ask the superintendent what that is, have him come up here and—"

"Get away from there!" he bellowed. She hung up as though she'd been bitten, turned to stare.

A second later he realized what a swell out that would have been to have the first report of the nuisance come from them themselves; he wished he had let her go ahead. It should have come from them. They were closest to the death-flat. If it came from somebody else further away—and they seemed not to have noticed it—that would be one more chip stacked up against him.

"All right, notify him if you want to," he countermanded.

"No, no, not if you don't want me to." She was frightened now. He had her all rattled. She moved away from the phone.

To bridge the awkward silence he said the one thing he didn't want to, the one thing of all he'd intended not to say. As though possessed of perverse demons, it came out before he could stop it: "Maybe it's from next-door." Then his eyes hopelessly rolled around in their sockets.

"How could it be?" she contradicted mildly. "That flat's been vacant for the past month or more—"

A clock they had in there in the room with them ticked on hollowly, resoundingly, eight, nine, ten times. Clack, clack, clack, as though it were hooked up to a loudspeaker. What a racket it was making! Couldn't hear yourself think.

"No one living in there, you say?" he said in a hoarse whisper after what seemed an hour ticked by.

"No, I thought you knew that. I forgot, you don't take much interest in the neighbors—"

Then who was he? Where had he come from? Not from the street, because he had been in his undershirt. "I dragged the guy back into the wrong apartment!" thought Harlan. He was lucky it was vacant! It gave him the shivers, even now, to think what might have happened if there had been somebody else in there that night! The more he puzzled over it, the cloudier the mystery got. That particular door had been ajar, the bed down out of the closet, and the guy had been pussyfooting back toward there. Then where did he belong, if not in there? He was obviously a lone wolf, or he would have been missed by now. Those living with him would have sent out an alarm the very next morning after it had happened. Harlan had been keeping close tab on the police calls on his radio and there hadn't been anything of the kind. And even if he had lived alone in one of the other flats, the unlatched door left waiting for his return would have attracted attention from the hall by now.

What was the difference where he came from anyway; it was where he was now that mattered! All he could get out of it was this: there would be no pay-off tomorrow after all. The agony would be prolonged now indefinitely—until prospective tenants were shown the place and sudden discovery resulted. He groaned aloud, took his next swig direct from the bottle without any tumbler for a go-between.

In the morning he could tell breakdown was already setting in. Between the nightly sousing, the unending mental strain, the lack of food, he was a doddering wreck when he got out of bed and staggered into his clothes. Mrs. Harlan said, "I don't think you'd better go to the office today. If you could see yourself—!" But he had to, anything was better than staying around here!

He opened the living-room door (he'd closed it on the two of them the night before) and the fetid air from inside seemed to hit him in the face, it was so strong. He reeled there in that corrupt, acrid draft, not because it was so difficult to breathe but because it was so difficult for *him* to breathe, knowing what he did about it. He stood there gagging, hand to throat; his wife had to come up behind him and support him with one arm for a minute, until he pulled himself together. He couldn't, of course, eat anything. He grabbed his hat and made for the elevator in a blind hurry that was almost panic. His head jerked toward that other door as he crossed the hall; it hadn't missed doing that once for three days and nights.

This time there was a difference. He swung back again in time to meet the superintendent's stare. The latter had just that moment come out of the elevator with a wad of rent receipts in his hand. You couldn't say that Harlan paled at the involuntary betrayal he had just committed because he hadn't been the color of living protoplasm in thirty-six hours now.

The super had caught the gesture, put his own implication on it. "That bothering you folks too?" he said. "I've had complaints from everyone else on this floor about it so far. I'm going in there right now and invest—"

The hallway went spinning around Harlan like a cyclorama. The superintendent reached out, steadied him by the elbow. "See that, it's got you dizzy already! Must be some kind of sewer-gas." He fumbled for a passkey. "That why you folks wanted to move earlier in the week?"

Harlan still had enough presence of mind left, just enough, to nod. "Why didn't you say so?" the super went on. Harlan didn't have enough left to answer that one. What difference did it make. In about a minute more it would be all over but the shouting. He groped desperately to get himself a minute more time.

"I guess you want the rent," he said with screwy matter-of-factness. "I got it right here with me. Better let me give it to you now. I'm going in to town—"

He paid him the fifty bucks, counted them three times, purposely let one drop, purposely fumbled picking it up. But the passkey still stayed ready in the super's hand. He leaned against the wall, scribbled a receipt, and handed it to Harlan. "Thanks, Mr. Harlan." He turned, started down the hall toward that door. That damnable doorway to hell!

Harlan was thinking: "I'm not going to leave him now. I'm going to stick with him when he goes in there. He's going to make the discovery, but it's never gonna get past him! I can't let it. He saw me look at that door just now. He'll read it all over my face. I haven't got the juice left to bluff it out. I'm going to kill him in there—with my bare hands." He let the rent receipt fall out of his hand, went slowly after the man like somebody walking in his sleep.

The passkey clicked, the super pushed the door open, light came out into the dimmer hallway from it, and he passed from sight. Harlan slunk through the doorframe after him and pushed the door back the other way, partly closing it after the two of them. It was only then that Harlan made an incomprehensible discovery. The air was actually clearer in here than in his own place—clearer even than out in the hall! Stale and dust-laden from being shut up for days, it was true, but odorless, the way air should be!

"Can't be in here, after all," the super was saying, a few paces ahead.

Harlan took up a position to one side of the bedcloset, murmuring to himself: "He lives—until he opens that!"

The super had gone into the bath. Harlan heard him raise and slap down the wooden bowl cover in there, fiddle with the washbasin stopper. "Nope, nothing in here!" he called out. He came out again, went into the postage-stamp kitchen, sniffed around in there, examining the sink, the gas-stove. "It *seemed* to come from in here," he said, showing up again, "I can't make head or tail out of it!"

Neither could Harlan. The only thing he could think of was: the bedding and the mattress, which were on *this* side of what was causing it, must have acted as a barricade, stuffing up the closet-door, and must have kept that odor from coming out into this room, sending it through the thin porous wall in the other direction instead, into his own place and from there out into the hall.

The super's eye roved speculatively on past him and came to rest on the closet door. "Maybe it's something behind that bed," he said.

Harlan didn't bat an eyelash, jerky as he had been before out in the hall. "You just killed yourself then, Mister," was his unheard remark. "This is it. Now!" He gripped the floor-boards with the soles of his feet through the shoe-leather, tensed, crouched imperceptibly for the spring.

The super stepped over, so did Harlan, diagonally, toward him. The super reached down for the knob, touched it, got ready to twist his wrist—

The house-phone in the entry-way buzzed like an angry hornet. Harlan went up off his heels, coming down again on them spasmodically. "Paging me, I guess. I told them I was coming in here," said the super, turning to go out there and answer it. "Okay, Molly," he said, "I'll be right down." He held the front door ready to show Harlan he wanted to leave and lock up again. "Somebody wants to see an apartment," he explained. The door clicked shut, the odors of decay swirled around them once more on the outside of it, and they rode down together in the car.

Something was dying in Harlan by inches—his reason maybe. "I can never go through that again," he moaned. The sweat did not start coming through his paralyzed pores until after he was seated in the train, riding in. Everything looked misshapen and out of focus.

He came back at twilight. In addition to the dusky amber hall lights, there was a fan of bright yellow spilling out of the death-door. Open again, and voices in there. Lined up along the wall outside the door were a radio cabinet, a bridge lamp, a pair of chairs compacted together seat to seat. An expressman in a dirty blue blouse came out, picked them up effortlessly with one arm, and slung them inside after him.

Harlan sort of collapsed against his own door. He scratched blindly for admittance, forgetting he had a key, too shell-shocked to use it even if he had taken it out.

Mrs. Harlan let him in, too simmering with the news she had to tell to notice his appearance or actions. "We've got new neighbors," she said almost before she had the door closed. "Nice young couple, they just started to move in before you got here—"

He was groping desperately for the bottle on the shelf, knocked down a glass and broke it. Then they hadn't found out yet; they hadn't taken down the bed yet! It kept going through his battered brain like a demoniac rhythm. He nearly gagged on the amount of whisky he was swallowing from the neck of the bottle all at one time. When room had been cleared for his voice, he panted: "What about that odor? You mean they took that place the way it—?"

"I guess they were in a hurry, couldn't be choosy. He sent his wife up to squirt deodorant around in the hall before they got here. What does he care, once he gets them signed up? Dirty trick, if you ask me."

He had one more question to ask. "Of course you sized up every stick of stuff they have. Did they—did they bring their own bed with them?"

"No, I guess they're going to use the one in there—"

Any minute now! His brain was fifty per cent blind unreasoning panic, unable to get the thing in the right perspective any more. That discovery itself wasn't necessarily fatal, but his own possible implication in it no longer seemed to register with him. He was confusing one with the other, unable to differentiate between them any more. Discovery had to be prevented, discovery had to be forestalled! Why? Because his own corrosive guilty conscience knew the full explanation of the mystery. He was forgetting that they didn't—unless he gave it to them himself.

Still sucking at the bottle, he edged back to the front door, turned sidewise to it, put his ear up against it.

"T'anks very much, buddy," he heard the moving man say gruffly, and the elevator-slide closed.

He opened the door, peered out. The last of the furniture had gone inside, the hall was clear now. The fumes of the disinfectant the super's wife had used were combating that other odor, but it was still struggling through—to his acute senses, at least. They had left their door open. Their voices were clearly audible as he edged further out. Two living people unsuspectingly getting settled in a room with an unseen corpse!

"Move that over a little further," he heard the woman say. "The bed has to come down there at nights. Oh, that reminds me! He couldn't get it open when he wanted to show it to me today. The door must be jammed. He promised to come back, but I guess he forgot—"

"Let's see what I can do with it," the husband's voice answered.

Harlan, like something drawn irresistibly toward its own destruction, was slinking nearer and nearer, edgewise along the corridor-wall. A tom-tom he carried with him was his heart.

A sound of bare hands pounding wood came through the bright-yellow gap in the wall ahead. Then a couple of heavier impacts, kicks with the point of a shoe.

"It's not locked, is it?"

"No, when I turn the knob I can see the catch slip back under the lock. Something's holding it jammed in there. The bed must be out of true or somebody closed it too hard the last time."

"What're we going to sleep on?" the woman wailed.

"If I can hit it hard enough, maybe the vibration'll snap it back. Run down a minute and borrow a hammer from the super, like a good girl."

Harlan turned and vanished back where he had come from. Through the crack of the door he saw the woman come out into the hall, stand waiting for the car, go down in it. He said to his wife, "Where's that hammer we used to have?" He found it in a drawer and went out with it.

He was no longer quite sane when he knocked politely alongside that open door down the hall. He knew what he was doing, but the motivation was all shot. The man, standing there in the middle of the lighted room staring helplessly at the fast closet-door, turned his head. He was just an ordinary man, coat off, tie off, suspenders showing; Harlan had never set eyes on him before, their paths were just now crossing for the first time. But discovery had to be prevented, discovery had to be prevented!

Harlan, smiling sleepily, said, "Excuse me. I couldn't help overhearing you ask your wife for a hammer. I'm your next-door neighbor. Having trouble with that bed-closet, I see. Here, I brought you mine."

The other man reached out, took it shaft-first the way Harlan was holding it. "Thanks, that's real swell of you," he grinned appreciatively. "Let's see what luck I have with it this time."

Harlan got in real close. The tips of his fingers kept feeling the goods of his suit. The other man started tapping lightly all up and down the joint of the door. "Tricky things, these beds," he commented.

"Yeah, tricky," agreed Harlan with that same sleepy, watchful smile. He came in a little closer. Something suddenly gave a muffled "Zing!" behind the door, like a misplaced spring or joint jumping back in place.

"That does it!" said the man cheerfully. "Now let's see how she goes. Better stand back a little," he warned. "It'll catch you coming out." He turned the knob with one hand and the door started opening. He passed the hammer back to Harlan, to free the other. Harlan moved around to the same side he was on until he was right at his neighbor's elbow. The door swung flat against the wall. The bed started to come down. The man's two arms went out and up to ease it, so it wouldn't fall too swiftly.

Just as the top-side of it got down to eye-level the hammer rose in Harlan's fist, described a swift arc, fell, crashed into the base of the other man's skull. He went down so instantaneously that the blow seemed not to have been interrupted, to have continued all the way to the floor in one swing. Again the red motes of anger, call them self-preservation this time—

A dull boom came through them first—the bed hitting the floor. They swirled thicker than ever; then screams and angry, frightened voices pierced them. They began to dissipate. He found himself kneeling there alongside the bed, gory hammer poised in his hand, facing them across it. There must have been other blows.

A woman lay slumped there by the door, moaning "My husband, my husband!" They were picking her up to carry her out.

Another woman further in the background was staring in, all eyes. Wait, he knew her—his wife. Someone out in the hall was saying, "Hurry up, hurry up! This way! In here!" and two figures in dark-blue flashed in, moving so swiftly that before he knew it they were behind him holding his arms. They took the hammer away. Nothing but voices, a welter of voices, heard through cotton-batting.

"This man is dead!"

"He didn't even know him. They just moved in. Went crazy, I guess."

He was being shaken back and forth from behind, like a terrier. "What'd you do it for? What'd you do it for?"

Harlan pointed at the bed. "So he wouldn't find out—"

"Find out what?" He was being shaken some more. "Find out what? Explain what you mean!"

Didn't they understand, with it staring them right in the face? His eyes came to rest on it. The bed was empty.

"God, I think I understand!" There was such sheer horror in the voice that even Harlan turned to see where it had come from. It was the superintendent. "There was a down-and-outer, a friend of mine. He didn't have a roof over his head—I know I had no right to, but I let him hang out in here nights the past couple weeks, while the apartment was vacant. Just common, ordinary charity. Then people started complaining about losing their milk, and I saw I'd get in trouble, so I told him to get out. He disappeared three days ago, I figured he'd taken me at my word, and then this morning I found out he was in the hospital with a slight head-concussion. I even dropped in for a few minutes to see how he was getting along. He wouldn't tell me how it happened, but I think I get it now. *He* must have done it to him, thought he'd killed him, hidden him there in that folding-bed. My friend got such a fright that he lammed out the minute he came to—"

Harlan was mumbling idiotically, "Then I didn't kill any-one?"

"You went to town on this one, all right," one of the men in
blue said. He turned to the second one, scornfully. "To cover up
a justified assault-and-battery, he pulls a murder!"

When another man, in mufti, took him out in the hall at the
end of two or three short steel links, he recoiled from the putrid
odor still clinging out there. "I thought they said he wasn't
dead—"

Somewhere behind him he heard the super explaining to one
of them: "Aw, that's just some sloppy people on the floor below
cooking corned-beef and cabbage alla time, we gave 'em a
dispossess for creating a nuisance in the building! He musta
thought it was—"

My father once told me of a factory where he worked for a while in
the Thirties: every so often the foreman would walk to the head of the
assembly line and spit, and the worker who was closest to where his
spit landed would be fired. That little story told me more about the
Depression than a volume of social history, and for me "The Corpse
Next Door" has this same quality of making us feel in the pit of our
stomach what it was like to scratch for life in the Depression. A fight
to the death over a bottle of milk, absurd though it may seem to young
readers today, is a superb reflection of the agonies of their fathers, and
the seedy apartment house a wondrous evocation of how their fathers
lived.

You'll Never See Me Again

It was the biscuits started it. How he wished, afterward, that she'd never made those biscuits! But she made them, and she was proud of them. Her first try. Typical bride-and-groom stuff. The gag everyone's heard for years, so old it has whiskers down to here. So old it isn't funny any more. No, it isn't funny; listen while it's told.

He wasn't in the mood for playing house. He'd been working hard all day over his drafting-board. Even if they'd been good he probably would have grunted, "Not bad," and let it go at that. But they weren't good, they were atrocious. They were as hard as gravel, they tasted like lye, she'd put in too much of

something and left out too much of something else, and life was
too short to fool around with them.

"Well, I don't hear you saying anything about them," she
pouted.

All he said was: "Take my advice, Smiles, and get 'em at the
corner bakery after this."

"That isn't very appreciative," she said. "If you think it was
much fun bending over that hot oven—"

"If you think it's much fun eating them—I've got a blueprint
to do tomorrow; I can't take punishment like this!"

One word led to another. By the time the meal was over, her
fluffy golden head was down inside her folded arms on the table
and she was making broken-hearted little noises.

Crying is an irritant to a tired man. He kept saying things he
didn't want to. "I could have had a meal in any restaurant
without this. I'm tired. I came home to get a little rest, not the
death scene from 'Camille' across the table from me."

She raised her head at that. She meant business now. "If I'm
annoying you, that's easily taken care of! You want it quiet; we'll
see that you *get* it quiet. No trouble at all about that."

She stormed into the bedroom and he could hear drawers
slamming in and out. So she was going to walk out on him, was
she? For a minute he was going to jump up and go in there after
her and put his arms around her and say: "I'm sorry, Smiles; I
didn't mean what I said." And that probably would have ended
the incident then and there.

But he checked himself. He remembered a well-meaning
piece of advice a bachelor friend of his had given him before
his marriage. And bachelors always seem to know so much
about marriage rules! "If she should ever threaten to walk out
on you, and they all do at one time or another," this sage had
counseled him, "there's only one way for you to handle that. Act
as though you don't care; let her go. She'll come back fast
enough, don't worry. Otherwise, if you beg her not to, she'll
have the upper hand over you from then on."

He scratched himself behind one ear. "I wonder if he was right?" he muttered. "Well, the only way to find out is to try it."

So he left the table, went into the living-room, snapped on a reading-lamp, sprawled back in a chair, and opened his evening paper, perfectly unconcerned to all appearances. The only way you could tell he wasn't, was by the little glances he kept stealing over the top of the paper every once in a while to see if she was really going to carry out her threat.

She acted as if she were. She may have been waiting for him to come running in there after her and beg for forgiveness, and when he didn't, forced herself to go through with it. Stubborn pride on both their parts. And they were both so young, and this was so new to them. Six weeks the day after tomorrow.

She came bustling in, set down a little black valise in the middle of the room, and put on her gloves. Still waiting for him to make the first overtures for reconciliation. But he kept making the breach worse every time he opened his mouth, all because of what some fool had told him. "Sure you've got everything?" he said quietly.

She was so pretty even when she was angry. "I'm glad you're showing your true colors; I'd rather find out now than later."

Someone should have pushed their two heads together, probably. But there wasn't anyone around but just the two of them. "You're making a mountain out of a molehill. Well, pick a nice comfortable hotel while you're at it."

"I don't have to go to a hotel. I'm not a waif. I've got a perfectly good mother who'll receive me with open arms."

"Quite a trip in the middle of the night, isn't it?" And to make matters worse, he opened his wallet as if to give her the money for her fare.

That put the finishing touch to her exasperation. "I'll get up there without any help from you, Mr. Ed Bliss! And I don't want any of the things you ever gave me, either! Take your old silver-fox piece!" *Fluff.* "And take your old diamond ring!" *Plink.*

"And take your old pin money!" *Scuff-scuff-slap.* "And you can take back that insurance policy you took out on me, too! Simon Legree! Ivan the Terrible!"

He turned the paper back to where the boxscores were. He only hoped that bachelor was right. "See you day after tomorrow, or whenever you get tired playing hide-and-seek," he said calmly.

"You'll never see me again as long as you live!" It rang in his ears for days afterward.

She picked up the valise, the front door went *boom!* and he was single again.

The thing to do now was to pretend he didn't care, and then she'd never try anything like this again. Otherwise his life would be made miserable. Every time they had the least little argument, she'd threaten to go back to her mother.

That first night he did all the things he'd always wanted to do, but they didn't stack up to so much after all. Took off his socks and walked around in his bare feet, let the ashes lie wherever they happened to drop off, drank six bottles of cold beer through their mouths and let them lie all over the room, and went to bed without bothering to shave.

He woke up about four in the morning, and it felt strange knowing she wasn't in the house with him, and he hoped she was all right wherever she was, and he finally forced himself to go back to sleep again. In the morning there wasn't anyone to wake him up. Her not being around didn't seem so strange then simply because he didn't have time to notice; he was exactly an hour and twenty-two minutes late for work.

But when he came back that night, it did seem strange, not finding anyone there waiting for him, the house dark and empty, and beer bottles rolling all around the living-room floor. Last night's meal, their last one together, was still strewn around on the table after twenty-four hours. He poked his finger at one of the biscuits, thought remorsefully, *I should have kept quiet. I could have pretended they were good, even if they weren't.* But it was too late now, the damage had been done.

He had to eat out at a counter by himself, and it was very depressing. He picked up the phone twice that evening, at 10:30 and again at 11:22, on the point of phoning up to her mother's place and making up with her, or at least finding out how she was. But each time he sort of slapped his own hand, metaphorically speaking, in rebuke and hung up without putting the call through. *I'll hold out until tomorrow,* he said to himself. *If I give in now, I'm at her mercy.*

The second night was rocky. The bed was no good; they needed to be made up about once every twenty-four hours, he now found out for the first time. A cop poked him in the shoulder with his club at about three in the morning and growled, "What's your trouble, bud?"

"Nothing that's got anything to do with what's in your rule book," Bliss growled back at him. He picked himself up from the curb and went back inside his house again.

He would have phoned her as soon as he woke up in the morning, but he was late again—only twelve minutes behind, this time, though—and he couldn't do it from the office without his fellow draftsmen getting wise she had left him.

He finally did it when he came back that evening, the second time, after eating. This was exactly 8:17 p.m. Thursday, two nights after she'd gone.

He said, "I want to talk to Mrs. Belle Alden, in Denby, this State. I don't know her number. Find it for me and give it to me." He'd never met Smiles's mother, incidentally.

While he was waiting for the operator to ring back, he was still figuring how to get out of it; find out how she was without seeming to capitulate. Young pride! *Maybe I can talk the mother into not letting on I called to ask about her, so she won't know I'm weakening. Let it seem like she's the first one to thaw out.*

The phone rang and he picked it up fast, pride or no pride. "Here's your party."

A woman's voice got on, and he said, "Hello, is this Mrs. Alden?"

The voice said it was.

"This is Ed, Smiles's husband."

"Oh, how is she?" she said animatedly.

He sat down at the phone. It took him a minute to get his breath back again. "Isn't she there?" he said finally.

The voice was surprised. "Here? No. Isn't she *there?*"

For a minute his stomach had felt all hollow. Now he was all right again. He was beginning to get it. Or thought he was. He winked at himself, with the wall in front of him for a reflector. So the mother was going to bat for her. They'd cooked up this little fib between them, to punish him. They were going to throw a little fright into him. He'd thought he was teaching her a lesson, and now she was going to turn the tables on him and teach him one. He was supposed to go rushing up there tearing at his hair and foaming at the mouth. "Where's Smiles? She's gone! I can't find her!" Then she'd step out from behind the door, crack her whip over his head, and threaten: "Are you going to behave? Are you ever going to do that again?" And from then on, she'd lead him around with a ring in his nose.

"You can't fool me, Mrs. Alden," he said self-assuredly. "I know she's there. I know she told you to say that."

Her voice wasn't panicky, it was still calm and self-possessed, but there was no mistaking the earnest ring to it. Either she was an awfully good actress, or this wasn't any act. "Now listen, Ed. You ought to know I wouldn't joke about a thing like that. As a matter of fact, I wrote her a long letter only yesterday afternoon. It ought to be in your mailbox by now. If she's not there with you, I'd make it my business to find out where she is, if I were you. And I wouldn't put it off, either!"

He still kept wondering: *Is she ribbing me or isn't she?* He drawled undecidedly, "Well, it's damned peculiar."

"I certainly agree with you," she said briskly.

He just chewed the inner tube of his cheek.

"Well, will you let me know as soon as you find out where she is?" she concluded. "I don't want to worry, and naturally I won't be able to help doing so until I hear that she's all right."

He hung up, and first he was surer than ever that it wasn't true she wasn't there. For one thing, the mother hadn't seemed *worried* enough to make it convincing. He thought, *I'll be damned if I call back again, so you and she can have the laugh on me. She's up there with you right now.*

But then he went outside and opened the mailbox, and there was a letter for Smiles with her mother's name on the envelope, and postmarked 6:30 the evening before.

He opened it and read it through. It was bona fide, all right; leisurely, chatty, nothing fake about it. One of those letters that are written over a period of days, a little at a time. There was no mistaking it; up to the time it had been mailed, she hadn't seen her daughter for months. And Smiles had left him the night before; if she'd gone up there at all, she would have been there long before then.

He didn't feel so chipper any more, after that. She wouldn't have stayed away this long if she'd been here in town, where she could walk or take a cab back to the house. There was nothing to be that sore about. And she'd intended going up there. The reason he felt sure of that was this. With her, it wasn't a light decision, lightly taken and lightly discarded. She hadn't been living home with her mother when he married her. She'd been on her own down here for several years before then. They corresponded regularly, they were on good terms, but the mother's remarriage had made a difference. In other words, it wasn't a case of flying straight back to the nest the first time she'd lost a few feathers. It was not only a fairly lengthy trip up there, but they had not seen each other for several years. So if she'd said she was going up there, it was no fleeting impulse, but a rational, clear-cut decision, and she was the kind of girl who would carry it out once she had arrived at it.

He put his hat on, straightened his tie, left the house, and

went downtown. There was only one way she could get anywhere near Denby, and that was by bus. It wasn't serviced by
train.

Of the two main bus systems, one ran an express line that
didn't stop anywhere near there; you had to go all the way to
the Canadian border and then double back nearly half of the
way by local, to get within hailing distance. The smaller line ran
several a day, in each direction, up through there to the nearest
large city beyond; they stopped there by request. It was obvious
which of the two systems she'd taken.

That should have simplified matters greatly for him; he found
out it didn't. He went down to the terminal and approached the
ticket seller.

"Were you on duty here Tuesday night?"

"Yeah, from six on. That's my shift every night."

"I'm trying to locate someone. Look. I know you're selling
tickets all night long, but maybe you can remember her." He
swallowed a lump in his throat. "She's young, only twenty, with
blond hair. So pretty you'd look at her twice, if you ever saw her
the first time; I know you would. Her eyes are sort of crinkly and
smiling. Even when her mouth isn't smiling, her eyes are. She
—she bought a ticket to Denby."

The man turned around and took a pack of tickets out of a
pigeon-hole and blew a layer of dust off them. "I haven't sold
a ticket to Denby in over a month." They had a rubber band
around them. All but the top one. That blew off with his breath.

That seemed to do something to his powers of memory. He
ducked down out of sight, came up with it from the floor. "Wait
a minute," he said, prodding his thumbnail between two of his
teeth. "I don't remember anything much about any eyes or
smile, but there *was* a young woman came up and priced the
fare to Denby. I guess it was night before last, at that. Seeing
this one ticket pulled loose out of the batch reminded me of it.
I told her how much it was, and I snagged out a ticket—this
loose one here. But then she couldn't make it; I dunno, she

didn't have enough money on her or something. She looked at her wrist watch, and asked me how late the pawnshops stay open. I told her they were all closed by then. Then she shoveled all the money she could round up across the counter at me and asked me how far that would take her. So I counted and told her, and she told me to give her a ticket to that far."

Bliss was hanging onto his words, hands gripping the counter until his knuckles showed white. "Yes, but where to?"

The ticket seller's eyelids drooped deprecatingly. "That's the trouble," he said, easing the back of his collar. "I can't remember that part of it. I can't even remember how much the amount came to, now, any more. If I could, I could get the destination by elimination."

If I only knew how much she had in her handbag when she left the house, Bliss thought desolately, *we could work it out together, him and me.* He prodded: "Three dollars? Four? Five?"

The ticket vendor shook his head baffledly. "No use, it won't come back. I'm juggling so many figures all night long, every night in the week—"

Bliss slumped lower before the sill. "But don't you keep a record of what places you sell tickets to?"

"No, just the total take for the night, without breaking it down."

He was as bad off as before. "Then you can't tell me for sure whether she did get on the bus that night or not?"

Meanwhile an impatient line had formed behind Bliss, and the ticket seller was getting fidgety.

"No. The driver might remember her. Look at it this way: she only stood in front of me for a minute or two at the most. If she got on the bus at all, she sat in back of him for anywhere from an hour to four hours. Remember, I'm not even guaranteeing that the party I just told you about is the same one you mean. It's just a vague incident to me."

"Would the same one that made Tuesday night's run be back by now?"

"Sure, he's going out tonight again." The ticket man looked at a chart. "Go over there and ask for No. 27. Next!"

No. 27 put down his coffee mug, swiveled around on the counter stool, and looked at his questioner.

"Yare, I made Tuesday night's upstate run."

"Did you take a pretty blond girl, dressed in a gray jacket and skirt, as far as Denby?"

No. 27 stopped looking at him. His face stayed on in the same direction, but he was looking at other things. "Nawr, I didn't."

"Well, was she on the bus at all?"

No. 27's eyes remained at a tangent from the man he was answering. "Nawr, she wasn't."

"What're you acting so evasive about? I can tell you're hiding something, just by looking at you."

"I said, 'Nawr, I didn't.' "

"Listen. I'm her husband. I've got to know. Here, take this, only tell me, will you? I've got to know. It's an awful feeling!"

The driver took a hitch in his belt. "I get good wages. A ten-dollar bill wouldn't make me say I sawr someone when I didn't. No, nor a twenty, nor a century either. That's an old one. It would only make me lose my rating with the company." He swung around on his stool, took up his coffee mug again. "I only sawr the road," he said truculently. "I ain't supposed to see who's riding in back of me."

"But you can't help seeing who gets off each time you stop."

This time No. 27 wouldn't answer at all. The interview was over, as far as he was concerned. He flung down a nickel, defiantly jerked down the visor of his cap, and swaggered off.

Bliss slouched forlornly out of the terminal, worse off than before. The issue was all blurred now. The ticket seller vaguely thought some girl or other had haphazardly bought a ticket for as much money as she had on her person that night, but without guaranteeing that she fitted his description of Smiles at all. The driver, on the other hand, definitely denied anyone like her had ridden with him, as far as Denby or anywhere else. What was he to think? Had she left, or hadn't she left?

Whether she had or not, it was obvious that she had never arrived. He had the testimony of her own mother, and that letter from her from upstate, to vouch for that. And who was better to be believed than her own mother?

Had she stayed here in the city then? But she hadn't done that, either. He knew Smiles so well. Even if she had gone to the length of staying overnight at a hotel that first night, Tuesday, she would have been back home with him by Wednesday morning at the very latest. Her peevishness would have evaporated long before then. Another thing, she wouldn't have had enough money to stay for any longer than just one night at even a moderately priced hotel. She'd flung down the greater part of her household expense money on the floor that night before walking out.

All I can do, he thought apprehensively, *is make a round of the hotels and find out if anyone like her was at any of them Tuesday night, even if she's not there now.*

He didn't check every last hotel in town, but he checked all the ones she would have gone to, if she'd gone to one at all. She wouldn't have been sappy enough to go to some rundown lodginghouse near the freight yards or longshoremen's hostelry down by the piers. That narrowed the field somewhat.

He checked on her triply: by name first, on the hotel registers for Tuesday night; then by her description, given to the desk clerks; and lastly by any and all entries in the registers, no matter what name was given. He knew her handwriting, even if she'd registered under an assumed name.

He drew a complete blank. No one who looked like her had come to any of the hotels, Tuesday night, or at any time since. No one giving her name. No one giving another name, who wrote like her. What was left? Where else could she have gone? Friends? She didn't have any. Not close ones, not friends she knew well enough to walk in on unannounced and stay overnight with.

Where was she? She wasn't in the city. She wasn't in the

country, up at Denby. She seemed to have vanished completely from the face of the earth.

It was past two in the morning by the time he'd finished checking the hotels. It was too late to get a bus any more that night, or he would have gone up to Denby then and there himself. He turned up his coat collar against the night mist and started disconsolately homeward. On the way he tried to buck himself up by saying: *Nothing's happened to her. She's just hiding out somewhere, trying to throw a scare into me. She'll show up, she's bound to.* It wouldn't work, much. It was two whole days and three nights now. Marriage is learning to know another person, learning to know by heart what he or she'd do in such-and-such a situation. They'd only been married six weeks, but, after all, they'd been going together nearly a year before that; he knew her pretty well by now.

She wasn't vindictive. She didn't nurse grievances, even imaginary ones. There were only two possible things she would have done. She would have either gotten on that bus red-hot, been cooled off long before she got off it again, but stayed up there a couple of days as long as she was once there. Or if she hadn't taken the bus, she would have been back by twelve at the latest right that same night, with an injured air and a remark like: "You ought to be ashamed of yourself letting your wife walk the streets like a vagrant!" or something to that effect. She hadn't, so she must have gone up there. Then he thought of the letter from her mother, and he felt good and scared.

The phone was ringing when he got back. He could hear it even before he got the front door open. He nearly broke the door down in his hurry to get at it. For a minute he thought—

But it was only Mrs. Alden. She said, "I've been trying to get you ever since ten o'clock. I didn't hear from you, and I've been getting more and more worried." His heart went down under his shoelaces. "Did you locate her? Is it all right?"

"I can't find her," he said, so low he had to say it over again so she could catch it.

She'd been talking fast until now. Now she didn't say anything at all for a couple of minutes; there was just an empty hum on the wire. Something came between them. They'd never seen each other face to face, but he could sense a change in her voice, a different sound to it the next time he heard it. It was as though she were drawing away from him. Not moving from where she stood, of course, but rather withdrawing her confidence. The beginnings of suspicion were lurking in it somewhere or other.

"Don't you think it's high time you got in touch with the police?" he heard her say. And then, so low that he could hardly get it: "If you don't, I will." *Click,* and she was gone.

He didn't take it the way he, perhaps, should have.

As he hung up, he thought, *Yes, she's right, I'll have to. Nothing else left to be done now. It's two full days now; no use kidding myself any more.*

He put on his hat and coat again, left the house once more. It was about three in the morning by this time. He hated to go to them. It seemed like writing finis to it. It seemed to make it so final, tragic, in a way. As though, once he notified them, all hope of her returning to him unharmed, of her own accord, was over. As though it stopped being just a little private, domestic matter any more and became a police matter, out of his own hands. Ridiculous, he knew, but that was the way he felt about it. But it had to be done. Just sitting worrying about her wasn't going to bring her back.

He went in between two green door lamps and spoke to a desk sergeant. "I want to report my wife missing." They sent a man out, a detective, to talk to him. Then he had to go down to the city morgue, to see if she was among the unidentified dead there, and that was the worst experience he'd had yet. It wasn't the sight of the still faces one by one; it was the dread, each time, that the next one would be hers. Half under his breath, each time he shook his head and looked at someone who had once been loved, he added, "No, thank God." She wasn't there.

Although he hadn't found her, all he could give when he left that place of the dead was a sigh of unutterable relief. She wasn't among the *found* dead, that was all this respite marked. But he knew, although he tried to shut the grisly thought out, that there are many dead who are *not* found. Sometimes not right away, sometimes never.

They took him around to the hospitals then, to certain wards, and though this wasn't quite so bad as the other place, it wasn't much better either. He looked for her among amnesia victims, would-be suicides who had not yet recovered consciousness, persons with all the skin burned off their faces, mercifully swathed in gauze bandaging and tea leaves. They even made him look in the alcoholic wards, though he protested strenuously that *she* wouldn't be there, and in the psychopathic wards.

The sigh of relief he gave when this tour was over was only less heartfelt than after leaving the morgue. She wasn't dead. She wasn't maimed or injured or out of her mind in any way. And still she wasn't to be found.

Then they turned it over to Missing Persons, had her description broadcast, and told him there wasn't anything he could do for the present but go home.

He didn't even try to sleep when he got back the second time. Just sat there waiting—for the call that didn't come and that he somehow knew wouldn't come, not if he waited for a week or a month.

It was starting to get light by that time. The third day since she'd been swallowed up bodily was dawning. She wasn't in the city, alive or dead, he was convinced. Why sit there waiting for them to locate her when he was sure she wasn't here? He'd done all he could at this end. He hadn't done anything yet at the other end. The thing was too serious now; it wasn't enough just to take the word of a *voice* over a telephone wire that she wasn't up there. Not even if the voice was that of her own mother, who was to be trusted if anyone was, who thought as

much of her as he did. He decided he'd go up there himself.
Anything was better than just sitting here waiting helplessly.

He couldn't take the early-morning bus, the way he wanted
to. Those building plans he was finishing up had to be turned
in today; there was an important contractor waiting for them.
He stood there poring over the blueprints, more dead than
alive between worry and lack of sleep, and when they were
finally finished, turned in, and O.K.'d, he went straight from the
office to the terminal and took the bus that should get in there
about dark.

Denby wasn't even an incorporated village, he found when
the bus finally got there, an hour late. It was just a place where
a turnpike crossed another road, with houses spaced at lengthy
intervals along the four arms of the intersection. Some of them
a quarter of a mile apart, few of them in full view of one another
due to intervening trees, bends in the roads, rises and dips of
the ground. A filling-station was the nearest thing to the crossroads, in one direction. Up in the other was a store, with living-
quarters over it. It was the most dispersed community he had
ever seen.

He chose the store at random, stopped in there, and asked,
"Which way to the Alden house?"

The storekeeper seemed to be one of those people who wear
glasses for the express purpose of staring over instead of
through them. Or maybe they'd slipped down on the bridge of
his nose. "Take that other fork, to your right," he instructed.
"Just keep going till you think there ain't going to be no more
houses, and you're sure I steered you wrong. Keep on going
anyway. When you least expect it, one last house'll show up,
round the turn. That's them. Can't miss it. You'll know it by the
low brick barrier wall runs along in front of it. He put that up
lately, just to keep in practice, I reckon."

Bliss wondered what he meant by that, if anything, but didn't
bother asking. The storekeeper was evidently one of these
loquacious souls who would have rambled on forever given the

slightest encouragement, and Bliss was tired and anxious to reach his destination. He thanked him and left.

The walk out was no picayune city block or two; it was a good stiff hike. The road stretched before him like a white tape under the velvety night sky, dark-blue rather than black, and stars twinkled down through the openings between the roadside-tree branches. He could hear countryside night noises around him, crickets or something, and once a dog barked 'way off in the distance, it sounded like miles away. It was lonely, but not particularly frightening; nature rarely is, it is man that is menacing.

Just the same, if she had come up here—and of course she hadn't—it wouldn't have been particularly prudent for a young girl alone like her to walk this distance at that hour of the night. She probably would have phoned out to them to come in and meet her at the crossroads, from either the store or that filling-station. And yet if both had been closed up by then—her bus wouldn't have passed through here until one or two in the morning—she would have had to walk it alone. But she hadn't come up so why conjure up additional dangers?

Thinking which, he came around the slow turn in the road and a low, elbow-height boundary wall sprang up beside him and ran down the road past a pleasant, white-painted two-story house, with dark gables, presumably green. They seemed to keep it in good condition. As for the wall itself, he got what the storekeeper's remark had intended to convey when he saw it. It looked very much as though Alden had put it up simply to kill time, give himself something to do, add a fancy touch to his property. For it seemed to serve no useful purpose. It was not nearly high enough to shut off the view, so it had not been built for privacy. It only ran along the front of the parcel, did not extend around the sides or to the back, so it was not even effective as a barrier against poultry or cattle, or useful as a boundary mark. It seemed to be purely decorative. As such, it was a neat, workmanlike job; you could tell Alden had been a

mason before his marriage. It was brick, smoothly, painstak-
ingly plastered over.

There was no gate in it, just a gap, with an ornamental willow
wicket arched high over it. He turned in through there. They
were up yet, though perhaps already on the point of retiring.
One of the upper-floor windows held a light, but with a blind
discreetly drawn down over it.

He rang the bell, then stepped back from the door and looked
up, expecting to be interrogated first from the window, particularly at this hour. Nothing of the kind happened; they evidently
possessed the trustfulness that goes with a clear conscience. He
could hear steps start down the inside stairs. A woman's steps,
at that, and a voice that carried out to where he was with
surprising clarity said, "Must be somebody lost their way, I
guess."

A hospitable little lantern up over the door went on from the
inside, and a moment later he was looking at a pleasant-faced,
middle-aged woman with soft gray eyes. Her face was long and
thin, but without the hatchet-sharp features that are so often an
accompaniment of that contour of face. Her hair was a graying
blond, but soft and wavy, not scraggly. Knowing who she was,
he almost thought he could detect a little bit of Smiles in her
face: the shape of the brows and the curve of the mouth, but
that might have been just autosuggestion.

"Hm-m-m?" she said serenely.

"I'm Ed, Mrs. Alden."

She blinked twice, as though she didn't get it for a minute. Or
maybe wasn't expecting it.

"Smiles's husband," he said, a trifle irritatedly. You're supposed to know your own in-laws. It wasn't their fault, of course,
that they didn't. It wasn't his, either. He and Smiles had been
meaning to come up here on a visit as soon as they could, but
they'd been so busy getting their own home together, and six
weeks is such a short time. Her mother had been getting over
a prolonged illness at the time of their wedding, hadn't been

strong enough for the trip down and back.

Both her hands came out toward his now, after that momentary blankness. "Oh, come in, Ed," she said heartily. "I've been looking forward to meeting you, but I *wish* it had been under other circumstances." She glanced past his shoulder. "She's not with you, I see. No word yet, Ed?" she went on worriedly.

He looked down and shook his head glumly.

She held her hand to her mouth in involuntary dismay, then quickly recovered her self-control, as though not wishing to add to his distress. "Don't know what to think," she murmured half audibly. "It's not like her to do a thing like that. Have you been to the police yet, Ed?"

"I reported it to them before daylight this morning. Had to go around to the different hospitals and places." He blew out his breath at the recollection. "Huff, it was ghastly."

"Don't let's give up yet, Ed. You know the old saying, 'No news is good news.' " Then: "Don't let me keep you standing out here. Joe's upstairs; I'll call him down."

As he followed her inside, his whole first impression of Smiles's mother was that she was as nice, wholesome, inartificial a woman as you could find anywhere. And first impressions are always half the battle.

She led him along a neat, hardwood-floored hall, varnished to the brightness of a mirror. An equally spotless white staircase rose at the back of it to the floor above.

"Let me take your hat," she said thoughtfully, and hung it on a peg. "You look peaked, Ed; I can tell you're taking it hard. That trip up is strenuous, too. It's awful; you know you read about things like this in the papers nearly every day, but it's only when it hits home you realize—"

Talking disconnectedly like that, she had reached the entrance to the living-room. She thrust her hand around to the inside of the door frame and snapped on the lights. He was standing directly in the center of the opening as she did so. There was something a little unexpected about the way they went on, but he couldn't figure what it was; it must have been just a subconscious impression on his part. Maybe they were a little brighter than he'd expected, and after coming in out of the dark—The room looked as though it had been painted fairly recently, and he supposed that was what it was, the walls and woodwork gave it back with unexpected dazzle. It was too small a detail even to waste time on. Or is any detail ever too small?

She had left him for a moment to go as far as the foot of the stairs. "Joe, Smiles's husband is here," he heard her call.

A deep rumbling voice answered, "She with him?"

She tactfully didn't answer that, no doubt to spare Bliss's feelings; she seemed to be such a considerate woman. "Come down, dear," was all she said.

He was a thick, heavy-set man, with a bull neck and a little circular fringe of russet-blond hair around his head, the crown of it bald. He was going to be the blunt, aggressive type, Bliss could see. With eyes too small to match it. Eyes that said, *Try and get past us*.

"So you're Bliss." He reached out and shook hands with him. It was a hard shake, but not particularly friendly. His hands were calloused to the lumpiness of alligator hide. "Well, you're taking it pretty calmly, it seems to me."

Bliss looked at him. "How do you figure that?"

"Joe!" the mother had remonstrated, but so low neither of them paid any attention.

"Coming up here like this. Don't you think it's your business to stick close down there, where you could do some good?"

Mrs. Alden laid a comforting hand on Bliss's arm. "Don't, Joe. You can tell how the boy feels by looking at him. I'm Smiles's mother and I know how it is; if she said she was coming up here, why, naturally—"

"I know you're Teresa's mother," he said emphatically, as if to shut her up.

A moment of awkward silence hung suspended in the air above their three heads. Bliss had a funny "lost" feeling for a minute, as though something had eluded him just then, some-thing had been a little askew. It was like when there's a word you are trying desperately to remember; it's on the tip of your tongue, but you can't bring it out. It was such a small thing, though—

"I'll get you something to eat, Ed," she said, and as she turned to go out of the room, Bliss couldn't help overhearing her say to her husband in a stage whisper: "Talk to him. Find out what really happened."

Alden had about as much finesse as a trained elephant doing the gavotte among ninepins. He cleared his throat judicially. "D'ja do something you shouldn't, that how it come about?"

"What do you mean?"

"Wull, *we* have no way of knowing what kind of a disposition you've got. Have you got a pretty bad temper, are you a little too quick with the flat of your hand?"

Bliss looked at him incredulously. Then he got it. "That's hardly a charge I expected to have to defend myself on. But if it's required of me—I happen to worship the ground my wife walks on. I'd sooner have my right arm wither away than—"

"No offense," said Alden lamely. "It's been known to happen before, that's all."

"Not in my house," Bliss said, and gave him a steely look.

Smiles's mother came in again at this point, with something on a tray. Bliss didn't even bother looking up to see what it was. He waved it aside, sat there with his arms dangling out over his knees, his head bent way over, looking straight down through them.

The room was a vague irritant. He kept getting it all the time, at least every time he raised his head and looked around, but he couldn't figure what was doing it. There was only one thing he was sure of, it wasn't the people in it. So that left it up to the room. Smiles's mother was the soothing, soft-moving type that it was pleasant to have around you. And even the husband, in spite of his brusqueness, was the stolid emotionless sort that didn't get on your nerves.

What was it, then? Was the room furnished in bad taste? It wasn't; it was comfortable and homey-looking. And even if it hadn't been, that wouldn't have done it. He was no interior decorator, allergic to anything like that. Was it the glare from the recent paint job? No, not that, either; now that he looked, there wasn't any glare. It wasn't even glossy paint, it was the dull kind without high lights. That had just been an optical illusion when the lights first went on.

He shook his head a little to get rid of it, and thought, *What's annoying me in here?* And he couldn't tell.

He was holding a lighted cigarette between his dangling fingers, and the ash was slowly accumulating.

"Pass him an ash tray, Joe," she said in a watery voice. She was starting to cry, without any fuss, unnoticeably, but she still had time to think of their guest's comfort. Some women are like that.

He looked and a whole cylinder of ash had fallen to the rug. It looked like a good rug, too. "I'm sorry," he said, and rubbed it out with his shoe. Even the rug bothered him in some way.

Pattern too loud? No, it was quiet, dark-colored, and in good taste. He couldn't find a thing the matter with it. But it kept troubling him just the same.

Something went *clang*. It wasn't in the same room with them, some other part of the house, faint and muffled, like a defective pipe joint settling or swelling.

She said, "Joe, when are you going to have the plumber in to fix that water pipe? It's sprung out of line again. You'll wait until we have a good-sized leak on our hands."

"Yeah, that's right," he said. It sounded more like an original discovery than a recollection of something overlooked. Bliss couldn't have told why, it just did. More of his occultism, he supposed.

"I'll have to get a fresh handkerchief," she said apologetically, got up and passed between them, the one she had been using until now rolled into a tight little ball at her upper lip.

"Take it easy," Alden said consolingly.

His eyes went to Bliss, then back to her again, as if to say: *Do you see that she's crying, as well as I do?* So Bliss glanced at her profile as she went by, and she was. She ought to have been, she was the girl's mother.

When she came in again with the fresh handkerchief she'd gone to get, he got to his feet.

"This isn't bringing her back. I'd better get down to the city again. They might have word for me by now."

Alden said, "Can I talk to you alone a minute, Bliss, before you go?"

The three of them had moved out into the hall. Mrs. Alden went up the stairs slowly. The higher up she got the louder her sobs became. Finally a long wail burst out, and the closing of a door cut it in half. A minute later bedsprings protested, as if someone had dropped on them full length.

"D'you hear that?" Alden said to him. Another of those never-ending nuances hit Bliss; he'd said it as if he were proud of it.

Bliss was standing in the doorway, looking back into the room. He felt as if he were glad to get out of it. And he still couldn't understand why, any more than any of the rest of it.

"What was it you wanted to say to me on the side?"

Blunt as ever, Alden asked, "Have you told us everything, or have you left out part of it? Just what went on between you and Teresa anyway?"

"One of those tiffs."

Alden's small eyes got even smaller, they almost creased out in his face. "It must have been *some* tiff, for her to walk out on you with her grip in her hand. She wasn't the kind—"

"How did you know she took her grip with her? I didn't tell you that."

"You didn't have to. She was coming up here, wasn't she?

They always take their grips when they walk out on you."

There wasn't pause enough between their two sentences to stick a bent comma. One just seemed to flow out of the other, only with a change of speakers. Alden's voice had gone up a little with the strain of the added pace he'd put into it, that was all. He'd spoken it a little faster than his usual cadence. Small things. Damn those small things to hell, torturing him like gnats, like gnats that you can't put your finger on!

Right under Bliss's eyes, a bead of sweat was forming between two of the reddish tufts of hair at the edge of Alden's hair line. He could see it oozing out of the pore. What was that from? Just from discussing what time his bus would get him back to the city, as they were doing now? No, it must have been from saying that sentence too fast a while ago—the one about the grip. The effects were only coming out now.

"Well," Bliss said, "I'd better get a move on, to catch the bus back."

Her door, upstairs, had opened again. It might have been just coincidental, but it was timed almost as though she'd been listening.

"Joe," she called down the stair well. "Don't let Ed start back down again right tonight. Two trips in one day is too much; he'll be a wreck. Why not have him stay over with us tonight, and take the early morning one instead?"

Bliss was standing right down there next to him. She could have spoken to him directly just as easily. Why did she have to relay it through her husband?

"Yeah," Alden said up to her, "that's just what I was thinking myself." But it was as though he'd said: *I get you.*

Bliss had a funny feeling they'd been saying something to one another right in front of his face without his knowing what it was.

"No," he said dolefully, "I'm worried about her. The sooner I get down there and get to the bottom of it—"

He went on out the door, and Alden came after him.

"I'll walk you down to the bus stop," he offered.

"Not necessary," Bliss told him curtly. After all, twice now this other man had tried to suggest he'd abused or maltreated his wife; he couldn't help resenting it. "I can find my way back without any trouble. You're probably tired and want to turn in."

"Just as you say," Alden acquiesced.

They didn't shake hands at parting. Bliss couldn't help noticing that the other man didn't even reach out and offer to. For his part, that suited him just as well.

After he'd already taken a few steps down the road, Alden called out after him, "Let us know the minute you get good news; I don't want my wife to worry any more than she has to. She's taking it hard."

Bliss noticed he didn't include himself in that. He didn't hold that against him, though; after all, there was no blood relationship there.

Alden turned as if to go back inside the house again, but when Bliss happened to glance back several minutes later, just before taking the turn in the road that cut the house off from sight, he could still detect a narrow up-and-down band of light escaping from the doorway, with a break in it at one point as though a protruding profile were obscuring it.

Wants to make sure I'm really on my way to take that bus, he said to himself knowingly. But suspicion is a two-edged sword that turns against the wielder as readily as the one it is wielded against. He only detected the edge that was turned toward him, and even that but vaguely.

He reached the crossroads and took up his position. He still had about five minutes to wait, but he'd hardly arrived when two yellow peas of light, swelling until they became great hazy balloons, came down the turnpike toward him. He thought it was the bus at first, ahead of its own schedule, but it turned out to be a coupé with a Quebec license. It slowed long enough for the occupant to lean out and ask:

"Am I on the right road for the city?"

"Yeah, keep going straight, you can't miss," Bliss said dully. Then suddenly, on an impulse he was unable to account for afterward, he raised his voice and called after him, "Hey! I don't suppose you'd care to give me a lift in with you?"

"Why not?" the Canuck said amiably, and slowed long enough for Bliss to catch up to him.

Bliss opened the door and sidled in. He still didn't know what had made him change his mind like this, unless perhaps it was the vague thought that he might make better time in with a private car like this than he would have with the bus.

The driver said something about being glad to have someone to talk to on the way down, and Bliss explained briefly that he'd been waiting for the bus, but beyond those few introductory remarks, they did not talk much. Bliss wanted to think. He wanted to analyze his impression of the visit he had just concluded.

It was pretty hopeless to do much involved thinking with a stranger at his elbow, liable to interrupt his train of thought every once in a while with some unimportant remark that had to be answered for courtesy's sake, so the most he could do was marshal his impressions, sort of document them for future reference when he was actually alone:

1. The lights seemed to go on in an unexpected way, when she first pressed the switch.

2. The room bothered him. It hadn't been the kind of room you feel at ease in. It hadn't been *restful*.

3. There had been some sort of faulty vocal co-ordination when she said, "I'm Smiles's mother," and he said, "I know you're Teresa's mother."

4. There had also been nuances in the following places: When Alden's eyes sought his, as if to assure himself that he, Bliss, saw that she was crying almost unnoticeably there in the room with them. When she ran whimpering up the stairs and threw herself on the bed, and he said, "Hear that?" And lastly when she called down and addressed her overnight invitation

to Alden, instead of Bliss himself, as though there were some intangible kernel in it to be extracted first before he passed on the dry husk of the words themselves to Bliss.

At this point, before he got any further, there was a thud, a long-drawn-out reptilian hiss, and a tire went out. They staggered to a stop at the side of the road.

"Looks like I've brought you tough luck," Bliss remarked.

"No," his host assured him, "that thing's been on its ninth life for weeks; I'm only surprised it lasted this long. I had it patched before I left Three Rivers this morning, thought maybe I could make the city on it, but it looks like no soap. Well, I have a spare, and now I *am* glad I hitched you on; four hands are better than two."

The stretch of roadway where it had happened was a particularly bad one, Bliss couldn't help noticing as he slung off his coat and jumped down to lend a hand; it was crying for attention, needled with small jagged rock fragments, either improperly crushed in the first place or else loosened from their bed by some recent rain. He supposed it hadn't been blocked off because there was no other branch road in the immediate vicinity that could take its place as a detour.

They'd hardly gotten the jack out when the bus overtook and passed them, wiping out his gain of time at a stroke. And then, a considerable time later, after they'd already finished the job and wiped their hands clean, some other anonymous car went steaming by, this time at a rate of speed that made the bus seem to have been standing still in its tracks. The Canadian was the only one in sight by the stalled car as its cometlike headlights flicked by. Bliss happened to be farther in off the road just then. He turned his head and looked after it, however, at the tornado-like rush of air that followed in its wake, and got a glimpse of it just before it hurtled from sight.

"That fellow's *asking* for a flat," the Canadian said, "passing over a stretch of fill like this at such a clip."

"He didn't have a spare on him, either," Bliss commented.

"Looked like he was trying to beat that bus in." Just an idle phrase, for purposes of comparison. It took on new meaning later, though, when Bliss remembered it.

They climbed in and started off again. The rest of the ride passed uneventfully. Bliss spelled his companion at the wheel, the last hour in, and let him take a little doze. He'd been on the road steadily since early that morning, he'd told Bliss.

Bliss woke him up and gave the car back to him when they reached the city limits. The Canadian was heading for a certain hotel all the way downtown, so Bliss wouldn't let him deviate from his course to take him over to his place; he got out instead at the nearest parallel point to it they touched, thanked him, and started over on foot.

He had a good stiff walk ahead of him, but he didn't mind that, he'd been sitting cramped up for so long. He still wanted to think things over as badly as ever, too, and he'd found out by experience that solitary walking helped him to think better.

It didn't in this case, though. He was either too tired from the events of the past few days, or else the materials he had were too formless, indefinite, to get a good grip on. He kept asking himself, *What was wrong up there? Why am I dissatisfied?* And he couldn't answer for the life of him. *Was anything wrong,* he was finally reduced to wondering, *or was it wholly imaginary on my part?* It was like a wrestling bout with shadows.

The night around him was dark-blue velvet, and as he drew near his own isolated semisuburban neighborhood, the silence was at least equal to that up at Denby. There wasn't a soul stirring, not even a milkman. He trudged onward under a leafy tunnel of sidewalk trees that all but made him invisible.

Leaving the coupé where he had, and coming over in a straight line this way, brought him up to his house from behind, on the street in back of it instead of the one running directly before it, which was an approach he never took at other times, such as when coming home from downtown. Behind it there was nothing but vacant plots, so it was a short-cut to cross diagonally behind the house next door and go through from the back instead of going all the way around the corner on the outside. He did that now, without thinking of anything except to save a few extra steps.

As he came out from behind the house next door, treading soundless on the well-kept backyard grass, he saw a momentary flash through one of his own windows that could only have been a pocket torch. He stopped dead in his tracks. *Burglars* was the first thought that came to him.

He advanced a wary step or two. The flash came again, but from another window this time, nearer the front. They were evidently on their way out, using it only intermittently to help find their way. He'd be able to head them off at the front door, as they stole forth.

There was a partition hedge between the two houses, running from front to back. He scurried along that, on his neighbor's side of it, keeping head and shoulders down, until he was on a line with his own front door. He crouched there, peering through.

They had left a lookout standing just outside his door. He could see the motionless figure. And then, as his fingers were about to part the hedge, to aid him in crashing through, the still form shifted a little, and the uncertain light struck a glint from a little wedge on its chest. At the same instant Bliss caught the outline of a visor above the profile. A cop!

One hand behind him, Bliss ebbed back again on his heels, thrown completely off balance by the unexpected revelation.

His own front door opened just then and two men came out, one behind the other. Without visors and without metallic gleams on their chests. But the cop turned and flipped up his nightstick toward them in semisalute; so, whatever they were, they weren't burglars, although one was unmistakably carrying something out of the house with him.

They carefully closed the front door behind them, even tried it a second time to make sure it was securely fastened. A snatch

of guarded conversation drifted toward him as they made their
way down the short front walk to the sidewalk. The uniformed
man took no part in it, only the two who had been inside.

"He's hot, all right," Bliss heard one say.

"Sure, he's hot, and he already knows it. You notice he wasn't
on that bus when it got in. I'll beat it down and get the Teletype
busy. You put a case on this place. Still, he might try to sneak
back in again later."

Bliss had been crouched there on his heels. He went forward
and down now on the flats of his hands, as stunned as though
he'd gotten a rabbit punch at the back of the neck.

Motionless there, almost dazed, he kept shaking his head
slightly, as though to clear it. They were after *him*, they thought
he'd—Not only that, but they'd been tipped off what bus he was
supposed to show up on. That could mean only one person, Joe
Alden.

He wasn't surprised. He could even understand his doing a
thing like that; it must seem suspicious to them up there the
way she'd disappeared, and Bliss's own complete lack of any
plausible explanation for it. He'd probably have felt the same
way about it himself, if he'd been in their place. But he did
resent the sneaky way Alden had gone about it, waiting until he
was gone and then denouncing him the minute his back was
turned. Why hadn't he tried to have him held by the locals
while he was right up there with them? He supposed, now, that
was the esoteric meaning in her invitation to him to stay over;
so Alden could go out and bring in the cops while he was asleep
under their roof. It hadn't worked because he'd insisted on
leaving.

Meanwhile, he continued watching these men before him
who had now, through no fault of his own, become his deadly
enemies. They separated. One of them, with the uniformed cop
trailing along with him, started down the street away from the
house. The other drifted diagonally across to the opposite side.
The gloom of an overshadowing tree over there swallowed him,

and he failed to show up again on the other side of it, where there was a little more light.

There was hardly any noise about the whole thing, hardly so much as a footfall. They were like shadows moving in a dream world. A car engine began droning stealthily, slurred away, from a short distance farther down the street, marking the point of departure of two out of the three. A drop of sweat, as cold as mercury, toiled sluggishly down the nape of Bliss's neck, blotted itself into his collar.

He stayed there where he was, on all fours behind the hedge, a few minutes longer. The only thing to do was go out and try to clear himself. The one thing *not* to do was turn around and slink off—though the way lay open behind him. But at the same time he had a chill premonition that it wasn't going to be so easy to clear himself; that once they got their hands on him—

But I've got to, he kept telling himself over and over. *They've got to help me, not go after me. They can't say I—did anything like that to Smiles! Maybe I can hit one of them that's fair minded, will listen to me.*

Meanwhile he had remained in the crouched position of a track runner waiting for the signal to start. He picked himself up slowly and straightened to his full height behind the hedge. That took courage, alone, without moving a step farther. "Well, here goes," he muttered, tightened his belt, and stuck a cigarette in his mouth. It was a crawly sort of feeling. He knew, nine chances to one, his freedom of movement was over the minute he stepped out from behind this hedge and went over toward that inky tree shadow across the street that was just a little too lumpy in the middle. He didn't give a rap about freedom of movement in itself, but his whole purpose, his one aim from now on, was to look for and find Smiles. He was afraid losing it would hamper him in that. She was his wife, he wanted to look for her himself, he didn't want other guys to do it for him whether they were professionals or not.

He lighted the cigarette when halfway across the street, but the tree shadow didn't move. The detective evidently didn't know him by sight yet, was on the lookout for someone coming from the other direction on his way to the house.

Bliss stopped right in front of him and said, "Are you looking for me? I'm Ed Bliss and I live over there."

The shadow up and down the tree trunk detached itself, became a man. "How'd you know anyone was looking for you?" It was a challenge, as though that were already an admission of guilt in itself.

Bliss said, "Come inside, will you? I want to talk to you."

They crossed over once more. Bliss unlocked the door for him, with his own key this time, and put on the lights. They went into the living-room. It was already getting dusty from not being cleaned in several days.

He looked Bliss over good. Bliss looked him over just as good. He wanted a man in this, not a detective.

The detective spoke first, repeated what he'd asked him outside on the street. "How'd you know we'd be looking for you when that bus got in?"

"I didn't. I just happened to take a lift down instead."

"What's become of your wife, Bliss?"

"I don't know."

"We think you do."

"I wish you were right. But not in the way you mean."

"Never mind what you wish. You know another good word for that? Remorse."

The blood in Bliss's face thinned a little. "Before you put me in the soup, just let me talk here quietly with you a few minutes. That's all I ask."

"When she walked out of here Tuesday night, what was she wearing?"

Bliss hesitated a minute. Not because he didn't know—he'd already described her outfit to them when he reported her missing—but because he could sense a deeper import lurking behind the question.

The detective took the hesitancy for an attempt at evasion, went on: "Now every man knows his wife's clothes by heart. You paid for every last one of them, you know just what she owned. Just tell me what she had on."

There was danger in it somewhere. "She had on a gray suit —jacket and skirt, you know. Then a pink silk shirtwaist. She threw her fur piece back at me, so that's about all she went out in. A hat, of course. One of those crazy hats."

"Baggage?"

"A black valise with tan binding. Oh, about the size of a typewriter case."

"Sure of that?"

"Sure of that."

The detective gave a kind of soundless whistle through his teeth. "Whe-ew!" he said, and he looked at Bliss almost as if he felt sorry for him. "You've sure made it tough for yourself this time! I didn't have to ask you that, because we know just as well as you what she had on."

"How?"

"Because we found every last one of those articles you just mentioned in the furnace downstairs in this very house, less than twenty minutes ago. My partner's gone down to headquarters with them. And a guy don't do that to his wife's clothes unless he's done something to his wife, too. What've you done with her, Bliss?"

The other man wasn't even in the room with him any more, so far as Bliss was concerned. A curtain of foggy horror had dropped down all around him. "My God!" he whispered hoarsely. "Something's happened to her, somebody's done something to her!" And he jumped up and ran out of the room so unexpectedly, so swiftly, that if his purpose had been to escape, he almost could have eluded the other man. Instead he made for the cellar door and ran down the basement steps. The detective had shot to his feet after him, was at his heels by the time he got down to the bottom. Bliss turned on the light and looked at the furnace grate, yawning emptily open—as though that could tell him anything more.

He turned despairingly to the detective. "Was there any blood on them?"

"Should there have been?"

"Don't! Have a heart," Bliss begged in a choked voice, and shaded his eyes. "Who put them in there? Why'd they bring them back here? How'd they get in while I was out?"

"Quit that," the headquarters man said dryly. "Suppose we get started. Our guys'll be looking all over for you, and it'll save them a lot of trouble."

Every few steps on the way back up those basement stairs, Bliss would stop, as though he'd run down and needed winding up again. The detective would prod him forward, not roughly, just as a sort of reminder to keep going.

"Why'd they put them *there?*" he asked. "Things that go in there are meant for fuel. That's what you came back for, to finish burning them, isn't it? Too late in the year to make a fire in the daytime without attracting attention."

"Listen. We were only married six weeks."

"What's that supposed to prove? Do you think there haven't been guys that got rid of their wives six *days* after they were married, or even six *hours?*"

"But those are fiends—monsters. *I* couldn't be one of them!"

And the pitiless answer was: "How do we know that? We can't tell, from the outside, what you're like on the inside. We're not X-ray machines."

They were up on the main floor again by now.

"Was she insured?" the detective questioned.

"Yes."

"You tell everything, don't you?"

"Because there's nothing to hide. I didn't just insure *her*, I insured us both. I took out twin policies, one on each of us. We were each other's beneficiaries. She wanted it that way."

"But you're here and she's not," the detective pointed out remorselessly.

They passed the dining-room entrance. Maybe it was the dishes still left on the table from that night that got to him. She came before him again, with her smiling crinkly eyes. He could see her carrying in a plate covered with a napkin. "Sit down there, mister, and don't look. I've got a surprise for you."

That finished him. That was a blow below the belt. He said, "You gotta let me alone a minute." And he slumped against the wall with his arm up over his face.

When he finally got over it, and it took some getting over, a sort of change had come over the detective. He said tonelessly, "Sit down a minute. Get your breath back and pull yourself together." He didn't sound like he meant that particularly, it was just an excuse.

He lighted a cigarette and then he threw the pack over at Bliss. Bliss let it slide off his thigh without bothering with it.

The detective said, "I've been a dick going on eight years now, and I never saw a guy who could fake a spell like you just had, and make it so convincing." He paused, then went on: "The reason I'm saying this is, once you go in you stay in, after what we found here in the house tonight. And, then, you did come up to me outside of your own accord, but of course that could have been just self-preservation. So I'm listening, for just as long as it takes me to finish this cigarette. By the time I'm through, if you haven't been able to tell me anything that changes the looks of things around, away we go." And he took a puff and waited.

"There's nothing I can tell you that I haven't already told you. She walked out of here Tuesday night at supper time. Said she was going to her mother's. She never got there. I haven't seen her since. Now you fellows find the things I saw her leave in, stuffed into the furnace in the basement." He pinched the bridge of his nose and kept it pinched.

The detective took another slow pull at his cigarette. "You've been around to the morgue and the hospitals. So she hasn't had any accident. Her things are back here again. So it isn't just a straight disappearance, or amnesia, or anything like that. That means that whatever was done to her or with her, was done against her will. Since we've eliminated accident, suicide, voluntary and involuntary disappearance, that spells murder."

"Don't!" Bliss said.

"It's got to be done." The detective took another puff. "Let's get down to motive. Now, you already have one, and a damned fine one. You'll have to dig up one on the part of somebody else that'll be stronger than yours, if you expect to cancel it out."

"Who could want to hurt her? She was so lovely, she was so beautiful—"

"Sometimes it's dangerous for a girl to be too lovely, too beautiful. It drives a man out of his mind, the man that can't have her. Were there any?"

"You're talking about Smiles now," Bliss growled dangerously, tightening his fist.

"I'm talking about a *case*. A case of suspected murder. And to us cases aren't beautiful, aren't ugly, they're just punishable." He puffed again. "'Did she turn anyone down to marry you?'"

Bliss shook his head. "She once told me I was the first fellow she ever went with."

The detective took another puff at his cigarette. He looked at it, shifted his fingers back a little, then looked at Bliss. "I seldom smoke that far down," he warned him. "I'm giving you a break. There's one more drag left in it. Anyone else stand to gain anything, financially, by her death, outside of yourself?"

"No one I know of."

The detective took the last puff, dropped the butt, ground it out. "Well, let's go," he said. He fumbled under his coat, took out a pair of handcuffs. "Incidentally, what was her real name? I have to know when I bring you in."

"Teresa."

"Smiles was just your pet name for her, eh?" The detective seemed to be just talking aimlessly, to try to take the sting out of the pinch, keep Bliss's mind off the handcuffs.

"Yeah," Bliss said, holding out his wrist without being told to.

"I was the first one called her that. She never liked to be called Teresa. Her mother was the one always stuck to that."

He jerked his wrist back in again.

"C'mon, don't get hard to handle," the detective growled, reaching out after it.

"Wait a minute," Bliss said excitedly, and stuck his hand behind his back. "Some things have been bothering me. You brought one of them back just then. I nearly had it. Let me look, before I lose it again. Let me look at that letter a minute that her mother sent her yesterday. It's here in my pocket."

He stripped it out of the envelope. *Smiles, dear,* it began.

He opened his mouth and looked at the other man. "That's funny. Her mother never called her anything but Teresa. I know I'm right about that. How could she? It was *my* nickname. And I'd never seen her until last night and—and Smiles hadn't been home since we were married."

The detective, meanwhile, kept trying to snag his other hand —he was holding the letter in his left—and bring it around in front of him.

"Wait a minute, wait a minute," Bliss pleaded. "I've got one of those things now. There was like a hitch in the flow of conversation, an air pocket. She said, 'I'm Smiles's mother,' and he said, 'You're *Teresa's* mother,' like he was reminding her what she always called Smiles. Why should he have to remind her of what she always called Smiles herself?"

"And that's supposed to clear you of suspicion, because her mother picks up your nickname for your wife, after she's been talking to you on the phone two or three days in a row? Anyone would be liable to do that. She did it to sort of accommodate you. Didn't you ever hear of people doing that before? That's how nicknames spread."

"But she caught it *ahead of time,* before she heard me call it to her. This letter heading shows that. She didn't know Smiles had disappeared yet, when she sent this letter. Therefore she hadn't spoken to me yet."

"Well, then, she got it from the husband, or from your wife's own letters home."

"But she never used it before; she disliked it until now. She wrote Smiles and told her openly it sounded too much like the nickname of a chorus girl. I can prove it to you. I can show you. Wait a minute, whatever your name is. Won't you let me see if I can find some other letter from her, just to convince myself?"

"My name is Stillman, and it's too small a matter to make any difference one way or the other. Now, come on, Bliss; I've tried to be fair with you until now—"

"Nothing is too small a matter to be important. You're a detective, do I have to tell you that? It's the little things in life that count, never the big ones. The little ones go to make up the big ones. Why should she suddenly call her by a nickname she never used before and disapproved of? Wait, let me show you. There must be one of her old letters upstairs yet, left around in one of the bureau drawers. Just let me go up and hunt for it. It'll just take a minute."·

Stillman went up with him, but Bliss could tell he was slowly souring on him. He hadn't changed over completely yet, but he was well under way. "I've taken all the stalling I'm going to from you," he muttered tight-lipped. "If I've got to crack down on you to get you out of here with me, I'll show you that I can do that, too."

Bliss was pawing through his wife's drawers meanwhile, head tensely lowered, knowing he had to beat his captor's change of mood to the punch, that in another thirty seconds at the most the slow-to-anger detective was going to yank him flat on the floor by the slack of the collar and drag him bodily out of the room after him.

He found one at last, almost when he'd given up hope. The same medium-blue ink, the same note paper. They hadn't corresponded with any great frequency, but they had corresponded regularly, about once every month or so.

"Here," he said relievedly, "here, see?" And he spread it out flat on the dresser top. Then he spread the one from his pocket alongside it, to compare. "See? 'Dearest Teresa.' What did I tell—"

He never finished it. They both saw it at once. It would have been hard to miss, the way he'd put both missives edge to edge. Bliss looked at the detective, then back to the dresser again.

Stillman was the first to put it into words. An expression of sudden concentration had come over his face. He elbowed Bliss a little aside, to get a better look. "See if you can dig up some more samples of her writing," he said slowly. "I'm not an expert, but, unless I miss my guess, these two letters weren't written by the same person."

Bliss didn't need to be told twice. He was frantically going through everything of Smiles's he could lay his hands on, all her keepsakes, mementos, accumulated belongings, scattering them around. He stopped as suddenly as he'd begun, and Stillman saw him standing there staring fixedly at something in one of the trinket boxes he had been plumbing through.

"What's the matter? Did you find some more?"

Bliss acted scared. His face was pale. "No, not writing," he said in a bated voice. "Something even—Look."

The detective's chin thrust over his shoulder. "Who are they?"

"That's evidently a snapshot of her and her mother, taken at a beach when she was a girl. I've never seen it before, but—"

"How do you know it's her mother? It could be some other woman, a friend of the family's."

Bliss had turned it over right while he was speaking. On the back, in schoolgirlish handwriting, was the notation: *Mamma and I, at Sea Crest, 19—*

Bliss reversed it again, right side forward.

"Well, what're you acting so scared about?" Stillman demanded impatiently. "You look like you've seen a ghost."

"Because this woman on the snapshot isn't the same woman I spoke to as her mother up at Denby tonight!"

"Now, wait a minute; hold your horses. You admit yourself you had never set eyes on her before until tonight; eight years is eight years. She's in a bathing-suit in this snapshot. She may have dyed or bleached her hair since, or it may have turned gray on her."

"That has nothing to do with it! I'm not looking at her hair or her clothes. The whole shape of her face is different. The bone structure is different. The features are different. This woman has a broad, round face. The one in Denby has a long, oval one. I tell you, it's not the same woman at all!"

"Gimme that, and gimme those." Stillman pocketed letters and snapshot. "Come on downstairs. I think I'll smoke another cigarette." His way of saying: *You've got yourself a reprieve.*

When they were below again, he sat down, with a misleading air of leisure. "Gimme your wife's family background, as much of it as you can, as much of it as she told you."

"Smiles was down here on her own when I met her. Her own father died when she was a kid, and left them comfortably well off, with their own house up in—"

"Denby?"

"No, it was some other place; I can't think of it offhand. While she was still a youngster, her mother gave Smiles her whole time and attention. But when Smiles had finished her schooling, about two years ago, the mother was still an attractive woman, young for her years, lively, good-hearted. It was only natural that she should marry again. Smiles didn't resent that, she'd expected her to. When the mother fell for this mason, Joe Alden, whom she first met when they were having some repairs made to the house, Smiles tried to like him. He'd been a good man in his line, too, but she couldn't help noticing that after he married her mother, he stopped dead, never did a stroke of work from then on; pretended he couldn't find any—when she knew for a fact that there was work to be had. That was the first thing she didn't like. Maybe he sensed she was onto him, but anyway they didn't rub well together. For her mother's sake, to avoid trouble, she decided to clear out, so her mother wouldn't have to choose between them. She was so diplomatic about it, though, that her mother never guessed what the real reason was.

"She came on down here, and not long ago Alden and her mother sold their old house and moved to a new one in Denby. Smiles said she supposed he did it to get away from the gossipy neighbors as much as anything else; they were probably beginning to criticize him for not at least making a stab at getting a job after he was once married."

"Did they come down when you married Smiles?"

"No. Smiles didn't notify them ahead; just sent a wire of announcement the day we were married. Her mother had been in poor health, and she was afraid the trip down would be more than she could stand. Well, there's the background."

"Nothing much there to dig into, at first sight."

"There never is, anywhere—at first sight," Bliss let him know. "Listen, Stillman. I'm going back up there again. Whatever's wrong is up at that end, not at this."

"I was detailed here to bring you in for questioning, you know." But he didn't move.

"Suppose I hadn't gone up to you outside in the street just now. Suppose I hadn't shown up around here for, say, another eight or ten hours. Can't you give me those extra hours? Come up there with me, never leave me out of your sight, put the bracelet on me, do anything you want, but at least let me go up there once more and confront those people. If you lock me up down at this end, then I've lost her sure as anything. I'll never find out what became of her—and you won't either. Something bothered me up there. A whole lot of things bothered me up there, but I've only cleared up one of them so far. Let me take a crack at the rest."

"You don't want much," Stillman said grudgingly. "D'ya know what can happen to me for stepping out of line like that? D'ya know I can be broken for anything like that?"

"You mean you're ready to ignore the discrepancy in handwriting in those two letters, and my assurance that there's someone up there that doesn't match the woman on that snapshot?"

"No, naturally not; I'm going to let my lieutenant know about both those things."

"And by that time it'll be too late. It's already three days since she's been gone."

"Tell you what," Stillman said. "I'll make a deal with you. We'll start out for headquarters now, and on the way we'll stop in at that bus terminal. If I can find any evidence, the slightest shred, that she started for Denby that night, I'll go up there with you. If not, we go over to headquarters."

All Bliss said was: "I know you'll find out she did leave."

Stillman took him without handcuffing him, merely remarking, "If you try anything, you'll be the loser, not me."

The ticket seller again went as far as he had with Bliss the time before, but still couldn't go any further than that. "Yeah, she bought a ticket for as far as the money she had on her would take her, but I can't remember where it was to."

"Which don't prove she ever hit Denby," Stillman grunted.

"Tackle the bus driver," Bliss pleaded. "No. 27. I know he was holding out on me. I could tell by the way he acted. She rode with him, all right, but for some reason he was cagey about saying so."

But they were out of luck. No. 27 was up at the other end, due to bring the cityward bus in the following afternoon.

Stillman was already trying to steer his charge out of the place and on his way over to headquarters, but Bliss wouldn't give up. "There must be someone around here that saw her get on that night. One of the attendants, one of the concessionaires that are around here every night. Maybe she checked her bag, maybe she drank a cup of coffee at the counter."

She hadn't checked her bag; the checkroom attendant couldn't remember anyone like her. She hadn't stopped at the lunch counter, either; neither could the counterman recall her. Nor the Negro that shined shoes. They even interrogated the matron of the restroom, when she happened to appear outside the door briefly. No, she hadn't noticed anyone like that, either.

"All right, come on," Stillman said, hooking his arm around Bliss's.

"One more spin. How about him, over there, behind the magazine stand?"

Stillman only gave in because it happened to be near the exit; they had to pass it on their way out.

And it broke! The fog lifted, if only momentarily, for the first time since the previous Tuesday night. "Sure I do," the vender said readily. "How could I help remembering? She came up to me in such a funny way. She said, 'I have exactly one dime left, which I overlooked when I was buying my ticket because it slipped to the bottom of my handbag. Let me have a magazine.' Naturally, I asked her which one she wanted. 'I don't care,' she said, 'so long as it lasts until I get off the bus. I want to be sure my mind is taken up.' Well, I've been doing business here for years, and it's gotten so I can clock the various stops. I mean, if they're riding a long distance, I give them a good thick magazine; if they're riding a short distance, I give them a skinny one. I gave her one for a medium distance—Denby; that was where she told me she was going."

All Stillman said was: "Come on over to the window while I get our tickets."

Bliss didn't say "Thanks." He didn't say anything. He didn't have to. The grateful look he gave the detective spoke for itself.

"Two to Denby, round," Stillman told the ticket seller. It was too late for the morning bus; the next one left in the early afternoon.

As they turned from the window, Bliss wondered aloud:

"Still and all, why was that driver so reluctant to admit she rode on the bus with him that night? And the ticket man claims she didn't buy a ticket to Denby, but to some point short of there."

"It's easy to see what it adds up to," Stillman told him. "She had a ticket for only part of the distance. She coaxed the driver into letting her ride the rest of the way to Denby. Probably explained her plight to him, and he felt sorry for her. That explains his reluctance to let you think she was on the bus at all. He must have thought you were a company spotter and naturally what he did would be against the regulations."

Tucking away the tickets in his inside coat pocket, the detective stood there a moment or two undecidedly. Then he said, "We may as well go back to your house. I might be able to turn up something else while we're waiting, and you can catch a nap. And, too, I'm going to call in, see if I can still make this detour up there and back legitimate while I'm about it."

When they got back to his house Bliss, exhausted, fell asleep in the bedroom. He remained oblivious to everything until the detective woke him up a half hour before bus time.

"Any luck?" Bliss asked him, shrugging into his coat.

"Nope, nothing more," Stillman said. Then he announced, "I've given my word to my lieutenant I'll show up at headquarters and have you with me, no later than nine tomorrow morning. He doesn't know you're with me right now; I let him think I got a tip where I could lay my hands on you. Leaving now, we will get up there around sunset, and we'll have to take the night bus back. That gives us only a few hours up there to see if we can find any trace of her. Pretty tight squeeze, if you ask me."

They boarded the bus together and sat down in one of the back seats. They didn't talk much during the long, monotonous ride up.

"Better take another snooze while you've got the chance," Stillman said.

Bliss thought he wouldn't be able to again, but, little by little, sheer physical exhaustion, combined with the lulling motion of the bus, overcame him and he dropped off.

It seemed like only five minutes later that Stillman shook him by the shoulder, rousing him. The sun was low in the west; he'd slept through nearly the entire trip. "Snap out of it, Bliss; we get off in another couple of minutes, right on time."

"I dreamed about her," Bliss said dully. "I dreamed she was in some kind of danger, needed me bad. She kept calling to me, 'Ed! Hurry up, Ed!' "

Stillman dropped his eyes. "I heard you say her name twice in your sleep: 'Smiles, Smiles,' " he remarked quietly. "Damned if you act like any guilty man I ever had in my custody before. Even in your sleep you sound like you were innocent."

"Denby!" the driver called out.

As the bus pulled away and left them behind at the crossroads, Stillman said, "Now that we're up here, let's have an understanding with each other. I don't want to haul you around on the end of a handcuff with me, but my job is at stake; I've got to be sure that you're still with me when I start back."

"Would my word of honor that I won't try to give you the slip while we're up here be worth anything to you?"

Stillman looked him square in the eye. "Is it worth anything to *you?*"

"It's about all I've got. I know I've never broken it."

Stillman nodded slowly. "I think maybe it'll be worth taking a chance on. All right, let me have it."

They shook hands solemnly.

Dusk was rapidly falling by now; the sun was already gone from sight and its afterglow fading out.

"Come on, let's get out to their place," Bliss said impatiently.

"Let's do a little inquiring around first. Remember, we have no evidence so far that she actually got off the bus here at all, let alone reached their house. Just her buying that magazine and saying she was coming here is no proof in itself. Now, let's see, she gets off in the middle of the night at this sleeping hamlet. Would she know the way out to their house, or would she have to ask someone?"

"She'd have to ask. Remember, I told you they moved here *after* Smiles had already left home. This would have been her first trip up here."

"Well, that ought to cinch it for us, if she couldn't get out there without asking directions. Let's try our luck at that filling-station first; it would probably have been the only thing open any more at the hour she came."

The single attendant on duty came out, said, "Yes, gents?"

"Look," Stillman began. "The traffic to and from here isn't exactly heavy, so this shouldn't be too hard. Think back to Tuesday night, the last bus north. Did you see anyone get off it?"

"I don't have to see 'em get off, I got a sure-fire way of telling whether anyone gets off or not."

"What's that?"

"Anyone that does get off, at least anyone that's a stranger here, never fails to stop by me and ask their way. That's as far as the last bus is concerned. The store is closed before then. And no one asked their way of me Tuesday night, so I figure no strangers got off."

"This don't look so good," murmured Stillman in an aside to Bliss. Then he asked the attendant, "Did you hear it go by at all? You must have, it's so quiet here."

"Yeah, sure, I did. It was right on time, too."

"Then you could tell if it stopped to let anyone down or went straight through without stopping, couldn't you?"

"Yeah, usually I can," was the disappointing answer. "But just that night, at that particular time, I was doing some repair work on a guy's car, trying to hammer out a bent fender for him, and my own noise drowned it out. As long as no one stopped by, though, I'm pretty sure it never stopped."

"Damn it," Stillman growled, as they turned away, "she couldn't have been more unseen if she was a ghost!"

After they were out of earshot of the filling-station attendant, Bliss said, "If Alden, for instance, had known she was coming and waited to meet her at the bus, that would do away with her having to ask anyone for directions. She may have telephoned ahead, or sent a wire up."

"If she didn't even have enough money to buy a ticket all the way, she certainly wouldn't have been able to make a toll call. Anyway, if we accept that theory, that means we're implicating them directly in her disappearance, and we have no evidence so far to support that. Remember, she may have met with foul play right here in Denby, along the road to their house, without ever having reached it."

It was fully dark by the time they rounded the bend in the road and came in sight of that last house of all, with the low brick wall in front of it. This time not a patch of light showed from any of the windows, upstairs or down, and yet it was earlier in the evening than when Bliss himself had arrived.

"Hello?" the detective said. "Looks like nobody home."

They turned in under the willow arch, rang the bell, and waited. Stillman pommeled the door and they waited some more. This was just perfunctory, however; it had been obvious to the two of them from the moment they first looked at the place that no one was in.

"Well, come on. What're we waiting for?" Bliss demanded. "I can get in one of the windows without any trouble."

Stillman laid a restraining hand on his arm. "No, you don't; that's breaking and entering. And I'm out of jurisdiction up here to begin with. We'll have to go back and dig up the local law; maybe I can talk him into putting the seal of official approval on it. Let's see if we can tell anything from the outside, first. I may be able to shine my torch in through one of the windows."

He clicked it on, made a white puddle against the front of the house, walked slowly in the wake of that as it moved along until it leaped in through one of the black window embrasures. They both edged up until their noses were nearly pressed flat against the glass, trying to peer through. It wouldn't work. The blinds were not down, but the closely webbed net curtains that hung down inside of the panes effectively parried its rays. They coursed slowly along the side of the house, trying it at window after window, each time with the same results.

Stillman turned away finally, but left his torch on. He splashed it up and down the short length of private dirt lane that ran beside the house, from the corrugated tin shack at the back that served Alden as a garage to the public highway in front. He motioned Bliss back as the latter started to step out onto it. "Stay off here a minute. I want to see if I can find out something from these tire prints their car left. See 'em?"

It would have been hard not to. The road past the house was macadamized, but there was a border of soft, powdery dust along the side of it, as with most rural roads. "I want to see if I can make out which way they turned," Stillman explained, strewing his beam of light along them and following offside. "If they went in to the city, to offer their co-operation to us down there, that would take them off to the right; no other way they could turn from here. If they turned to the left, up that way, it was definitely a lam, and it changes the looks of things all around."

The beam of his light, coursing along the prints like quicksilver in a channel, started to curve around *toward the right* as it followed them up out of sight on the hard-surfaced road. There was his answer.

He turned aimlessly back along them, light still on. He stopped parallel to the corner of the house, strengthened the beam's focus by bringing the torch down closer to the ground. "Here's something else," Bliss heard him say. "Funny how you can notice every little thing in this fine floury dust. His front left tire had a patch on it, and a bad one, too. See it? You can tell just what they did. Alden evidently ran the car out of the shed alone, ahead of his wife. She got in here at the side of the house, to save time, instead of going out the front way; they were going down the road the other way, anyway. His wheel came to rest with the patch squarely under it. That's why it shows so plain in this one place. Then he took his brake off and the car coasted back a little with the tilt of the ground. When he came forward again, the position of his wheel diverged a little, missed erasing its own former imprint. Bet they have trouble with that before the night's over."

He spoke as though it were just a trivial detail. But is anything, Bliss was to ask himself later, a trivial detail?

"Come on," Stillman concluded, pocketing his light, "let's go get the law and see what it looks like on the inside."

The constable's name was Cochrane, and they finally located him at his own home. "Evening," Stillman introduced himself, "I'm Stillman of the city police. I was wondering if there's some way we could get a look inside that Alden house. Their—er—stepdaughter has disappeared down in the city; she was supposed to have started for here, and this is just a routine check. Nothing against them. They seem to be out, and we have to make the next bus back."

Cochrane plucked at his throat judiciously. "Well, now, I guess I can accommodate you, as long as it's done in my presence. I'm the law around here, and if they've got nothing to hide, there's no reason why they should object. I'll drive ye back in my car. This feller here your subordinate, I s'pose?"

Stillman said, "Um," noncommittally, favored Bliss with a nudge. The constable would have probably balked at letting a man already wanted by the police into these people's house, they both knew, even if he was accompanied by a bona fide detective.

He stopped off at his office first to get a master key, came back with the remark: "This ought to do the trick." They were back at the Alden place once more inside of ten minutes, all told, from the time they had first left it.

Cochrane favored them with a sly grimace as they got out and went up to the house. "I'm sort of glad you fellers asked me to do this, at that. Fact is, we've all been curious about them folks ourselves hereabouts for a long time past. Kind of unsociable;

keep to themselves a lot. This is as good a time as any to see if
they got any skeletons in the closet."

Bliss shuddered involuntarily at the expression.

The constable's master key opened the door without any
great difficulty, and the three of them went in.

They looked in every room in the place from top to bottom,
and in every closet of every room, and not one of the "skeletons" the constable had spoken of turned up, either allegorical
or literal. There wasn't anything out of the way, and nothing to
show that anything had ever been out of the way, in this house.

In the basement, when they reached it, were a couple of
sagging, half-empty bags of cement in one corner, and pinkish
traces of brick dust and brick grit on the floor, but that was
easily accounted for. "Left over from when he was putting up
that wall along the roadside a while back, I guess," murmured
Cochrane.

They turned and went upstairs again. The only other discovery of any sort they made was not of a guilty nature, but simply
an indication of how long ago the occupants had left. Stillman
happened to knuckle a coffeepot standing on the kitchen range,
and it was still faintly warm from the residue of liquid left in it.

"They must have only just left before we got here," he said
to Bliss. "Missed them just by minutes."

"Funny; why did they wait until after dark to start on a long
trip like that? Why didn't they leave sooner?"

"That don't convict them of anything, just the same," Stillman maintained obdurately. "We haven't turned up a shred of
evidence that your wife ever saw the inside of this house. Don't
try to get around that."

The local officer, meanwhile, had gone outside to put some
water in his car. "Close the door good after you as you come
out," he called out to them.

They were already at the door, but Bliss unaccountably
turned and went back inside again. When Stillman followed
him a moment later, he was sitting there in the living-room

raking his fingers perplexedly through his hair.

"Come on," the detective said, as considerately as he could, "let's get going. He's waiting for us."

Bliss looked up at him helplessly. "Don't you get it? Doesn't this room bother you?"

Stillman looked around vaguely. "No. In what way? What's wrong with it? To me it seems clean, well kept, and comfortable. All you could ask for."

"There's something about it annoys me. I feel ill at ease in it. It's not *restful,* for some reason. And I have a peculiar feeling that if I could figure out *why* it isn't restful, it would help to partly clear up this mystery about Smiles."

Stillman sliced the edge of his hand at him scornfully. "Now you're beginning to talk plain crazy, Bliss. You say this room isn't restful. The room has nothing to do with it. It's you. You're all tense, jittery, about your wife. Your nerves are on edge, frayed to the breaking point. That's why the room don't seem restful to you. Naturally it don't. No room would."

Bliss kept shaking his head baffledly. "No. No. That may sound plausible, but I know that isn't it. It's not *me,* it's the room itself. I'll admit I'm all keyed up, but I noticed it already the other night when I wasn't half so keyed up. Another thing, I don't get it in any of the other rooms in this house, I only get it in here."

"I don't like the way you're talking; I think you're starting to crack up under the strain," Stillman let him know, but he hung around in the doorway for a few minutes, watching him curiously, while Bliss sat there motionless, clasped hands hanging from the back of his neck now.

"Did you get it yet?"

Bliss raised his head, shook it mutely, chewing the corner of his mouth. "It's one of those things; when you try too hard for it, it escapes you altogether. It's only when you're sort of not thinking about it, that you notice it. The harder I try to pin it down, the more elusive it becomes."

"Sure," said Stillman with a look of sympathetic concern, "and if you sit around in here brooding about it much more, I'll be taking you back with me in a straitjacket. Come on, we've only got ten more minutes to make that bus."

Bliss got reluctantly to his feet. "There it goes," he said. "I'll never get it now."

"Ah, you talk like these guys that keep trying to communicate with spirits through a ouija board," Stillman let him know, locking up the front door after them. "The whole thing was a wild-goose chase."

"No, it wasn't."

"Well, what'd we get out of it?"

"Nothing. But that doesn't mean it isn't around here waiting to be seen. It's just that we've missed seeing it, whatever it is."

"There's not a sign of her around that house. Not a sign of her ever having been there. Not a sign of violence."

"And I know that, by going away from here, we're turning our backs on whatever there is to be learned about what became of her. We'll never find out at the other end, in the city. I nearly had it, too, when I was sitting in there. Just as I was about to get it, it would slip away from me again. Talk about torture!"

Stillman lost his temper. "Will you lay off that room! If there was anything the matter with it, I'd notice it as well as you. My eyes are just as good, my brains are just as good. What's the difference between you and me?" The question was only rhetorical.

"You're a detective and I'm an architect," Bliss said inattentively, answering it as asked.

"Are you fellows going to stand there arguing all night?" the constable called from the other side of the wall.

They went out and got into the open car, started off. Bliss felt like groaning: "Good-by, Smiles." Just as they reached the turn of the road that would have swept the house out of sight once they rounded it, Stillman happened to glance back for no particular reason, at almost the very last possible moment that it could still be seen in a straight line behind them.

"Hold it," he ejaculated, thumbing a slim bar of light narrowed by perspective. "We left the lights on in that last room we were in."

The constable braked promptly. "Have to go back and turn them off, or they'll—"

"We haven't time now, we'll miss the bus," Stillman cut in. "It's due in six more minutes. Drive us down to the crossroads first, and then you come back afterward and put them out yourself."

"No!" Bliss cried out wildly, jumping to his feet. "This has a meaning to it! I'm not passing this up! I want another look at those lights; they're asking me to, they're begging me to!" Before either one of them could stop him, he had jumped down from the side of the car without bothering to unlatch the door. He started to run back up the road, deaf to Stillman's shouts and imprecations.

"Come back here, you welsher! You gave me your word of honor!"

A moment later the detective's feet hit the ground and he started after his prisoner. But Bliss had already turned in through the opening in the wall, was flinging himself bodily against the door, without waiting for any master key this time. The infuriated detective caught him by the shoulder, swung him violently around, when he had reached him.

"Take your hands off me!" Bliss said hoarsely. "I'm going to get in there!"

Stillman swung at him and missed. Instead of returning the blow, Bliss threw his whole weight against the door for the last time. There was a rending and splintering of wood, and it shot inward, leaving the whole lock intact against the frame. Bliss went flailing downward on his face into the hallway. He scrambled erect, reached the inner doorway, put his hand inside, and put the lights out without looking into the room.

"It's when they go on that counts," he panted.

The only reason Stillman wasn't grappling with him was that he couldn't locate him for a minute in the dark. The switch clicked a second time. Light flashed from the dazzlingly calcimined ceiling. Bliss was standing directly in the middle of the opening as it did so, just as he had been the first night.

Stillman was down the hall a few steps, couldn't see his face for a minute. "Well?" he asked.

Bliss turned to him without saying anything. The look on his face answered for him. He'd gotten what he wanted.

"Why, they're not in the center of the ceiling! They're offside. That's what made them seem glaring, unexpected. They took my eyes by surprise. I've got professionally trained eyes, remember. They didn't go on where I expected them to, but a little farther over. And now that I have that much, I have it all." He gripped Stillman excitedly by the biceps. "Now I see what's wrong with the room. Now I see why I found it so unrestful. It's out of true."

"What?"

"Out of proportion. Look. Look at that window. It's not in the center of that wall. And d'you see how cleverly they've tried to cover the discrepancy? A thin, skinny, up-and-down picture on the short side; a big, wide, fat one on the longer side. That creates an optical illusion, makes both sides seem even. Now come over here and look this way." He pulled the detective in after him, turned him around by the shoulder. "Sure, same thing with the door frame; that's not dead center, either. But the door opens inward into the room, swings to that short side and partly screens it, throws a shadow over it, so that takes care of that. What else? What else?"

He kept pivoting feverishly, sweeping his glance around on all sides. "Oh, sure, the rug. I was sitting here and I dropped some ashes and looked down at the floor. See what bothered me about that? Again there's an unbalance. See the margin of polished woodwork running around on three sides of it? And on the fourth side it runs right smack up against the baseboard of the wall. Your eye wants proportion, symmetry; it's got to have it in all things. If it doesn't get it, it's uncomfortable. It wants that dark strip of woodwork on all *four* sides, or else the rug should touch all four baseboards, like a carpet—"

He was talking slower and slower, like a record that's running down. Some sort of tension was mounting in him, gripping him, Stillman could tell by looking at him. He panted the last few words out, as if it took all his strength to produce them, and then his voice died away altogether, without a period.

"What're you getting so white around the gills for?" the detective demanded. "Suppose the room is lopsided, what then? Your face is turning all green—"

Bliss had to grab him by the shoulder for a minute for support. His voice was all furry with dawning horror. "Because—because—don't you see what it means? Don't you see *why* it's that way? One of these walls is a dummy wall, built out *in front* of the real one." His eyes were dilated with unbelieving horror. He clawed insensately at his own hair. "It all hangs together so damnably! He was a mason before he married her mother, I told you that. The storekeeper down at the crossroads said that Alden built a low brick wall in front of the house, 'just to keep in practice,' he guessed. No reason for it. It wasn't high enough for privacy, it didn't even run around all four sides of the plot.

"He didn't build it just to keep in practice! He did it to get the bricks in here from the contractor. More than he needed. He put it up just to have an excuse to order them. Who's going to count—Don't stand there! Get an ax, a crowbar; help me break this thing down! Don't you see what this dummy wall is for? Don't you see what we'll find—"

The detective had been slower in grasping it, but he finally got it, too. His own face went gray. "Which one is it?"

"It must be on this side, the side that's the shortest distance from the window, door, and light fixture." Bliss rushed up to it, began to pound it with his clenched fists, up and down, sounding it out. Sweat flew literally off his face like raindrops in a stiff wind.

The detective bolted out of the room, sent an excited yell at the open front door:

"Cochrane! Come in here, give us a hand, bring tools!"

Between the two of them they dug up a hatchet, a crowbar, cold chisel, and bung starter. "That wall," the detective explained tersely for the constable's benefit, without going into details. Cochrane didn't argue; one look at both their faces must have told him that some unspeakable horror was on the way to revelation.

Bliss was leaning sideways against it by now, perfectly still, head lowered almost as though he were trying to hear something through it. He wasn't. His head was lowered with the affliction of discovery. "I've found it," he said stifledly. "I've found—the place. Listen." He pounded once or twice. There was the flat impact of solidity. He moved farther over, pounded again. This time there was the deeper resonance of a partly, or only imperfectly, filled orifice. "Half bricks, with a hollow behind them. Elsewhere, whole bricks, mortar behind them."

Stillman stripped his coat off, spit on his hands. "Better get out of the room—in case you're right," he suggested, flying at it with the hatchet, to knock off the plaster. "Wait outside the door; we'll call you—"

"No! I've got to know, I've got to see. Three of us are quicker than two." And he began chipping off the plaster coating with the cutting edge of the chisel. Cochrane cracked it for them with the bung starter. A cloud of dust hovered about them while they hacked away. Finally, they had laid bare an upright, *coffin-shaped* segment of pinkish-white brickwork in the plaster finish of the wall.

They started driving the chisel in between the interstices of the brick ends, Stillman steadying it, Cochrane driving it home with the bung starter. They changed to the crowbar, started to work that as a lever, when they'd pierced a big enough space.

"Look out. One of them's working out."

A fragment of brick ricocheted halfway across the room, dropped with a thud. A second one followed. A third. Bliss started to claw at the opening with his bare nails, to enlarge it faster.

"You're only impeding us, we can get at it faster this way," Stillman said, pushing him aside. A gray fill of imperfectly dried clayey mortar was being laid bare. It was only a shell; flakes of it, like dried mud, had begun dropping off and out, some of their own weight, others with the impact of their blows, long before they had opened more than a "window" in the brickwork façade.

"Get back," Stillman ordered. His purpose was to protect Bliss from the full impact of discovery that was about to ensue.

Bliss obeyed him at last, staggered over to the other end of the room, stood there with his back to them as if he were looking out of the window. Only the window was farther over. A spasmodic shiver went down his back every so often. He could hear the pops and thuds as brick fragments continued to drop out of the wall under the others' efforts, then a sudden engulfing silence.

He turned his head just in time to see them lowering something from the niche in the wall. An upright something. A rigid, mummified, columnar something that resembled nothing so much as a log covered with mortar. The scant remainder of bricks that still held it fast below, down toward the floor, shattered, spilled down in a little freshet as they wrenched it free. A haze of kindly concealing dust veiled them from him. For a minute or two they were just white shadows working over something, and then they had this thing lying on the floor. A truncated thing without any human attributes whatever, like the mold around a cast metal statue—but with a core that was something else again.

"Get out of here, Bliss," Stillman growled. "This is no place for you!"

Wild horses couldn't have dragged Bliss away. He was numbed beyond feeling now, anyway. The whole scene had been one that could never again be forgotten by a man who had once lived through it.

"Not with that!" he protested, as he saw the crouching Stillman flick open the large blade of a penknife.

"It's the only thing I *can* use! Go out and get us some water, see if we can soften this stuff up a little, dissolve it."

When Bliss came back with a pail of it, Stillman was working away cautiously at one end of the mound, shaving a little with the knife blade, probing and testing with his fingers. He desisted suddenly, flashed the constable a mutely eloquent look, shifted up to the opposite end. Bliss, staring with glazed eyes, saw a stubby bluish-black wedge peering through where he had been working—the tip of a woman's shoe.

"Upside down at that," grunted Cochrane, trying not to let Bliss overhear him. The latter's teeth were chattering with nervous shock.

"I told you to get out of here!" Stillman flared for the third and last time. "Your face is driving me crazy!" With as little effect as before.

Fine wires seemed to hold some of it together, even after he had pared it with the knife blade. He wet the palms of his hands in the pail of water, kneaded and crumbled it between them in those places. What had seemed like stiff wires was strands of human hair.

"That's enough," he said finally in a sick voice. "There's someone there; that's all I wanted to be sure of. I don't know how to go about the rest of it, much; an expert'll have to attend to that."

"Them devils," growled Cochrane deep in his throat.

Bliss suddenly toppled down between them, so abruptly they both thought he had fainted for a minute. "Stillman!" he said in a low throbbing voice. He was almost leaning across the thing. "These wisps of hair— Look! They show through dark, bluish-black! *She was blond!* Like an angel. It's somebody else!"

Stillman nodded, held his forehead dazedly. "Sure, it must be. I don't have to go by that; d'you know what should have told me from the beginning? Your wife's only been missing since Tuesday night, three days ago. The condition of the mortar shows plainly that this job's been up for weeks past. Why, the paint on the outside of the wall would have hardly been dry yet,' let alone the fill in back of it. Apart from that, it would have been humanly impossible to put up such a job single-handed in three days. We both lost our heads; it shows you it doesn't pay to get excited.

"It's the mother, that's who it is. There's your answer for the discrepancy in the handwriting on the two notes, the snapshot, and that business about the nickname that puzzled you. Come on, stand up and lean on me, we're going to find out where he keeps his liquor. You need a drink if a man ever did!"

They found some in a cupboard out in the kitchen, sat down for a minute. Bliss looked as if he'd been pulled through a knothole. The constable had gone out on wobbly legs to get a breath of fresh air.

Bliss put the bottle down and started to look alive again.

"I think I'll have a gulp myself," Stillman said. "I'm not a drinking man, but that was one of the nastiest jobs in there just now I've ever been called on to participate in."

The constable rejoined them, his face still slightly greenish. He had a drink, too.

"How many of them were there when they first moved in here?" Stillman asked him.

"Only two. Only him and his wife, from first to last."

"Then you never saw her; they hid her from sight, that's all."

"They've been kind of stand-offish, no one's ever been inside the place until tonight."

"It's her, all right, the real mother," Bliss said, as soon as he'd gotten his mental equilibrium back. "I don't have to see the face, I know I'm right. No, no more. I'm O.K. now, and I want to be able to think clearly. Don't you touch any more of it, either, Still. That's who it must be. Don't you see how the whole things hangs together? Smiles *did* show up here Tuesday night, or rather in the early hours of Wednesday morning; I'm surer than ever of it now. You asked me, back at my house, for a motive that would overshadow that possible insurance one of mine. Well, here it is; this is it. She was the last one they expected to see, so soon after her own marriage to me. She walked in here and found an impostor in the place of her own mother, a stranger impersonating her. They had to shut her up quick, keep her from raising an alarm. There's your motive as far as Smiles is concerned."

"And it's a wow," concurred Stillman heartily. "The thing is, what've they done with her, where is she? We're no better off than before. She's not around here; we've cased the place from cellar to attic. Unless there's another of those trick walls that we've missed spotting."

"You're forgetting that what you said about the first one still goes. There hasn't been time enough to rig up anything that elaborate."

"I shouldn't have taken that drink," confessed Stillman.

"I'm convinced she *was* here, though, as late as Thursday night, and still alive in the place. Another of those tantalizing things just came back to me. There was a knock on one of the water pipes somewhere; I couldn't tell if it was upstairs or down. I bet she was tied up someplace, the whole time I was sitting here."

"Did you hear one or more than one?"

"Just one. The woman got right up and went out, I noticed, giving an excuse about getting a fresh handkerchief. They probably had her doped, or under some sedative."

"That's then, but now?"

"There's a lot of earth around outside, acres of it, miles of it," Cochrane put in morbidly.

"No, now wait a minute," Stillman interjected. "Let's get this straight. If their object was just to make her disappear, clean vanish, as in the mother's case, that would be one thing. Then I'm afraid we might find her lying somewhere around in that earth you speak of. But you're forgetting that her clothes turned up in your own furnace at home, Bliss—showing they didn't want her to disappear, they wanted to pin her death definitely on you."

"Why?"

"Self-preservation, pure and simple. With a straight disappearance, the investigation would have never been closed. In the end it might have been directed up this way, resulted in unearthing the first murder, just as we did tonight. Pinning it on you would have not only obviated that risk, but eliminated you as well—cleaned the slate for them. A second murder to safeguard the first, a legal execution to clinch the second. But —to pin it successfully on you, that body has to show up down around where you are, and not up here at all. The clothes were a forerunner of it."

"But would they risk taking her back to my place, knowing it was likely to be watched by you fellows, once they had denounced me to you themselves? That would be like sticking their own heads in a noose. They might know it would be kept under surveillance."

"No, it wouldn't have been. You see, your accidental switch to that hitchhike from the bus resulted in two things going wrong. We not only went out to your house to look for you when you didn't show up at the terminal, but, by going out there, we found the clothes in the furnace sooner than they wanted us to. I don't believe they were meant to be found until—the body was also in position."

"Then why make two trips, instead of just one? Why not take poor Smiles at the same time they took her clothes?"

"He had to make a fast trip in, the first time, to beat that bus. They may have felt it was too risky to take her along then. He also had to familiarize himself with your premises, find some way of getting in, find out if the whole thing was feasible or not before going ahead with it. They felt their call to us—it wasn't an accusation at all, by the way, but simply a request that we investigate—would get you out of the way, clear the coast for them. They expected you to be held and questioned for twenty-four, forty-eight hours, straight. They thought they'd given themselves a wide enough margin of safety. But your failure to take the bus telescoped it."

Bliss rose abruptly. "Do you think she's—yet?" He couldn't bring himself to mention the word.

"It stands to reason that they'd be foolish to do it until the last possible moment. That would increase the risk of transporting her a hundredfold. And they'd be crazy to do it anywhere else but on the exact spot where they intend her to be found eventually. Otherwise it would be too easy for us to reconstruct the fact that she was killed somewhere else and taken there afterward."

"Then the chances are she was still alive when they left here with her! There may still be time even now; she may still be alive! What are we sitting here like this for?"

They both bolted out together, but Bliss made for the front door, Stillman headed for the phone in the hall.

"What're you doing that for?"

"Phone in an alarm to city headquarters. How else can we hope to save her? Have them throw a cordon around your house—"

Bliss pulled the instrument out of his hands. "Don't! You'll only be killing her quicker that way! If we frighten them off, we'll never save her. They'll lose their heads, kill her anywhere and drop her off just to get rid of her. This way, at least we know it'll be in or somewhere around my house."

"But, man, do you realize the head start they've had?"

"We only missed them by five or ten minutes. Remember that coffeepot on the stove?"

"Even so, even with a State police escort, I doubt if we can get in under a couple of hours."

"And I say that we've got to take the chance! You noticed their tire treads before. He has a walloping bad patch, and he's never going to make that bad stretch on the road with it. I saw his car last night when it raced past, and he had no spares up. There's no gas station for miles around there. All that will cut down their head start."

"You're willing to gamble your wife's life against a flat tire?"

"There isn't anything else I *can* do. I'm convinced if you send an alarm ahead and have a dragnet thrown around my house, they'll scent it and simply shy away from there and go off someplace else with her where we *won't* be able to get to her in time, because we won't know where it is. Come on, we could be miles away already, for the time we've wasted talking."

"All right," snapped the detective, "we'll play it your way! Is this car of yours any good?" he asked Cochrane, hopping in.

"Fastest thing in these parts," said the constable grimly, slithering under the wheel.

"Well, you know what you've got to do with it: cut down their head start to nothing flat; less than nothing, you've got to get us there five minutes to the good."

"Just get down low in your seats and hang onto your back teeth," promised Cochrane. "What we just turned up in there happened in my jurisdiction, don't forget—and the law of the land gives this road to us tonight!"

It was an incredible ride; incredible for the fact that they stayed right side up on the surface of the road at all. The speedometer needle clung to stratospheric heights throughout. The scenery was just a blurred hiss on both sides of them. The wind pressure stung the pupils of their eyes to the point where they could barely hold them open. The constable, luckily, used glasses for reading and had happened to have them about him when they started. He put them on simply in order to make sure of staying on the road at all.

They had to take the bad stretch at a slower speed in sheer self-defense, in order not to have the same thing happen to them that they were counting on having happened to the Alden car. An intact tire could possibly get over it unharmed, but one that was already defective was almost sure to go out.

"Wouldn't you think he'd have remembered about this from passing over it last night, and taken precautions?" Stillman yelled above the wind at Bliss.

"He took a chance on it just like we're doing now. Slow up a minute at the first gas station after here, see if he got away with it or not." He knew that if he had, that meant they might just as well turn back then and there; Smiles was as good as dead already.

It didn't appear for another twenty minutes, even at the clip they had resumed once the bad stretch was past. With a flat, or until a tow car was sent out after anyone, it would have taken an hour or more to make it.

"Had a flat to fix, coming from our way, tonight?" Stillman yelled out at the attendant.

"And how!" the man yelled back, jogging over to them. "That was no flat! He wobbled up here with ribbons around his wheel. Rim all flattened, too, from riding so long on it."

"*He?*" echoed Stillman. "Wasn't there two women, or anyway one, with him?"

"No, just a fellow alone."

"She probably waited for him up the road out of sight with Smiles," Bliss suggested in an undertone, "to avoid being seen; then he picked them up again when the job was finished. Or if Smiles was able to walk, maybe they detoured around it on foot and rejoined the car farther down."

"Heavy-set man with a bull neck, and little eyes, and scraggly red hair?" the constable asked the station operator.

"Yeah."

"That's him. How long ago did he pull out of here?"

"Not more than an hour ago, I'd say."

"See? We've already cut their head start plenty," Bliss rejoiced.

"There's still too damn much of it to suit me," was the detective's answer.

"One of you take the wheel for the next lap," Cochrane said. "The strain is telling on me. Better put these on for goggles." He handed Stillman his reading-glasses.

The filling-station and its circular glow of light whisked out behind them and they were on the tear once more. They picked up a State police motorcycle escort automatically within the next twenty minutes, by their mere speed in itself; simply tapered off long enough to show their badges and make their shouts of explanation heard. This was all to the good, it cleared their way through such towns and restricted-speed belts as lay in their path. Just to give an idea of their pace, there were times, on the straightaway, when their escort had difficulty in keeping up with them. And even so, they weren't making good enough time to satisfy Bliss. He alternated between fits of optimism, when he sat crouched forward on the edge of the seat, fists clenched, gritting: "We'll swing it; we'll get there in time; I know it!" and fits of despair, when he slumped back on his shoulder blades and groaned, "We'll never make it! I'm a fool, I should have let you phone in ahead like you wanted to! Can't you make this thing *move* at all?"

"Look at that speedometer," the man at the wheel suggested curtly. "There's nowhere else for the needle to go but off the dial altogether! Take it easy, Bliss. They can't possibly tear along at this clip; we're official, remember. Another thing, once they get there, they'll do a lot of cagey reconnoitering first. That'll eat up more of their head start. And finally, even after they get at it, they'll take it slow, make all their preparations first, to make it look right. Don't forget, they think they've got all night; they don't know we're on their trail."

"And it's still going to be an awful close shave," insisted Bliss through tightly clenched teeth.

Their State police escort signed off at the city limits with a wave of the arm, a hairpin turn, and left them on their own.

They had to taper down necessarily now, even though traffic was light at this night hour. Bliss showed Stillman the shortcut over that would bring them up to his house from the rear. A block and a half away Stillman choked off their engine, coasted to a stealthy stop under the overshadowing trees, and the long grueling race against time was over—without their knowing as yet whether it had been successful or not.

"Now follow me," Bliss murmured, hopping down. "I hope we didn't bring the car in too close; sounds carry so at an hour like this."

"They won't be expecting us." One of Stillman's legs gave under him from his long motionless stint at the wheel; he had to hobble along slapping at it until he could get the circulation back into it. Cochrane brought up at the rear.

When they cleared the back of the house next door to Bliss's and could look through the canal of separation to the street out in front, Bliss touched his companions on the arm, pointed meaningly. The blurred outline of a car was visible, parked there under the same leafy trees where Stillman himself had hidden when he was waiting for Bliss. They couldn't make out its interior.

"Someone in it," Cochrane said, breathing hard. "I think it's a woman, too. I can see the white curve of a bare arm on the wheel."

"You take that car, we'll take the house; he must be in there with her long ago at this stage of the game," Stillman muttered. "Can you come up on it quietly enough so she won't have time to sound the horn or signal him in any way?"

"I'll see to it I do!" was the purposeful answer. Cochrane turned back like a wraith, left the two of them alone.

They couldn't go near the front of the house because of the lookout, and there was no time to wait for Cochrane to incapacitate her. "Flatten out and do like I do," Bliss whispered. "She's probably watching the street out there more than this lot behind the house." He crouched, with his chin nearly down to his knees, darted across the intervening space to the concealment provided by the back of his own house.

"We can get in through the kitchen window," Bliss instructed, when Stillman had made the switch-over after him.
"The latch never worked right. Give me a folder of matches,
and make a footrest with your hands."

When he was up with one foot on the outside of the sill, his
companion supporting the other, Bliss tore off and discarded
the sandpaper and matches adhering to it, used the cardboard
remainder as a sort of impromptu jimmy, slipping it down into
the seam between the two window halves, and pushing the
fastening back out of the way with it. A moment later he had
the lower pane up and was inside the room, stretching down his
hands to Stillman to help him up after him.

They both stood perfectly still there for a minute in the
gloom, listening for all they were worth. Not a sound reached
them, not a chink of light showed. Bliss felt a cold knife of doubt
stab at his heart.

"Is he in here at all?" He breathed heavily. "That may be
somebody else's car out there across the way."

At that instant there was the blurred but unmistakable sound
that loose, falling earth makes, dropping back into a hollow or
cavity. You hear it on the streets when a drainage ditch is being
refilled. You hear it in a cemetery when a grave is being covered up. In the silence of this house, in the dead of night, it had
a knell-like sound of finality. *Burial.*

Bliss gave a strangled gasp of horror, lurched forward in the
darkness. "He's already—through!"

The sound had seemed to come from somewhere underneath
them. Bliss made for the basement door. Stillman's heavy footfalls pounded after him, all thought of concealment past.

Bliss clawed open the door that gave down to the cellar, flung
it back. For a split second, and no more, dull-yellow light
gleamed up from below. Then it snuffed out, too quickly to
show them anything. There was pitch blackness below them, as
above, and an ominous silence.

Something clicked just over Bliss's shoulder, and the pale

moon of Stillman's torch glowed out from the cellar floor below them, started traveling around, looking for something to center on. Instantly a vicious tongue of flame spurted toward the parent orb, the reflector, and something flew past Bliss, went *spat* against the wall, as a thunderous boom sounded below.

Bliss could sense, rather than tell, that Stillman was raising his gun behind him. He clawed out, caught the cuff of the detective's sleeve, brought it down. "Don't! She may be down there somewhere in the line of fire!"

Something shot out over his shoulder. Not a gun or slug, but the torch itself. Stillman was trying to turn it into a sort of readymade star shell, by throwing it down there still lighted. The light pool on the floor streaked off like a comet, flicked across the ceiling, dropped down on the other side, and steadied itself against the far wall—with a pair of trouser legs caught squarely in the light, from the knees down. They buckled to jump aside out of the revealing beam, but not quickly enough. Stillman sighted his gun at a kneecap and fired. The legs jolted, wobbled, folded up forward toward the light, bringing a torso and head down into view on the floor. When the fall ended, the beam of the torch was weirdly centered on the exact crown of a bald head surrounded by a circular fringe of reddish hair. It rolled from side to side like a giant ostrich egg, screaming agonizedly into the cellar floor.

"I'll take him," Stillman grunted. "You put on that light!"

Bliss groped for the dangling light cord that had proved such a hindrance to them just now by being down in the center of the basement instead of up by the doorway where they could get at it. He snagged it, found the finger switch, turned it. Horror flooded the place at his touch, in piebald tones of deep black shadow and pale yellow. The shovel Alden had just started to wield when he heard them coming lay half across a mound of freshly disinterred earth. Near it were the flat flagstones that had topped it, flooring the cellar, and the pickax that had loosened them. He must have brought the tools with him in the car, for they weren't Bliss's.

And on the other side of that mound—the short but deep hole the earth had come out of. Alden must have been working away down here for some time, to get so much done singlehanded. And yet, though they had arrived before he'd finished, they were still too late—for in the hole, filling it to within an inch or two of the top, and fitting the sides even more closely, rested a deep old-fashioned trunk that had probably belonged to Smiles's mother and come down in the trunk compartment of the car. And four-square as it was, it looked ominously small for anyone to fit into—whole.

Bliss pointed down at it, moaned sickly. "She—she—"

He wanted to fold up and let himself topple inertly across the mound of earth before it. Stillman's sharp, whiplike command kept him upright. "Hang on! Coming!"

He had clipped the back of Alden's skull with his gun butt, to put him out of commission while their backs were turned. He leaped up on the mound of earth, and across the hole to the opposite side, then dropped down by the trunk, tugging at it.

"There's no blood around; he may have put her in alive. Hurry up, help me to get the lid up! Don't waste time trying to lift the whole thing out; just the lid. Get some air into it—"

It shot up between the two of them, and within lay a huddled bulk of sacking, pitifully doubled around on itself. *It was still moving feebly.* Fluttering spasmodically, rather than struggling any more.

The blade of the penknife Stillman had already used once before tonight flew out, slashed furiously at the coarse stuff. A contorted face was revealed through the rents, but not recognizable as Smiles's any more—a face black with suffocation, in which the last spark of life had been about to go out. And still might, if they didn't coax it back in a hurry.

They got her up out of it between them and straightened her out flat on the floor. Stillman sawed away at the short length of rope cruelly twisted around her neck, the cause of suffocation, severed it after seconds that seemed like centuries, unwound it, flung it off. Bliss, meanwhile, was stripping off the tattered remnants of the sacking. She was in a white silk slip.

Stillman straightened up, jumped for the stairs. "Breathe into her mouth like they do with choking kids. I'll send out a call for a Pulmotor."

But the battle was already won by the time he came trooping down again; they could both tell that, laymen though they were. The congested darkness was leaving her face little by little, her chest was rising and falling of its own accord, she was coughing distressedly, and making little whimpering sounds of returning consciousness. They carried her up to the floor above when the emergency apparatus arrived, nevertheless, just to make doubly sure. It was while they were both up there, absorbed in watching the Pulmotor being used on her, that a single shot boomed out in the basement under them, with ominous finality.

Stillman clapped a hand to his hip. "Forgot to take his gun away from him. Well, there goes one of Cochrane's prisoners!"

They ran for the basement stairs, stopped halfway down them, one behind the other, looking at Alden's still form lying there below. It was still face-down, in the same position as before. One arm, curved under his own body at chest level, and a lazy tendril of smoke curling up around his ribs, told the difference.

"What a detective I am!" Stillman said disgustedly.

"It's better this way," Bliss answered, tight lipped. "I think I would have killed him with my own bare hands, before they got him out of here, after what he tried to do to her tonight!"

By the time they returned upstairs again, Cochrane had come in with the woman. They were both being iodined and bandaged by an intern.

"What happened?" Stillman asked dryly. "Looks like she gave you more trouble than he gave us."

"Did you ever try to hang onto the outside of a wild car while the driver tried to shake you off? I'd gotten up to within one tree length of her, when the shots down in the basement tipped her off Alden was in for it. I just had time to make a flying tackle for the baggage rack before she was off a mile a minute. I had to work my way forward along the running-board, with her swerving and flinging around corners on two wheels. She finally piled up against a refuse-collection truck; dunno how it was we both weren't killed."

"Well, she's all yours, Cochrane," Stillman said. "But first I'm going to have to ask you to let me take her over to headquarters with me. You, too, Bliss." He looked at his watch. "I promised my lieutenant I'd be in with you by nine the latest, and I'm a stickler for keeping a promise. We'll be a little early, but unforeseen circumstances came up."

At headquarters, in the presence of Bliss, Stillman, Cochrane, the lieutenant of detectives, and the necessary police stenographer, Alden's accomplice was prevailed on to talk.

"My name is Irma Gilman," she began, "and I'm thirty-nine years old. I used to be a trained nurse on the staff of one of the large metropolitan hospitals. Two of my patients lost their lives through carelessness on my part, and I was discharged.

"I met Joe Alden six months ago. His wife was in ill health, so I moved in with them to look after her. Her first husband had left her well off, with slews of negotiable bonds. Alden had already helped himself to a few of them before I showed up, but now that I was there, he wanted to get rid of her altogether, so that we could get our hands on the rest. I told him he'd never get away with anything there, where everybody knew her; he'd have to take her somewhere else first. He went looking for a house, and when he'd found one that suited him, the place in Denby, he took me out to inspect it, without her, and palmed me off on the agent as his wife.

"We made all the arrangements, and when the day came to move, he went ahead with the moving van. I followed in the car with her after dark. That timed it so that we reached there late at night; there wasn't a soul around any more to see her go in. And from then on, as far as anyone in Denby knew, there were only two of us living in the house, not three. We didn't keep her locked up, but we put her in a bedroom at the back, where she couldn't be seen from the road, and put up a fine-meshed screen on the window. She was bed-ridden a good part of the time, anyway, and that made it easier to keep her presence concealed.

"He started to make his preparations from the moment we moved in. He began building this low wall out in front, as an excuse to order the bricks and other materials that he needed for the real work later on. He ordered more from the contractor than he needed, of course.

"Finally it happened. She felt a little better one day, came downstairs, and started checking over her list of bonds. He'd persuaded her when they were first married not to entrust them to a bank; she had them in an ordinary strongbox. She found out some of them were already missing. He went in there to her, and I listened outside the door. She didn't say very much, just: 'I thought I had more of these thousand-dollar bonds.' But that was enough to show us that she'd caught on. Then she got up very quietly and went out of the room without another word.

"Before we knew it, she was on the telephone in the hall— trying to get help, I suppose. She didn't have a chance to utter a word, he was too quick for her. He jumped out after her and pulled it away from her. He was between her and the front door, and she turned and went back upstairs, still without a sound, not even a scream. Maybe she still did not realize she was in bodily danger, thought she could get her things on and get out of the house.

"He said to me, 'Go outside and wait in front. Make sure there's no one anywhere in sight, up and down the road or in the fields.' I went out there, looked, raised my arm and dropped it, as a signal to him to go ahead. He went up the stairs after her.

"You couldn't hear a thing from inside. Not even a scream, or a chair falling over. He must have done it very quietly. In a while he came down to the door again. He was breathing a little fast and his face was a little pale, that was all. He said, 'It's over. I smothered her with one of the bed pillows. She didn't have much strength.' Then he went in again and carried her body down to the basement. We kept her down there while he went to work on this other wall; as soon as it was up high enough, he put her behind it and finished it. He repainted the whole room so that one side wouldn't look too new.

"Then, without a word of warning, the girl showed up the other night. Luckily, just that night Joe had stayed down at the hotel late having a few beers. He recognized her as she got off the bus and brought her out with him in the car. That did away with her having to ask her way of anyone. We stalled her for a few minutes by pretending her mother was fast asleep, until I had time to put a sedative in some tea I gave her to drink. After that it was easy to handle her; we put her down in the basement and kept her doped down there.

"Joe remembered, from one of her letters, that she'd said her husband had insured her, so that gave us our angle. The next day I faked a long letter to her and mailed it to the city, as if she'd never shown up here at all. Then when Bliss came up looking for her, I tried to dope him, too, to give us a chance to transport her back to his house during his absence, finish her off down there, and pin it on him. He spoiled that by passing the food up and walking out on us. The only thing left for us to do after that was for Joe to beat the bus in, plant her clothes ahead of time, and put a bee in the police's bonnet. That was just to get Bliss out of the way, so the coast would be left clear to get her in down there.

"We called his house from just inside the city limits when we got down here with her tonight. No one answered, so it seemed to have worked. But we'd lost a lot of time on account of that blowout. I waited outside in the car, with her covered up on the floor, drugged. When Joe had the hole dug, he came out and took her in with him.

"We thought all the risk we had to run was down at this end. We were sure we were perfectly safe up at the other end; Joe had done such a bang-up job on that wall. I still can't understand how you caught onto it so quick."

"I'm an architect, that's why," Bliss said grimly. "There was something about that room that bothered me. It wasn't on the square."

Smiles was lying in bed when Bliss went back to his own house, and she was pretty again. When she opened her eyes and looked up at him, they were all crinkly and smiling just as they used to be.

"Honey," she said, "it's so good to have you near me. I've learned my lesson. I'll never walk out on you again."

"That's right, you stay where you belong, with Ed," he said soothingly, "and nothing like that'll ever happen to you again."

In 1929, while in Hollywood working on the film version of his novel *Children of the Ritz,* the young Woolrich after a whirlwind courtship married a producer's daughter. She left him after a few weeks and the marriage was later annulled. Not too many years thereafter Woolrich wrote "You'll Never See Me Again," in which the protagonist's marriage takes the same course (up to a point) as the author's. Those who know Woolrich's work superficially might expect his treatment of the theme would be mawkish, self-pitying, sickeningly sentimental; in reality, the story is among his very finest, his control is complete at almost every step of the way, and his narrative magic defies you to lay the tale down unfinished.

II

DEATH AND THE CITY

Dusk to Dawn

It was just beginning to grow dark when Lew Stahl went in to the Odeon picture theater where his roommate Tom Lee worked as an usher. It was exactly 6:15.

Lew Stahl was twenty-five, out of work, dead broke and dead honest. He'd never killed anyone. He'd never held a deadly weapon in his hand. He'd never even seen anyone lying dead. All he wanted to do was see a show, and he didn't have the necessary thirty cents on him.

The man on door duty gave him a disapproving look while Lew was standing out there in the lobby waiting for Tom to slip him in free. Up and down, and up again the doorman walked like "You gotta nerve!" But Stahl stayed pat. What's the use having a pal as an usher in a movie house if you can't cadge an admission now and then?

Tom stuck his head through the doors and flagged him in. "Friend of mine, Duke," he pacified the doorman.

"Are you liable to get called down for this?" Stahl asked as he followed him in.

Tom said, "It's O.K. as long as the manager don't see me. It's between shows anyway; everyone's home at supper. The place is so empty you could stalk deer up in the balcony. Come on up, you can smoke up there."

Stahl trailed him upstairs, across a mezzanine, and out into the darkness of the sloping balcony. Tom gave the aisle his torch so his guest could see. On the screen below a woman's head was wavering, two or three times larger than life. A metallic voice clanged out, echoing sepulchrally all over the house, like a modern Delphic Oracle. "Go back, go back!" she said. "This is no place for you!"

Her big luminous eyes seemed to be looking right at Lew Stahl as she spoke. Her finger came out and pointed, and it seemed to aim straight at him and him alone. It was weird; he almost stopped in his tracks, then went on again. He hadn't eaten all day; he figured he must be woozy, to think things like that.

Tom had been right; there was only one other guy in the whole balcony. Kids went up there, mostly, during the matinees, and they'd all gone home by now, and the evening crowd hadn't come in yet.

Stahl picked the second row, sat down in the exact middle of it. Tom left him, saying, "I'll be back when my five-minute relief comes up."

Stahl had thought the show would take his mind off his troubles. Later, thinking back over this part of the evening, he was willing to admit he hadn't known what real trouble was yet. But all he could think of was he hadn't eaten all day, and how hungry he was; his empty stomach kept his mind off the canned story going on on the screen.

He was beginning to feel weak and chilly, and he didn't even have a nickel for a cup of hot coffee. He couldn't ask Tom for any more money, not even that nickel. Tom had been tiding him over for weeks now, carrying his share of the room rent, and all he earned himself was a pittance. Lew Stahl was too decent, too fair-minded a young fellow, to ask him for another penny, not even if he dropped in his tracks from malnutrition. He couldn't get work. He couldn't beg on the street corner; he hadn't reached that point yet. He'd rather starve first. Well, he was starving already.

He pulled his belt over a notch to make his stomach seem tighter, and shaded his hand to his eyes for a minute.

That lone man sitting back there taking in the show had looked prosperous, well fed. Stahl wondered if he'd turn him down, if he went back to him and confidentially asked him for a dime. He'd probably think it was strange that Stahl should be in a movie house if he were down and out, but that couldn't be helped. Two factors emboldened him in this maiden attempt at panhandling. One was it was easier to do in here in the dark than out on the open street. The second was there was no one around to be a witness to his humiliation if the man bawled him out. If he was going to tackle him at all, he'd better not sit thinking about it any longer, he'd better do it before the house started to fill up, or he knew he'd never have the nerve. You'd be surprised how difficult it is to ask alms of a stranger when you've never done it before, what a psychological barrier separates the honest man from the panhandler.

Lew Stahl turned his head and glanced back at the man, to try and measure his chances ahead of time. Then he saw to his surprise that the man had dozed off in his seat; his eyes were closed. And suddenly it was no longer a matter of asking him for money, it was a matter of taking it, helping himself while the man slept. Tom had gone back to the main floor, and there was no one else up there but the two of them. Before he knew it he had changed seats, was in the one next to the sleeper.

"A dollar," he kept thinking, "that's all I'll take, just a dollar, if he has a wallet. Just enough to buy a big thick steak and . . ."

His stomach contracted into a painful knot at the very thought, and salt water came up into his mouth, and his hunger was so great that his hand spaded out almost of its own accord and was groping toward the inner pocket of the man's coat.

The coat was loosely buttoned and bulged conveniently open the way the man was sitting, and Stahl's downward dipping fingers found the stiff grained edge of a billfold without much trouble. It came up between his two fingers, those were all he'd dared insert in the pocket, and it was promisingly fat and heavy.

A second later the billfold was down between Lew's own legs and he was slitting it edgewise. The man must have been sweating, the leather was sort of sticky and damp on one side only, the side that had been next to his body. Some of the stickiness adhered to Stahl's own fingertips.

It was crammed with bills, the man must have been carrying between seventy and eighty dollars around with him. Stahl didn't count them, or even take the whole batch out. True to his word, he peeled off only the top one, a single, tucked it into the palm of his hand, started the wallet back where he'd found it.

It was done now; he'd been guilty of his first criminal offense.

He slipped it in past the mouth of the pocket, released it, started to draw his arm carefully back. The whole revere on that side of the man's coat started to come with Lew's arm, as though the two had become glued together. He froze, held his arm where it was, stiffly motionless across the man's chest. The slightest move, and the sleeper might awake. The outside button on Lew's cuff had freakishly caught in the man's lapel button hole, twisted around in some way. And it was a defective, jagged-edged button, he remembered that now well; it had teeth to hang on by.

He tried to slip his other hand in between the lapel and his arm and free them. There wasn't enough room for leverage. He tried to hold the man's lapel down and pull his own sleeve free, insulating the tug so it wouldn't penetrate the sleeper's consciousness. The button held on, the thread was too strong to break that way.

It was the most excruciating form of mental agony. Any minute he expected the sleeper's eyes to pop open and fasten on him accusingly. Lew had a disreputable penknife in his pocket. He fumbled desperately for it with one hand, to cut the damnable button free. He was as in a strait-jacket; he got it out of his right-hand pocket with his left hand, crossing one arm over the other to do so. At the same time he had to hold his prisoned arm rigid, and the circulation was already leaving it.

He got the tarnished blade open with his thumbnail, jockeyed the knife around in his hand. He was sweating profusely. He started sawing away at the triple-ply button-thread that had fastened them together. The knife blade was none too keen, but it finally severed. Then something happened; not the thing he'd dreaded, not the accusation of suddenly opened eyes. Something worse. The sleeper started sagging slowly forward in his seat. The slight vibration of the hacking knife must have been transmitted to him, dislodged him. He was beginning to slop over like a sandbag. And people don't sleep like that, bending over at the floor.

Stahl threw a panicky glance behind him. And now accusing eyes did meet him, from four or five rows back. A woman had come in and taken a seat some time during the past minute or two. She must have seen the jockeying of a knife blade down there, she must have wondered what was going on. She was definitely not looking at the screen, but at the two of them.

All presence of mind gone, Lew tried to edge his crumpled seat-mate back upright, for appearances' sake. Pretend to her they were friends sitting side by side; anything, as long as she didn't suspect he had just picked his pocket. But there was something wrong—the flabbiness of muscle, the lack of heavy breathing to go with a sleep so deep it didn't break no matter how the sleeper's body fell. That told him all he needed to know; he'd been sitting quietly for the past five minutes next to a man who was either comatose or already a corpse. Someone who must have dropped dead during the show, without even falling out of his seat.

He jumped out into the aisle past the dead man, gave him a startled look, then started excitedly toward the back to tip off Tom or whomever he could find. But he couldn't resist looking back a second time as he went chasing off. The woman's eyes strayed accusingly after him as he flashed by.

Tom was imitating a statue against the wall of the lounge, beside the stairs.

"Come back there where I was sitting!" Lew panted. "There's a guy next to me out cold, slopping all over!"

"Don't start any disturbance," Tom warned in an undertone.

He went back with Lew and flashed his torch quickly on and off, and the face it high-lighted wasn't the color of anything living; it was like putty.

"Help me carry him back to the restroom," Tom said under his breath, and picked him up by the shoulders. Lew took him by the legs, and they stumbled back up the dark aisle with the corpse.

The woman who had watched all this was feverishly gathering up innumerable belongings, with a determination that almost approached hysteria, as if about to depart forthwith on a mission of vital importance.

Lew and Tom didn't really see it until they got him in the restroom and stretched him out on a divan up against the wall —the knife-hilt jammed into his back. It didn't stick out much, was in at an angle, nearly flat up against him. Sidewise from right to left, but evidently deep enough to touch the heart; they could tell by looking at him he was gone.

Tom babbled, "I'll get the manager! Stay here with him a

second. Don't let anyone in!" He grabbed up a "No Admittance" sign on his way out, slapped it over the outside doorknob, then beat it.

Lew had never seen a dead man before. He just stood there, and looked and looked. Then he went a step closer, and looked some more. "So that's what it's like!" he murmured inaudibly. Finally Lew reached out slowly and touched him on the face, and cringed as he met the clammy feel of it, pulled his hand back and whipped it down, as though to get something off it. The flesh was still warm and Lew knew suddenly he had no time alibi.

He threw something over that face and that got rid of the awful feeling of being watched by something from the other world. After that Lew wasn't afraid to go near him; he just looked like a bundle of old clothes. The dead man was on his side, and Lew fiddled with the knife-hilt, trying to get it out. It was caught fast, so he let it alone after grabbing it with his fingers from a couple of different directions.

Next he went through his pockets, thinking he'd be helping to identify him.

The man was Luther Kemp, forty-two, and he lived on 79th Street. But none of that was really true any more, Lew thought, mystified; he'd left it all behind. His clothes and his home and his name and his body and the show he'd paid to see were here. But where the hell had he gone to, anyway? Again that weird feeling came over Lew momentarily, but he brushed it aside. It was just that one of the commonest things in life—death—was still strange to him. But after strangeness comes familiarity, after familiarity, contempt.

The door flew open, and Tom bolted in again, still by himself and panting as though he'd run all the way up from the floor below. His face looked white, too.

"C'mere!" he said in a funny, jerky way. "Get outside, hurry up!"

Before Lew knew what it was all about, they were both outside, and Tom had propelled him all the way across the dimly lighted lounge to the other side of the house, where there was another branch of the staircase going down. His grip on Lew's arm was as if something were skewered through the middle of it.

"What's the idea?" Lew managed to get out.

Tom jerked his head backward. "You didn't really do that, did you? To that guy."

Lew nearly dropped through the floor. His answer was just a welter of words.

Tom telescoped it into "No," rushed on breathlessly, "Well, then all the more reason for you to get out of here quick! Come on down on this side, before they get up here! I'll tell you about it down below."

Half-way down, on the landing, Tom stopped a second time, motioned Lew to listen. Outside in the street some place the faint, eery wail of a patrol-car siren sounded, rushed to a crescendo as it drew nearer, then stopped abruptly, right in front of the theater itself.

"Get that? Here they are now!" Tom said ominously, and rushed Lew down the remaining half-flight, around a turn to the back, and through a door stenciled "Employees Only."

A flight of steps led down to a sub-basement. He pushed Lew ahead of him the rest of the way down, but Tom stayed where he was. He pitched something that flashed, and Lew caught it adroitly before he even knew what it was. A key.

"Open twelve, and switch to my blue suit," Tom said. "Leave that gray of yours in the locker."

Lew took a step back toward him, swung his arm back. "I haven't done anything! What's the matter with you? You trying to get me in a jam?"

"You're in one already, I'm trying to get you out of it!" Tom snapped. "There's a dame out there hanging onto the manager's neck with both arms, swears she saw you do it. Hallucinations, you know the kind! Says he started falling asleep on you,

and you gave him a shove, one word led to another, then you
knifed him. Robbed him, too. She's just hysterical enough to
believe what she's saying herself."

Lew's knees gave a dip. "But holy smoke! Can't you tell 'em
I was the first one told you about it myself? I even helped you
carry him back to the rest-room! Does that look like I—"

"It took me long enough to get this job," Tom said sourly. "If
the manager finds out I passed you in free—what with this
giving his house a bad name and all—I can kiss my job good-by!
Think of my end of it, too. Why do they have to know anything
about you? You didn't do it, so all right. Then why be a chump
and spend the night in a station-house basement? By tomorrow
they'll probably have the right guy and it'll be all over with."

Lew thought of that dollar he had in his pocket. If he went
back and let them question him, they'd want to know why he
hadn't paid his way in, if he had a buck on him. That would tell
them where the buck came from. He hated to pony up that
buck now that he had it. And he remembered how he'd tam-
pered with the knife-hilt, and vaguely knew there was something called fingerprints by which they had a way of telling who
had handled it. And then the thought of bucking that woman
—from what he remembered of the look on her face—took
more nerve than he had. Tom was right, why not light out and
steer clear of the whole mess, as long as he had the chance? And
finally this argument presented itself: If they once got hold of
him and believed he'd done it, that might satisfy them, they
mightn't even try to look any further, and then where would he
be? A clear conscience doesn't always make for courage, sometimes it's just the other way around. The mystic words "circumstantial evidence" danced in front of his eyes, paralyzing him.

"Peel!" Tom said. "The show breaks in another couple minutes. When you hear the bugles bringing on the newsreel, slip
out of here and mingle with the rest of them going out. She's
tagged you wearing a gray suit, so it ought to be easy enough
to make it in my blue. They won't think of busting open the

lockers to look. Wait for me at our place." Then Tom ducked
out and the passageway-door closed noiselessly after him.

Lew didn't give himself time to think. He jumped into the
blue suit as Tom had told him to, put on his hat and bent the
brim down over his eyes with fingers that were shaking like
ribbons in a breeze. He was afraid any minute that someone,
one of the other ushers, would walk in and catch him. What was
he going to say he was doing in there?

He banged the locker closed on his own clothes, just as a
muffled *ta-da* came from the screen outside. In another minute
there were feet shuffling by outside the door and the hum of
subdued voices. He edged the door open, and pressed it shut
behind him with his elbow. The few movie goers who were
leaving were all around him, and he let them carry him along
with them. They didn't seem to be aware, down below here, of
what had happened up above so short a time ago. Lew didn't
hear any mention of it.

It was like running the gauntlet. There were two sets of doors
and a brightly lighted lobby in between. One of the detectives
was standing beside the doorman at the first set of doors. The
watchful way he scanned all faces told Lew what he was. There
was a second one outside the street doors. He kept looking so
long at each person coming out—that told what he was.

Lew saw them both before he got up to them, through the
clear glass of the inner doors. The lights were on their side, Lew
was in the dark, with the show still going on in back of him. His
courage froze, he wanted to stay in there where he was. But if
he was going to get out at all, now was the time, with the
majority of the crowd, not later on when he'd be more conspicuous.

One thing in his favor was the color of his suit. He saw the
detectives stopping all the men in gray and motioning them
aside; he counted six being sidetracked before he even got out
into the lobby. They weren't interfering with anyone else.

But that ticket-taker was a bigger risk than either of the plainclothes-men. So was the doorman. Before he'd gone in he'd been standing right under both their eyes a full five minutes waiting for Tom to come down. He'd gone in without paying, and that had burned the ticket-taker up. But going past them, Lew had to walk slow, as slowly as everyone else was walking, or he'd give himself away twice as quick. He couldn't turn around now and go back any more, either; he was too close to the detectives and they'd notice the maneuver.

A clod-hopper in front of him came to his rescue just when he thought he was a goner. The clod-hopper stepped backward unexpectedly to take a look at something, and his whole hoof landed like a stone-cutter's mallet across Lew's toes. Lew's face screwed up uncontrollably with pain, and before he straightened it out again, the deadly doorman's gaze had swept harmlessly over it without recognition, and Lew was past him and all he could see was the back of Lew's head.

Lew held his breath. Nothing happened. Right foot forward, left foot forward, right foot forward. . . . The lobby seemed to go on for miles. Someone's hand touched him, and the mercury went all the way down his spine to the bottom, but it was only a woman close behind him putting on her gloves.

After what seemed like an eternity of slow motion, he was flush with the street-doors at last. Only that second detective out there to buck now, and he didn't worry him much. He drifted through with all the others, passed close enough to the detective to touch him, and he wasn't even looking at Lew. His eyes were on the slap-slap of the doors as they kept swinging to and fro with each new egress.

Lew moved from under the revealing glare of the marquee lights into the sheltering darkness. He didn't look back, and presently the hellish place was just a blob of light far behind him. Then it wasn't even that any more.

He kept dabbing his face, and he felt limp in the legs for a long time afterwards. He'd made it, but whew! what an experience; he said to himself that he'd undergone all the emotions of a hunted criminal, without having committed a crime.

Tom and Lew had a cheap furnished room in a tenement about half an hour's walk away. Lew walked there unhesitatingly now, in a straight line from the theater. As far as he could see, it was all over, there wasn't anything to worry about now any more. He was out of the place, and that was all that mattered. They'd have the right guy in custody, maybe before the night was over, anyway by tomorrow at the latest.

He let himself into the front hallway with the key, climbed the stairs without meeting anyone, and closed the room door behind him. He snapped on the fly-blown bulb hanging from the ceiling, and sat down to wait for Tom.

Finally the clock rotated to 11 P.M. The last show broke at 11:30, and when Tom got here it would be about twelve.

About the time Tom should have been showing up, a newspaper delivery truck came rumbling by, distributing the midnight edition. Lew saw it stop by a stand down at the corner and dump out a bale of papers. On an impulse he got up and went down there to get one, wondering if it would have the story in it yet, and whether they'd caught the guy yet. He didn't open it until he'd got back.

It hadn't made a scare-head, but it had made a column on the front page. "Man stabbed in movie house; woman sees crime committed." Lew got sort of a vicarious thrill out of it for a minute, until he read further along. They were *still* looking for a guy just his height and build, wearing a gray suit, who had bummed his way in free. The motive—probably caught by the victim in the act of picking his pocket while he slept. In panic, Lew doused the light.

From then on it was a case of standing watching from behind the drawn shade and standing listening behind the door, and wearing down the flooring in between the two places like a caged bear. He knew he was crazy to stay there, and yet he didn't know where else to go. It would be even crazier, he thought, to roam around in the streets, he'd be sure to be picked up before morning. The sweat came out of every pore hot, and then froze cold. And yet never once did the idea of walking back there of his own accord, and saying to them, "Well, here I am; I didn't do it," occur to him. It looked too bad now, the way he'd changed clothes and run out. He cursed Tom for putting him up to it, and himself for losing his head and listening to him. It was too late now. There's a finality about print, especially to a novice; because that paper said they were looking for him, it seemed to kill Lew's last chance of clearing himself once and for all.

He didn't see Tom coming, although he was glancing out through a corner of the window the whole time; Tom must have slunk along close to the building line below. There was a sudden scurry of quick steps on the stairs, and Tom was trying the door-knob like fury. Lew had locked it on the inside when he'd put the light out.

"Hurry up, lemme in!" Tom panted. And then when Lew had unlocked the door: "Leave that light out, you fool!"

"I thought you'd never get here!" Lew groaned. "What'd they do, give a midnight matinee?"

"Down at Headquarters, they did!" Tom said resentfully. "Hauled me down there and been holding me there ever since! I'm surprised they let me go when they did. I didn't think they were gonna." He threw the door open. "You gotta get out of here!"

"Where'm I gonna go?" Lew wailed. "You're a fine louse of a friend!"

"Suppose a cop shows up here all of a sudden and finds you here, how's that gonna make it look for me? How do I know I wasn't followed coming back here? Maybe that's why they let me go!"

Tom kept trying to shoulder Lew out in the hall, and Lew kept trying to hang onto the door-frame and stay in; in a minute more they would have been at it hot and heavy, but suddenly there was a pounding at the street-door three floors below. They both froze.

"I knew it!" Tom hissed. "Right at my heels!"

The pounding kept up. "Coming! Wait a minute, can't you?" a woman's voice said from the back, and bedroom-slippers went slapping across the oilcloth. Lew was out on the landing now of his own accord, scuttling around it like a mouse trying to find a hole.

Tom jerked his thumb at the stairs going up. "The roof!" he whispered. "Maybe you can get down through the house next door." But Lew could see all he cared about was that he was out of the room.

Tom closed the door silently but definitely. The one below opened at the same instant, to the accompaniment of loud beefs from the landlady, that effectively covered the creaking of the stairs under Lew's flying feet.

"The idea, getting people out of their beds at this hour! Don't you tell me to pipe down, detective or no detective! This is a respectable hou—"

Lew was up past the top floor by that time. The last section was not inclined stairs any more but a vertical iron ladder, ending just under a flat, lead skylight, latched on the underside. He flicked the latch open, climbed up a rung further and lowered his head out of the way, with the thing pressing across his shoulders like Atlas supporting the world. He had to stay there like that till he got in out of the stair-well; he figured the cop would hear the thing creak and groan otherwise. It didn't have hinges, had to be displaced bodily.

There was a sudden commanding knock at Tom's door on the third, and an "Open up here!" that left no room for argument. Tom opened it instantly, with a whining, "What do you want this time?" Then it closed again, luckily for Lew, and the detective was in there with Tom.

Lew heaved upward with all his might, and felt as if he were lifting the roof bodily off the house. His head and shoulders pushed through into the open night. He caught the two lower corners of the thing backhanded so it wouldn't slam down again as he slipped out from under it, and eased it down gently on its frame. Before the opening had quite closed, though, he had a view down through it all the way to the bottom of the stair-well, and half-way along this, at the third floor, a face was sticking out over the bannister, staring up at him. The landlady, who had stayed out there eavesdropping. She had the same bird's-eye view of him that he had of her.

He let go the skylight cover and pounded across the graveled tar toward the next roof for all he was worth. The detective would be up here after him in a minute now.

The dividing line between the two roofs was only a knee-high brick parapet easy enough to clear, but after that there was only one other roof, instead of a whole block-length of them. Beyond the next house was a drop of six stories to a vacant lot. The line of roofs, of varying but accessible heights, lay behind him in the other direction; he'd turned the wrong way in the dark. But it didn't matter, he thought, as long as he could get in through the twin to the skylight he'd come out of.

He couldn't. He found it by stubbing his toe against it and falling across it, rather than with the help of his eyes. Then when he knelt there clawing and tugging at it, it wouldn't come up. Latched underneath like the first one had been!

There wasn't any time to go back the other way now. Yellow light showed on the roof behind him as the detective lifted the trap. First a warning thread of it, then a big gash, and the dick was scrambling out on the roof-top. Lew thought he saw a gun in his hand, but he didn't wait to find out. There was a three-foot brick chimney a little ways behind Lew. He darted behind it while his pursuer's head was still turned up the other way. But the gravel under him gave a treacherous little rattle as he carried out the maneuver.

There was silence for a long time. He was afraid to stick his head out and look. Then there was another of those little give-away rustles, not his this time, coming from this same roof, from the other side of the chimney.

Then with a suddenness that made him jump, a new kind of planet joined the stars just over his head, blazed out and spotted him from head to foot. A pocket-torch. Lew just pressed his body inward, helpless against the brick work.

"Come on, get up," the detective's voice said without any emotion, somewhere just behind the glare. To Lew it was like the headlight of a locomotive; he couldn't see a thing for a minute. He straightened up, blinking; even thought he was going to be calm and resigned for a minute. "I didn't do it," he said. "Honest, I didn't do it! Gimme a break, will you?"

The detective said mockingly that he would, sure he would, using an expression that doesn't bear repetition. He collared Lew with one hand, by both sides of his coat at once, pulling the reveres together close up under Lew's chin. Then he balanced the lighted torch on the lip of the chimney-stack, so that it stayed pointed at Lew and drenched him all over. Then he frisked him with that hand.

"I tell you I was just sitting next to him! I didn't touch him, I didn't put a finger on him!"

"And that's why you're hiding out on the roof, is it? Changed your suit, too, didn't you? I'll beat the truth out of you, when I get you where we're going!"

It was that, and the sudden sight of the handcuffs twinkling in the rays of the torch, that made Lew lose his head. He jerked backwards in the detective's grip, trying to get away from him. His back brushed the brick work. The flashlight went out suddenly, and went rattling all the way down inside the chimney. Lew was wedged in there between the detective and the stack. He raised the point of his knee suddenly, jabbed it upward between them like a piston. The detective let go Lew's collar, the manacles fell with a clink, and he collapsed at Lew's feet, writhing and groaning. Agonized as he was, his hand sort of flailed helplessly around, groping for something; Lew saw that even in the dark. Lew beat him to it, tore the gun out of his pocket, and pitched it overhand and backwards. It landed way off somewhere behind Lew, but stayed on the roof.

The detective had sort of doubled up in the meantime, like a helpless beetle on its back, drawing his legs up toward his body. They offered a handle to grab him by. Lew was too frightened to run away and leave him, too frightened that he'd come after him and the whole thing would start over. It was really an excess of fright that made him do it; there is such a thing. He grabbed the man around the ankles with both hands, started dragging him on his back across the gravel toward the edge of the roof, puffing, "You're not gonna get *me!* You're not gonna get *me!* You're not taking *me* with ya while I know it!"

Toward the side edge of the building he dragged the detective. He didn't bother looking to see what was below; just let go the legs, spun the detective around on his behind, so that the loose gravel shot out from under him in all directions, grabbed him by the shoulders, and pushed him over head-first. The dick didn't make a sound. Lew didn't know if he was still conscious or had fainted by now from the blow in the groin Lew had given him. Then he was snatched from sight as if a powerful magnet had suddenly pulled him down.

Then Lew did a funny thing. The instant after the detective was gone, Lew stretched out his arms involuntarily toward where he'd been, as if to grab him, catch him in time to save him. As though he hadn't really realized until then the actual meaning of what he was doing. Or maybe it was his last inhibition showing itself, before it left him altogether. A brake that would no longer work was trying to stop him after it was too late. The next minute he was feeling strangely light-headed, dizzy. But not dizzy from remorse, dizzy like someone who's been bound fast and is suddenly free.

Lew didn't look down toward where the man had gone, he looked up instead—at the stars that must have seen many another sight like the one just now, without blinking.

"Gosh, it's easy!" he marveled, openmouthed. "I never knew before how easy it is to kill anyone! Twenty years to grow 'em, and all it takes is one little push!"

He was suddenly drunk with some new kind of power, undiscovered until this minute. The power of life and death over his fellowmen! Everyone had it, everyone strong enough to raise a violent arm, but they were afraid to use it. Well, he wasn't! And here he'd been going around for weeks living from hand to mouth, without any money, without enough food, when everything he wanted lay within his reach all the while! He *had* been green all right, and no mistake about it!

Death had become familiar. At seven it had been the most mysterious thing in the world to him, by midnight it was already an old story.

"Now let 'em come after me!" he thought vindictively, as he swayed back across the roof toward the skylight of the other house. "Now I've given 'em a real reason for trying to nab me!" And he added grimly, "If they can!"

Something flat kicked away from under his foot, and he stopped and picked up the gun that he'd tossed out of reach. He looked it over after he was through the skylight and there was light to examine it by. He'd never held one in his hand before. He knew enough not to squint down the bore, and that was about all he knew.

The stair-well was empty; the landlady must have retreated temporarily to her quarters below to rouse her husband, so he wouldn't miss the excitement of the capture and towing away. Lew passed Tom's closed door and was going by it without stopping, going straight down to the street and the new career that awaited him in the slumbering city, when Tom opened it himself and looked out. He must have heard a creak and thought it was the detective returning, thought Lew, and figured a little bootlicking wouldn't hurt any.

"Did you get him—?" Tom started to say. Then he saw who it was, and saw what Lew was holding in his hand.

Lew turned around and went back to him. "No, he didn't get me," he said, ominously quiet, "I got him." He went in and closed the door of the room after him. He kept looking at Tom, who backed away a little.

"Now you've finished yourself!" Tom breathed, appalled.

"You mean I'm just beginning," Lew said.

"I'm going to get out of here!" Tom said, in a sudden flurry of panic, and tried to circle around Lew and get to the door.

Lew waved him back with the gun. "No, you're not, you're going to stay right where you are! What'd you double-cross me for?"

Tom got behind a chair and hung onto it with both hands— as though that was any good! Then almost hysterically, as he read Lew's face: "What's the matter, ya gone crazy? Not *me*, Lew! Not *me!*"

"Yes, you!" Lew said. "You got me into it. You knew they'd follow you. You led 'em to me. But they still don't know what I look like—but you do! That one went up there after me can't tell now what I look like, but you still can! They can get me on sight, while you're still around."

Tom was holding both palms flat out toward Lew, as though Lew thought they could stop or turn aside a bullet! Tom had time to get just one more thing out: "You're not human at all!"

Then Lew pulled the trigger and the whole room seemed to lift with a roar, as though blasting were going on under it. The gun bucked Lew back half a step; he hadn't known those things had a kick to them. When he looked through the smoke, Tom's face and shoulders were gone from behind the chair, but his forearms were still hanging across the top of it, palms turned downward now, and all the fingers wiggling at once. Then they fell off it, went down to join the rest of him on the floor.

Lew watched him for a second, what he could see of him. Tom didn't move any more. Lew shook his head slowly from side to side. "It sure is easy all right!" he said to himself. And this had been even less dramatic than the one up above on the roof.

Familiarity with death had already bred contempt for it.

He turned, pitched the door open, and went jogging down the stairs double-quick. Doors were opening on every landing as he whisked by, but not a move was made to stop him—which was just as well for them. He kept the gun out in his hand the whole time and cleared the bottom steps with a short jump at the bottom of each flight. Bang! and then around to the next.

The landlady had got herself into a bad position. She was caught between him and the closed street-door as he cleared the last flight and came down into the front hall. If she'd stayed where she belonged, Lew said to himself, she could have ducked back into her own quarters at the rear when he came down. But now her escape was cut off. When she saw it was Lew, and not the detective, she tried to get out the front way. She couldn't get the door open in time, so then she tried to turn back again. She dodged to one side to get out of Lew's way, and he went to that side too. Then they both went to the other side together and blocked each other again. It was like a game of puss-in-the-corner, with appalled faces peering tensely down the stair-well at them.

She was heaving like a sick cat in a sand-box, and Lew decided she was too ludicrous to shoot. New as he was at the game of killing, he had to have dignity in his murders. He walloped her back-handed aside like a gnat, and stepped over her suddenly upthrust legs. She could only give a garbled description of him any way.

The door wasn't really hard to open, if you weren't frightened, like Lew wasn't now. Just a twist of the knob and a wrench. A voice shrieked down inanely from one of the upper floors, "Get the cops! He's killed a fellow up here!" Then Lew was out in the street, and looking both ways at once.

A passerby who must have heard the shot out there had stopped dead in his tracks, directly opposite the doorway on the other side of the street, and was gawking over. He saw Lew and called over nosily: "What happened? Something wrong in there?"

It would have been easy enough to hand him some stall or other, pretend Lew was himself looking for a cop. But Lew had this new contempt of death hot all over him.

"Yeah!" he snarled viciously. "I just shot a guy! And if you stand there looking at me like that, you're gonna be the next!"

He didn't know if the passerby saw the gun or not in the dark, probably not. The man didn't wait to make sure, took him at his word. He bolted for the nearest corner. *Scrunch*, and he was gone!

"There," Lew said to himself tersely, "is a sensible guy!"

Black window squares here and there were turning orange as the neighborhood began belatedly to wake up. A lot of interior yelling and tramping was coming from the house Tom and Lew had lived in. He made for the corner opposite from the one his late questioner had fled around, turned it, and slowed to a quick walk. He put the gun away; it stuck too far out of the shallow side-pocket of Tom's suit, so he changed it to the inner breast-pocket, which was deeper. A cop's whistle sounded thinly behind him, at the upper end of the street he'd just left.

A taxi was coming toward him, and he jumped off the side-walk and ran toward it diagonally. The driver tried to swerve without stopping, so he jumped up on the running-board and wrenched the wheel with his free hand. He had the other spaded into his pocket over the gun again. "Turn around, you're going downtown with me!" he said. A girl's voice bleated in the back. "I've got two passengers in there already!" the driver said, but he was turning with a lurch that nearly threw Lew off.

"I'll take care of that for you!" he yanked the back door open and got in with them. "Out you go, that side!" he ordered. The fellow jumped first, as etiquette prescribed, but the girl clung to the door-strap, too terrified to move, so Lew gave her a push to help her make up her mind. "Be a shame to separate the two of you!" he called after her. She turned her ankle, and went down kerplunk and lay there, with her escort bending over her in the middle of the street.

"Wh-where you want me to g-go with you, buddy?" chattered the driver.

"Out of this neighborhood fast," Lew said grimly.

He sped along for a while, then whined: "I got a wife and kids, buddy—"

"You're a very careless guy," Lew said to that.

He knew they'd pick up his trail any minute, what with those two left stranded in the middle of the street to direct them, so he made for the concealing labyrinth of the park, the least policed part of the city.

"Step it down a little," he ordered, once they were in the park. "Take off your shoes and throw them back here." The driver's presence was a handicap, and Lew had decided to get rid of him, too. Driving zig-zag along the lane with one hand, the cabbie threw back his shoes. One of them hit Lew on the knee as it was pitched through the open slide, and for a minute Lew nearly changed his mind and shot him instead, as the easiest way out after all. The cabbie was half dead with fright by this time, anyway. Lew made him take off his pants, too, and then told him to brake and get out.

Lew got in at the wheel. The driver stood there on the asphalt in his socks and shirt-tails, pleading, "Gee, don't leave me in the middle of the park like this, buddy, without my pants and shoes, it'll take me all night to get out!"

"That's the main idea," Lew agreed vindictively, and added: "You don't know how lucky you are! You're up against Death's right-hand man. Scram, before I change my mind!"

The cabbie went loping away into the dark, like a bow-legged scarecrow and Lew sat at the wheel belly-laughing after him. Then he took the cab away at top speed, and came out the other end about quarter of an hour later.

He was hungry, and decided the best time to eat was right

then, before daylight added to the risk and a general alarm had time to circulate. The ability to pay, of course, was no longer a problem in this exciting new existence that had begun for him tonight. He picked the most expensive place open at that hour, an all-night delicatessen, where they charged a dollar for a sandwich and named it after a celebrity. A few high-hats were sitting around having bacon and eggs in the dim, artificial blue light that made them look like ghosts.

He left the cab right at the door and sat down where he could watch it. A waiter came over who didn't think much of him because he didn't have a boiled shirt. He ran his finger down the list and picked a five-dollar one.

"What's a Jimmy Cagney? Gimme one of them."

"Hard-boiled egg with lots of paprika." The waiter started away.

Lew picked up a glass of water and sloshed it across the back of his neck. "You come back here! Do that over, and say sir!" he snarled.

"Hard-boiled egg with lots of paprika, sir," the waiter stuttered, squirming to get the water off his backbone.

When he was through, Lew leaned back in his chair and thumbed him over. "How much do you take in here a night?"

"Oh, around five hundred when it's slow like this." He took out a pad and scribbled "5.00" at the bottom, tore it off and handed it to Lew.

"Lend me your pencil," Lew said. He wrote "Pay me" in front of it, and rubbed out the decimal point. "I'll take this over to the cashier myself," he told the waiter.

Then as he saw the waiter's glance sweep the bare table-top disappointedly, "Don't worry, you'll get your tip; I'm not forgetting you."

Lew found the tricky blue lighting was a big help. It made everyone's face look ghastly to begin with and you couldn't tell when anyone suddenly got paler. Like the cashier, when he looked up from reading the bill Lew presented and found the

bore of the gun peering out from Lew's shirt at him like some
kind of a bulky tie pin.

He opened the drawer and started counting bills out. "Quit
making your hands shake so," Lew warned him out of the corner of his mouth, "and keep your eyes down on what you're
doing, or you're liable to short-change me!"

Lew liked doing it that way, adding to the risk by standing
there letting the cashier count out the exact amount, instead of
just cleaning the till and lamming. What was so hectic about a
hold-up, he asked himself. Every crime seemed so simple, once
you got the hang of it. He was beginning to like this life, it was
swell!

There were thirty or so bucks left in the drawer when the
cashier got through. But meanwhile the manager had got curious about the length of time Lew had been standing up there
and started over toward them. Lew could tell by his face he
didn't suspect even yet, only wanted to see if there was some
difficulty. At the same time Lew caught sight of the waiter
slinking along the far side of the room, toward the door in back
of him. He hadn't been able to get over to the manager in time,
and was going to be a hero on his own, and go out and get a cop.

So Lew took him first. The waiter was too close to the door
already for there to be any choice in the matter. Lew didn't
even aim, just fired what he'd heard called a snap-shot. The
waiter went right down across the doorsill, like some new kind
of a lumpy mat. Lew didn't even feel the thing buck as much
as when he'd shot Tom. The cashier dropped too, as though the
same shot had felled him. His voice came up from the bottom
of the enclosure, "There's your money, don't shoot me, don't
shoot me!" Too much night-work isn't good for a guy's guts,
Lew mused.

There was a doorman outside on the sidewalk. Lew got him
through the open doorway just as he got to the curb, in the act
of raising his whistle to his lips. He stumbled, grabbed one of the
chromium stanchions supporting the entrance canopy, and

went slipping down like a fireman sliding down a pole. The manager ducked behind a table, and everyone else in the place went down to floor-level with him, as suddenly as though they were all puppets jerked by strings. Lew couldn't see a face left in the room; just a lot of screaming coming from behind empty chairs.

Lew grabbed up the five hundred and sprinted for the door. He had to hurdle the waiter's body and he moved a little as Lew did so, so he wasn't dead. Then Lew stopped just long enough to peel off a ten and drop it down on him. "There's your tip, chiseler!" Lew hollered at him, and beat it.

Lew couldn't get to the cab in time, so he had to let it go, and take it on foot. There was a car parked a few yards in back of it, and another a length ahead, that might have blocked his getting it out at the first try, and this was no time for lengthy extrications. A shot came his way from the corner, about half a block up, and he dashed around the next one. Two more came from that, just as he got to the corner ahead, and he fired back at the sound of them, just on general principle. He had no aim to speak of, had never held one of the things in his hand until that night.

He turned and sprinted down the side street, leaving the smoke of his shot hanging there disembodiedly behind him like a baby cloud above the sidewalk. There were two cops by now, but the original one was in the lead and he was a good runner. He quit shooting and concentrated on taking Lew the hard way, at arms' length. Lew turned his head in time to see him tear through the smoke up there at the corner and knock it invisible. He was a tall limber guy, must have been good in the heats at police games, and he came hurtling straight toward Death. Tick, tick, tick, his feet went, like a very quick clock.

A fifth shot boomed out in that instant, from ahead of Lew this time, down at the lower corner. Somebody had joined in from that direction, right where Lew was going toward. They had him sewn up now between them, on this narrow sidestreet.

One in front, two behind him—and to duck in anywhere was curtains.

Something happened, with that shot, that happens once in a million years. The three of them were in a straight line—Lew in the middle, the sprinter behind him, the one who had just fired coming up the other way. Something spit past Lew's ear, and the tick, tick behind him scattered into a scraping, thumping fall—*plump!*—and stopped. The runner had been hit by his own man, up front.

He didn't look, his ears had seen the thing for him. He dove into a doorway between the two of them. Only a miracle could save him, and it had no more than sixty seconds in which to happen, to be any good.

His star, beaming overtime, made it an open street door, indicative of poverty. The street was between Second and Third Avenues, and poverty was rampant along it, the same kind of poverty that had turned Lew into a ghoul, snatching a dollar from a dead man's pocket, at six-thirty this night. He punched three bell-buttons as he flashed by.

"If they come in here after me," he sobbed hotly, "there's going to be shooting like there never was before!" And they would, of course. The header-offer down at Second, who had shot his own man, must have seen which entrance he'd dived for. Even if he hadn't, they'd dragnet all of them.

Lew reached in his pocket as he took the stairs, brought out a fistful of the money and not the gun for once. At least a hundred's worth came up in his paw. One of the bills escaped, fluttered down the steps behind him like a green leaf. What's ten, or even twenty, when you've got sixty seconds to buy your life?

"In there!" One of the winded, surviving cops' voices rang out clearly, penetrated the hall from the sidewalk. The screech of a prowl car chimed in.

He was holding the handful of green dough up in front of him, like the olive branch of the ancients, when the first of the three doors opened before him, second-floor front. A man with a curleycue mustache was blinking out as he raced at him.

"A hundred bucks!" Lew hissed. "They're after me! Here, hundred bucks if you lemme get in your door!"

"Whassa mat'?" he wanted to know, startled wide awake.

"Cops! Hundred bucks!" The space between them had been used up, Lew's whole body hit the door like a projectile. The man was holding onto it on the inside, so it wouldn't give. The impact swung Lew around sideways, he clawed at it with one hand, shoved the bouquet of money into the man's face with the other. "Two hundred bucks!"

"Go 'way!" the man cried, tried to close Lew out. Lew had decided to shoot him out of the way if he couldn't buy his way in.

A deep bass voice came rumbling up behind him. *"Che cosa, Mario?"*

"Two hundred bucks," Lew strangled, reaching for the gun with his left hand.

"Due cento dollari!" The door was torn away from him, opened wide. An enormous, mustached, garlicky Italian woman stood there. "Issa good? Issa rill?" Lew jammed them down her huge bosom as the quickest way of proving their authenticity. Maybe Mario Jr. had had a run-in with cops about breaking a window or swiping fruit from a pushcart; maybe it was just the poverty. She slapped one hand on her chest to hold the money there, grabbed Lew's arm with the other. *"Si! Vene presto!"* and spat a warning *"Silenzio! La porta!"* at her reluctant old man.

She pounded down the long inner hall, towing Lew after her. The door closed behind them as the stairway outside was started vibrating with ascending feet—flat feet.

The bedroom was pitch black. She let go of him, gave him a push sideways and down, and he went sprawling across an enormous room-filling bed. A cat snatched itself out of the way and jumped down. He hoisted his legs up after him, clawed, pulled a garlicky quilt up to his chin. He began to undress hectically under it, lying on his side. She snapped a light on and was standing there counting the money. *"Falta cento—"* she growled aggressively.

"You get the other hundred after they go 'way." He stuck his hand out under the cover, showed it to her. He took the gun out and showed her that too. "If you or your old man give me away—!"

Pounding had already begun at their door. Her husband was standing there by it, not making a sound. She shoved the money down under the same mattress Lew was on. He got rid of his coat, trousers and shoes, pitched them out on the other side of him, just as she snapped out the light once more. He kept the gun and money with him, under his body.

The next thing he knew, the whole bed structure quivered under him, wobbled, all but sank flat. She'd got in alongside of him! The clothes billowed like sails in a storm, subsided. She went, "Ssst!" like a steam radiator, and the sound carried out into the hall. Lew heard the man pick up his feet two or three times, plank them down again, right where he was standing, to simulate trudging toward the door. Then he opened it, and they were in. Lew closed his eyes, spaded one hand under him and kept it on the gun.

"Took you long enough!" a voice said at the end of the hall. "Anyone come in here?"

"Nome-body."

"Well, we'll take a look for ourselves! Give it the lights!"

The lining of Lew's eyelids turned vermilion, but he kept them down. The mountain next to him stirred, gyrated. *"Che cosa, Mario?"*

"Polizia, non capisco."

Kids were waking up all over the place, in adjoining rooms, adding to the anvil chorus. It would have looked phony to go on sleeping any longer in that racket. Lew squirmed, stretched, blinked, yawned, popped his eyes in innocent surprise. There were two cops in the room, one of them standing still, looking at him, the other sticking his head into a closet.

Lew had black hair and was sallow from undernourishment, but he didn't know a word of Italian.

"Who's this guy?" the cop asked.

"Il mio fratello." Her brother. The volume of noise she and Mario and the kids were making covered him.

The first cop went out. The second one came closer, pulled the corner of the covers off Lew. All he saw was a skinny torso in an undershirt. Lew's outside shirt was rolled in a ball down by his feet. His thumb found and went into the hollow before the trigger underneath him. If he said "Get up outa there," those would be the last words he ever said.

He said, "Three in a bed?" disgustedly. "Sure y'ain't got your grandfather in there, too? These guineas!" He threw the covers back at Lew and went stalking out.

Lew could hear him through the open door tramp up the stairs after the others to the floor above. A minute later their heavy footsteps sounded on the ceiling right above his head.

A little runty ten-year-old girl peered in at him from the doorway. He said, "Put that light out! Keep them kids outa here! Leave the door open until they go! Tell your old man to stand there rubber-necking out, like all the others are doing!"

They quit searching in about fifteen minutes, and Lew heard them all go trooping down again, out into the street, and then he could hear their voices from the sidewalk right under the windows.

"Anything doing?" somebody asked.

"Naw, he musta got out through the back yard and the next street over."

"O'Keefe hurt bad?"

"Nicked him in the dome, stunned him, that was all." So the cop wasn't dead.

When Mario came out the front door at eight-thirty on his way to the barber shop where he worked, his "brother-in-law"

was with him, as close to him as sticking plaster. Lew had on an
old felt hat of Mario's and a baggy red sweater that hid the coat
of Tom's blue suit. It would have looked too good to come
walking out of a building like that on the way to work. That red
sweater had cost Lew another fifty. The street looked normal,
one wouldn't have known it for the shooting gallery it had been
at four that morning. They walked side by side up toward Second, past the place where O'Keefe had led with his chin, past
the corner where the smoke of Lew's shot had hung so ghostily
in the lamplight. There was a newsstand open there now, and
Lew bought a paper. Then he and Mario stood waiting for
the bus.

It drew up and Lew pushed Mario on alone, and jerked his
thumb at the driver. It went sailing off again, before Mario had
time to say or do anything, if he'd wanted to. It had sounded to
Lew, without knowing Italian, as though the old lady had been
coaching Mario to get a stranglehold on the rest of Lew's
money. Lew snickered aloud, ran his hand lightly over the
pocket where the original five-hundred was intact once more.
It had been too good to miss, the chance she'd given him of
sneaking it out of the mattress she'd cached it under and putting it back in his pocket again, while her back was turned.
They'd had all their trouble and risk for nothing.

Lew made tracks away from there, went west as far as Third
and then started down that. He stayed with the sweater and hat,
because they didn't look out of character on Third. The cops
had seen him in the blue suit when they chased him from
Rubin's; they hadn't seen him in this outfit. And no matter how
the *signora* would blaze when she found out how Lew had
gypped them, she couldn't exactly report it to the police, and
tell them what he was wearing, without implicating herself and
her old man.

But there was one thing had to be attended to right off, and
that was the matter of ammunition. To the best of Lew's calcu-
lations (and so much had happened, that they were already

pretty hazy) he had fired four shots out of the gun from the time he had taken it over from the dick on the roof. One at Tom, two in Rubin's, and one on the street when they'd been after him. There ought to be two left in it, and if the immediate future was going to be like the immediate past, he was going to need a lot more than that. He not only didn't know where any could be bought, he didn't even know how to break the thing and find out how many it packed.

He decided a pawnshop would be about the best bet, not up here in the mid-town district, but down around the lower East Side or on the Bowery somewhere. And if they didn't want to sell him any, he'd just blast and help himself.

He took a street car down as far as Chatham Square. He had a feeling that he'd be safer on one of them than on the El or the subway; he could jump off in a hurry without waiting for it to stop, if he had to. Also, he could see where he was going through the windows and not have to do too much roaming around on foot once he alighted. He was a little dubious about hailing a cab, dressed the way he now was. Besides, he couldn't exactly tell a hackman, "Take me to a pawnshop." You may ride in a taxi coming out of one, you hardly ride in a taxi going to one.

He went all the way to the rear end and opened the newspaper. He didn't have to hunt it up. This time it *had* made a scare-head. "One-Man Crime Wave!" And then underneath, "Mad dog gunman still at large somewhere in city." Lew looked up at the oblivious backs of the heads up forward, riding on the same car with Lew. Not one of them had given him a second glance when he'd walked down the aisle in the middle of all of them just now. And yet more than one must be reading that very thing he was at the moment; he could see the papers in their hands. That was he, right in the same trolley they were, and they didn't even know it! His contempt for death was beginning to expand dangerously toward the living as well, and the logical step beyond that would be well past the confines of sanity—a superman complex.

Fortunately, he never quite got to it. Something within this same paper itself checked it, before it got well started. Two things that threw cold water over it, as it were. They occurred within a paragraph of each other, and had the effect of deflating his ego almost to the point at which it had been last night, before he'd touched that dead man's face in the theater restroom. The first paragraph read: "The police, hoping that young Tom Lee might unknowingly provide a clue to the suspect's whereabouts, arranged to have him released at Headquarters shortly after midnight. Detective Walter Daly was detailed to follow him. Daly trapped Stahl on the roof of a tenement, only to lose his balance and fall six stories during the scuffle that ensued. He was discovered unconscious but still alive sometime after the young desperado had made good his second escape, lying with both legs broken on an ash-heap in a vacant lot adjoining the building."

That was the first shock. Still alive, eh? And he'd lost his balance, huh? A line or two farther on came the second jolt:

"Stahl, with the detective's gun in his possession, had meanwhile made his way down the stairs and brutally shot Lee in his room. The latter was rushed to the hospital with a bullet wound in his neck; although his condition is critical, he has a good chance to survive. . . ."

Lew let the thing fall to the floor and just sat there, stunned. Tom wasn't dead either! He wasn't quite as deadly as he'd thought he was; death wasn't so easy to dish out, not with the aim he seemed to have. A little of his former respect for death came back. Step one on the road to recovery. He remembered that waiter at Rubin's, flopping flat across the doorway; when he'd jumped over him, he'd definitely cringed—so he hadn't finished him either. About all he'd really managed to accomplish, he said to himself, was successfully hold up a restaurant, separate a cab driver from his pants and his machine, and outsmart the cops three times—at the theater, on the roof, and in the Italians' flat. Plenty for one guy, but not enough to turn him into a Manhattan Dillinger by a long shot.

A lot of his self-confidence had evaporated and he couldn't seem to get it back. There was a sudden, sharp increase of nervousness that had been almost totally lacking the night before.

He said to himself, "I need some bullets to put into this gun! Once I get them, I'll be all right, that'll take away the chills, turn on the heat again!"

He spotted a likely looking hockshop, and hopped off the car.

He hurried in through the swinging doors of the pawnshop and got a lungful of camphor balls. The proprietor came up to him on the other side of the counter. He leaned sideways on his elbow, tried to stop the shaking that had set in, and said: "Can you gimme something to fit this?" He reached for the pocket he'd put the gun in.

The proprietor's face was like a mirror. Expectancy, waiting to see what it was; then surprise, at how white his customer was getting; then astonishment, at why Lew should grip the counter like that, to keep from falling.

It was gone, it wasn't there any more. The frisking of the rest of his pockets was just reflex action; the emptiness of the first one told the whole story. He thought he'd outsmarted that Italian she-devil; well, she'd outsmarted him instead! Lifted the gun from him while she was busy seeming to straighten this old red sweater of her husband's on him. And the motive was easy to guess: So that Mario wouldn't be running any risk when he tried to blackmail Lew out on the street for the rest of the five hundred, like she'd told him to. Lew had walked a whole block with him, ridden all the way down here, and never even missed it until now! A fine killer he was!

He could feel what was left of his confidence crumbling away inside him, as though this had been the finishing touch it needed. Panic was coming on. He got a grip on himself; after all, he had five hundred in his pocket. It was just a matter of buying another gun and ammunition, now.

"I wanna buy a revolver. Show me what you've got."

"Show me your license," the man countered.

"Now, listen," he was breathing hard, "just skip that part of it. I'll pay you double." He brought out the money.

"Yeah, skip it," the proprietor scoffed. "And then what happens to me, when they find out where you got it? I got myself to think of."

Lew knew he had some guns; the very way he spoke showed he did. He sort of broke. "For the love of Gawd, lemme have a gun!" he wailed.

"You're snowed up, mac," he said. "G'wan, get out of here."

Lew clenched his teeth. "You lemme have a gun, or else—" And he made a threatening gesture toward the inside of his coat. But he had nothing to threaten with; his hand dropped limply back again. He felt trapped, helpless. The crumbling away kept on inside him. He whined, pleaded, begged.

The proprietor took a step in the direction of the door. "Get out of here now, or I'll call the police! You think I want my license taken away?" And then with sudden rage, "Where's a cop?"

Police. Cops. Lew turned and powdered out like a streak.

And Lew knew then what makes a killer; not the man himself, just the piece of metal in his hand, fashioned by men far cleverer than he. Without that, just a snarling cur, no match even for a paunchy hockshop owner.

Lew lost track of what happened immediately after that. Headlong, incessant flight—from nothing, to nothing. He didn't actually run, but kept going, going, like a car without a driver, a ship without a rudder.

It was not long after that he saw the newspaper. Its headline screamed across the top of the stand where it was being peddled. "Movie Murderer Confesses." Lew picked it up, shaking all over.

The manager of Tom's theater. Weeks, his name was. Somebody'd noticed that he'd been wearing a different suit during the afternoon show than the one he'd had on earlier. The seat behind Kemp's, the dead man's, had had chewing gum on it. They'd got hold of the suit Weeks had left at the dry-cleaner's, and that had chewing gum on the seat of the trousers, too. He'd come in in a hurry around six, changed from one to the other right in the shop, the tailor told them. He'd had one there, waiting to be called for. He admitted it now, claimed the man had been breaking up his home.

Lew dropped the paper and the sheets separated, fell across his shoes.

It stuck to his shoe and Lew was like someone trudging through snow. "Movie Murderer Confesses—Murderer Confesses—Confesses. . . ."

Subconsciously he must have known where he was going, but he wasn't aware of it, was in a sort of fog in the broad daylight. The little blue and white plaque on the lamp-post said "Center Street." He went slowly down it. He walked inside between the two green lamps at the police station entrance and went up to the guy at the desk and said, "I guess you people are looking for me. I'm Lew Stahl."

Somehow, Lew knew it would be better if they put him away for a long while, the longer the better. He had learned too much that one night, got too used to death. Murder might be a habit that, once formed, would be awfully hard to break. Lew didn't want to be a murderer.

Night, death, the city; a mood of mingled seediness and terror; a little guy trapped in the Depression and running for his life—these ingredients become magic in Woolrich's hands, as you have just seen. The story's structure is similar to that of the much better-known "Murder Always Gathers Momentum" (*Detective Fiction Weekly*, 12/14/40), and the evocation and creative use of the inside of a movie house also appear in "Double Feature" (*Detective Fiction Weekly*, 5/15/36); but Woolrich didn't mechanically repeat himself, he reworked his material thoroughly, and over the years he contributed at least as much as Hammett and Chandler (who also reworked material regularly) toward making the pulps the repository of staggeringly good stories that they were and still are.

Murder at the Automat

Nelson pushed through the revolving-door at twenty to one in the morning, his squadmate, Sarecky, in the compartment behind him. They stepped clear and looked around. The place looked funny. Almost all the little white tables had helpings of food on them, but no one was at them eating. There was a big black crowd ganged up over in one corner, thick as bees and sending up a buzz. One or two were standing up on chairs, trying to see over the heads of the ones in front, rubbering like a flock of cranes.

The crowd burst apart, and a cop came through. "Now, stand back. Get away from this table, all of you," he was saying.

"There's nothing to see. The man's dead—that's all."

He met the two dicks halfway between the crowd and the door. "Over there in the corner," he said unnecessarily. "Indigestion, I guess." He went back with them.

They split the crowd wide open again, this time from the outside. In the middle of it was one of the little white tables, a dead man in a chair, an ambulance doctor, a pair of stretcher-bearers, and the automat manager.

"He gone?" Nelson asked the interne.

"Yep. We got here too late." He came closer so the mob wouldn't overhear. "Better send him down to the morgue and have him looked at. I think he did the Dutch. There's a white streak on his chin, and a half-eaten sandwich under his face spiked with some more of it, whatever it is. That's why I got in touch with you fellows. Good night," he wound up pleasantly and elbowed his way out of the crowd, the two stretcher-bearers tagging after him. The ambulance clanged dolorously outside, swept its fiery headlights around the corner, and whined off.

Nelson said to the cop: "Go over to the door and keep everyone in here, until we get the three others that were sitting at this table with him."

The manager said: "There's a little balcony upstairs. Couldn't he be taken up there, instead of being left down here in full sight like this?"

"Yeah, pretty soon," Nelson agreed, "but not just yet."

He looked down at the table. There were four servings of food on it, one on each side. Two had barely been touched. One had been finished and only the soiled plates remained. One was hidden by the prone figure sprawled across it, one arm out, the other hanging limply down toward the floor.

"Who was sitting here?" said Nelson, pointing to one of the unconsumed portions. "Kindly step forward and identify yourself." No one made a move. "No one," said Nelson, raising his voice, "gets out of here until we have a chance to question the three people that were at this table with him when it happened."

Someone started to back out of the crowd from behind. The woman who had wanted to go home so badly a minute ago, pointed accusingly. *"He* was—that man there! I remember him distinctly. He bumped into me with his tray just before he sat down."

Sarecky went over, took him by the arm, and brought him forward again. "No one's going to hurt you," Nelson said, at sight of his pale face. "Only don't make it any tougher for yourself than you have to."

"I never even saw the guy before," wailed the man, as if he had already been accused of murder, "I just happened to park my stuff at the first vacant chair I—" Misery liking company, he broke off short and pointed in turn. *"He* was at the table, too! Why doncha hold him, if you're gonna hold me?"

"That's just what we're going to do," said Nelson dryly. "Over here, you," he ordered the new witness. "Now, who was eating spaghetti on his right here? As soon as we find that out, the rest of you can go home."

The crowd looked around indignantly in search of the recalcitrant witness that was the cause of detaining them all. But this time no one was definitely able to single him out. A white-uniformed busman finally edged forward and said to Nelson: "I think he musta got out of the place right after it happened. I looked over at this table a minute before it happened, and he was already through eating, picking his teeth and just holding down the chair."

"Well, he's not as smart as he thinks he is," said Nelson. "We'll catch up with him, whether he got out or didn't. The rest of you clear out of here now. And don't give fake names and addresses to the cop at the door, or you'll only be making trouble for yourselves."

The place emptied itself like magic, self-preservation being stronger than curiosity in most people. The two table-mates of the dead man, the manager, the staff, and the two dicks remained inside.

An assistant medical examiner arrived, followed by two men with the usual basket, and made a brief preliminary investigation. While this was going on, Nelson was questioning the two witnesses, the busman, and the manager. He got an illuminating composite picture.

The man was well known to the staff by sight, and was considered an eccentric. He always came in at the same time each night, just before closing time, and always helped himself to the same snack—coffee and a bologna sandwich. It hadn't varied for six months now. The remnants that the busman removed from where the man sat each time, were always the same. The manager was able to corroborate this. He, the dead man, had raised a kick one night about a week ago, because the bologna-sandwich slots had all been emptied before he came in. The manager had had to remind him that it's first come, first served, at an automat, and you can't reserve your food ahead of time. The man at the change-booth, questioned by Nelson, added to the old fellow's reputation for eccentricity. Other, well-dressed people came in and changed a half-dollar, or at the most a dollar bill. He, in his battered hat and derelict's overcoat, never failed to produce a ten and sometimes even a twenty.

"One of these misers, eh?" said Nelson. "They always end up behind the eight-ball, one way or another."

The old fellow was removed, also the partly consumed sandwich. The assistant examiner let Nelson know: "I think you've got something here, brother. I may be wrong, but that sandwich was loaded with cyanide."

Sarecky, who had gone through the man's clothes, said: "The name was Leo Avram, and here's the address. Incidentally, he had seven hundred dollars, in C's, in his right shoe and three hundred in his left. Want me to go over there and nose around?"

"Suppose I go," Nelson said. "You stay here and clean up."

"My pal," murmured the other dick dryly.

The waxed paper from the sandwich had been left lying under the chair. Nelson picked it up, wrapped it in a paper-napkin, and put it in his pocket. It was only a short walk from the automat to where Avram lived, an outmoded, walk-up building, falling to pieces with neglect.

Nelson went into the hall and there was no such name listed. He thought at first Sarecky had made a mistake, or at least been misled by whatever memorandum it was he had found that purported to give the old fellow's address. He rang the bell marked *Superintendent*, and went down to the basement-entrance to make sure. A stout blond woman in an old sweater and carpet-slippers came out.

"Is there anyone named Avram living in this building?"

"That's my husband—he's the superintendent. He's out right now, I expect him back any minute."

Nelson couldn't understand, himself, why he didn't break it to her then and there. He wanted to get a line, perhaps, on the old man's surroundings while they still remained normal. "Can I come in and wait a minute?" he said.

"Why not?" she said indifferently.

She led him down a barren, unlit basement-way, stacked with empty ashcans, into a room green-yellow with a tiny bud of gaslight. Old as the building upstairs was, it had been wired for electricity, Nelson had noted. For that matter, so was this basement down here. There was a cord hanging from the ceiling ending in an empty socket. It had been looped up out of reach. "The old bird sure was a miser," thought Nelson. "Walking around on one grand and living like this!" He couldn't help feeling a little sorry for the woman.

He noted to his further surprise that a pot of coffee was boiling on a one-burner gas stove over in the corner. He wondered if she knew that he treated himself away from home each night. "Any idea where he went?" he asked, sitting down in a creaking rocker.

"He goes two blocks down to the automat for a bite to eat every night at this time," she said.

"How is it," he asked curiously, "he'll go out and spend money like that, when he could have coffee right here where he lives with you?"

A spark of resentment showed in her face, but a defeated resentment that had long turned to resignation. She shrugged. "For himself, nothing's too good. He goes there because the light's better, he says. But for me and the kids, he begrudges every penny."

"You've got kids, have you?"

"They're mine, not his," she said dully.

Nelson had already caught sight of a half-grown girl and a little boy peeping shyly out at him from another room. "Well," he said, getting up, "I'm sorry to have to tell you this, but your husband had an accident a little while ago at the automat, Mrs. Avram. He's gone."

The weary stolidity on her face changed very slowly. But it did change—to fright. "Cyanide—what's that?" she breathed, when he'd told her.

"Did he have any enemies?"

She said with utter simplicity. "Nobody loved him. Nobody hated him that much, either."

"Do you know of any reason he'd have to take his own life?"

"Him? Never! He held on tight to life, just like he did to his money."

There was some truth in that, the dick had to admit. Misers seldom commit suicide.

The little girl edged into the room fearfully, holding her hands behind her. "Is—is he dead, Mom?"

The woman just nodded, dry-eyed.

"Then, can we use this now?" She was holding a fly-blown electric bulb in her hands.

Nelson felt touched, hard-boiled dick though he was. "Come down to headquarters tomorrow, Mrs. Avram. There's some

money there you can claim. G'night." He went outside and
clanged the basement-gate shut after him. The windows alongside him suddenly bloomed feebly with electricity, and the
silhouette of a woman standing up on a chair was outlined
against them.

"It's a funny world," thought the dick with a shake of his
head, as he trudged up to sidewalk-level.

It was now two in the morning. The automat was dark when
Nelson returned there, so he went down to headquarters. They
were questioning the branch-manager and the unseen counterman who prepared the sandwiches and filled the slots from the
inside.

Nelson's captain said: "They've already telephoned from the
chem lab that the sandwich is loaded with cyanide crystals. On
the other hand, they give the remainder of the loaf that was
used, the leftover bologna from which the sandwich was prepared, the breadknife, the cutting-board, and the scraps in the
garbage-receptacle—all of which we sent over there—a clean
bill of health. There was clearly no slip-up or carelessness in the
automat pantry. Which means that cyanide got into that sandwich on the consumer's side of the apparatus. He committed
suicide or was deliberately murdered by one of the other customers."

"I was just up there," Nelson said. "It wasn't suicide. People
don't worry about keeping their light bills down when they're
going to take their own lives."

"Good psychology," the captain nodded. "My experience is
that miserliness is simply a perverted form of self-preservation,
an exaggerated clinging to life. The choice of method wouldn't
be in character, either. Cyanide's expensive, and it wouldn't be
sold to a man of Avram's type, just for the asking. It's murder,
then. I think it's highly important you men bring in whoever
the fourth man at that table was tonight. Do it with the least
possible loss of time."

A composite description of him, pieced together from the few scraps that could be obtained from the busman and the other two at the table, was available. He was a heavy-set, dark-complected man, wearing a light-tan suit. He had been the first of the four at the table, and already through eating, but had lingered on. Mannerisms—had kept looking back over his shoulder, from time to time, and picking his teeth. He had had a small black satchel, or sample-case, parked at his feet under the table. Both survivors were positive on this point. Both had stubbed their toes against it in sitting down, and both had glanced to the floor to see what it was.

Had he reached down toward it at any time, after their arrival, as if to open it or take anything out of it?

To the best of their united recollections—no.

Had Avram, *after* bringing the sandwich to the table, gotten up again and left it unguarded for a moment?

Again, no. In fact the whole thing had been over with in a flash. He had noisily unwrapped it, taken a huge bite, swallowed without chewing, heaved convulsively once or twice, and fallen prone across the tabletop.

"Then it must have happened right outside the slot—I mean the inserting of the stuff—and not at the table, at all," Sarecky told Nelson privately. "Guess he laid it down for a minute while he was drawing his coffee."

"Absolutely not!" Nelson contradicted. "You're forgetting it was all wrapped up in wax-paper. How could anyone have opened, then closed it again, without attracting his attention? And if we're going to suspect the guy with the satchel—and the cap seems to want us to—he was already *at* the table and all through eating when Avram came over. How could he know ahead of time which table the old guy was going to select?"

"Then how did the stuff get on it? Where did it come from?" the other dick asked helplessly.

"It's little things like that we're paid to find out," Nelson reminded him dryly.

"Pretty large order, isn't it?"

"You talk like a layman. You've been on the squad long enough by now to know how damnably unescapable little habits are, how impossible it is to shake them off, once formed. The public at large thinks detective work is something miraculous like pulling rabbits out of a silk-hat. They don't realize that no adult is a free agent—that they're tied hand and foot by tiny, harmless little habits, and held helpless. This man has a habit of taking a snack to eat at midnight in a public place. He has a habit of picking his teeth after he's through, of lingering on at the table, of looking back over his shoulder aimlessly from time to time. Combine that with a stocky build, a dark complexion, and you have him! What more d'ya want—a spotlight trained on him?"

It was Sarecky, himself, in spite of his misgivings, who picked him up forty-eight hours later in another automat, sample-case and all, at nearly the same hour as the first time, and brought him in for questioning! The busman from the former place, and the two customers, called in, identified him unhesitatingly, even if he was now wearing a gray suit.

His name, he said, was Alexander Hill, and he lived at 215 Such-and-such a street.

"What business are you in?" rapped out the captain.

The man's face got livid. His Adam's apple went up and down like an elevator. He could barely articulate the words. "I'm— I'm a salesman for a wholesale drug concern," he gasped terrifiedly.

"Ah!" said two of his three questioners expressively. The sample-case, opened, was found to contain only tooth-powders, aspirins, and headache remedies.

But Nelson, rummaging through it, thought: "Oh, nuts, it's too pat. And he's too scared, too defenseless, to have really done it. Came in here just now without a bit of mental build-up prepared ahead of time. The real culprit would have been all primed, all rehearsed, for just this. Watch him go all to pieces. The innocent ones always do."

The captain's voice rose to a roar. "How is it everyone else stayed in the place that night, but you got out in such a hurry?"

"I—I don't know. It happened so close to me, I guess I—I got nervous."

That wasn't necessarily a sign of guilt, Nelson was thinking. It was his duty to take part in the questioning, so he shot out at him: "You got nervous, eh? What reason d'you have for getting nervous? How'd *you* know it wasn't just a heart attack or malnutrition—unless you were the cause of it?"

He stumbled badly over that one. "No! No! I don't handle that stuff! I don't carry anything like that—"

"So you know what it was? How'd you know? We didn't tell you," Sarecky jumped on him.

"I—I read it in the papers next morning," he wailed.

Well, it had been in all of them, Nelson had to admit.

"You didn't reach out in front of you—toward him—for anything that night? You kept your hands to yourself?" Then, before he could get a word out, *"What about sugar?"*

The suspect went from bad to worse. "I don't use any!" he whimpered.

Sarecky had been just waiting for that. "Don't lie to us!" he yelled, and swung at him. "I watched you for ten full minutes tonight before I went over and tapped your shoulder. You emptied half the container into your cup!" His fist hit him a glancing blow on the side of the jaw, knocked him and the chair he was sitting on both off-balance. Fright was making the guy sew himself up twice as badly as before.

"Aw, we're just barking up the wrong tree," Nelson kept saying to himself. "It's just one of those fluke coincidences. A drug salesman happens to be sitting at the same table where a guy drops from cyanide poisoning!" Still, he knew that more than one guy had been strapped into the chair just on the strength of such a coincidence and nothing more. You couldn't expect a jury not to pounce on it for all it was worth.

The captain took Nelson out of it at this point, somewhat to his relief, took him aside and murmured: "Go over there and give his place a good cleaning while we're holding him here. If you can turn up any of that stuff hidden around there, that's all we need. He'll break down like a stack of cards." He glanced over at the cowering figure in the chair. "We'll have him before morning," he promised.

"That's what I'm afraid of," thought Nelson, easing out. "And then what'll we have? Exactly nothing." He wasn't the kind of a dick that would have rather had a wrong guy than no guy at all, like some of them. He wanted the right guy—or none at all. The last he saw of the captain, he was stripping off his coat for action, more as a moral threat than a physical one, and the unfortunate victim of circumstances was wailing, "I didn't do it, I didn't do it," like a record with a flaw in it.

Hill was a bachelor and lived in a small, one-room flat on the upper West Side. Nelson let himself in with the man's own key, put on the lights, and went to work. In half an hour, he had investigated the place upside-down. There was not a grain of cyanide to be found, nor anything beyond what had already been revealed in the sample-case. This did not mean, of course, that he couldn't have obtained some either through the firm he worked for, or some of the retail druggists whom he canvassed. Nelson found a list of the latter and took it with him to check over the following day.

Instead of returning directly to headquarters, he detoured on an impulse past the Avram house, and, seeing a light shining in the basement windows, went over and rang the bell.

The little girl came out, her brother behind her. "Mom's not in," she announced.

"She's out with Uncle Nick," the boy supplied.

His sister whirled on him. "She told us not to tell anybody that, didn't she!"

Nelson could hear the instructions as clearly as if he'd been in the room at the time, "If that same man comes around again, don't you tell him I've gone out with Uncle Nick, now!"

Children are after all very transparent. They told him most of what he wanted to know without realizing they were doing it. "He's not really your uncle, is he?"

A gasp of surprise. "How'd you know that?"

"Your ma gonna marry him?"

They both nodded approvingly. "He's gonna be our new Pop."

"What was the name of your real Pop—the one before the last?"

"Edwards," they chorused proudly.

"What happened to him?"

"He died."

"In Dee-troit," added the little boy.

He only asked them one more question. "Can you tell me his full name?"

"Albert J. Edwards," they recited.

He gave them a friendly push. "All right, kids, go back to bed."

He went back to headquarters, sent a wire to the Bureau of Vital Statistics in Detroit, on his own hook. They were still questioning Hill down to the bone, meanwhile, but he hadn't caved in yet. "Nothing," Nelson reported. "Only this account-sheet of where he places his orders."

"I'm going to try framing him with a handful of bicarb of soda, or something—pretend we got the goods on him. I'll see if that'll open him up," the captain promised wrathfully. "He's not the push-over I expected. You start in at seven this morning and work your way through this list of retail druggists. Find out if he ever tried to contract them for any of that stuff."

Meanwhile, he had Hill smuggled out the back way to an

outlying precinct, to evade the statute governing the length of time a prisoner can be held before arraignment. They didn't have enough of a case against him yet to arraign him, but they weren't going to let him go.

Nelson was even more surprised than the prisoner at what he caught himself doing. As they stood Hill up next to him in the corridor, for a minute, waiting for the Black Maria, he breathed over his shoulder, "Hang on tight, or you're sunk!"

The man acted too far gone even to understand what he was driving at.

Nelson was present the next morning when Mrs. Avram showed up to claim the money, and watched her expression curiously. She had the same air of weary resignation as the night he had broken the news to her. She accepted the money from the captain, signed for it, turned apathetically away, holding it in her hand. The captain, by prearrangement, had pulled another of his little tricks—purposely withheld one of the hundred-dollar bills to see what her reaction would be.

Halfway to the door, she turned in alarm, came hurrying back. "Gentlemen, there must be a mistake! There's—there's a hundred-dollar bill here on top!" She shuffled through the roll hastily. "They're all hundred-dollar bills!" she cried out aghast. "I knew he had a little money in his shoes—he slept with them under his pillow at nights—but I thought maybe, fifty, seventy dollars—"

"There was a thousand in his shoes," said the captain, "and another thousand stitched all along the seams of his overcoat."

She let the money go, caught the edge of the desk he was sitting behind with both hands, and slumped draggingly down it to the floor in a dead faint. They had to hustle in with a pitcher of water to revive her.

Nelson impatiently wondered what the heck was the matter with him, what more he needed to be convinced she hadn't known what she was coming into? And yet, he said to himself,

how are you going to tell a real faint from a fake one? They close
their eyes and they flop, and which is it?

He slept three hours, and then he went down and checked
at the wholesale-drug concern Hill worked for. The firm did not
handle cyanide or any other poisonous substance, and the man
had a very good record there. He spent the morning working
his way down the list of retail druggists who had placed their
orders through Hill, and again got nowhere. At noon he quit,
and went back to the automat where it had happened—not to
eat but to talk to the manager. He was really working on two
cases simultaneously—an official one for his captain and a private one of his own. The captain would have had a fit if he'd
known it.

"Will you lemme have that busman of yours, the one we had
down at headquarters the other night? I want to take him out
of here with me for about half an hour."

"You're the Police Department," the manager smiled ac-
quiescently.

Nelson took him with him in his streetclothes. "You did a
pretty good job of identifying Hill, the fourth man at that table,"
he told him. "Naturally, I don't expect you to remember every
face that was in there that night. Especially with the quick
turnover there is in an automat. However, here's what you do.
Go down this street here to Number One-twenty-one—you can
see it from here. Ring the superintendent's bell. You're looking
for an apartment, see? But while you're at it, you take a good
look at the woman you'll see, and then come back and tell me
if you remember seeing her face in the automat that night or
any other night. Don't stare now—just size her up."

It took him a little longer than Nelson had counted on. When
he finally rejoined the dick around the corner, where the latter
was waiting, he said: "Nope, I've never seen her in our place,
that night or any other, to my knowledge. But don't forget—I'm
not on the floor every minute of the time. She could have been

in and out often without my spotting her."

"But not," thought Nelson, "without Avram seeing her, if she went anywhere near him at all." She hadn't been there, then. That was practically certain. "What took you so long?" he asked him.

"Funny thing. There was a guy there in the place with her that used to work for us. He remembered me right away."

"Oh, yeah?" The dick drew up short. "Was *he* in there that night?"

"Naw, he quit six months ago. I haven't seen him since."

"What was he, sandwich-maker?"

"No, busman like me. He cleaned up the tables."

Just another coincidence, then. But, Nelson reminded himself, if one coincidence was strong enough to put Hill in jeopardy, why should the other be passed over as harmless? Both cases—his and the captain's—now had their coincidences. It remained to be seen which was just that—a coincidence and nothing more—and which was the McCoy.

He went back to headquarters. No wire had yet come from Detroit in answer to his, but he hadn't expected any this soon —it took time. The captain, bulldog-like, wouldn't let Hill go. They had spirited him away to still a third place, were holding him on some technicality or other that had nothing to do with the Avram case. The bicarbonate of soda trick hadn't worked, the captain told Nelson ruefully.

"Why?" the dick wanted to know. "Because he caught on just by looking at it that it wasn't cyanide—is that it? I think that's an important point, right there."

"No, he thought it was the stuff all right. But he hollered blue murder it hadn't come out of his room."

"Then if he doesn't know the difference between cyanide and bicarb of soda at sight, doesn't that prove he didn't put any on that sandwich?"

The captain gave him a look. "Are you for us or against us?" he wanted to know acidly. "You go ahead checking that list of retail druggists until you find out where he got it. And if we can't dig up any other motive, unhealthy scientific curiosity will satisfy me. He wanted to study the effects at first hand, and picked the first stranger who came along."

"Sure, in an automat—the most conspicuous, crowded public eating-place there is. The one place where human handling of the food is reduced to a minimum."

He deliberately disobeyed orders, a thing he had never done before—or rather, postponed carrying them out. He went back and commenced a one-man watch over the basement-entrance of the Avram house.

In about an hour, a squat, foreign-looking man came up the steps and walked down the street. This was undoubtedly "Uncle Nick," Mrs. Avram's husband-to-be, and former employee of the automat. Nelson tailed him effortlessly on the opposite side, boarded the same bus he did but a block below, and got off at the same stop. "Uncle Nick" went into a bank, and Nelson into a cigar-store across the way that had transparent telephone-booths commanding the street through the glass front.

When he came out again, Nelson didn't bother following him any more. Instead, he went into the bank himself. "What'd that guy do—open an account just now? Lemme see the deposit-slip."

He had deposited a thousand dollars cash under the name of Nicholas Krassin, half of the sum Mrs. Avram had claimed at headquarters only the day before. Nelson didn't have to be told that this by no means indicated Krassin and she had had anything to do with the old man's death. The money was rightfully hers as his widow, and, if she wanted to divide it with her groom-to-be, that was no criminal offense. Still, wasn't there a stronger motive here than the "unhealthy scientific curiosity" the captain had pinned on Hill? The fact remained that she wouldn't have had possession of the money had Avram still

been alive. It would have still been in his shoes and coat-seams
where she couldn't get at it.

Nelson checked Krassin at the address he had given at the
bank, and, somewhat to his surprise, found it to be on the level,
not fictitious. Either the two of them weren't very bright, or
they were innocent. He went back to headquarters at six, and
the answer to his telegram to Detroit had finally come. "Exhu-
mation order obtained as per request stop Albert J. Edwards
deceased January 1936 stop death certificate gives cause fall
from steel girder while at work building under construction
stop—autopsy—"

Nelson read it to the end, folded it, put it in his pocket without changing his expression.

"Well, did you find out anything?" the captain wanted to
know.

"No, but I'm on the way to," Nelson assured him, but he may
have been thinking of that other case of his own, and not the
one they were all steamed up over. He went out again without
saying where.

He got to Mrs. Avram's at quarter to seven, and rang the bell.
The little girl came out to the basement-entrance. At sight of
him, she called out shrilly, but without humorous intent, "Ma,
that man's here again."

Nelson smiled a little and walked back to the living-quarters.
A sudden hush had fallen thick enough to cut with a knife.
Krassin was there again, in his shirt-sleeves, having supper with
Mrs. Avram and the two kids. They not only had electricity now
but a midget radio as well, he noticed. You can't arrest people
for buying a midget radio. It was silent as a tomb, but he let the
back of his hand brush it, surreptitiously, and the front of the
dial was still warm from recent use.

"I'm not butting in, am I?" he greeted them cheerfully.

"N-no, sit down," said Mrs. Avram nervously. "This is Mr.
Krassin, a friend of the family. I don't know your name—"

"Nelson."

Krassin just looked at him watchfully.

The dick said: "Sorry to trouble you. I just wanted to ask you a couple questions about your husband. About what time was it he had the accident?"

"You know that better than I," she objected. "You were the one came here and told me."

"I don't mean Avram, I mean Edwards, in Detroit—the riveter that fell off the girder."

Her face went a little gray, as if the memory were painful. Krassin's face didn't change color, but only showed considerable surprise.

"About what time of day?" he repeated.

"Noon," she said almost inaudibly.

"Lunch-time," said the dick softly, as if to himself. "Most workmen carry their lunch from home in a pail—" He looked at her thoughtfully. Then he changed the subject, wrinkled up his nose appreciatively. "That coffee smells good," he remarked.

She gave him a peculiar, strained smile. "Have a cup, Mr. Detective," she offered. He saw her eyes meet Krassin's briefly.

"Thanks, don't mind if I do," drawled Nelson.

She got up. Then, on her way to the stove, she suddenly flared out at the two kids for no apparent reason: "What are you hanging around here for? Go in to bed. Get out of here now, I say!" She banged the door shut on them, stood before it with her back to the room for a minute. Nelson's sharp ears caught the faint but unmistakable click of a key.

She turned back again, purred to Krassin: "Nick, go outside and take a look at the furnace, will you, while I'm pouring Mr. Nelson's coffee? If the heat dies down, they'll all start complaining from upstairs right away. Give it a good shaking up."

The hairs at the back of Nelson's neck stood up a little as he watched the man get up and sidle out. But he'd asked for the cup of coffee, himself.

He couldn't see her pouring it—her back was turned toward him again as she stood over the stove. But he could hear the splash of the hot liquid, see her elbow-motions, hear the clink of the pot as she replaced it. She stayed that way a moment longer, after it had been poured, with her back to him—less than a moment, barely thirty seconds. One elbow moved slightly. Nelson's eyes were narrow slits. It was thirty seconds too long, one elbow-motion too many.

She turned, came back, set the cup down before him. "I'll let you put your own sugar in, yes?" she said almost playfully. "Some like a lot, some like a little." There was a disappearing ring of froth in the middle of the black steaming liquid.

Outside somewhere, he could hear Krassin raking up the furnace.

"Drink it while it's hot," she urged.

He lifted it slowly to his lips. As the cup went up, her eyelids went down. Not all the way, not enough to completely shut out sight, though.

He blew the steam away. "Too hot—burn my mouth. Gotta give it a minute to cool," he said. "How about you—ain't you having any? I couldn't drink alone. Ain't polite."

"I had mine," she breathed heavily, opening her eyes again. "I don't think there's any left."

"Then I'll give you half of this."

Her hospitable alarm was almost overdone. She all but jumped back in protest. "No, no! Wait, I'll look. Yes, there's more, there's plenty!"

He could have had an accident with it while her back was turned a second time, upset it over the floor. Instead, he took a kitchen-match out of his pocket, broke the head off short with his thumbnail. He threw the head, not the stick, over on top of the warm stove in front of which she was standing. It fell to one side of her, without making any noise, and she didn't notice it. If he'd thrown stick and all, it would have clicked as it dropped and attracted her attention.

She came back and sat down opposite him. Krassin's footsteps could be heard shuffling back toward them along the cement corridor outside.

"Go ahead. Don't be bashful—drink up," she encouraged. There was something ghastly about her smile, like a death's-head grinning across the table from him.

The match-head on the stove, heated to the point of combustion, suddenly flared up with a little spitting sound and a momentary gleam. She jumped a little, and her head turned nervously to see what it was. When she looked back again, he already had his cup to his lips. She raised hers, too, watching him over the rim of it. Krassin's footfalls had stopped somewhere just outside the room door, and there wasn't another sound from him, as if he were standing there, waiting.

At the table, the cat-and-mouse play went on a moment longer. Nelson started swallowing with a dry constriction of the throat. The woman's eyes, watching him above her cup, were greedy half-moons of delight. Suddenly, her head and shoulders went down across the table with a bang, like her husband's had at the automat that other night, and the crash of the crushed cup sounded from underneath her.

Nelson jumped up watchfully, throwing his chair over. The door shot open, and Krassin came in, with an ax in one hand and an empty burlap-bag in the other.

"I'm not quite ready for cremation yet," the dick gritted, and threw himself at him.

Krassin dropped the superfluous burlap-bag, the ax flashed up overhead. Nelson dipped his knees, down in under it before it could fall. He caught the shaft with one hand, midway between the blade and Krassin's grip, and held the weapon teetering in mid-air. With his other fist he started imitating a hydraulic drill against his assailant's teeth. Then he lowered his barrage suddenly to solar-plexus level, sent in two bodyblows that caved his opponent in—and that about finished it.

Out in the wilds of Corona, an hour later, in a sub-basement locker-room, Alexander Hill—or at least what was left of him—was saying: "And you'll lemme sleep if I do? And you'll get it over real quick, send me up and put me out of my misery?"

"Yeah, yeah!" said the haggard captain, flicking ink out of a fountain pen and jabbing it at him. "Why dincha do this days ago, make it easier for us all?"

"Never saw such a guy," complained Sarecky, rinsing his mouth with water over in a corner.

"What's that man signing?" exploded Nelson's voice from the stairs.

"Whaddye think he's signing?" snarled the captain. "And where you been all night, incidentally?"

"Getting poisoned by the same party that croaked Avram!" He came the rest of the way down, and Krassin walked down alongside at the end of a short steel link.

"Who's this guy?" they both wanted to know.

Nelson looked at the first prisoner, in the chair. "Take him out of here a few minutes, can't you?" he requested. "He don't have to know all our business."

"Just like in the story-books," muttered Sarecky jealously. "One-Man Nelson walks in at the last minute and cops all the glory."

A cop led Hill upstairs. Another cop brought down a small brown-paper parcel at Nelson's request. Opened, it revealed a small tin that had once contained cocoa. Nelson turned it upside down and a few threads of whitish substance spilled lethargically out, filling the close air of the room with a faint odor of bitter almonds.

"There's your cyanide," he said. "It came off the shelf above Mrs. Avram's kitchen-stove. Her kids, who are being taken care

of at headquarters until I can get back there, will tell you it's
roach-powder and they were warned never to go near it. She
probably got it in Detroit, way back last year."

"She did it?" said the captain. "How could she? It was on the
automat-sandwich, not anything he ate at home. *She* wasn't at
the automat that night, she was home, you told us that yourself."

"Yeah, she was home, but she poisoned him at the automat
just the same. Look, it goes like this." He unlocked his manacle,
refastened his prisoner temporarily to a plumbing-pipe in the
corner. He took a paper-napkin out of his pocket, and, from
within that, the carefully preserved waxpaper wrapper the
death-sandwich had been done in.

Nelson said: "This has been folded over twice, once on one
side, once on the other. You can see that, yourself. Every crease
in it is double-barreled. Meaning what? The sandwich was
taken out, doctored, and rewrapped. Only, in her hurry, Mrs.
Avram slipped up and put the paper back the other way
around.

"As I told Sarecky already, there's death in little habits. Avram was a miser. Bologna is the cheapest sandwich that automat
sells. For six months straight, he never bought any other kind.
This guy here used to work there. He knew at what time the
slots were refilled for the last time. He knew that that was just
when Avram always showed up. And, incidentally, the old man
was no fool. He didn't go there because the light was better—
he went there to keep from getting poisoned at home. Ate all
his meals out.

"All right, so what did they do? They got him, anyway—like
this. Krassin, here, went in, bought a bologna sandwich, and
took it home to her. She spiked it, rewrapped it, and, at eleven-
thirty, he took it back there in his pocket. The sandwich-slots
had just been refilled for the last time. They wouldn't put any
more in till next morning. There are three bologna-slots. He
emptied all three, to make sure the victim wouldn't get any but

the lethal sandwich. After they're taken out, the glass slides remain ajar. You can lift them and reach in without inserting a coin. He put his death-sandwich in, stayed by it so no one else would get it. The old man came in. Maybe he's near sighted and didn't recognize Krassin. Maybe he didn't know him at all—I haven't cleared that point up yet. Krassin eased out of the place. The old man is a miser. He sees he can get a sandwich for nothing, thinks something went wrong with the mechanism, maybe. He grabs it up twice as quick as anyone else would have. There you are.

"What was in his shoes is this guy's motive. As for her, that was only partly her motive. She was a congenital killer, anyway, outside of that. He would have married her, and it would have happened to him in his turn some day. She got rid of her first husband, Edwards, in Detroit that way. She got a wonderful break. He ate the poisoned lunch she'd given him way up on the crossbeams of a building under construction, and it looked like he'd lost his balance and toppled to his death. They exhumed the body and performed an autopsy at my request. This telegram says they found traces of cyanide poisoning even after all this time.

"I paid out rope to her tonight, let her know I was onto her. I told her her coffee smelled good. Then I switched cups on her. She's up there now, dead. I can't say that I wanted it that way, but it was me or her. You never would have gotten her to the chair, anyway. She was unbalanced of course, but not the kind that's easily recognizable. She'd have spent a year in an institution, been released, and gone out and done it all over again. It grows on 'em, gives 'em a feeling of power over their fellow human beings.

"This louse, however, is *not* insane. He did it for exactly one thousand dollars and no cents—and he knew what he was doing from first to last. So I think he's entitled to a chicken-and-ice-cream-dinner in the death-house, at the state's expense."

"The Sphinx," growled Sarecky under his breath, shrugging

into his coat. "Sees all, knows all, keeps all to himself."

"Who stinks?" corrected the captain, misunderstanding. "If anyone does, it's you and me. He brought home the bacon!"

One would have thought the "impossible crime" story to be a type most uncongenial to Woolrich's talents—which shows how much more skilled and versatile he was than most readers realize. Along with the neat puzzle, Woolrich gives us a rich evocation of that seedy automat and its habitués, and some fine night scenes of the city during the Depression, and that characteristic touch of the police threat to frame the most likely suspect—adding up to an excellent tale, untouched since its original appearance.

Death in the Air

Inspector Stephen Lively, off-duty and homeward-bound, stopped at the newsstand underneath the stairs leading up to the Elevated station and selected one of the following day's newspapers and one of the following month's magazines for purposes of relaxation. His nightly trip was not only lengthy, it was in two parts—from headquarters to South Ferry by "El" and from there to Staten Island by ferry—hence the two separate items of reading-matter; one for each leg of the way.

Given a combination of two such names as his and, human nature being what it is, what else can you expect in the way of a nickname but—Step Lively? It had started at the age of seven or thereabouts when he stood up in school and pronounced his first name the wrong way; he finally quit struggling against it when it followed him onto the squad and he realized that he was stuck with it for the rest of his days, like it or not.

It wouldn't have been so bad, only it was altogether inappropriate. Step Lively had never made a quick motion in his life. To watch him was to think of an eight-times-slowed-down film or a deep-sea diver wading through seaweed on the ocean floor; he gave the impression of having been born lazy and getting more so all the time. And the nickname probably made this trait more glaring.

He was not, strangely enough, obese along with it—just the opposite, tall and spare, concave at the waist where others bulge. He carried his head habitually bent forward a little, as though it were too much trouble to hold it up straight. He not only walked slowly, he even talked slowly. What mattered chiefly was that he thought fast; as far as results went, his record on the force seemed to prove that the race isn't always to the swift. He'd been known to bring in some of the nimblest, most light-footed gentry on record.

Like a steam-roller pursuing a motorcycle; it can't keep up with it, but it can keep remorselessly after it, wear it down, slowly overtake it, and finally flatten it out. So Step's superiors didn't let it worry them too much that he was the despair of traffic-cops crossing a busy street, or that he sent people waiting on line behind him out of their minds. It takes more than that to spoil a good detective.

Step entered the lighted stairway-shed and sighed at the sight of the climb that awaited him, as it did every night. An escalator, like some of the other stations had, would have been so much easier on a man.

The subway, which would have gotten him to the ferry considerably quicker, he eschewed for two very good reasons. One was that he'd have to walk a whole additional block eastward to get to it. And secondly, even though you descended to it instead of climbing at this end, you had to climb up out of it at the other end anyway; he preferred to get the hard work over with at the start, and have a nice restful climb down waiting for him when he got off.

He slowly poised one large, paddle-like foot on the bottom step and eight minutes later he was upstairs on the platform, the ordeal of the ascent safely behind him until tomorrow night. As he stepped out from behind the turnstile, a Sixth Avenue train was standing by with its gates in the act of closing. Step could have made it; a man who had come up behind him darted across and did. Step preferred not to. It would have meant hurrying. There'd be another one along in a minute. The old adage about cars and women was good common horse sense.

This was 59th, and the trains alternated. The next would be a Ninth Avenue. They separated at 53rd, but both wound up together again at South Ferry, so it didn't matter which he took. More seats on the Ninth anyway. And so, because he refused to bestir himself—this story.

A three-car Ninth flashed in in due course. Step got up off the bench—it wouldn't have been like him to stand waiting—and leisurely strolled across to it. He yawned and tapped his mouth as he perambulated sluggishly down the aisle. The crabby, walrus-mustached conductor, who had had to hold the gate for him, felt a sudden unaccountable urge to stick a pin in him and see if he really could move fast or not, but wisely restrained the impulse, maybe because he had no pin.

The first car had a single occupant, sitting on one of the lengthwise seats, visible only up to the waist. The rest of him was buried behind an outspread newspaper, expanded to its full length. Step sprawled out directly opposite him with a grunt of satisfaction, opened his own paper, and got busy relaxing. All the windows were open on both sides of the car, and it was a pleasant, airy way to ride home on a warm night. Two pairs of legs and two tents of newsprint on opposite sides of the aisle were all that remained visible. The conductor, maybe because

Step irritated him vaguely, retired to the second car, between stations, instead of this one.

The train coasted down Ninth Avenue sixty feet in the air, with the buildings that topped it by a story or two set back at a respectable distance from its roadbed. But then at Twelfth Street, it veered off into Greenwich Street and a change in spacing took place. The old mangy tenements closed in on it on both sides, narrowing into a bottleneck and all but scraping the sides of the cars as they threaded through them. There was, at the most, a distance of three yards between the outer rail of the super-structure and their fourth-floor window-ledges, and where fire-escapes protruded only half that much.

What saved them from incessant burglarizing in this way was simply that there was nothing to burglarize. They were not worth going after. Four out of five were tenantless, windows either boarded up or broken-glass cavities yawning at the night. Occasionally a dimly-lighted one floated by, so close it gave those on the train a startling impression of being right in the same room with those whose privacy they were cutting across in this way. A man in his underwear reading a paper by a lamp, a woman bent over a washtub in a steaming kitchen. Their heads never turned at the streaming, comet-like lights or the roar of the wheels going by. They were so used to it they never gave it a thought. It was just part of their surroundings. Nor did those on the train show any interest either, as a rule. The few there were at this hour had their papers up and their backs to the passing scene. There isn't anything pretty about the lower West Side of New York. The river a block over is blotted out by docks, and the connecting side-streets are roofed with produce-sheds.

In the front car, the two solitary occupants continued immersed in their reading-matter. Christopher and Houston had gone by, and they pulled into Desbrosses Street. As they cleared it again a moment later, the train slackened briefly, slowed down without coming to a full halt, then almost immediately picked up speed once more. Perhaps some slight hitch on the part of a track-signal or a momentary break in the "shoe" gripping the third rail. Step took his eyes off his paper and glanced around over his shoulder, not because of that, but to find out how near his destination he was.

There was an open window staring him in the face, flush with the car-window that framed him, and so close it was almost like a continuation of it, a connecting-tunnel into the tenement's front room. There was no light in the first room, but light shone feebly in from the room beyond through an open doorway. At the same time the train-lights swept in and washed across the walls like a sort of lantern-slide, from left to right.

In the double glare, fore and aft, two forms could be glimpsed, moving unsteadily about together. A man and woman dancing drunkenly in the dark, with exaggerated motions of their arms and heads. Lurching, reeling, pressed tightly together. "Wonder what the big idea of that is?" Step thought tolerantly. "Too warm for lights, I guess—" The noise of the cars drowned out whatever music was being supplied them for their strange activities.

Just as the two superimposed windows slipped apart out of perspective, the wheels of the train cracked loudly as though passing over a defect in the rails. At the same time, one of the shadow-dancers struck a match and it went right out again, just a stab of orange, and some water-borne insect or other winged into the car past Step's face. He slapped vaguely at it, went back to his newspaper. The train picked up speed and headed down the track for Franklin Street.

The party across the aisle had fallen asleep, Step noticed when next he glanced over across the top of his paper. He grinned broadly at the sight he presented. There was a man after his own heart. Too much trouble even to fold up his paper and put it away. The breeze coming in on Step's side of the car had slapped it back against his face and shoulders; his hands were no longer holding it up, had dropped limply to his lap. His legs had sprawled apart, were wobbling loosely in and out like rubber with the motion of the car.

Step wondered how he could breathe with the layers of paper flattened that way across his nose and mouth, you could actually see the indentation his nose made through it. And that insect that had blown in—it looked like a large black beetle—was perched there on the paper just above it. Step thought of the innumerable comedy-gags he'd seen where someone tried to swat a fly on a sleeper's face, and of course the sleeper got the full impact of it. If he only knew the guy, he'd be tempted to try that now himself. Still, it was an awful lot of effort to reach across a car-aisle just to swat a horse-fly.

As they began drawing up for Franklin, the air-current of their own momentum rushed ahead, outdistanced them. It tugged loose the outside paper of the sleeper's outspread newspaper, no longer clamped down by his fingers, and sent it whirling up the aisle. Step blinked and went goggle-eyed. The black bug was still there, on the page underneath, as though it had bored its way through! A second sheet loosened, went skimming off. The damn thing was still there, as though it were leaping invisibly from one page to the other!

Step got to his feet, and though the motion was slow enough, there was a certain tenseness about him. He wasn't grinning any more. Just as he did so, the train came to a halt. The jolt threw the sleeper over on the side of his face, and all the rest of the newspaper went fluttering off, separating as it went. The black bug had leaped the last gap, was in the exact middle of the sleeper's forehead now, this time red-rimmed and with a thread of red leading down from it alongside his nose, like a weird eyeglass-string, to lose itself in the corner of his mouth. Step had seen too many of them not to know a bullet-hole when he saw one. The sleeper was dead. He didn't have to put his hand in under his coat, nor touch the splayed hand, caught under his body and dangling down over the aisle like a chicken-claw, to make sure of that. Death had leaped out at him from the very print he was reading. Such-and-such, then—period! A big black one, right into the brain. He'd never known what had hit him, had died instantly, sitting up. It wasn't the breeze that had slapped the paper up against him; it was the bullet. It wasn't an insect that had winged past Step's shoulder that time; it was the bullet.

Step reached up leisurely and tugged twice at the emergency-cord overhead. The gates had closed on Franklin, and the train had already made a false start ahead, checked immediately with a lurch. The handlebar-mustached conductor came running in from the platform, the motorman looked out from his booth at the upper end of the car.

"What's the idea? What's going on in here?" The conductor's words spattered like buckshot around the heedless Step.

"Hold the train," he drawled almost casually. "Here's a man been shot dead." Then as the blue-coated one began panting down the back of his neck and elbowing him aside, he remonstrated mildly, "Now don't crowd like that. There's nothing *you* can do. What y'getting so excited about? Just lemme try to find out who he is first—"

The motorman said from the other side of him, "Get him off. We can't stand here all night. We're on a schedule; we'll tie up the whole line into a knot behind us."

"Stand aside! Who do you think you are anyway?" the fiery conductor demanded.

Step said wearily, "Oh, do I have to go through that again?" and absentmindedly palmed his badge to him, backhand, while he continued bending over the prostrate form. From then on there was nothing but a respectful silence all around while he went on going through the corpse's pockets with maddening deliberation.

His mind, however, was anything but sluggish, was crackling like a high-tension wire. The sound of the shot? There didn't necessarily have to be any in this case, but that crack of the car-wheels over a split in the rails had probably been it. And the

match that one of those two tipsy dancers had struck in the
darkened tenement-room back there hadn't been a match at
all, hadn't glowed steadily enough nor lasted long enough,
couldn't have been anything but the flash of the shot, the results
of which he was now beholding.

Drinking, carousing, then entertaining themselves by taking
pot-shots out the window at passing trains, were they? Well, a
nice little manslaughter rap would take the high spirits out of
them, for some time to come, whoever they were.

"Dudley Wall," he said, reading from an envelope. "Lives on
Staten Island like me. Shame, poor fella. All right, take him by
the feet and help me get him outside to the waiting-room." And
as the conductor moved backwards before him down the aisle,
with the body between them, he rebuked: "Don't walk so fast.
He ain't going to get away from us!" They moved at a snail's
pace thereafter, to suit Step, out through the gate and across the
platform with their burden. Stretched him out on one of the
benches inside by the change-booth, and then Step strolled
inside with the agent and sent in his report over the latter's
phone.

"That guy," whispered the conductor darkly to the motorman on their way back to their posts, "has sleeping sickness, you
can't tell me different!"

"Maybe it's ringworm," hazarded the motorman. They
pulled out, and the two or three other trains that had ganged
up behind them flashed by one after the other without stopping, to make up for lost time.

"I gotta get back to Desbrosses Street," Step remarked, coming out again. "You keep an eye on him till they get here." He
felt sure he'd know the tenement window again when he saw
it, whether they were still there or not.

"Well, you'll have to go down to the street, cross over, and
then climb to the uptown side," the agent explained, wondering what he was waiting for.

Step looked horrified. "And then when I get there climb

down again? And climb up four flights of stairs inside that building? Oh, golly, I'm just tuckered out. I couldn't make it. I'll walk
back along the track, only way I can see. That's bad enough."

He sighed deeply, took a tuck in his belt, and made his way
to the far end of the platform. He descended the short ladder
to the track-level and struck out from there, trudging doggedly
along with one hand trailing along beside him on the guard-rail.

"Watch the trains!" the agent shouted after him warningly.

Step didn't answer out loud, that was too much trouble, but
to himself he muttered: "This is one time I'm glad I'm good and
thin!"

One of them caught him halfway between the two stations,
and the sight of it looming up on him was fairly terrifying to one
unused to track-walking. He began to wobble unsteadily on the
cat-walk, which seemed only inches wide, and realizing that he
would either topple dizzily in front of it or fall down to the
street if he kept looking at it head-on, he wisely turned his back
to it, grabbed the guard-rail with both hands, and stared intently out at the roof-tops, ignoring it till it had hurtled by. Its
velocity nearly seemed to pull the coat off his back.

He stared after it disapprovingly. "Such a town. Everything
always in a hurry to get somewhere else!" Then he resumed his
laborious progress alongside the tracks, feeling sorry for his feet
and hoping the sniper in the tenement had no firearms license,
so he could also tack a stiff Sullivan-Law charge on him.

The two lighted halves of the Desbrosses Street platform
loomed toward him, lighted under the apron like the footlights
of a stage. It ought to be about here. They'd already pulled out,
he remembered, when he'd turned around to look. Dark-red
brick it had been, but then the whole row was that. No fire-
escape, either. Wait a minute, there'd been a sign up on the
cornice of the building next-door, but on which side of it, he
couldn't recall. Nor what it had said, until suddenly it was staring him in the face once more, with that vague familiarity that
only twice-seen things can have. Then he knew that was it.

PICKLED AND SALTED FISH in tarnished metal capitals with rain-streaks under them, each letter separately clamped to the brickwork, in the style of the nineteenth-century advertiser. He stopped in front of the building next to it, on the Desbrosses side. This had almost certainly been it. There was the same wide-open window through which he'd seen them dancing. But no light was coming in from the other room now. It was dark and deserted, just a gap in the façade.

It looked near enough to touch, but actually was far more inaccessible from where he now was, than it had seemed from the train-window. The gap was just wide enough to fall to your death in without half-trying, and the ledge was just over his head, now that he was down at track-level.

Step Lively had the courage of his convictions. He was going to get in this way, without going all the way down to the street and climbing up inside that dump, if he died in the attempt. He looked around him vaguely but determinedly. They had been repairing the track-bed near here somewhere, and there was a neat, handy little stack of short planks piled up, almost directly across the way from him—but with two third-rails in-between.

He didn't hesitate for a minute. What was a third rail compared to climbing four flights of stairs and getting all out of breath? Besides, they had guards on top of them, like covered troughs. There wasn't anything coming on this side, so he started across on one of the ties, and arched respectfully over the deadly metal when he came to it. So much for the downtown track. An uptown train was pulling out of Franklin, but it wouldn't get here for awhile yet. Plenty of time to get back and across.

He reached the opposite catwalk safely, picked up the top plank, and tucked it broadside under his arm. The on-coming train was still at a respectable distance, although its lights were getting brighter by the moment. He started back over, the plank swaying up and down in his grasp like a see-saw. It wasn't the actual weight of it that hampered him, it was that its length

threw him off-balance. He was like a tightrope-walker with too
long a pole. He didn't have it right in the middle, and it kept
tipping him forward. The train was big as a barn by now, he
hadn't calculated on how quickly it would cover the short distance between the two stations. You could already look right
down the lighted aisle of the first car, through the open ves-
tibule-door. But this was no time for surveying. He lifted one
foot clear of the contact-rail, set it down on the other side, then
tried to bring the second one over after it. It wouldn't come. He
must have given it just the wrong kind of a little half-turn. It was
stuck between the two ties.

He didn't do anything at all for just a split second, which is
sometimes the wisest possible course—and came easiest to him,
anyway. However, there weren't many of them left, split or
otherwise. The roar of the train was rising to a crescendo. The
first thing almost anyone else would have done in his fix would
have been to yank and tug at the recalcitrant foot—and wedge
it in irretrievably. Step Lively was a slow mover but a quick
thinker. He used his split-second to turn his head and stare
down one hip at the treacherous hoof. The heel had dipped
down into the space between the two ties and jammed. It ought
to come out again easy enough, if he did the right thing. And
there wasn't time to do the wrong thing. So he started turning
back again on it, as if he were going to step right in front of the
train. That reversed whatever twist had originally trapped it; it
came up free, smooth as pie, and he stepped backwards with it
out of death's path, face turned toward the train as it rushed
abreast of him, brakes that wouldn't have been in time to save
him screeching. He had presence of mind enough to point the
plank skyward, like a soldier presenting arms, so the train
wouldn't sideswipe it and throw him. The cars seemed to take
the skin off his nose.

The damn thing stopped a car-length away, but whether on
his account or the station's he didn't know and didn't bother
finding out. He got back the rest of the way to the other side

of the tracks on knees that made him ashamed of them, they jogged so.

"Now just for that," he growled unreasonably at the blank window, "I'm gonna slap you up plenty for attempting to escape while under arrest, or something!"

The plank, when he paid it out, bridged the gap neatly, but at rather a steep incline, the window-ledge being higher than the guard-rail of the "El" structure. The distance, however, was so short that this didn't worry him. He took the precaution of taking out his gun, to forestall any attempt to shake him off his perch before he could grab the window-sash, but so far there had been no sign of life from within the room. They were probably sleeping it off.

He got up on the bottom rail, put his knee on the plank, and a minute later was groveling across it in mid-air, above the short but very deep chasm. It slipped diagonally downward toward the "El" a little under his weight, but not enough to come off the ledge. The next minute he had his free hand hooked securely around the wooden window-frame and was over and in.

He took a deep breath of relief, but still wouldn't have been willing to admit that this was a lot of trouble to go to just to get out of climbing a flock of stairs. He was that way. Without looking down just now, he'd been dimly aware of people milling about on the street below him, shouting up. They'd taken him for crazy, he supposed.

A downtown train careened past just behind his back right then, and lighted up the interior of the room for him nicely, better than a pocket-flash. It also did something else—as though all these trains tonight bore him a personal grudge. It struck the lower edge of the plank he had just used, which extended too far in past the rail, with a crack and sent it hurtling down to the street below. As long as he hadn't been on it at the time, being cut off like this didn't worry him particularly—he'd intended walking down anyway. He only hoped those on the sidewalk would see it coming in time to dodge. They ought to, looking up the way they had been.

But before he could give it another thought, the flickering train-lights washing across the walls showed him that he wasn't alone in the room after all.

One-half of his quarry was lying there face-down across the bed. It was the lady-souse, and judging by the way her arms hung down on one side and her feet on the other she was more soused than ladylike. Step took his eye off her and followed the phantom yellow-square the last car-window made as it traveled around three of the walls after its mates and then flickered out in the opposite direction from the train. It had shown him a switch by the door. So the place was wired for electricity, decrepit as it was. There was a moment of complete darkness, and then he had the room-light on.

He turned back to her. "Hey, you!" he growled. "Where's that guy that was in here with you a couple minutes ago? Get up offa there and answer me before I—!"

But she wasn't answering anybody any more. The bullet-hole under her left eye answered for her, when he tilted her face. It said: *Finished!* The cheek was all pitted with powder-burns. There was a playing-card symbol, the crimson ace of diamonds, on the white counterpane where the wound had rested. His eye traveled around the room. No radio, nothing to make music. They hadn't been dancing. That had been her death-struggle in his arms. The first shot had missed her, had killed the man named Wall in the first car of the "El" instead; the second one must have come a split-second after Step's car-window passed beyond range. The same bullet hadn't killed both; hers was still in her head. There was no wound of egress.

Step didn't bother playing detective, snooping around, even examining the remaining rooms of the tawdry little flat. His technique would have astounded a layman, horrified a rookie, probably only have made his superior sigh resignedly and shrug. "Well, that's Step for you." What he did about getting after the culprit, in a murder that had been committed so recently it was still smoking, was to pull over a warped rocking-chair, sit down, and begin rolling a cigarette. His attitude implied that it had tired him plenty to walk the tracks all the way back here, and everything could wait until he'd rested up a little. An occasional flickering of the eyelids, however, betokened that all was not as quiet on the inside of his head as on the outside.

The woman's hands seemed to fascinate him. The tips of her fingers were touching the floor, as though she were trying to balance herself upside-down. He took them up in his own and looked more closely. The nails were polished and well cared for. He turned them palm-up. The skin was not coarse and reddened, by dishwashing and housework. "You didn't belong here on Greenwich Street," he remarked. "Wonder who you were hiding from?"

A long spike of ash had formed on the end of his cigarette, and crummy as the place was, he looked around for something to park it in. No ashtrays in sight; evidently the dead lady hadn't been a smoker. He flicked the ash off into space, and as he did so, his eyes traveled down the seam between two of the unpainted floor-boards. Wedged into it was a butt. He got it out with the aid of a pin from his lapel. The mouth-end was still damp. Her lips, he had noticed, had been reddened fairly recently. But there wasn't a fleck of color on this. Not hers, therefore.

He dropped the cigarette he had been smoking and crushed it out, then passed the other one back and forth under his nose a couple of times. An acrid odor immediately took the place of the aroma of his familiar Virginia tobacco. He went a step further, put a lighted match to the end of it and tried to draw on it without actually touching it to his lips, still holding it on the pin. He had to suck mightily to start it glowing. Instantly there were results. His lungs smarted. And yet it wasn't the smoke of the burning paper he was getting, as in the case of an ordinary cigarette. That was escaping at both ends. It was the vapor of the weed that filled it.

Marihuana—crazy-weed. And unwittingly he'd gone about

just the right way of smoking it, not letting it come into contact with his lips. A vacuous, boisterous laugh wrenched from him abruptly, over the slain woman's head. Nothing to laugh at, and here he was roaring. He dropped the damned thing precipitately, trod on it as though it were a snake, opened his mouth and fanned pure air into it. The booming laugh subsided to a chortle, ebbed away. He mopped his forehead, got up, and went unsteadily toward the outer door of the flat.

The din down below in the street seemed to have increased a hundredfold, meanwhile; he couldn't be sure whether it actually had or it was just the after-effects of the drugged cigarette making it seem so. Sirens screeching, bells clanging, voices yelling—as though there were a whole crowd milling around out there.

He opened the flat door, and you couldn't see your hand in front of your face. No lights out in the hall. Then he saw a peculiar hazy blur just a few feet away, up overhead, and realized that there *were* lights—but the building was on fire. It wasn't darkness he'd stepped out into, but a solid wall of smoke.

He could possibly have gotten out, still made the street from where he was, by a quick dash down the stairs then and there. Step Lively plus several whiffs of a drugged cigarette, however, was no combination calculated to equal a quick dash in any direction, up or down. He turned around coughing and shuffled back into the flat he had just emerged from, closing the door on the inferno outside.

To do him justice, it wasn't simply inertia or laziness this time that kept him up there where he was. Hundreds of men in hundreds of fires have hung back to drag somebody living out with them. But very few have lingered to haul out somebody already dead. That, however, was precisely what Step had gone back for. The lady was his corpus delicti and he wasn't leaving her there to be cremated.

That a fire should start up here and now, in the very building where a murder had been committed, was too much of a coinci-

dence. It was almost certainly a case of incendiarism on the
murderer's part, perpetrated in hopes of obliterating all traces
of his crime. "And if he was smoking that devilish butt I picked
up," he said to himself, "he wouldn't stop to worry about
whether anybody else was living in the building or not!"

He retrieved it a second time, what there was left of it, and
dropped it in his pocket, pin and all. Then he wrapped the
counterpane with the ace-of-diamonds symbol on it around the
woman, turning her into a bundle of laundry, and moved toward the door with her. The current failed just as he was fumbling at it with one hand, under her, and the room went black.

A dull red glow shone up the stairwell, though, when he got
it open. It would have been all right to see by, but there wasn't
anything to breathe out there any more, just blistering heat and
strangling smoke. Spearheads of yellow started to shoot up
through it from below, like an army with bayonets marching up
the stairs. He got back inside again, hacking and with water
pouring out of his eyes, but hanging onto her like grim death,
as though she were some dear one instead of just a murdered
stranger he had happened to find.

The room was all obliterated with haze now, like the hallway
had been the first time, but he groped his way through it to the
window. He didn't lose his head; didn't even get frightened.
That was all right for women or slobs in suspenders, trapped on
the top floor of a blazing tenement. "I didn't come in through
the door, anyway," he growled. He was good and sore, though,
about all this hectic activity he was having to go through. "I
should 'a' been home long ago, and had my shoes off—" he was
thinking as he leaned out across the sill and tried to signal to the
mob that he could hear, but no longer see, down on the street.

He was hidden from them, and they from him, by the smoke
billowing out from the windows below him. It formed a regular
blanket between—but not the kind that it paid to jump into.
Still, the apparatus must be ganged up down there by this time.
You'd think they'd do something about helping a fellow get

down, whether they could see him or not. Somebody must have almost certainly spotted him climbing in. . . .

Even if he still had the plank, he couldn't have made it across on that any more. He not only had *her* now, but his lungs and eyes were going all wacky with this damn black stuff; he'd have toppled off it in a minute. The crack he'd just made to himself about having his shoes off at home registered. He parked her across the sill, bunched one leg, and started unlacing. It took him about forty-five seconds to undo the knot and slip the oxford off—which for him was excellent time. He poised it and flung it down through the smoke. If it would only bean somebody now, they'd stop and think maybe that shoes don't come flying down out of a fire unless there's somebody up there in it alive.

It did. A section of ladder shot up out of the swirling murk just as it left his hand. The helmeted figure scampering up monkeylike met the shoe halfway, with the bridge of his nose, and nearly went off into space. He flailed wildly with one propeller-like arm, caught the ladder once more in the nick of time, and resumed his ascent—a brief nosebleed to add to his troubles. Such language Step had rarely heard before. "Oops," he murmured regretfully. "Shows it never pays to be too hasty. What I've always said."

The fireman wiped his mouth, growled: "C'mon, step out and over, the roof's gonna go any minute." He was on a level with Step's eyes now, outside the window. The room was about ready to burst with heat; you could hear the floor-boards cracking as they expanded.

Step reared the mummy-like figure, thrust it across the sill into the smoke-eater's arms. "Take this stiff and be careful of her," he coughed. "She's valuable. I'll be right down on top of you."

The fireman, hooked onto the ladder by his legs, slung the burden over his shoulder, clamped it fast with one arm, and started down. Step started to climb over the sill backwards. The smoke was worse out here than in the room, he couldn't see the ladder any more. A silvery lining to the smoke, like a halo all around him, showed they were training a searchlight up from below, but it couldn't get through the dense, boiling masses. He found a rung with his one stockinged foot, made passes at the air until he'd finally connected with one of the invisible shafts —and the rest was just a switch over. Try it sometime yourself.

Then he stayed where he was until he'd shrugged his coat half-off his shoulders and hooded it completely over his head. Then he went down slowly, blind, deaf, seared, and breathing into worsted a little at a time. He went down ten stories, twenty, fifty—and still the ground wouldn't come up and meet him. He decided the place must have been the Empire State in disguise. One time he passed through a spattering of cool, grateful spray blown off one of the hose-lines and almost felt like sticking around in it, it felt so good. Just about the time he decided that the ladder must be slowly moving upward under him, like a belt-line or treadmill, and that was why he wasn't getting anywhere, hands grabbed him at the ankles and shoulders and he was hoisted to terra firma a yard below.

"Bud," said the Fire Chief patiently, "as long as you were in shape to climb down on your own, couldn't you have made it a *little* faster? I'm a very nervous man."

Step disengaged his head from his coat, kissed himself on the knuckles, bent down and rapped them against the Greenwich Street sidewalk. Then he straightened up and remonstrated: "I never was rushed so in my life as I been for the past half-hour!" He glanced upward at the haze-blurred building, whose outline was beginning to emerge here and there from the haze of smoke.

"The fire," the Chief enlightened him, turning away, "was brought under control during the half-hour you were passing the third floor. We finally put it out during the, er, forty-five minutes it took you getting from there down. The assistant marshal's in there now conducting an investigation—" Which may have leaned more toward sarcasm than accuracy, but was a good example of the impression Step made upon people the very first time they encountered him.

"Tell him for me," Step said, "it was arson—nothing else but. He mayn't be able to find any evidence, but that doesn't alter the fact any."

"A firebug, you think?"

"Something just a step worse. A murderer. A pyromaniac is irresponsible, afflicted, can't help himself. This dog knew just what he was doing, killed his conscience for both acts ahead of time with marihuana." He pointed to the muffled figure on the stretcher. "That woman was shot dead a good quarter of an hour before the fire was discovered. I was a witness to it. I'm Lively, of the —th Precinct, uptown."

The fire chief muttered something that sounded like: "You may be attached to that precinct, but you're not lively." But he was diplomatic enough to keep it blurred. "But if you were a witness," he said aloud, "how is it the guy—?"

"Powdered? I wasn't in the room with them, I glimpsed it from an 'El' train that stalled for a minute opposite the window! You go in there and tell your marshal not to bother looking for gasoline cans or oil-soaked rags. He didn't have time for a set-up like that, must have just put a match to a newspaper running down the stairs. Where's the caretaker or janitor, or didn't the dump have one?"

"Over behind the ropes there, in the crowd across the street. Take him over and point out the guy to him, Marty."

Step trailed the fireman whom he had clouted with his shoe —which incidentally had vanished—limping on his one unshod foot, and ducked under the rope beside a grizzled, perspiring little man. Palmed his badge at him to add to his terror, and asked, while his eyes roved the crowd that hemmed them in: "Who was the woman top-floor front?"

"Insoorance?" whined the terrified one.

"No, police department. Well, come on—"

"Smiff. Miss Smiff."

Step groaned. But he'd figured she'd been hiding out anyway, so it didn't really matter much. "How long she been living up there in your house?"

"Ten day."

"Who visited her, see anybody?"

"Nome-body. She done even go out; my wife bring food."

Good and scared, reflected Step. Scared stiff, but it hadn't saved her. "Did you hear anything tonight just before the fire? Were you in the building? Hear a couple shots? Hear any screams?"

"No hear no-thing, train make too much noise. Only hear fella laff coming downstairs, like somebody tell-im good joke. Laff, laff, laff, all the way out to street—"

The marihuana, of course. Just two drags had affected his own risibilities. The effects of a whole reefer ought to last hours, at that rate. Step shoved away from the futile janitor, flagged one of the patrolmen holding the crowd in check behind the rope-barrier, introduced himself. The excitement was tapering off, now that everyone was out of the house and the fire had been subdued, it was only a matter of minutes before they'd start melting away. Overhead the "El" trains, which had been held back at Desbrosses Street while the smoke had been at its thick-est, were again being allowed through, although surface traffic was still being detoured.

"Who's on this job with you?" Step asked the cop in a low voice.

"One other guy, down at the other end."

"Think the two of you can keep 'em in like they are, another couple minutes?"

The cop looked insulted. "That's what we been doing. You don't see anybody edging out into the middle of the street, do ya?"

"No, you don't understand what I mean. Can you put up another rope at each side, hem them in where they are, keep

them from strolling off just a little while longer till I get a chance
to take a careful look through them all?"

"I'm not authorized to keep people from going about their
business, as long as they don't hamper the fire apparatus—"

"I'll take the responsibility. There's someone I'm out to get,
and I've got a very good hunch he's right here looking on.
Firebugs are known to do that, murderers too when they think
they're safe from discovery. When you've got a combination of
both, the urge to stay and gloat ought to be twice as strong!

"Bawl me out," he added abruptly, "so it don't look too
phony, my standing talking to you like this."

The cop swung his club at him, barked: "Get back there!
Whaddya think that rope's for? Get back there before I—"

Step cringed away from him, began to elbow his way deeper
into the tightly-packed crowd jamming the narrow sidewalk.
He did this as slow as he did everything else, didn't seem like
anyone who had a definite place to go, just a rubber-necker
working his way toward a better vantage-point. From time to
time he glanced over at the gutted building, or what could be
seen of it under the shadowy "El" structure that bisected the
street vertically. Torches blinked deep within the front hallway
of it, as firemen passed in and out, still veiled by the haze that
clung to it.

There wasn't, however, enough smoke left in the air, certainly not this close to the ground, to send anyone into parox-
ysms of strangled coughing. Such as that individual just ahead
was experiencing, handkerchief pressed to mouth. Step himself
had inhaled as much smoke as anyone, and his lungs were back
on the job again as good as ever. He kept facing the burned
building from this point on, edging over sidewise to the afflicted
one. The spasms would stop and he'd lower the handkerchief;
then another one would come on and he'd raise it again and
nearly spill himself into it. Step was unobtrusively at his elbow
by now.

When a person is suffering from a coughing-fit, two ways of

assisting them will occur to almost anybody. Offer them a drink of water or slap them helpfully on the back. Step didn't have any water to offer, so he chose the second means of alleviation. Slapped the tormented one between the shoulder-blades: but just once, not several times, and not nearly forcefully enough to do any good. "You're under arrest," he said desultorily, "come on."

The concealing handkerchief dropped—this time all the way to the ground. "What for? What're you talking about?"

"For two murders and an arson," drawled the wearied Step. "I'm talking about you. And don't be afraid to laugh right out. No need to muffle it with your handkerchief and try to change it into a cough any more. That was what gave you away to me. When you've been smoking marihuana, you've just gotta laugh or else— But watching fires isn't the right place to do your laughing. And if it had been real coughing, you wouldn't have stayed around where the smoke irritated you that much. Now show me where you dropped the gun before you came back here to watch, and then we'll get in a taxi. I wouldn't ask my feet to carry me another step tonight."

His prisoner bayed uncontrollably with mirth, then panted: "I never was in that building in my life—" Writhed convulsively.

"I saw you," said Step, pushing him slowly before him through the crowd, "through the window from an 'El' train as I was going by." He knew the soporific effect the drug was likely to have, its blunting of the judgment. "She came to us and told us she was afraid of this happening to her, asked for protection, and we been giving it to her. Did you think you could get away with it?"

"Then what'd she rat on Plucky at his trial for? She knew what to expect. He sent out word—"

"Oh, that vice trial. And she was one of the witnesses? I see." Step slammed the door of the cab on the two of them. "Thanks for telling me; now I know who she was, who you are, and why it was done. There is something to be said for marihuana after all. Not much, but maybe just a little."

When he stepped out of the cab with his handcuffed quarry at the foot of the Franklin Street station four blocks away, he directed the driver: "Now sound your horn till they come down off of up there." And when they did, his mates found Inspector Stephen Lively seated upon the bottom step of the station-stairs, his prisoner at his side.

"Fellas," he said apologetically, "this is the guy. And if I gotta go up there again to the top, I wonder could you two make a saddle with your hands and hoist me between you. I'm just plumb tuckered out!"

The fast-action whizbang, very simply plotted but tied to a specific and unusual background, was a Woolrich specialty. His best-known story in this vein is "You Pays Your Nickel" (*Argosy*, 8/22/36, later retitled "Subway"), but several others remain uncollected: "The Show-boat Murders" (*Detective Fiction Weekly*, 12/14/35), "Murder on the Night Boat" (*Black Mask*, 2/37), and (until now) the above story. Although dozens of mysteries have been set on trains, and Ellery Queen's *The Tragedy of X* (1932) makes brilliant use of the streetcar, the elevated train system has never been integral to a crime story except for "Death in the Air." The almost cinematic evocation of the El, and of what one could see through its windows during the Depression, marks the story as distinctively Woolrichian, and the treatment of marijuana as some sort of devil's brew (which Woolrich repeated in his great story "Marihuana") places the tale as of a time before the facts about pot became common knowledge.

Mamie 'n' Me

She kept reading about it all through the meal. She even cried a little, thinking about it. On account of our own, I guess. She got up twice and went in to look, to see if ours was all right, sleeping in there in the dark. She came back and said, "I'm going to lock the door good and tight, after you go to work."

"It wouldn't happen to people like us," I tried to point out. "It's only when you've got a lot of money they do that to you."

"I don't care, money or no money, it's the most unforgivable crime there is, Terry." Her eyes got all bright blue and blazing, like they do whenever she gets good and sore about something. "I could forgive anything quicker than that. I could understand

272

a man robbing a bank, or even taking another man's life, but to take a poor helpless little mite like that from its mother! I keep thinking what she must be feeling all day today, since she first went in to look at it this morning and found it gone."

I sort of hung my head. It did get you. It was lousy. It was the lowest thing under God's sun to do to anyone. I wasn't trying to say it wasn't. I was only trying to say there was nothing poor devils like us could do about it.

"And it'll die on their hands, poor little thing!" she went on. She slapped at the newspaper. "Look there! It's got to have a special diet. It's got to have that new kind of milk with codliver oil in it. She's asked the papers to print that, hoping it'll catch their eye. As though *they* care, or know enough to look after it!"

It was nearly midnight on the alarm, and I had to go. I felt bad as she did, but I had one of my own to provide for. I stuck my hand in the sugar bowl and couldn't get it out again. That cheered her up a little. She laughed. "That Mamie, always eating me out of house and home!" Then when I got it out and started filling my pockets, she cracked my hand one. "Two's enough now!" she said, and put the lid back on the bowl.

"I like her better than I do you," I said, picking up my cap. "She's my real girl."

"Why didn't you marry her, then?" she snapped. She held her face up to me at the door.

"Don't keep thinking about the Ellerton case," I said. "Try to get some sleep. See you in the morning."

But I heard her turn the lock and put on the safety catch after the door was closed.

It was a swell night, clear and crisp, and all the stars were out. I took the subway to the division stable. Everybody in the car was reading about it. "No Word Yet," one scarehead said. I heard one man say to another, "They'll be afraid to bring it back now, even after they get the money; afraid of their own precious skins. It'll be the same thing over again, like so many times before."

I thought, pumping the china ring I was holding back and forth, "I'd like to get my hands on 'em!" A million other guys like me must have been saying that all over the city tonight. Day dreams.

Mamie was sure glad to see me when I got to the stable. She whinnied and pawed and her little ears stuck up straight. I said, "How's my best girl? Lemme see if I got something for my best girl." I pretended I couldn't find anything, and she stuck her head down to my pocket and snuffled. She knew where I carried the sugar all right.

I harnessed her myself. I always did; she liked me to better than the stableman, although he was around her more than me. But I was her best beau, I took her out stepping. We rolled out of the stable and down to the plant, and got on line back of the loading-platforms to wait our turn at filling-up.

All the guys were talking about it too. Michaelman said, "Just the same it's a great boost for our Sun-Ray milk, her mentioning the kid has to have it, in all the papers like that. Wait'll you see the calls that start to come in for it."

We all gave him cold looks, like he was out of order. Somebody said, "The firm don't need business that bad, if it's got to be built up on somebody's grief," and I wished it had been me. I'd been thinking that, but I hadn't been able to put the words together right.

I left Mamie on line and went to take a look in my order-drawer in the office. New orders and cancellations, you know. Once in awhile extras too, but mostly those are asked for by note outside the customer's door. There wasn't very much doing and it kind of worried me. Part of the job is to get new customers, see. Not by direct soliciting, like a salesman, but just sort of intangibly, by the kind of service you give your old ones. Promotion depends on three things in my line: getting new orders, getting the old ones paid up on time, and the number of empties you collect and turn in.

I went back shaking my head to myself; not a new order in the drawer. As soon as I got my load stowed aboard and checked, Mamie and me started out. She knew the way down to where the route began, I just held the reins on one finger and let her take her own head. There was no one much but us on the streets any more, no lights to stop for; and her hoofbeats rang out clear and loud on the quiet air. They had a soothing sound to me, but I guess everyone's different; I wasn't in bed trying to get some sleep. When we got there she swung into the first route-block and stopped dead in front of the right door, of her own accord.

I only had a two-block route, most of them are short like that in the built-up parts of town, but it wasn't the cream of the bottle by any means. Deliveries were swiped right and left, and it was a tough neighborhood to make collections in. I always expected to be held up, even in the daytime, before I got back to the office with my receipts.

I loaded up my trays, gave Mamie her second piece of sugar, and climbed up five flights. You work walk-ups from the top down, elevator-buildings from the bottom up. Don't ask me why. There wasn't an elevator on my whole route.

The Flannery girl on the fourth floor had been out with the young fellow her Ma didn't like again, and was getting it laced into her while she undressed. You could hear it all up and down the hall.

"I'm telling ye for the last time, he'll nivver amount to nothing, you mark my words, young lady! Barney I can't get ye to go out with, no, it's always a headache ye've got, but this good-for-nothing ye'll gallivant with until al' hours of the night!"

And then a plaintive little whine, "But Ma, if you could only see how he does the Big Apple—"

I came out again, and Mamie had moved down one door without being told and was waiting for me to catch up with her. I filled up again and went in the second house. There was a fellow sleeping on the stairs between the third and fourth, all huddled up in a knot. I thought he was a drunk at first, and stepped over him without disturbing him, which is no cinch carrying fifty pounds of loaded baskets. But when I came down again, he woke up and looked at me kind of scared. He was just a kid, eighteen or nineteen, and he looked all in.

"What's matter, got no place to sleep?" I asked him.

"No," he admitted, sort of frightened, as though he thought I was going to turn him over to a cop or something. "I been walking around all day and—"

I went on down a couple of steps, then I stopped and looked back at him again. I caught him looking at my tray and kind of swallowing hard. "When'd you eat last?" I said curtly.

He seemed to have a hard time remembering for a minute. "Yesterday morning," he faltered finally.

"Here, wrap yourself around this," I said. I passed him a pint I happened to have on my tray. It was only a dime out of my own pocket, anyway. He started to pull at the hinge cap like he couldn't get it off fast enough. He needed it so bad he even forgot to say thanks, which is needing a thing bad all right.

"Take it easy," I warned him gruffly, "or you'll give yourself the bends. Bring me down the empty when you're through."

Afterward I watched him meander on up the street away from there. I don't feel sorry for him, I said to myself, he's only eighteen or nineteen; couple years from now he'll be making more than I do myself.

Mamie turned her head around and looked at me, much as to say: You're telling me?

I ran into a sort of minor commotion on the second floor, half a dozen houses further along. A guy was trying to get in Mrs. Hatchett's door. He belonged in there, but she wouldn't let him come in. He was plenty lush.

"I warned you!" her voice came back shrilly from the inside, "I warned you next time you came home in that condition I'd lock you out!"

He heard me going by on my way up, and took me into his confidence a hall-length away. " 'S a disgrashe, tha's what it is! Her own husband!"

"Sure," I said inattentively. "Sure," and went on up.

When I came down again, he was very quiet all of a sudden, and I thought the light on the hall walls looked different, kind of flickering. I dropped my trays with a bang and sprinted down to him. He'd hauled some newspapers up against the doorseam and put a match to them. I stiff-armed him away and he toppled over into a sitting position. I stamped them out, and then I hammered good and businesslike on the door myself. She seemed to know the difference right away, she came back again.

"You better take him inside with you, lady, before he burns the building down!" I said.

"Oh, so tha's the kind of a guy you are!" he said offendedly. "Well now I don't wanna go in no more, how do you like that?"

She opened the door, cracked a whiplike "Get in here!" at him, that brought him submissively to his feet and made him sidle cringingly by her without a word. She only came up to his shoulders.

"Sometimes," I told Mamie downstairs, "I don't think I appreciate you half enough."

I'd never liked the next house over. It was as old as all the others, but had been done over to comply with the housing regulations. That only made it worse, it attracted a lot of fly-by-nights who weren't bound by leases, here today and gone tomorrow; they were always skipping out and gypping me out of my collections. I'd been held up in here once too, six months before, and I hadn't forgotten it.

I only needed one tray for this house; most of the tenants weren't great milk-drinkers. I only had one customer on the whole top floor and she was three weeks overdue on her bill. I delivered her order, and a note with it. "No doubt it has escaped your attention—" Like hell it had. You couldn't get her to answer her doorbell on collection days; she lay low in there. At least she hadn't moved out, that was something.

On the floor below, the fifth, I had a new customer, dating from the previous week. When I went over to the door, they'd left a note out for me—in the neck of a beer-bottle!

Lieve us a bottle of your Sun-Ray milk, we would like to try it out.
                                                                    E-5.

While I was standing there puzzling out the scrawl—and it took plenty of puzzling out the way it was written—I could hear the faint wail of a kid coming from inside the flat. Like a kitten left out in the rain, that weak and thin.

It was a sad sort of sound; made me feel sorta blue.

I hadn't really expected any orders for Sun-Ray, not around this district. It cost twenty-two a quart, pretty steep for these kind of people. I'd brought just one bottle along with me in the wagon, in case I needed it. I went downstairs again to get it. I thought: Michaelman was right, they are starting to call for it, like he said. Starting early—

That reminded me of the Ellerton case. The photostat of the ransom note she'd found this morning in the kid's bed, which all the papers had shown, came before me again like when Mil had shown it to me. "Lieve the money—" These people upstairs didn't know how to spell that word either. Such an easy word, too, you wouldn't think anyone would trip over it. And here were two different note-writers, both in the same day, doing it.

Two *different* note-writers—?

That started a new train of thought, and my jaw sagged.

I looked up at the windows from the sidewalk. One was lit up, with the shade down all the way, but the other was dark. I was thinking. Funny, there was no kid around when I was in there Monday collecting for the first week. Now they've got one all of a sudden, just like that! And even if it was out being aired when I was up there, there would have been some of its clothes or something around, and there weren't any. Ours always has its—those whaddye-call-it three-cornered things—hanging all around the place. And then I was remembering something else, even stranger. When she left me for a minute to get the change to pay me, I spotted all the milk I'd delivered up to then, five bottles of it, standing untouched under the sink. If they didn't use it, why did they order it and pay for it? Unless they expected ahead of time to need some milk in the place, but didn't know just when it was going to be, and wanted to be ready with it when the time came.

There was something sort of chilly about that thought.

I went upstairs again with the delivery they'd asked for. The wailing was still going on, until I got right opposite the door. Then I heard a woman's voice say, "Close that door, it drives me nuts!" and the sound died down, you couldn't hear it any more. So the kid wasn't in the same room with them.

That diet that Mrs. Ellerton had asked the papers to print for her, it had something else in it too. Oh yeah, oranges. A lot of orange juice.

There was an incinerator door down the hall. I went down there and opened it quietly and looked in. The kind of people that lived here were too lazy to throw the stuff down the chute, just chucked it in behind the door. There was a bag in the corner that had split open from its own fall; it had half-a-dozen orange rinds in it.

I went downstairs again. I felt nervous and spooky, and wished I knew what to do. I wondered if I was making a fool out of myself, and half of me said I was, and the other half of me said I wasn't.

It was the kind of a toss-up that makes a man pretty darned uncomfortable.

Mamie started to amble down to the next stop when she saw me. I said, "Whoa," and she stayed where she was, but turned to look around at me kind of questioningly, as if to say, "What's taking you so long in there tonight?"

I lit a cigarette and stared inside of my wagon, without seeing anything, if you know what I mean. All of a sudden I'd thrown the cigarette down and was going inside a third time, without exactly knowing how it happened. My feet seemed to carry me along of their own accord. I'd left my trays outside.

I went all the way up to the roof this time. The roof-door was only held by a hook on the inside. I got out through it without any trouble. I tiptoed across the tar and gravel and started climbing down the fire escape that served the front windows of the house. I had to go real slow, I wasn't much used to fire escapes. I thought, "If a cop comes along and looks up and sees me—" but I kept going down anyway.

When I got down level with the fifth floor, I couldn't see in the lighted window, the shade was fitted to it skin-tight. I was scared stiff the thing would creak under me. I crept over to the dark one next to it. I put the edge of my hands up against the pane and tried to squint through them. All I could make out was a couple of white shapes like beds. But the window was open a couple of inches from the top, and I could hear that same faint wail out here like I had in the hall.

I saw myself landed in jail, with my job gone and Mil worried sick, but somehow I went ahead and started inching the lower pane up from the bottom. It was like something had hold of me that was beyond my control, wouldn't let me quit. I think it was that wailing, that seemed to keep asking for help and nobody listened.

It was making me feel sorta crazy. I had to stop it, somehow. . . .

When I had the lower pane even with the top, I eased across onto the floor, but careful where I put my feet. You could see an orange line along the floor where the door to the next room was, and you could hear their voices clear and loud every once in awhile, like they were playing cards.

One bed was empty but the other had a bundle of old clothes on it. The wailing was coming right from the middle of them.

I shifted my body between them and the room door, and lit a match, and held it covered by my hands so it wouldn't glow much. There was a little bit of a crinkled red face staring up at me from the middle of all the blankets and things. The top one was pinned down on both sides so it couldn't fall off the bed. It had a pale-blue initial down in the corner of it; E.

Their name, here, was supposed to be Harris; I had it on my order slip. E. Ellerton began with E. Something tickled my forehead for a minute, and it was a drop of sweat.

I don't think I'd have had the nerve to go ahead and do it, if they'd kept quiet. I think I'd have backed out again the way I came in, and maybe just gone looking for the cop on the beat and told him what I suspected. Because if I took it out of here without being sure, it meant I was just doing to them what somebody else had done to the Ellertons. Lots of people give their kids oranges and special milk, and the blanket could have been borrowed from a relative.

But all of a sudden a man's voice said real irritable in the next room, "Can't you do something to shut it up? I'm going wacky! Go out and see if the milkman left that bilge you ast for, maybe that'll quiet it." I kind of lost my head altogether when I heard her footsteps tap-tap down the hall to the front-door. I knew I had to get out in a hurry, couldn't stand there trying to make up my mind any more, and it took all my presence of mind away. Before I knew what I was doing I started unfastening the safety-pins; I never knew how tricky they were to open until then, it seemed to take me a week to get rid of them.

Then I grabbed up the whole bundle of blankets, kid and all, and backed out the window with them.

It was shorter to go back up to the roof with it than to try to climb all the way down the front of the building to the street. I went up the tricky iron slats fast this time, noise or no noise, and across, and down the inside stairs. I had to get down past their floor before they came out and cut me off.

I just made it. I could hear the commotion, hear the woman yelp, "It's gone!" as I flashed down and around the landing, but they hadn't opened their door yet. It was wailing the whole time, but in broken snatches now, not one long stretch, like it liked the hurry and shaking I was giving it.

I ran faster.

I tore out to the wagon with it and shoved it in. It had to go right on the ice, where the butter and stuff was, and I knew that wasn't going to be good for it, but it couldn't be helped. Maybe the cold would take awhile to work through all those layers of blankets.

They came racing out right at my heels. All I had time to do was go, "Chk chk" to Mamie and get her to start on with it, reach down to pick up my trays, when they were standing all around me. There were three of them and they were still all in their shirt sleeves. One of them had a gun out in his hand and didn't care who saw it.

He snarled, "Hey, you! Did anybody just come out of that door?"

He had a real ugly look to him. "Well, did they or didn't they?" he said again.

When he put it that way, why should I say no? "Yeah," I said, "a fellow just came out ahead of you, carrying some laundry. He went up that way." I pointed to the opposite direction from Mamie. The clop-clop of her hoofs and the creak of the wheels drowned out the wailing, from where we were standing. She was starting to slow again, at the next house down, so I went, "Chk chk" again. She turned and looked back at me, as if to say: "Are you crazy, skipping our next stop like this?" but she went on toward the corner.

I didn't think they'd believe me, Mil says she can always tell when I'm lying, but I guess they didn't know me as well as she does.

"Laundry, eh?" the one with the gun said viciously, and they turned and went streaming up toward where I'd pointed, one

behind the other. "Hijacked right under our noses!" I heard one
of them mutter.

The other one cursed back over his shoulder as they ran.

The woman came out just as they started off. She wasn't
crying or anything, she just looked sore and mean. "I'm not
staying up there to hold the bag!" she said, and went skittering
after them.

I picked up my trays and started after Mamie and the wagon,
but I kept going, "Chk chk" so she wouldn't stop and uncover
that wailing sound. A minute after they'd gone around that
upper corner I heard a shot ring out. Maybe they'd run into the
cop on the beat, and he didn't like people to come around
corners with guns in their hands at that hour. But by that time
I'd caught up to the wagon and climbed up behind Mamie. I
didn't hang around waiting to find out what it was, I passed up
all the rest of my deliveries and lit out.

Mamie put on speed willingly enough, but I had a hard time
with her. She kept trying to head back to the division stable, like
other nights when we got through. The papers had said the
Ellertons lived at 75 Mount Pleasant Drive. I didn't have any
trouble remembering that, it had been repeated over and over.
It was on the outskirts of the city, along Jorgensen's route.

The nearer I got to it, the more scared I got. I was more
scared now than even when I took it out of the room and up the
fire-escape with me. Suppose—suppose it wasn't the one? That
was why I didn't stop and turn it over to a cop on the way; *he*
wouldn't know any more than I did, Mrs. Ellerton was the only
one would know for sure, and I wanted to get the suspense over
with as quickly as I could.

A block away from where they lived I remembered to take
it up off the ice. I laid it across my lap on the driver's seat and
kept it from falling off with one hand. The outside blanket was
kind of cold already, but the inside ones were still warm. It quit
wailing and looked up at me with its weazened little face, like

it enjoyed riding like that. I grinned at it and it kind of opened
its mouth and grinned back, only it didn't have any teeth.

Their place was all lit up when I got there, with a bunch of
cars lined up in front of it. I found a place for Mamie to pull
up in, and got down and carried it up to the house with me
under one arm. I noticed it was facing upside down, so I stopped
a minute and turned it right side up so they wouldn't get sore.

A man opened the door the minute I rang the bell, like he'd
been standing there waiting all night. I started, "Will you ask
Mrs. Ellerton if this is her baby—?" but I never got any further
than that. He snatched it away from me before I knew what
happened. So fast, in fact, that the whole outside blanket fell off
it onto the floor.

There were a lot of people in the room behind him, and they
all started to get very excited. A man started to call someone's
name in a thick, choked voice, and a lady in a pink dressing
gown came flying down the stairs so fast it's a wonder she didn't
trip.

She never said from first to last whether it was hers or not,
all she did was grab it up and hold it to her and sort of waltz
around with it, so I guess it was.

A couple of the men there, detectives I guess, were standing
in the doorway asking me where I found it and all about it,
when suddenly she came rushing over to me, and before I could
stop her grabbed up my hand and started to kiss it. "Aw, don't,
lady," I said. "I haven't washed 'em since I left home to go to
work."

I couldn't get away until long after the sun came up. I kept
trying to tell them I still had some deliveries to make, and all
they kept saying was couldn't they do something for me? Well,
when they put it that way, why should I be bashful?

"Sure," I said finally, "if it's no trouble, you could let me have
a couple pieces of sugar for Mamie, this part of town is off her
route and she probably feels pretty strange out there."

They all stood there looking at me like I'd said something wonderful. I don't see anything wonderful about that, do you?

Here for the first and only time in this book Woolrich is fully at peace with the world, telling a gentle little story about a gentle little man and making magic with both, evoking the city before dawn and making the phantoms vanish with the sunrise. This is the shortest story in the book and one of the most rewarding.

III

THE BUTCHERS
AND THE TRAPPED

The Screaming Laugh

A call came into constabulary headquarters, at the county seat, about seven one morning. It was from Milford Junction, a local doctor named Johnson reporting the death of one Eleazar Hunt sometime during the night. Just a routine report, as required by law.

"And have you ascertained the causes?" asked the sheriff.

"Yes, I just got through examining him. I find he had burst a blood vessel—laughing too hard. Nothing out of the usual about it, but of course that's for you to decide."

"Well, I'll send a man over to check." The sheriff turned to Al Traynor, one of the members of his constabulary, who had

just come in. "Drive down Milford Junction way, Al. Local resi-
dent near there, name of Eleazar Hunt, died from laughing too
hard. Look things over just for the record."

"Laughing too hard?" Traynor looked at him when he heard
that. Then he shrugged. "Well, I suppose if you've got to go, it's
better to go laughing than crying."

He returned to his car and started off for Milford Junction. It
was about three quarters of an hour's drive by the new State
highway that had been completed only two or three years
before, although the hamlet itself wasn't directly on this, had to
be reached by a dirt feeder road that branched off it. The Hunt
place was about half a mile on the other side of it, near a point
where the highway curved back again to rejoin the short cut,
cutting a corner off the late Mr. Hunt's acreage.

The white painted farmhouse with its green shutters gleamed
dazzlingly in the early morning sunshine. Peach trees, bursting
into bloom before it, hid the roof and cast blue shade on the
ground. A wire fence at the back enclosed a poultry yard, and
beyond that were hen houses, a stall from which a black and
white cow looked plaintively forth, a toolshed, a roofed well, a
vegetable garden. It was an infinitely pleasant-looking little
property, and if death had struck there at all, there was no
outward sign.

There was a coupé standing in the road before the house,
belonging to the doctor who had reported the death, presumably. Traynor coasted up behind it, braked, got out, and went in
through the gate. He had to crouch to pass under some of the
low hanging peach boughs. There was a cat sunning itself on the
lower doorstep. He reached down to tickle it and a man came
around the corner of the house just then, stood looking at him.

He was sunburned, husky, and about thirty. He wore overalls
and was carrying an empty millet sack in his hand. Judging by
the commotion audible at the back, he had just finished feeding
the poultry. His eyes were shrewd and lidded in a perpetual
squint that had nothing to do with the sun.

"You the undertaker already?" he wanted to know.

"Sheriff's office," snapped Traynor, none too pleased at the comparison. "You work here?"

"Yep. Hired man."

"How long?"

" 'Bout six months."

"What's your name?"

"Dan Fears."

"He keep anybody else on?"

Fears answered indirectly, with a scornful gesture toward the back. "Not enough to keep one man busy as it is. Tend one cow and pick up a few eggs."

It occurred to Traynor if there was that little to do, why hadn't the cow been led out to pasture by now and the poultry fed earlier? He went on in, stepping high over the cat. She looked indolently upward at his heel as it passed over her.

A shaggy, slow moving man was coming toward the screen door to meet Traynor as he pushed through it with a single cursory knock at its frame. Johnson was a typical country doctor, of a type growing scarcer by the year. You could tell by looking at him that he'd never hurried or got excited in his life. You could surmise that he'd never refused a middle-of-the-night call from miles away in the dead of winter either. He was probably highly competent, in spite of his misleading rusticity.

"Hello, son." He nodded benignly. "You from the sheriff's office? I was just going back to my own place to make out the death certificate."

"Can I see him?"

"Why, shore. Right in here." The doctor parted a pair of old-fashioned sliding doors and revealed the "front parlor" of the house. Across the top of each window was stretched a valance of faded red plush, ending in a row of little plush balls. On a table stood an oil lamp—there was no electricity this far out —with a frosted glass dome and a lot of little glass prisms dangling from it.

There was an old-fashioned reclining chair with an adjustable back near the table and lamp. Just now it was tilted only slightly, at a comfortable reading position. It was partly covered over with an ordinary bed sheet, like some furniture is in summertime, only the sheet bulged in places and a clawlike hand hung down from under it, over the arm of the chair. Traynor reached down, turned back the upper edge of the sheet. It was hard not to be jolted. The face was a cartoon of frozen hilarity. It wasn't just that death's-head grimace that so often, because of bared teeth, faintly suggests a grin. It was the real thing. It was Laughter, permanently photographed in death. The eyes were creased into slits; you could see the dried but still faintly glistening saline traces of the tears that had overflowed their ducts down alongside his nose. The mouth was a vast upturned crescent full of yellowish horse teeth. The whole head was thrown stiffly back at an angle of uncontrollable risibility. It was uncanny only because it was so motionless, so silent, so permanent.

"You found him just like this?"

"Shore. Had to examine him, of course, but rigor had already set in, so I figger nothing I did disturbed him much." Johnson chuckled inside himself, gave Traynor a humorously reproachful look. "Why, son, you don't think this is one of *those* things? Shame on you!"

He saw that he hadn't convinced the younger man by his raillery. "Why, I examined him thoroughly, son," he protested gently. "I know my business as well as the next man. I tell you not a finger was laid on this man. Nothing's happened to him but what I said. He burst a blood vessel from laughing too hard. Course, if you want me to perform a complete autopsy, send his innards and the contents of his stomach down to the State laboratory—" It was said with an air of paternal patience, as if he were humoring a headstrong boy.

"I'm not discrediting your competence, doctor. What's this?" Traynor picked up a little booklet, lying open tent-shaped on the table. "Joe Miller's Joke Book," it said on the cover, and the copyright was 1892.

"That's what he was reading. That's what got him, I reckon. Found it lying on the floor under his right hand. Fell from his fingers at the moment of death, I guess."

"Same page?"

"Same one it's open at now. You want to find the exact joke he was reading when he passed away, that what you're aiming at, son?" More of that paternal condescension.

Traynor evidently did, or at least an approximation of what type of killing humor this was. He stopped doing anything else and stood there stock-still for five minutes, conscientiously reading every joke on the two open pages, about a dozen altogether. The first one read:

Pat: Were you calm and collected when the explosion occurred?
Mike: I wuz calm and Murphy wuz collected.

The others were just about as bad, some even staler.

"Do me a favor, doc," he said abruptly, passing the booklet over. "Read these for yourself."

"Oh, now, here—" protested Johnson, with a rueful glance at the still form in the chair, but he went ahead and did what Traynor requested.

Traynor watched his expression closely. He'd only just met the man, but he could already tell he was full of a dry sort of humor. But not a gleam showed, his face never changed from first to last; it became, if anything, sort of mournful.

"D'you see what I mean?" was all Traynor said, taking the booklet back and tossing it aside.

Johnson shook his head. "No two people have the same sense of humor, remember that, son. What's excruciatingly funny to one man goes right over another's head. Likely, these jokes were new to him, not mossbacked like they are to you and me."

"Did you know him at all, doc?"

"Just to say howdy to on the road."

"Ever see him smile much?"

"Can't say I did. But there's nothing funny about saying

howdy. What is it you're driving at, son?"

Traynor didn't answer. He went over to the corpse, unbuttoned its shirt, and scrutinized the under arms and ribs with exhaustive intentness.

The doctor just stood looking on. "You won't find any marks of violence, son. I've been all over that."

Next Traynor squatted down by the feet, drew up one trousers leg to the knees, then the other. Johnson by this time, it was plain to see, considered him a bad case of dementia detectivis. Traynor seemed to see something at last; he smiled grimly. All Johnson could see were a pair of shanks encased in wool socks, supported by garters. Patent garters, sold by the million, worn by the million.

"Found something suspicious?" he asked, but without conviction, it was easy to see.

"Suspicious isn't the word," Traynor murmured low. "Damning."

"Damning whom—and of what?" said Johnson dryly.

Again Traynor didn't answer.

He hurriedly unlaced both of Hunt's shoes, dropped them off. Then he unfastened one garter and stripped the sock off his foot. Turned it inside out and peered at the sole. Peered at the sole of the foot itself too. He stripped the other one off and went through the same proceeding. Johnson, meanwhile, was shaking his head disapprovingly, as if his patience were being overtaxed.

"You are the most pee-culiar young fellow I ever hope to meet," he sighed.

Traynor balled up the two socks, and thrust one into each pocket of his coat, garter and all. They were black—fortunately. He flipped the sheet back over the bared feet, concealing them. A little wisp of something rose in the air as he did so, disturbed by the draft of his doing that, fluttered, winged downward again. A little bit of fluff, it seemed to be. He went after it, nevertheless, retrieved it, took an envelope out of his pocket, and thrust it in.

Johnson was past even questioning his actions by now; he was convinced they were unaccountable by all rational standards, anyway. "Would you care to talk to Mrs. Hunt?" he asked.

"Yes, I sure would," Traynor said curtly.

Johnson went out to the hall, called respectfully up the stairs: "Mrs. Hunt, honey."

She was very ready to come down, Traynor noticed. Her footsteps began to descend almost before the words were out of the doctor's mouth. As though she'd been poised right up above at the head of the staircase, waiting for the summons.

He couldn't help a slight start of surprise as she came into sight; he had expected someone near Hunt's own age. She was about twenty-eight, the buxom blond type. "Second wife," Traynor thought.

She had reached the bottom by now, and the doctor introduced them.

"This is Mr. Traynor of the sheriff's office."

"How do you do?" she said mournfully. But her eyes were clear, so she must have stopped crying some time before. "Did you want to talk to me?"

"Just to ask you the main facts, that's all."

"Oh. Well, let's go outdoors, huh? It—it sort of weighs you down in here." She glanced toward the partly open parlor doors, glanced hurriedly away again.

They went outside, began to stroll aimlessly along the front of the house, then around the corner and along the side. He could see Fears out there in the sun, beyond the poultry yard, hoeing the vegetable patch. Fears turned his head, looked over his shoulder at them as they came into sight, then looked down again. Hunt's widow seemed unaware of his existence.

"Well," she was saying, "all I can tell you is, I went upstairs to bed about ten o'clock last night, left him down there reading by the lamp. I'm a sound sleeper, and before I knew it, it was daybreak and the roosters woke me up. I saw he'd never come up to bed. I hurried down, and there he was just like I'd left him, lamp still lit and all, only the book had fallen out of his hand. He had this broad grin on his face and—"

"He did?" he interrupted.

"Yes. Isn't it spooky?" She shuddered. "Did you see it?"

"I did. And spooky," he said slowly, "is a very good word for it."

If he meant anything by that, she seemed to miss it completely.

She wound up the little there was left of her story. "I tried to wake him, and when I couldn't, I knew what it was. I called to Fears, but he was out back some place, so I ran all the way down the road to Doctor Johnson's house myself and brought him back."

"Did he usually stay down alone like that, nights, and read?"

"Yes. Only in the beginning, when I first married him, he used to read things like mail order catalogues and such. Well, I'd tried to liven him up a little lately. I bought that joke book for him and left it lying around, tried to coax him to read it. He wouldn't have any part of it at first, pretended not to be interested, but I think on the sly he began to dip into it after I'd go upstairs at nights. He wasn't used to laughing and he got a stitch or something, I guess. Maybe he was ashamed to have me catch him at it and tried to hold it in—and that's what happened to him."

They were lingering under the parlor windows. He'd stopped unnoticeably, so she had too, perforce. He was gazing blankly around, eyes on the treetops, the fleecy clouds skimming by, everywhere but the right place. He'd seen something on the ground, and the job was to retrieve it right under her eyes without letting her see him do it.

"Do you mind?" he said, and took out a package of cigarettes. It was crumpled from being carried around on his person for days, and in trying to shake one out, he lost nearly the whole contents. He bent down and picked them up again one by one, with a fine disregard for hygiene, and each time something else as well. It was very neatly done. It went over her head completely.

They turned around and went slowly back to the front of the house again. As they were rounding the corner once more, Traynor looked back. He saw Fears raise his head and look after them at that moment. "Very allergic to my being here," Traynor thought to himself.

Johnson came out of the door.

"The undertaker's here."

And he looked questioningly at Traynor; the latter nodded his permission for removal.

She said, "Oh, I'd better get upstairs; I don't want to—see him go," and hurriedly ran inside.

Traynor didn't hang around to watch, either. He drifted back around the side of the house again. He let himself through the poultry yard, and out at the far side of it, where Fears was puttering around. He approached him with a fine aimlessness, like a man who has nothing to do with himself and gravitates toward the nearest person in sight to kill time chatting.

"He had a nice place here," he remarked.

Fears straightened, leaned on his hoe, drew his sleeve across his forehead. "No money in it, though." He was looking the other way, off from Traynor.

"What do you figure she'll do, keep on running it herself now that he's gone?"

The question should have brought the other's head around toward him, at least. It didn't. Fears spat reflectively, still kept looking stubbornly away from him.

"I don't think she's cut out for it, don't think she'd make a go of it."

There's something in this direction, away from where he's looking, that he doesn't want me to notice, Traynor told himself. He subtly jockeyed himself around so that he could look behind him without turning his entire head.

There was a toolshed there. Implements were stacked up against the wall at the back of it. The door was open and the sun shone sufficiently far in to reveal them. It glinted from the working edges of shovels, rakes, spades. But he noted a trowel with moist clayey soil drying out along its wedge; it was drying to a dirty gray white color.

"That looks like the well," he thought. Aloud he said: "Sun's getting hotter by the minute. Think I'll have a drink."

Fears dropped the hoe handle, stooped and got it again.

"I'd advise you to get it from the kitchen," he said tautly. "Well's all stirred up and muddy, 'pears like part of the sides must have crumbled. Have to 'low it to settle."

"Oh, I'm not choosy," Traynor remarked, strolling toward it. It hadn't rained in weeks. He shifted around to the far side of the structure, where he could face Fears while he pretended to dabble with the chained drinking cup.

There could be no mistaking it, the man was suddenly tense, rigid, out there in the sun, even while he went ahead stiffly hoeing. Every play of his shoulders and arms was forced. He wasn't even watching what he was doing, his hoe was damaging some tender young shoots. Traynor didn't bother getting his drink after all. He knew all he needed to know now. What's Fears been up to down there that he don't want me to find out about?—Traynor wondered. And more important still, did it have anything to do with Eleazar Hunt's death? He couldn't answer the first—yet—but he already had more than a sneaking suspicion that the answer to the second was yes.

He sauntered back toward the tiller.

"You're right," he admitted; "it's all soupy."

With every step that took him farther away from the well rim, he could see more and more of the apprehension lift from Fears. It was almost physical, the way he seemed to straighten out, loosen up there under his eyes, until he was all relaxed again.

"Told you so," Fears muttered, and once again he wiped his

forehead with a great wide sweep of the arm. But it looked more like relief this time than sweat.

"Well, take it easy." Traynor drifted lethargically back toward the front of the house once more. He knew Fears's eyes were following him every step of the way; he could almost feel them boring into the back of his skull. But he knew that if he turned and looked, the other would lower his head too quickly for him to catch him at it, so he didn't bother.

Hunt's body had been removed now and Doctor Johnson was on the point of leaving. They walked out to the roadway together toward their cars.

"Well, son," the doctor wanted to know, "still looking for something ornery in this or are you satisfied?"

"Perfectly satisfied now," Traynor assured him grimly, but he didn't say in which way he meant it. "Tell the truth, doc," he added. "Did you ever see a corpse grin that broadly before?"

"There you go again," sighed Johnson. "Well, no, can't say I have. But there is such a thing as cadaveric spasm, you know."

"There is," Traynor agreed. "And this isn't it. In fact this is so remarkable I'm going to have it photographed before I let the undertaker put a finger to him. I'd like to keep a record of it."

"Shucks," the doctor scoffed as he got in his coupé. "Why, I bet there never was a normal decease yet that couldn't be made to 'pear onnatural if you tried hard enough."

"And there never was an unnatural one yet," Traynor answered softly, "that couldn't be made to appear normal—if you were willing to take things for granted."

After he had arranged for the photographs to be taken, he dropped in at the general store. A place like that, he knew, was the nerve center, the telephone exchange, of the village, so to speak. The news of Eleazar Hunt's death had spread by now, and the cracker barrel brigade were holding a post-mortem. Traynor, who was not known by sight to anyone present, for his duties had not brought him over this way much, did not identify himself for fear of making them self-conscious in the presence of the law. He hung around, trying to make up his mind between two brands of plug tobacco, neither of which he intended buying, meanwhile getting an earful.

"Waal," said one individual, chewing a straw, "guess we'll never know now whether he actually did git all that money from the highway commission folks claim he did, for slicin' off a corner of his propitty to run that new road through."

"He always claimed he didn't. Not a penny of it ever showed up in the bank. My cousin works there and he'd be the first one to know it if it did."

"They say he tuck and hid it out at his place, that's why. Too mean to trust the bank, and he didn't want people thinking he was rich."

An ancient of eighty stepped forth, right angled over a hickory stick, and tapped it commandingly to gain the floor. "Shows ye it don't pay to teach an old dog new tricks! I've knowed Eleazar Hunt since he was knee-high to a grasshopper, and this is the first time I ever heard tell of him even smiling, let alone laughing fit to kill like they claim he done. Exceptin' just once, but that were beyond his control and didn't count."

"When was that?" asked Traynor, chiming in carefully casual. He knew by experience the best way to bring out these villagers' full narrative powers was to act bored stiff.

The old man fastened on him eagerly, glad of an audience. "Why, right in here where we're standing now, 'bout two years ago. Him and me was both standing up to the counter to git waited on, and Andy took me first and asked me what I wanted. So I raised this here stick of mine to point up at the shelf and without meaning to, I grazed Eleazar's side with the tip of it— I can't see so good any more, you know. Well, sir, for a minute I couldn't believe my ears. Here he was, not only laughing, but giggling like a girl, clutching at his ribs and shying away from me. Then the minute he got free of the stick, he changed right back to his usual self, mouth turned down like a horseshoe, snapped, 'Careful what you're doing, will you!' Ticklish, that's all it was. Some's more so than others."

"Anyone else see that but you?"

"I saw it," said the storekeeper. "I was standing right behind the counter when it happened. I never knew that about him until then myself. Funny mixture, to be ticklish with a glum disposition like he had."

"And outside of that, you say you never saw him smile?"

"Not even as a boy!" declared the old man vehemently.

"*She* was livening him up, though, lately," qualified the storekeeper. "Heard she was making right smart progress too."

"Who told you?" asked Traynor, lidding his eyes.

"Why, she did herself."

Traynor just nodded to himself. Buildup beforehand, he was thinking.

"Yes, and that's what killed him!" insisted the garrulous old man. "Way I figger it, he'd never used them muscles around the mouth that you shape smiles with and so they'd gone useless on him from lack of practice. Just like if you don't use your right arm for fifty years, it withers on you. Then she comes along and starts him to laughing at joke books and whatnot, and the strain was too much for him. Like I said before, you can't teach an old dog new tricks! These old codgers that marry young chickens!"

All Traynor did, after the old man had stumped out with an accurate shot at the brass receptacle inside the door, was get his name from the storekeeper and jot it down in his notebook, without letting anyone see him do it. The ancient one just might come in handy as a witness, if a murder trial was to come up— provided of course that he lasted that long.

"Well, how does it look?" the sheriff asked Traynor when he finally got back to headquarters.

"It doesn't look good," was the grim answer. "It was murder."

The sheriff drew in his breath involuntarily. "Got any evidence?" he said finally.

His eyes opened wide in astonishment as a small joke book, a handful of chicken feathers, and a pair of black socks with garters still attached, descended upon his desk. "What've these got to do with it?" he asked in stupefaction. "You don't mean to tell me—this is your evidence, do you?"

"It certainly is," said Traynor gloomily. "It's all the evidence there is or ever will be. This, and photographs I've had taken of his face. It's the cleverest thing that was ever committed under the sun. But not quite clever enough."

"Well, don't you think you'd better at least tell me what makes you so sure? What did you see?"

"All right," said Traynor irritably, "here's what I saw—and I know you're going to say right away it didn't amount to a row of pins. I saw a dead man with a broad grin on his face, too broad to be natural. I saw chicken feathers lying scattered around the ground—"

"It's a poultry farm, after all; they raise chickens there."

"But their tips are all bent over at right angles to the quill; show me the chicken that can do that to itself. And they were lying *outside* the wired enclosure, under the window of the room in which the dead man was."

"And?" said the sheriff, pointing to the socks.

"A few fibers of the same chicken feathers, adhering to the soles. The socks are black, luckily! I could see them with my naked eye."

"But isn't it likely that this Hunt might potter around in his stocking feet, even outdoors—where there are chicken feathers lying around?"

"Yes. But these fibers are on the linings of the socks, not the outsides of the soles. I reversed them pulling them off his feet."

"Anything else?"

"Not directly bearing on the commission of the murder itself, but involved in it. I saw a trowel with white clay drying on its edges, and a pair of thick gauntlets, used for spraying something on the peach trees, hanging up in the toolshed. Now tell me all this is no good to us."

"It certainly isn't!" declared the sheriff emphatically. "Why, I'd be laughed out of office if I moved against anyone on the strength of evidence such as this! You're talking in riddles, man! I can't make anything out of this. You not only haven't told me whom you suspect, but you haven't even given me the method used, or the motive."

Traynor drummed his finger tips on the desk. "And yet I'm dead sure. I'm as sure of it right now as if I'd seen it with my own eyes. I can give you the method right now, but what's the use? You'd only laugh at me, I can tell by the look on your face. I could name the motive and the suspects too, but until I've got the one, there's no use bringing in the others; there wouldn't be enough to hold them on."

"Well"—his superior shrugged, turning up his palms—"what do you want me to do?"

"Very little," muttered Traynor, "except lend me a waterproof pocket flashlight, if you've got one. And stick around till I come back; I've got an idea I won't be coming alone. There might be matters discussed that you'd be interested in."

"Where'll you be in the meantime?" the sheriff called after him as he pocketed the light and headed for the door.

"Down in Eleazar Hunt's well," was the cryptic answer. "And not because I'm thirsty, either."

Traynor coasted to a noiseless stop, well down the road from the Hunt place and out of sight of it, at about ten thirty that night. He snapped off his headlights, got out, examined the torch the sheriff had lent him to make sure it was in good working order, then cut across into the trees on foot, and made his way along under them parallel to the road but hidden from it.

There were no lights showing by the time he'd come in sight

of the house. Death or no death, people in the country retire early. He knew there was no dog on the place so he didn't hesitate in breaking cover and skirting the house around to the back. The story was Hunt had been too stingy to keep one, begrudging the scraps it would have required to feed it. His sour face, was the general verdict, was enough to frighten away any trespasser.

He found the poultry yard locked, but his business wasn't with that; he detoured around the outside of it in the pale moonlight, treading warily in order not to make his presence known. He played his light briefly on the toolshed door; it was closed but not locked, fortunately. He eased it open, caught up the trowel and rope ladder he had noticed yesterday morning, and hurried over to the well with them. He mightn't need the trowel, but he took it with him to make sure. The clay, incidentally, had been carefully scraped off it now—but too late to do Fears any good; the damage had already been done.

Traynor clamped the iron hooks on the end of the ladder firmly to the rim of the well, paid it out all the way down the shaft until he heard it go in with a muffled splash. It sounded deeper than he enjoyed contemplating, but if Fears had gone down in there, dredging, then he could do it too.

He clicked his light on, tucked it firmly under his left armpit, straddled the well guard, and started climbing down, trowel wedged in his coat pocket. The ladder pivoted lightly from side to side under his weight, but so long as it didn't snarl up altogether, that was all right. He stopped every few rungs to play the light around the shaft in a circle. Nothing showed above the water line, any more than it had yesterday morning, but that trowel hadn't had clay on it, and the water hadn't been all muddied up, for nothing.

The water hit him unexpectedly and he jolted at the knifelike cold of it. He knew he couldn't stay in it very long without numbing, but he kept going down rung by rung. It came up his legs, hit his kidneys, finally rose above the light under his arm.

That was waterproof, didn't go out. He stretched one leg downward off the ladder, feeling for the bottom. No bottom; the shaft
seemed to go to China. One sure thing was, *he* couldn't—and
keep on breathing.

He explored the wall of the well under the water line with
his free hand, all around him and down as far as he could reach.
The clay was velvet smooth, unmarred. Another rung—they
were widely spaced—would take his head under, and he didn't
like to risk it; he was already beginning to get numb all over.

Then suddenly the leg that he was using for a depth finder
struck something like a plank. But across the shaft, behind him.
He'd attached the ladder to the wrong side of the well rim. Still,
it was fairly accessible; the circumference of the bore wasn't
unduly large. He adjusted his leg to its height and got his heel
on it. Tested its sustaining powers and it didn't crumble in spite
of the fact that it must have been water-logged for years. It was
evidently inserted solidly into the clay, like a sort of shelf, more
of it bedded than actually protruding. Still it was a risky thing
to trust oneself to; he had an idea it was meant more for a
marker than to be used to stand on. He turned his body outward
to face it, got across to it without mishap, but bringing the
ladder with him over his shoulder as a precaution. He was
mostly under water during the whole maneuver, and rapidly
chilling to the bone. That Fears before him had been through
all this without some good, all powerful reason, he refused to
believe.

He found a large cavity on that side of the well almost at once.
It was just a few inches above the plank, a large square recess
gouged out of the compact clay. It was, as far as his waterlogged
finger tips could make out, a large empty biscuit tin wedged in
flush with the well wall, open end outward. A sort of handmade
but none the less efficient safe deposit box, so to speak.

But the important thing was that he could feel a heavy rub-
bery bulk resting within it. Flat, pouch shaped. He drew this

out, teeth chattering as the water momentarily rose into his nostrils, and finding it was too bulky to wedge into his pocket, tucked it into his submerged waistband, not caring to run the risk of bringing it up under his arm and perhaps dropping it to the bottom of the well just as he neared the top. The trowel, which he found he had not needed after all, he tossed over his shoulder into watery oblivion. The light, though it hampered him the way he kept it pinned against his side, he retained because it was not his but the sheriff's.

He renewed his grip on the transported ladder, took his feet off the scaffolding, and let the ladder swing back with him to its original side of the well. He didn't feel the slight collision at all, showing how thoroughly numbed he was by now, and showing what a risk he was running every moment of having his hold on it automatically relax and drop him into the depths. Nor could he tell the difference when his body was finally clear of the water. Meaning he'd better get out of there fast.

But it was twice as slow getting up as it had been getting down. He couldn't tell, through shoes and all, when each successive rung was firmly fixed under the arches of his feet, he kept making idiotic pawing gestures with his whole leg each time before it would finally catch on. That should have looked very funny, but not down there where he was.

Finally the cloying dampness of the air began to lift a little and he knew he must be nearing the top. Then a whiff of a draft, that he would never have felt if he'd been dry, struck through his drenched clothes like ice cold needles, and that proved it. His teeth were tapping together like typewriter keys.

There was something else, some faint warning that reached him. Not actually heard so much as sensed. As if someone's breath were coming down the shaft from just over his head, slightly amplified as if by a sounding board. He acted on it instantly, more from instinct than actual realization of danger. Unsheathed the light from under his arm and pointed it upward. He was closer to the top than he'd thought, scarcely a yard below it. The beam illumined Fears's face, bent low above him, contorted into a maniacal grimace of impending destruction, both arms high over his head wielding something. It looked like the flat of a shovel, but there was no time to find out, do anything but get out of its way. It came hissing down in a big arc against the well shaft. It would have smashed his skull like an egg, ground the fragments into the clay—great whipcords of straining muscle stood out on the arms wielding it—but he swerved his body violently sidewise off the ladder, hanging on just by one hand and one foot, and it cycloned by, missing him by fractions of inches, and battered into the clay with a pulpy whack.

Fears had been in too much of a hurry; if he'd let him get up a single rung higher, so that his head showed above the well rim, nothing could have saved him from being brained by the blow. The torch, of course, went skittering down into oblivion with a distant *plink!* The shovel followed it a second later; Fears didn't trouble to bring it up again from striking position, let go of it, perhaps under the mistaken impression that it had served its purpose and the only reason the victim didn't topple was that his stunned body had become tangled in the ropes.

Traynor could feel the ladder jar under him as his would-be destroyer sought to detach the hooks that clasped the well rim and throw the whole structure snaking down to the bottom. The very weight of his own body, on the inside, pinning it down close to the shaft, defeated the first try, gave him an added second's grace. To free the hooks, Fears had to raise the climber's whole weight first, ladder and all, to get enough slack into it.

There wasn't enough time to finish climbing out. Traynor vaulted up one more rung with the agility of desperation, so that his head cleared the shaft rim; he flung up his arm and caught Fears's lowered head, bent down to his task, toward him in a riveted headlock that was like a drowning man's. Fears gave a muffled howl of dismay, tried to arch his slumped back against it. There was a brief equipoise, then gravity and their combined topheavy positions had their way. Fears came floundering over into the mouth of the well, nearly broke Traynor's back by the shift of weight to the other side of him, tore him off his own precarious foothold, and they both went plunging sickeningly down off the ladder together. Their two yells of approaching destruction blended hollowly into one.

Numb and half frozen as Traynor already was, the shock of submersion was evidently less for him than for Fears, plunging in with his pores wide open and possibly overheated from hurrying out to the well from a warm bed. Traynor had been in the water once already, felt it less than he would have the first time. The way people condition their bodies to frigid water by wetting themselves before they dive off a board, for instance.

He never touched bottom, even now. He came up alone—the fall must have loosened the bear hug he'd had on the other man —struck out wildly all around him, aware that if he went down again— The radius of the confining wall was luckily narrow. He contacted the ladder, sealed his hands to it in a hold that blow torches couldn't have pried off, got on it again, and quickly pulled himself up above the water.

He waited there a minute, willing to stretch out a hand, but unable to do more than that. Fears never came up. Not a sound broke the inky black silence around Traynor but the slow heave of the disturbed water itself. The shock had either made the man lose consciousness or he'd struck his head against his own shovel at the bottom. If there was a bottom, which Traynor was beginning to doubt.

Go in again after him and try to find him, he couldn't. He got the warning from every cramped muscle in his body, and his restricted lungs and pounding heart. It meant his own sure death, inevitably. There are times one can tell. He wasn't even sure that he could get up any more, unaided.

But he finally did, tottering painfully rung by rung and feeling as if he'd been doing this all night. He flung himself across the well rim, crawled clear of it on his belly like some half drowned thing, then turned over on his back and did nothing else much but just breathe. Gusts of uncontrollable shivering swept over him every once in a while. Finally he sat up, pulled off his soaked coat, shirt, and even undershirt, and began beating himself all over the body with them to bring back the circulation.

It was only when he'd started it going again that he remembered to feel for the rubber pouch that had cost two lives so far, and nearly a third—his own. If he'd lost it down there, he'd had all his trouble for nothing. But instead of falling out, it had slipped down under his waistband and become wedged in the top of one trousers leg, too bulky to go any farther. There wasn't enough sensation left in his leg to tell him it was there until he'd pried it out with both hands.

"Money," he murmured, when he'd finally stripped it open and examined it. He turned his head and looked toward that sinister black opening in the ground. "I thought it was that. It almost always is."

There were seventy-five thousand dollars in it, so well protected they weren't even damp after three years' immersion.

He put on his coat and made his way back toward the house. One of the upper story window sashes eased up and a voice whispered cautiously down in the stillness:

"Did you get him, Dan?"

"No, Dan didn't get him, Mrs. Hunt," he answered in full speaking tone. "Put on something and come down; I'm taking you in to the sheriff's office with me. And don't keep me waiting around down here; I'm chilled to the bone."

The sheriff awoke with a start when Traynor thrust open his office door and ushered Mrs. Hunt in ahead of him.

"Here's one," he said, "and the other one's at the bottom of the well with the rest of the slimy things where he belongs. Sit

down, Mrs. Hunt, while I run through the facts for the benefit
of my superior here.

"I'll begin at the beginning. The State built a spanking fine
concrete highway that sliced off a little corner of Eleazar Hunt's
property. He had the good luck—or bad luck, as it now turns
out to have been—to collect seventy-five thousand dollars for it.
Here it is." He threw down the waterlogged package. "There's
your motive. First of all, it got him a second wife, almost before
he knew it himself. Then, through the wife, it got him a hired
man. Then, through the hired man *and* the wife, it got him—
torture to the death."

He turned to the prisoner, who was sitting nervously shred-
ding her handkerchief. "You want to tell the rest of it, or shall
I? I've got it on the tip of my tongue, you know—and I've got
it straight."

"I'll tell it," she said dully. "You seem to know it anyway."

"How'd you catch on he was hypersensitive to tickling?"

"By accident. I was sitting on the arm of his chair one evening, trying to vamp it out of him—where the money was, you
know. I happened to tickle him under the chin, and he jumped
a mile. Dan saw it happen and that gave him the idea. He built
it up to me for weeks. 'If he was tied down,' he said, 'in one place
so he couldn't get away from it, he couldn't hold out against it
very long, he'd have to tell you. It'd be like torture, but it
wouldn't hurt him.' It sounded swell, so I gave in.

"But, honest, I didn't know Dan meant to kill him. He was the
one did it. I didn't! I thought he only meant for us to take the
money and lam, and leave El tied up."

"Never mind that; go ahead."

"Dan had it all thought out beautiful. He had me go around
the village first building it up that I was getting El to laugh and
liven up. He even had me buy the joke book at the general
store. Then last night about ten thirty when El was sitting by
the lamp reading some seed catalogues, I gave the signal and
Dan came up behind him with rope and pillows from the bed

and insect spray gauntlets. He held him while I put the gauntlets on him—they're good thick buckram, you know—so no
rope burns would show from his struggles, and then he tied his
hands to the arms of the chair, over the gauntlets. The pillows
we used over his waist and thighs, for the same reason, to
deaden the ropes. Then he let the chair back down nearly flat,
and he took off El's shoes and socks, and brought in a handful
of chicken feathers from the yard, and squatted down in front
of him like an Indian, and started to slowly stroke the soles of
his feet back and forth. It was pretty awful to watch and listen
to: I hadn't thought it would be. But that screaming laugh!
Tickling doesn't sound so bad, you know.

"Every time Dan blunted a feather, he'd throw it away and
start in using a new one. And he said in his sleepy way: 'Care
to tell us where it is now? No? Wa-al, mebbe you know best.' I
wanted to bring him water once, but Dan wouldn't let me, said
that would only help him hold out longer.

"El was such a stubborn fool. He didn't once say he didn't
have the money, he only said he'd see us both in hell before he
told us where it was. He fainted away, the first time, about
twelve. After that he kept getting weaker all the time, couldn't
laugh any more, just heave his ribs.

"Finally he gave in, whispered it was in a tin box plastered
into the well, below the water line. He told us there was a rope
ladder he'd made himself to get down there, hidden in the attic.
Dan lowered himself down, and got it out, brought it up, and
counted it. I wanted to leave right way, but he talked me out
of it. He said: 'We'll only give ourselves away if we do that. We
know where it is now. Let's leave it there a mite longer; he
mayn't live *as long as you'd expect.*' I see now what he meant;
I still didn't then. Well, I listened to him; he seemed to have the
whole thing lined up so cleverly. He climbed back with it and
left it down there. Then we went back to the house. I went
upstairs, and I no sooner got there than I heard El start up this
whimpering and cooing again, like a little newborn baby. I

quickly ran down to try and stop him, but it was too late. Just as I got there, El overstrained himself and suddenly went limp. That little added extra bit more killed him, and Dan Fears had known it would, that's why he did it!

"I got frightened, but he told me there was nothing to worry about, everything was under control, and they'd never tumble in a million years. We took the ropes and pillows and gauntlets off him, of course, and no marks were left. We raised the chair back to reading position, and dropped the joke book by his hand, and I put on his shoes and socks. The only thing was, after he'd been a dead a little while, his face started to relapse to that sour, scowly look he always had all his life, and that didn't match the joke book. Well, Dan took care of that too. He waited until just before he was starting to stiffen, and then he arranged the lips and mouth with his hands so it looked like he'd been laughing his head off; and they hardened and stayed that way. Then he sent me out to fetch the doctor." She hung her head. "It seemed so perfect. I don't know how it is it fell through."

"How did you catch on so quick, Al?" the sheriff asked Traynor, while they were waiting for a stenographer to come and take down her confession.

"First of all, the smile. You could see his features had been rearranged after death. Before rigor sets in, there's a relaxation to the habitual expression. Secondly, the jokes were no good. Fears may have thought a sour puss wouldn't match them, but it would have matched them lots better than the one they gave him. Thirdly, when I hitched up the cuffs of his trousers, I saw that his socks had been put on wrong, as if in a hurry by someone who wasn't familiar with things like that—therefore presumably it was a woman. The garter clasps were fastened at the insides of the calves, but the original indentations still showed on the outsides. Fourthly, the bent chicken feathers. I still didn't quite get it, though, until I learned this afternoon at the general store that he was supersensitive to tickling. That gave me the whole picture, intact. I'd already seen the clay on the

trowel, and Fears did his level best to keep me away from the
well, so it didn't take much imagination to figure where the
money was hidden. The marks of the ropes may not have shown
on his hands, but the gauntlets were scarred by their friction,
I could see that plainly even by the light of the torch when I
went back to the toolshed tonight.

"It was pretty good, I'll give it that. If they'd only left his face
alone. I don't think my suspicions would have been awakened
in the first place. They spoiled it by overdoing it; just a mere
inference of how he'd died wasn't enough—they had guilty
consciences, so they wanted to make sure of getting their point
across, hitting the onlooker in the eye with it. And that was the
one thing he'd never had in life—a sense of humor. The joke
wasn't really in the book after all. The joke was on them."

Woolrich wrote a huge number of stories I call the " 'Suicide? Accident? No, it was murder! ' said the dick knowingly" type; and by quirk
of fate some of the worst of these, such as "What the Well-Dressed
Corpse Will Wear" (*Dime Detective*, 3/44) and "U, As in Murder"
(*Dime Detective*, 3/41), have won the relative permanence of inclusion
in collections of his short fiction. His best story in this vein, which you
have just read, came from a cheap and obscure pulp called *Clues
Detective*, and was never reprinted until now—a shocking oversight,
since its *frisson* of horror at the denouement is for me the equal of that
in Stanley Ellin's "The Specialty of the House" or of Woolrich's own
classic "The Customer's Always Right" (*Detective Tales*, 7/41, better
known as "The Fingernail").

One and a Half Murders

"A fine how-d'ye-do," Mike Travis scowled at his blubbering sister across the kitchen table. "I come down here for a little rest and a breath of sea-air, and I run into this smelly mess! Right in my own family. You could have knocked me over with a feather! And that's a fine way to hear it, too, from the kids on the street when I asked them the way to your house!"

"I wrote you," gurgled Mrs. Murray. "Didn't you get my let—?"

"No," barked Travis, jerking his cup away. "And quit crying into my coffee, it's weak enough as it is!"

"I thought maybe you could do something for him, working

with a private detective agency like you do," sniffled Mrs. Murray.

"Used to, y'mean! I was let out only last week, that's why I'm here. After the depresh is over everywhere else, it suddenly hits the investigation business as an afterthought. And at my age, too!" His face grew beet-red to the roots of his snow-white hair and his cigar-stub jerked from the left corner of his mouth to the right without his lifting a finger at it. "Too old, they think! Not up-to-date enough!"

His sister was the sort who could always spare a word for somebody else's troubles, even in the midst of her own. "You could fall back on barbering; you once took a course in that, didn't you, before you went into the detective business?" She dabbed her apron to her face and went back to her grief once more. "Frank's a good lad, he wouldn't kill anybody in cold blood like that. I know he didn't do it."

"Suppose you tell me just what happened," said Mike impatiently. "I ain't in the fortune-telling business."

His sister took a deep breath. "Well, you know how crazy he is about dancin'. There's no harm in that, is there? Well, one night—" and she launched into the past.

The rich girl hurried through the crowded lobby, holding her breath for fear of being recognized and stopped. Just when she thought she had made it, as she came out of the hotel, she met Arnold face to face. Her parents weren't with him for once.

"I couldn't sleep," she explained hastily. "Arnold, don't let on you saw me go out. I'll explain when I come back—"

He put out his hand and tried to stop her. "A girl your age shouldn't be out alone, at this hour, with a diamond bracelet like that on your wrist. Be careful, Sylvia, this is a bad town. Let me go with you—"

She turned away. "I can take care of myself. And if you breathe a word about this, I'll never speak to you again."

As she lost herself in the crowd moiling slowly along the

thronged Boardwalk, she had a feeling that he was coming after her, keeping her in sight. But she didn't look back.

Young Murray was waiting for her just outside the Million-Dollar Pier and he had the admission tickets in his hand. He didn't look like he could afford even the fifty-cents apiece it cost to enter. She took his arm with a smile and they went in.

It stretches way out over the Atlantic, and most of it is the big dancing-pavilion under colored lights. But at the back there is a verandah or promenade-deck, purposely left dark at all times. And along both sides there are two more. Anyone who's ever been there knows the set-up.

They had nothing to check, so they stepped right off and went to it. After about five minutes, she slipped the diamond bracelet off her wrist and asked him to carry it in his pocket for her. "The catch needs to be fixed, I'm afraid I'll lose it," she said. "Don't let me go home without it, they're real."

He gave her a look when he heard that, but he did what she asked. She'd only known him for three nights—but she was very young, and he danced so well.

When they stopped for a minute between numbers, a girl with too much eyeshadow on came over to where they were standing clapping.

"You can't ditch me like this!" she said to Murray. "Doing pretty good for yourself, aren't you!" She turned to the girl then, and her voice rose to a yell. "Watch yourself with this guy, Miss Millionbucks! Remember I told you so. He's death to dames!" Everyone around them heard her say it.

Somebody came after her and pulled her away, but she shouted back: "I'll fix you, Murray, if it's the last thing I do!"

"Brrh!" the rich girl said, and pretended to shiver. But many a truth is spoken in jest.

Half an hour later they left the floor together, he and she, to rest for awhile. They went out on the darkened end of the Pier, away from all the lights and noise. There was no one around out there just then. No one ever saw her alive again.

Yet how could anything happen to her, with hundreds of people within reach of her voice? Thoughts of death must have been very far from her mind. But a noisy jazz-band can drown out the loudest scream. The tune it was pounding out was "I'm The Boogy Man."

She murmured, "I'm thirsty, will you get me a drink of water?"

As he got up, he leaned across the back of her deck-chair and slipped both arms around her shoulders, in a double embrace from behind. She turned to look up at him. A cloud hid the moon for a moment, and they were both in pitch-darkness.

The eye-shadow girl came out on the left-hand "porch" of the Pier with someone, to get a breath of air. The moon was behind a cloud and the water was black.

"Wait, I'm not through with him!" she burned. "I'll get even—" She broke off suddenly and grew rigid. "What was that? D'ja hear that splash just then? Sounded like someone fell in."

"Just a wave slapping up against one of the piles," the fellow with her said.

"It came from down the end there. Let's go look."

She hurried away from him and turned the corner. She didn't come back and he finally had to go after her. When he got there she was leaning over the railing scanning the water.

Just then the moon came out again. She jerked back and caught him by the sleeve. "You look, is there anything down there? I thought I saw a white arm reaching up out of the water just now!"

Silvery patches appeared here and there, dazzling to the eyes. "It's the reflection of the moon," he said.

"Guess you're right. But gosh, it had me for a minute! Let's go back and dance."

As she turned to go, she saw something lying on a deck-chair, a tiny ball of white, and stopped to pick it up. A girl's handkerchief dropped by somebody, a costly one too. She was a thrifty soul and she took it with her; once it was laundered it would be as good as new. Her companion, who had gone ahead, didn't see her do it.

As she followed him in to the dance-floor, she said once more: "I'll get even with that two-timer yet!"

Meanwhile, someone had tapped Frank Murray on the shoulder as he bent over the water-cooler beside the illuminated fish-tanks at the rear of the dance-floor. Even before he looked up to see who it was, some of the water spilled out of the wax-paper cup he was filling; his hand didn't seem to be very steady.

His eyes lifted, and he didn't know the man.

The other's voice was dangerously low. "You came in here an hour ago with a girl in a white satin dress. What've you done with her? I'm taking her back with me, she doesn't belong in a place like this. Now, don't fool around with dynamite. I don't know if she's told you her name or not, but that's Sylvia Reading, the chain-store man's girl."

Murray wasn't holding the cup straight enough, more water slopped out of it. His wrist was jerking like a piston. His voice was steely enough when it came, though. "I know all about who she—" His teeth clamped tight and bit off the rest of it short. Finally he said, "You're wasting your time. She left half-an-hour ago."

"No, that doesn't go," the stranger said. "You were taking that drink to her, see? You're too crummy to spend a penny on yourself, you'd put your mouth right down on the tap, but for her you'd shoot a whole Lincoln-head at once. She's out there in back, I guess, waiting for you." He didn't wait for the answer.

The cup folded up in Murray's fist and the water spurted out and he went after him.

She wasn't out there. The other guy was standing there in the dark squinting all around and calling, "Come on, Syl, snap out of it. If your people ever find out about this—"

He hardly turned his head at all to meet the sudden on-slaught. There was a smack, and Murray was staring dazedly up at him, stiff-armed against the floor.

"I learned to box at Princeton," the stranger informed him, fastidiously shaking out his cuff, "not in poolrooms." He swooped down on him all at once, straightened up again, holding something in his hand. Something that sparkled. "What's this, that fell out of your pocket? Seems to me I've seen it before." He turned the bracelet slowly around. "So she went home half-an-hour ago, did she? And left this with you for a souvenir, I suppose. You robbed her while you were dancing with her, you little sewer-rat!"

Murray scrambled to his feet, face whiter than the moonlight. The palsy that had afflicted his wrist awhile ago had now spread to his whole body. His tone had changed to one of frightened pleading. "I didn't, Jack, I swear I didn't! Don't start anything like that, gimme a break, will ya? She handed it to me to hold for her. I left her waiting out here only a minute ago—"

"A five-thousand-dollar piece of jewelry she handed to you? Oh, of course! Just like that—I don't think!"

But Murray didn't wait to hear any more. A sense of his own predicament swept over him suddenly. That blind, unreasoning fear of the law, that claustrophobia, that the young, the poorly-educated, are always more susceptible to than others, struck him like lightning. The sight of the diamonds in the other's hand seemed to rob him of all reasoning power. He turned and fled in silent panic out toward the crowded dance-floor and the escape that lay beyond.

But Arnold's rasping shout had reached it ahead of him. "Stop that man! Hold him, somebody!"

As the fugitive flashed out under the pitiless, revealing lights, zig-zagging like a black bullet crashing through a bouquet of flowers, the music was already dying into a succession of discordant notes and the packed dancers were coming to an uncertain stop all over the huge place.

Arms reached out to grab him, always just too late. In his wake sprawling figures stumbled to regain their balance. But his impetus began to slow, the size of the crowd was against him.

And then a small, vindictive satin slipper slithered out between his racing feet like a spoke. He plunged flat on his face, with such force that his own legs went curling up in back of him, in what was almost a forward-somersault. When the shock had cleared, his eyes followed that treacherous little slipper from the floor on up to the malignant face of the eye-shadow girl. He was lying within five yards of the outer lobby, that would have led to the Boardwalk and freedom—if he had made it. She and her partner had been the last of all the couples barring his way!

"Thanks, pal, that was something to be proud of!" he panted, chin on floor.

He was jerked to his feet and pummeled around a lot before the pier attendants could extricate him. A couple of blue-coats were already rushing in from the Boardwalk outside, with a noisy mob of celebrators at their heels.

"Hold him, now!" warned Arnold, "until I have a chance to find out—" He raced to a booth and dialed Sylvia Reading's hotel.

Murray was moaning, "Oh my God, I didn't do anything!" when he came back. They were all standing around him thick as bees.

"He's a dip, he lifted a twenty-grand bracelet," someone volunteered. Its value had quadrupled inside of five minutes. The Pier manager was blue in the face, with two windmills for arms. "You couldn't take him nowhere else, you gotta hold jail right here in the middle? Look, millions of 'em in here without a ticket! Shoo, go home! No more dancing! We close for the night! I sue the municipality!"

Arnold came back slow and came back white. "She hasn't

gone back there, I just had her people on the wire! And it's only
a couple of blocks' walk from here. She's vanished!"

"You the complainant?" a cop asked. "What charges—theft?"

"My fiancée—ask him what he did with her. I saw her come
in here with him with my own eyes, now she's gone, no trace
of her! The bracelet was in his pocket—"

"Look in his other pocket, maybe you'll find the girl," someone wisecracked.

"Better still," a harsh voice said, "look in the water, out at the
end there." The little lady with the eyeshadow edged her way
forward with business-like determination. Twice as much eye-
shadow wouldn't have softened her eyes just then. "I saw him
with her. And a little later I was outside there myself, and I
heard a loud splash in the water. Ask this guy with me. Then
when I go look, I see a white arm sticking up out of the water.
And I picked this up."

She held up a crumpled ball of handkerchief. Her baleful
basilisk-eyes never once left Murray's shivering face.

Arnold caught at it, his face went gray. "That's hers," he
whispered. "Look in the corner, see the S and R embroidered
there. Sylvia Reading. Smell it. Gardenia—what she always
used." They had to hold him back from Murray. "You asked
what charges? Suspicion of murder. I'll bring the accusation
myself. That girl is gone!"

A sudden hush fell on the crowd. Murray's choked whimper
was all that could be heard as they dragged him away. Over and
over: "I didn't do anything, I didn't do anything—"

Sylvia Reading's body was washed up on the beach down at
Ventnor two days later, obviously carried there by the current.
Arnold identified it at once. The satin dress hadn't even lost its
sheen yet. The very rouge that had outlined her mouth could
still be discerned; "waterproof" was its trademark. The autopsy
showed that she had been in the water those two full days. And
there was only a little water in her lungs; *life had not been quite*

extinct when she was thrown in. She had been garrotted, strangled to death, with the silken shoulder-straps of her own dress,
caught from behind in a noose, and twisted. The marks showed
plainly on her throat.

Murray, whom she had last been seen alive with, was indicted
for murder in the first degree and held for trial. He had stopped
saying "I didn't do anything" now. It had gotten him too many
wallops. He didn't say anything at all any more.

"Well, if he didn't he probably did something else some other
time," commented Mike Travis unfeelingly, and stood up. He
reached for his hat. "He oughta get a good swift kick anyway,
going there night after night to dance like a jack-in-the-box!"

Mrs. Murray had uncovered one eye, hopefully. "Where you
going?" she sobbed.

"Down to the morgue," said Mike grudgingly.

As the door banged after him she gave a deep sigh. Strangely
enough, it sounded like a sigh of relief and renewed confidence.

Sylvia Reading lay there on the slab like a statue, and her
beauty was only a memory now, and all her father's millions
couldn't bring her back again. Mike stood looking down at her.

"No," he said over his shoulder, "I'm not a relative. I'm a
private investigator retained by Murray's family. Empire State
Agency, New York."

It didn't deter him that that had ceased to be a fact a week
ago. He'd kept the badge; that was about all he had to show for
twenty-five years' work. "Let me see her things," he said.

The cobwebby stockings didn't even have a run in them.
There was a green grease-spot on one, probably from brushing
one of the mildewed piles imbedded deep down in the water
where she'd first sunk.

He handed them back. "Run along, don't hang around me,"
he said impatiently. "I'm not a body-snatcher. Oh, so it's an
open-and-shut case, is it, and I'm just wasting my time here, am
I? Well, it's my time! Skate me in a chair, I'm not as young as
you lads."

The purplish discolorations were still clearly visible, where the treacherous ribbons had cut life short. Still, there must have been a moment's time, time enough to make just one gesture of resistance. What would be anyone's involuntary, spasmodic gesture at such a time? To reach for the thing that was stifling you, try to drag it away. And that failing, as of course it had—

He withdrew one of her hands from under the rubber sheet and looked at it. She probably had a manicure every day of her life, he told himself. But there was a little dirt, an almost invisible line of black, under the tapered, unbroken thumb-nail. He reached for the other hand and looked. Two of them had it on that hand.

"Hand him a deck of cards," somebody smirked in back of him, "maybe he wants to play honeymoon bridge with her!" He paid no attention.

Maybe sitting there at the end of the Pier with Murray that night she'd let her hands stray along the railing, had gotten a little dirt under her nails. But why just three fingers, why not all ten? He took a quill toothpick from his pocket and stripped the paper jacket from it. He held the lifeless hand up and prodded under the thumb-nail. The whole line of blackness moved at one time; as he withdrew the quill it had vanished from the nail—and he was holding a short human hair before his eyes. The other two nails each produced the same object. So it hadn't been dirt after all—and Sylvia Reading's last gesture, after trying to drag away the noose that was throttling her, had been to reach blindly upward and clutch at the head of her assailant in her death-throes.

He carefully put the three hairs away in the paper that had held the toothpick; then he got up and left. The morgue-attendants tapped their foreheads significantly as he slouched out. "Cracked," was their verdict.

Murray thought so too when Mike showed up to visit him in his cell later in the day. "Well," was Mike's dour greeting, "you're a credit! What'd you do it for anyway?"

Murray blasted him with a look. " 'Cause she stepped on my toes while we were dancing." As he turned his head impatiently away he felt three sharp twinges at the top of his scalp, and saw his uncle putting something into a cigarette-paper.

He sprang to his feet, his face violently contorted. "McGuffy!" he squalled through the bars, rattling them. "McGuffy!" And when the keeper came hustling along, "Throw this pest outa my cell! I got some rights, haven't I?" The turnkey had to come between them. "Kibitzer!" shouted Murray after his departing visitor.

"Ah, youth, hot-tempered youth," murmured Mike tolerantly as he shuffled down the corridor.

He next popped up at the barber shop of the Claymore Hotel. "Naw," he said as three barbers sprang to attention beside their chairs, "I don't want a workout, I want a job."

"Got references?" said the manager unwillingly, when Mike had buttonholed him. "I can't just hire anyone that comes in off the street—" He glanced at the dog-eared memorandum Mike passed to him. Mike was testing a pair of clippers with practiced fingers.

"Oh, you worked at the Grand Central Terminal in New York. That's more like it! And it says here you quit of your own accord." He glanced at Mike almost in awe. "Ain't many do that these days."

The three assistants gathered round, craning their necks to read the unparalleled statement with their own eyes. Mike was triumphantly warming up, snipping at an imaginary customer with a pair of shears.

Suddenly someone's finger pointed at an upper corner of the paper. The manager let out a howl. "These references are dated 1913! Get out, get out before I—"

Mike caught the folded credentials as they came flying back at him. "All right, if that's the way you feel about it," he said stiffly. At the door he turned to deliver a parting thrust. "A good barber improves with age, like wine!"

They were still snickering under their breaths about it a few minutes later, when one exclaimed, "I'm missing a pair of clippers!"

"Who took my shears?" another wanted to know.

"Holy smoke!" reported the third, "my spare jacket's gone from the hook!"

The shears, the clippers and the jacket all appeared simultaneously at the door of Room 1115, upstairs in the hotel, a little while later, and Mike, who was in the middle of all of them, knocked. It had cost him three dollars to check in just now and he was still muttering about it, but they didn't let you get past the reception-desk unquestioned unless you had a room of your own you were going to.

The door of eleven-fifteen opened and its occupant stared coldly out at him.

"Afternoon, Mr. Arnold," Mike said softly. "Little trim, hot towel, mud pack, nice cool shave—anything I can do for you? Compliments of the management."

"What's all this? I didn't send for any barber!" Arnold scowled. He got ready to close the door.

"I know you didn't, sir," said Mike ingratiatingly, "but we've installed one on each floor, we want our guests to be as comfortable as possible—"

Arnold ran a hand across his scratchy chin, motioned him in unwillingly. "All right, get it over with."

Mike deftly tucked a towel, snipped experimentally at the air with his shears. He hadn't done this in over twenty years, but it all came back to him little by little. His fingers lost their rustiness; he began to remember, each time, just what to do next. Sometimes, of course, the knowledge came a little too late; he saw that he shouldn't have run his clippers all the way up to the top of the head in the back; it looked too much like a convict-haircut. That was too bad, but the hair would all grow back again in a few weeks.

Arnold twitched and said: "Ow! What're you doing?"

Mike peered closely at the place. "Sorry, sir, I didn't notice. You have a little half-healed scratch there just under the hairline; I must have raked it with my comb just now."

Arnold was suddenly silent, didn't answer. You could have sliced the silence with a knife; it spoke louder than words. Mike cleaned the comb carefully, and the hairs that had caught between its teeth he removed and wrapped in a cigarette-paper behind the man's back.

"Speed it up!" Arnold said impatiently. "Is it going to take you all day?"

Mike quietly removed the towel, pocketed his implements, and moved toward the door without waiting for that finishing-touch to the tonsorial profession—the customer's verdict. Which was just as well.

It caught up with him, however, halfway down the corridor. The door flew open a second time, hair-raising imprecations pursued him, as well as a shoe and a thick glass ashtray which just missed him by inches. He dove discreetly down a staircase and sought his own room two floors below.

He pinned a note to the rolled-up white jacket and implements: "Return to hotel barber shop with apologies." Then he left, with half-a-dozen human hairs in a cigarette-paper, all he had to show for his three dollars. "We'll see what the little glass slides have to say," he murmured.

"And what do you want me to do with these?" demanded the A.C. Police Commissioner dryly. "Stuff a pillow with 'em, or put 'em in a locket for a keepsake?"

"Just send 'em to Washington for me and have the Department of Justice experts find out which matches which. Be sure not to get the tags mixed. A," he explained, "was taken from under the fingernails of the body—I have witnesses at the morgue to verify that. Group B is from the head of the accused, C from that of the chief State's witness. The analysis ought to show which matches which."

"Thanks for A, anyway," the Commissioner nodded, "it's one bet our examiner overlooked. It ought to come in handy at the trial. I'll do it for you, though, Travis."

"Have 'em send you a wire," pleaded Mike. "They can forward the full report later. I know the suspect you have now will stay put, but in case it turns out to be somebody else—you can reach me at my sister's house, South Carolina Avenue."

"You have my word on it," repeated the Commissioner.

Then he added, not unkindly, "I don't like to tell you this, old-timer, but that boy's as good as dead already. It's one of the strongest circumstantial cases we've had here in years."

Mike left, thinking, "And I'm counting on three hairs to outweigh it!"

He plodded along the Boardwalk, head down. It was hopeless. Even if the report that came back was favorable, what chance had the kid against that young swell, with all his money and influence? The dead girl's own people would probably back him up if it came to a showdown. He thought of Murray having him thrown out of his cell, and grinned. Spunky, fiery, even in the shadow of death. Then he thought of the other youth, nervous, fidgety, in his luxurious hotel-room. There had been something soft and flabby there just under the surface, Mike had sensed it. Too much money, maybe. Why not dig in, maybe he'd get something! Why wait for the hairs to tell the story? Maybe he could get something more, to back them up with. Why wait for the phalanx of high-priced lawyers that would close in around him, shielding him the moment he was legally jeopardized?

Arnold was ramming eighty-odd neckties into a valise when the knock came on his door. He thought it was the bellhop for

his baggage, and unsuspectingly went to open it. By the time
he saw that it wasn't, it was too late to close it again, they were
in already.

There were three of them, and he recognized the one in the
middle and knew then for a certainty what he'd already suspected all along, that his barber of awhile before had been
something more than a barber. The suspicion alone had jittered
him to the point of getting ready to take a run-out powder until
the trial came up; the certainty of it now paralyzed him to the
point of helplessness. It was characteristic of his fiber that instead of trying to bar their way he fell back flabby and limp as
a rag. Sylvia Reading had known her men, she had known what
she was doing when she refused to marry him. "Soft and no
good." She had carried the knowledge to her grave with her.
He was vanquished before the blow was even struck.

The men closed the door behind them. One stayed beside it.
One went over to the telephone and moved it out of the way.
Arnold's way.

"Remember me?" said Mike.

Arnold nodded, ashen.

Mike flashed some kind of a badge, took in the readied luggage. "So you were going away?" he drawled.

"Why? What do you want?" stammered the playboy.

"Funny you should be going away right at this time. Funny
you should have that little scratch on your scalp, just above the
hair-line. By the time you came back it would've healed,
wouldn't it?"

There was a bottle on the table, and a glass. Arnold said,
"Lemme have another drink, will you? Lemme talk to the Commissioner, will you?" He sounded out-of-breath.

The one by the telephone took it up with both hands, swung
downward with it. The wires came flying loose out of the sound-
box. Then he handed it to Arnold.

"You're going to talk to the Commissioner," Mike promised.
"That's why we're here. He sent us to get you."

Arnold gave a hiss of relief. "Nobody has to know, do they? I can explain to him—but it won't get in the papers, will it, your taking me there like this?"

"Won't it?" grinned Mike. "Won't it? Every leg-man in Atlantic City's ganged up down at the door, there's a camera waiting behind every post to get you—"

A cry broke from him. "I can't stand it! Photographers, my name in all the papers—it'll ruin my life! Can't you take me down the back way? Let me get hold of a lawyer, at least! Oh, my God, let me have a drink!"

Mike moved the bottle away. "I'll make a bargain with you," he said quietly. "You can have a drink, and we'll take you out the back way. Just take a sheet of that stationery and write, 'I killed Sylvia Reading,' and sign your name under it."

Arnold jumped back as though he'd been bitten. "No!" he yelled. "No! I didn't do it! You can't make me say I did! You're trying to catch me, aren't you! You can't pin it on me—"

"Can't we?" said Mike. "We have already. We've proved who killed her! Show him, Lane."

The one by the door fished out two little paper packets, undid them.

Mike said, "Your hair's been tested, since I was here this afternoon. You didn't know I helped myself to some, did you? It matches the specimens we found under her fingernails. Murray's doesn't! She reached up in her death-struggle and clawed at your head; she not only made that little scratch I reopened today, she tore out several of your hairs by the roots. They stayed under her nails, even the water didn't dislodge them. It's not the word of a friendless little dance-hall lizard against yours any more, it's the word of an expert at the Department of Justice in Washington! Come on—and hold your chin up when you hear the camera-shutters go click-click!"

He looked all around him, blindly, as though he couldn't see them any more. Suddenly he was talking through his hands, face hidden. "I couldn't stand it, to see her night after night with that cheap— She had no use for me, and it rankled. She wouldn't listen to me, wouldn't get up and leave when I found her sitting there alone. I started to shake her by the shoulders, I only wanted to shake some sense into her—and then, before I knew it, it had happened! I tell you, she drove me to it, she wouldn't take me seriously— Please," he slobbered, "let me have a drink—"

"Do like I told you," said Mike, "and we'll even wait outside the door for you, let you finish the bottle in peace."

Arnold's face stopped twitching for a moment. "You'll—wait —outside the door?" He snatched at a sheet of hotelpaper, scrawled two lines on it. His voice was just a whisper. "Here— now let me have my drink."

Outside the door Mike folded the paper and put it away. "Soft and no good," he murmured. He motioned his two companions toward the elevator.

"Ain't you gonna wait?" one whispered curiously.

"What for?" said Mike. "He's down there on the Boardwalk already, ahead of us."

"You knew that—and you let him?"

"It's the kindest thing anyone coulda done for him," Mike answered. "Funny how too much money takes all the backbone outa you. I gotta go over to the Commissioner with this confession."

The second one crumpled the two little paper packets and threw them away disgustedly. "I ain't getting bald fast enough," he complained, "I gotta yank out the few I got left. He didn't even look at 'em!"

"Quit beefing; here's your twenty apiece," said Mike, "and stay away from that cheesy confidence-racket of yours on the Boardwalk, or next time I will turn you both in like I threatened to!"

The Commissioner just sat back and whistled after he'd scanned Arnold's confession. "I don't know just how you got this out of him, brother," he said meaningfully, "but you don't know how lucky it is for you you did!" He passed an opened telegram across the desk to him. "Cast your eyes on that!"

Mike's face paled as he read. It was the D. of J. expert's preliminary report. "Group B, from head of accused, does not check with A, from fingernails victim, neither follicles, texture, nor color. Neither does Group C, from second suspect."

Mike just stood there swallowing. The chief clues had gone haywire. The specimens of hair had probably been off the dead girl's own head.

"We're dismissing the case against young Murray, all right," said the Commissioner sombrely, "but if it wasn't for these five scribbled words, 'I killed Sylvia Reading, J. Arnold,' you brought me in just now, we'd have had half a case of murder against you yourself for whatever it was you did to him made him jump out the window like he did. In fact, for all I know, we probably still have at that—but I'm not going to do anything about it." He stared curiously at Mike. "I suppose all that matters is results— but talk about putting the cart before the horse!"

"So you got your job back," beamed Mike's sister happily across the kitchen-table. "They must have read all about it in the papers. Special delivery, and signed by the head of the agency himself!"

"Yeah," scoffed Mike, "took 'em long enough to find out how good I am. Well, I'll take my time about answering, they can wait till I'm good and ready." He took the reply he had prepared from his pocket and hurriedly sealed it. "Got an air-mail stamp?" he wanted to know.

"One and a Half Murders" is among the least-known of Woolrich's stories, but it combines a fantastic number of distinctively Woolrichian elements, such as the Jersey shore setting, the dance hall, the Depression, extremes of wealth and poverty, murder for love, and some incredibly brutal policework. What has preserved the story indelibly in my mind, however, is a lingering suspicion (which I hope some of you may share) that maybe, just maybe, the man on whom the murder is pinned at the end was (although weak and frightened enough to sign a false confession under duress) no more guilty than the first apparent murderer. And if that suspicion is grounded, then we can see in the story a grimly Woolrichian image of justice, with the exoneration of one innocent man achieved by the destruction of another.

Dead on Her Feet

"And another thing I've got against these non-stop shindigs," orated the chief to his slightly bored listeners, "is they let minors get in 'em and dance for days until they wind up in a hospital with the D. T.'s, when the whole thing's been fixed ahead of time and they haven't a chance of copping the prize anyway. Here's a Missus Mollie McGuire been calling up every hour on the half-hour all day long, and bawling the eardrums off me because her daughter Toodles ain't been home in over a week and she wants this guy Pasternack arrested. So you go over there and tell Joe Pasternack I'll give him until tomorrow morning to fold up his contest and send his entries home. And tell him for me he can shove all his big and little silver loving-cups—"

For the first time his audience looked interested, even expectant, as they waited to hear what it was Mr. P. could do with his loving-cups, hoping for the best.

"—back in their packing-cases," concluded the chief chastely, if somewhat disappointingly. "He ain't going to need 'em any more. He has promoted his last marathon in this neck of the woods."

There was a pause while nobody stirred. "Well, what are you all standing there looking at me for?" demanded the chief testily. "You, Donnelly, you're nearest the door. Get going."

Donnelly gave him an injured look. "Me, Chief? Why, I've got a red-hot lead on that payroll thing you were so hipped about. If I don't keep after it it'll cool off on me."

"All right, then you Stevens!"

"Why, I'm due in Yonkers right now," protested Stevens virtuously. "Machine-gun Rosie has been seen around again and I want to have a little talk with her—"

"That leaves you, Doyle," snapped the merciless chief.

"Gee, Chief," whined Doyle plaintively, "gimme a break, can't you? My wife is expecting—" Very much under his breath he added: "—me home early tonight."

"Congratulations," scowled the chief, who had missed hearing the last part of it. He glowered at them. "I get it!" he roared. "It's below your dignity, ain't it! It's too petty-larceny for you! Anything less than the St. Valentine's Day massacre ain't worth going out after, is that it? You figure it's a detail for a bluecoat, don't you?" His open palm hit the desk-top with a sound like a firecracker going off. Purple became the dominant color of his complexion. "I'll put you all back where you started, watching pickpockets in the subway! I'll take some of the high-falutinness out of you! I'll—I'll—" The only surprising thing about it was that foam did not appear at his mouth.

It may have been that the chief's bark was worse than his

bite. At any rate no great amount of apprehension was shown by the culprits before him. One of them cleared his throat inoffensively. "By the way, Chief, I understand that rookie, Smith, has been swiping bananas from Tony on the corner again, and getting the squad a bad name after you told him to pay for them."

The chief took pause and considered this point.

The others seemed to get the idea at once. "They tell me he darned near wrecked a Chinese laundry because the Chinks tried to pass him somebody else's shirts. You could hear the screeching for miles."

Doyle put the artistic finishing touch. "I overheard him say he wouldn't be seen dead wearing the kind of socks you do. He was asking me did I think you had lost an election bet or just didn't know any better."

The chief had become dangerously quiet all at once. A faint drumming sound from somewhere under the desk told what he was doing with his fingers. "Oh he did, did he?" he remarked, very slowly and very ominously.

At this most unfortunate of all possible moments the door blew open and in breezed the maligned one in person. He looked very tired and at the same time enthusiastic, if the combination can be imagined. Red rimmed his eyes, blue shadowed his jaws, but he had a triumphant look on his face, the look of a man who has done his job well and expects a kind word. "Well, Chief," he burst out, "it's over! I got both of 'em. Just brought 'em in. They're in the back room right now—"

An oppressive silence greeted him. Frost seemed to be in the air. He blinked and glanced at his three pals for enlightenment.

The silence didn't last long, however. The chief cleared his throat. "*Hrrrmph.* Zat so?" he said with deceptive mildness. "Well now, Smitty, as long as your engine's warm and you're hitting on all six, just run over to Joe Pasternack's marathon dance and put the skids under it. It's been going on in that old armory on the west side—"

Smitty's face had become a picture of despair. He glanced mutely at the clock on the wall. The clock said four—A. M., not P. M. The chief, not being a naturally hard-hearted man, took time off to glance down at his own socks, as if to steel himself for this bit of cruelty. It seemed to work beautifully. "An election bet!" he muttered cryptically to himself, and came up redder than ever.

"Gee, Chief," pleaded the rookie, "I haven't even had time to shave since yesterday morning." In the background unseen nudgings and silent strangulation were rampant.

"You ain't taking part in it, you're putting the lid on it," the chief reminded him morosely. "First you buy your way in just like anyone else and size it up good and plenty, see if there's anything against it on moral grounds. Then you dig out one Toodles McGuire from under, and don't let her stall you she's of age either. Her old lady says she's sixteen and she ought to know. Smack her and send her home. You seal everything up tight and tell Pasternack and whoever else is backing this thing with him it's all off. And don't go 'way. You stay with him and make sure he refunds any money that's coming to anybody and shuts up shop good and proper. If he tries to squawk about there ain't no ordinance against marathons just lemme know. We can find an ordinance against anything if we go back far enough in the books—"

Smitty shifted his hat from northeast to southwest and started reluctantly toward the great outdoors once more. "Anything screwy like this that comes up, I'm always It," he was heard to mutter rebelliously. "Nice job, shooing a dancing contest. I'll probably get bombarded with powder-puffs—"

The chief reached suddenly for the heavy brass inkwell on his desk, whether to sign some report or to let Smitty have it, Smitty didn't wait to find out. He ducked hurriedly out the door.

"Ah me," sighed the chief profoundly, "what a bunch of

crumbs. Why didn't I listen to me old man and join the fire department instead!"

Young Mr. Smith, muttering bad language all the way, had himself driven over to the unused armory where the peculiar enterprise was taking place.

"Sixty cents," said the taxi-driver.

Smitty took out a little pocket account-book and wrote down —*Taxi-fare—$1.20.* "Send me out after nothing at four in the morning, will he!" he commented. After which he felt a lot better.

There was a box-office outside the entrance but now it was dark and untenanted. Smitty pushed through the unlocked doors and found a combination porter and doorman, a gentleman of color, seated on the inside, who gave him a stub of pink pasteboard in exchange for fifty-five cents, then promptly took the stub back again and tore it in half. "Boy," he remarked affably, "you is either up pow'ful early or up awful late."

"I just is plain up," remarked Smitty, and looked around him.

It was an hour before daylight and there were a dozen people left in the armory, which was built to hold two thousand. Six of them were dancing, but you wouldn't have known it by looking at them. It had been going on nine days. There was no one watching them any more. The last of the paid admissions had gone home hours ago, even the drunks and the Park Avenue stay-outs. All the big snow-white arc lights hanging from the rafters had been put out, except one in the middle, to save expenses. Pasternack wasn't in this for his health. The one remaining light, spitting and sizzling way up overhead, and sending down violet and white rays that you could see with the naked eye, made everything look ghostly, unreal. A phonograph fitted with an amplifier was grinding away at one end of the big hall, tearing a dance-tune to pieces, giving it the beating of its life. Each time the needle got to the end of the record it was swept back to the beginning by a sort of stencil fitted over the turn-table.

Six scarecrows, three men and three girls, clung ludicrously together in pairs out in the middle of the floor. They were not dancing and they were not walking, they were tottering by now, barely moving enough to keep from standing still. Each of the men bore a number on his back. *3, 8,* and *14* the numbers were. They were the "lucky" couples who had outlasted all the others, the scores who had started with them at the bang of a gun a week and two days ago. There wasn't a coat or vest left among the three men—or a necktie. Two of them had replaced their shoes with carpet-slippers to ease their aching feet. The third had on a pair of canvas sneakers.

One of the girls had a wet handkerchief plastered across her forehead. Another had changed into a chorus-girl's practice outfit—shorts and a blouse. The third was a slip of a thing, a mere child, her head hanging limply down over her partner's shoulder, her eyes glazed with exhaustion.

Smitty watched her for a moment. There wasn't a curve in her whole body. If there was anyone here under age, it was she. She must be Toodles McGuire, killing herself for a plated loving-cup, a line in the newspapers, a contract to dance in some cheap honky-tonk, and a thousand dollars that she wasn't going to get anyway—according to the chief. He was probably right, reflected Smitty. There wasn't a thousand dollars in the whole set-up, much less three prizes on a sliding scale. Pasternack would probably pocket whatever profits there were and blow, letting the fame-struck suckers whistle. Corner-lizards and dance-hall belles like these couldn't even scrape together enough to bring suit. Now was as good a time as any to stop the lousy racket.

Smitty sauntered over to the bleachers where four of the remaining six the armory housed just then were seated and sprawled in various attitudes. He looked them over. One was an aged crone who acted as matron to the female participants during the brief five-minute rest-periods that came every half-hour. She had come out of her retirement for the time being, a towel of dubious cleanliness slung over her arm, and was absorbed in the working-out of a crossword puzzle, mumbling to herself all the while. She had climbed halfway up the reviewing stand to secure privacy for her occupation.

Two or three rows below her lounged a greasy-looking counterman from some one-arm lunchroom, guarding a tray that held a covered tin pail of steaming coffee and a stack of wax-paper cups. One of the rest periods was evidently approaching and he was ready to cash in on it.

The third spectator was a girl in a dance dress, her face twisted with pain. Judging by her unkempt appearance and the scornful bitter look in her eyes as she watched the remaining dancers, she had only just recently disqualified herself. She had one stockingless foot up before her and was rubbing the swollen instep with alcohol and cursing softly under her breath.

The fourth and last of the onlookers (the fifth being the darky at the door) was too busy with his arithmetic even to look up when Smitty parked before him. He was in his shirt-sleeves and wore blue elastic armbands and a green celluloid eye-shade. A soggy-looking stogie protruded from his mouth. A watch, a megaphone, a whistle, and a blank-cartridge pistol lay beside him on the bench. He appeared to be computing the day's receipts in a pocket notebook, making them up out of his head as he went along. "Get out of my light," he remarked ungraciously as Smitty's shadow fell athwart him.

"You Pasternack?" Smitty wanted to know, not moving an inch.

"Naw, he's in his office taking a nap."

"Well, get him out here, I've got news for him."

"He don't wanna hear it," said the pleasant party on the bench.

Smitty turned over his lapel, then let it curl back again. "Oh, the lor," commented the auditor, and two tens left the day's receipts and were left high and dry in Smitty's right hand. "Buy yourself a drop of schnapps," he said without even looking up. "Stop in and ask for me tomorrow when there's more in the kitty—"

Smitty plucked the nearest armband, stretched it out until it would have gone around a piano, then let it snap back again. The business manager let out a yip. Smitty's palm with the two sawbucks came up flat against his face, clamped itself there by the chin and bridge of the nose, and executed a rotary motion, grinding them in. "Wrong guy," he said and followed the financial wizard into the sanctum where Pasternack lay in repose, mouth fixed to catch flies.

"Joe," said the humbled side-kick, spitting out pieces of ten-dollar-bill, "the lor."

Pasternack got vertical as though he worked by a spring. "Where's your warrant?" he said before his eyes were even open. "Quick, get me my mouth on the phone, Moe!"

"You go out there and blow your whistle," said Smitty, "and call the bally off—or do I have to throw this place out in the street?" He turned suddenly, tripped over something unseen, and went staggering halfway across the room. The telephone went flying out of Moe's hand at one end and the sound-box came ripping off the baseboard of the wall at the other. *"Tch, tch,* excuse it please," apologized Smitty insincerely. "Just when you needed it most, too!"

He turned back to the one called Moe and sent him headlong out into the auditorium with a hearty shove at the back of the neck. "Now do like I told you," he said, "while we're waiting for the telephone repairman to get here. And when their dogs have cooled, send them all in here to me. That goes for the cannibal and the washroom dame, too." He motioned toward the desk. "Get out your little tin box, Pasternack. How much you got on hand to pay these people?"

It wasn't in a tin box but in a briefcase. "Close the door," said

Pasternack in an insinuating voice. "There's plenty here, and plenty more will be coming in. How big a cut will square you? Write your own ticket."

Smitty sighed wearily. "Do I have to knock your front teeth down the back of your throat before I can convince you I'm one of these old-fashioned guys that likes to work for my money?"

Outside a gun boomed hollowly and the squawking of the phonograph stopped. Moe could be heard making an announcement through the megaphone. "You can't get away with this!" stormed Pasternack. "Where's your warrant?"

"Where's your license," countered Smitty, "if you're going to get technical? C'mon, don't waste any more time, you're keeping me up! Get the dough ready for the pay-off." He stepped to the door and called out into the auditorium: "Everybody in here. Get your things and line up." Two of the three couples separated slowly like sleepwalkers and began to trudge painfully over toward him, walking zig-zag as though their metabolism was all shot.

The third pair, Number 14, still clung together out on the floor, the man facing toward Smitty. They didn't seem to realize it was over. They seemed to be holding each other up. They were in the shape of a human tent, their feet about three feet apart on the floor, their faces and shoulders pressed closely together. The girl was that clothes-pin, that stringbean of a kid he had already figured for Toodles McGuire. So she was going to be stubborn about it, was she? He went over to the pair bellicosely. "C'mon, you heard me, break it up!"

The man gave him a frightened look over her shoulder. "Will you take her off me please, Mac? She's passed out or something, and if I let her go she'll crack her conk on the floor." He blew out his breath. "I can't hold her up much longer!"

Smitty hooked an arm about her middle. She didn't weigh any more than a discarded topcoat. The poor devil who had been bearing her weight, more or less, for nine days and nights on end, let go and folded up into a squatting position at her feet like a shriveled Buddha. "Just lemme stay like this," he moaned, "it feels so good." The girl, meanwhile, had begun to bend slowly double over Smitty's supporting arm, closing up like a jackknife. But she did it with a jerkiness, a deliberateness, that was almost grisly, slipping stiffly down a notch at a time, until her upside-down head had met her knees. She was like a walking doll whose spring has run down.

Smitty turned and barked over one shoulder at the washroom hag. "Hey you! C'mere and gimme a hand with this girl! Can't you see she needs attention? Take her in there with you and see what you can do for her—"

The old crone edged fearfully nearer, but when Smitty tried to pass the inanimate form to her she drew hurriedly back. "I —I ain't got the stren'th to lift her," she mumbled stubbornly. "You're strong, you carry her in and set her down—"

"I can't go in there," he snarled disgustedly. "That's no place for me! What're you here for if you can't—"

The girl who had been sitting on the sidelines suddenly got up and came limping over on one stockingless foot. "Give her to me," she said. "I'll take her in for you." She gave the old woman a long hard look before which the latter quailed and dropped her eyes. "Take hold of her feet," she ordered in a low voice. The hag hurriedly stooped to obey. They sidled off with her between them, and disappeared around the side of the orchestra-stand, toward the washroom. Their burden sagged low, until it almost touched the floor.

"Hang onto her," Smitty thought he heard the younger woman say. "She won't bite you!" The washroom door banged closed on the weird little procession. Smitty turned and hoisted the deflated Number 14 to his feet. "C'mon," he said. "In you go, with the rest!"

They were all lined up against the wall in Pasternack's "office," so played-out that if the wall had suddenly been taken away they would have all toppled flat like a pack of cards. Pasternack and his shill had gone into a huddle in the opposite corner, buzzing like a hive of bees.

"Would you two like to be alone?" Smitty wanted to know,

parking Number 14 with the rest of the droops.

Pasternack evidently believed in the old adage, "He who fights and runs away lives to fight, etc." The game, he seemed to think, was no longer worth the candle. He unlatched the briefcase he had been guarding under his arm, walked back to the desk with it, and prepared to ease his conscience. "Well folks," he remarked genially, "on the advice of this gentleman here" (big pally smile for Smitty) "my partner and I are calling off the contest. While we are under no legal obligation to any of you" (business of clearing his throat and hitching up his necktie) "we have decided to do the square thing, just so there won't be any trouble, and split the prize money among all the remaining entries. Deducting the rental for the armory, the light bill, and the cost of printing tickets and handbills, that would leave—"

"No you don't!" said Smitty, "That comes out of your first nine-days profits. What's on hand now gets divvied without any deductions. Do it your way and they'd all be owing you money!" He turned to the doorman. "You been paid, sunburnt?"

"Nossuh! I'se got five dolluhs a night coming at me—"

"Forty-five for you," said Smitty.

Pasternack suddenly blew up and advanced menacingly upon his partner. "That's what I get for listening to you, know-it-all! So New York was a sucker town, was it! So there was easy pickings here, was there! Yah!"

"Boys, boys," remonstrated Smitty, elbowing them apart.

"Throw them a piece of cheese, the rats," remarked the girl in shorts. There was a scuffling sound in the doorway and Smitty turned in time to see the lamed girl and the washroom matron each trying to get in ahead of the other.

"You don't leave me in there!"

"Well I'm not staying in there alone with her. It ain't my job! I resign!"

The one with the limp got to him first. "Listen, mister, you better go in there yourself," she panted. "We can't do anything with her. I think she's dead."

"She's cold as ice and all stiff-like," corroborated the old woman.

"Oh my God, I've killed her!" someone groaned. Number 14 sagged to his knees and went out like a light. Those on either side of him eased him down to the floor by his arms, too weak themselves to support him.

"Hold everything!" barked Smitty. He gripped the pop-eyed doorman by the shoulder. "Scram out front and get a cop. Tell him to put in a call for an ambulance, and then have him report in here to me. And if you try lighting out, you lose your forty-five bucks and get the electric chair."

"I'se pracktilly back inside again," sobbed the terrified darky as he fled.

"The rest of you stay right where you are. I'll hold you responsible, Pasternack, if anybody ducks."

"As though we could move an inch on these howling dogs," muttered the girl in shorts.

Smitty pushed the girl with one shoe ahead of him. "You come and show me," he grunted. He was what might be termed a moral coward at the moment; he was going where he'd never gone before.

"Straight ahead of you," she scowled, halting outside the door. "Do you need a road-map?"

"C'mon, I'm not going in there alone," he said and gave her a shove through the forbidden portal.

She was stretched out on the floor where they'd left her, a bottle of rubbing alcohol that hadn't worked uncorked beside her. His face was flaming as he squatted down and examined her. She was gone all right. She was as cold as they'd said and getting more rigid by the minute. "Overtaxed her heart most likely," he growled. "That guy Pasternack ought to be hauled up for this. He's morally responsible."

The cop, less well-brought-up than Smitty, stuck his head in the door without compunction.

"Stay by the entrance," Smitty instructed him, "Nobody

leaves." Then, "This was the McGuire kid, wasn't it?" he asked
his feminine companion.

"Can't prove it by me," she said sulkily. "Pasternack kept
calling her Rose Lamont all through the contest. Why don't-cha
ask the guy that was dancing with her? Maybe they got around
to swapping names after nine days. Personally," she said as she
moved toward the door, "I don't know who she was and I don't
give a damn!"

"You'll make a swell mother for some guy's children," commented Smitty following her out. "In there," he said to the
ambulance doctor who had just arrived, "but it's the morgue
now, and not first-aid. Take a look."

Number 14, when he got back to where they all were, was
taking it hard and self-accusing. "I didn't mean to do it, I didn't
mean to!" he kept moaning.

"Shut up, you sap, you're making it tough for yourself," someone hissed.

"Lemme see a list of your entries," Smitty told Pasternack.
The impresario fished a ledger out of the desk drawer and
held it out to him. "All I got out of this enterprise was kicks in
the pants! Why didn't I stick to the sticks where they don't drop
dead from a little dancing? Ask me, why didn't I!"

"Fourteen," read Smitty. "Rose Lamont and Gene Monahan.
That your real name, guy? Back it up." 14 jerked off the coat that
someone had slipped around his shoulders and turned the inner
pocket inside out. The name was inked onto the label. The
address checked too. "What about her, was that her real tag?"

"McGuire was her real name," admitted Monahan, "Toodles
McGuire. She was going to change it anyway, pretty soon, if
we'dda won that thousand"—he hung his head—"so it didn't
matter."

"Why'd you say you did it? Why do you keep saying you didn't
mean to?"

"Because I could feel there was something the matter with
her in my arms. I knew she oughtta quit, and I wouldn't let her.

I kept begging her to stick it out a little longer, even when she didn't answer me. I went crazy, I guess, thinking of that thousand dollars. We needed it to get married on. I kept expecting the others to drop out any minute, there were only two other couples left, and no one was watching us any more. When the rest-periods came, I carried her in my arms to the washroom door, so no one would notice she couldn't make it herself, and turned her over to the old lady in there. She couldn't do anything with her either, but I begged her not to let on, and each time the whistle blew I picked her up and started out from there with her—"

"Well, you've danced her into her grave," said Smitty bitterly. "If I was you I'd go out and stick both my feet under the first trolley-car that came along and hold them there until it went by. It might make a man of you!"

He went out and found the ambulance doctor in the act of leaving. "What was it, her heart?"

The A.D. favored him with a peculiar look, starting at the floor and ending at the top of his head. "Why wouldn't it be? Nobody's heart keeps going with a seven- or eight-inch metal pencil jammed into it."

He unfolded a handkerchief to reveal a slim coppery cylinder, tapering to needle-like sharpness at the writing end, where the case was pointed over the lead to protect it. It was aluminum—encrusted blood was what gave it its copper sheen. Smitty nearly dropped it in consternation—not because of what it had done but because he had missed seeing it.

"And another thing," went on the A.D. "You're new to this sort of thing, aren't you? Well, just a friendly tip. No offense, but you don't call an ambulance that long after they've gone, our time is too val—"

"I don't getcha," said Smitty impatiently. "She needed help; who am I supposed to ring in, potter's field, and have her buried before she's quit breathing?"

This time the look he got was withering. "She was past help hours ago." The doctor scanned his wrist. "It's five now. She's been dead since three, easily. I can't tell you when exactly, but your friend the medical examiner'll tell you whether I'm right or not. I've seen too many of 'em in my time. She's been gone two hours anyhow."

Smitty had taken a step back, as though he were afraid of the guy. "I came in here at four thirty," he stammered excitedly, "and she was dancing on that floor there—I saw her with my own eyes—fifteen, twenty minutes ago!" His face was slightly sallow.

"I don't care whether you saw her dancin' or saw her doin' double-hand-springs on her left ear, she was dead!" roared the ambulance man testily. "She was celebrating her own wake then, if you insist!" He took a look at Smitty's horrified face, quieted down, spit emphatically out of one corner of his mouth, and remarked: "Somebody was dancing with her dead body, that's all. Pleasant dreams, kid!"

Smitty started to burn slowly. "Somebody was," he agreed, gritting his teeth. "I know who Somebody is, too. His number was Fourteen until a little while ago; well, it's Thirteen from now on!"

He went in to look at her again, the doctor whose time was so valuable trailing along. "From the back, eh? That's how I missed it. She was lying on it the first time I came in and looked."

"I nearly missed it myself," the interne told him. "I thought it was a boil at first. See this little pad of gauze? It had been soaked in alcohol and laid over it. There was absolutely no external flow of blood, and the pencil didn't protrude, it was in up to the hilt. In fact I had to use forceps to get it out. You can see for yourself, the clip that fastens to the wearer's pocket, which would have stopped it halfway, is missing. Probably broken off long before."

"I can't figure it," said Smitty. "If it went in up to the hilt, what room was there left for the grip that sent it home?"

"Must have just gone in an inch or two at first and stayed

there," suggested the interne. "She probably killed herself on it by keeling over backwards and hitting the floor or the wall, driving it the rest of the way in." He got to his feet. "Well, the pleasure's all yours." He flipped a careless salute, and left.

"Send the old crow in that had charge in here," Smitty told the cop.

The old woman came in fumbling with her hands, as though she had the seven-day itch.

"What's your name?"

"Josephine Falvey—Mrs. Josephine Falvey." She couldn't keep her eyes off what lay on the floor.

"It don't matter after you're forty," Smitty assured her drily. "What'd you bandage that wound up for? D'you know that makes you an accessory to a crime?"

"I didn't do no such a—" she started to deny whitely.

He suddenly thrust the postage-stamp of folded gauze, rusty on one side, under her nose. She cawed and jumped back. He followed her retreat. "You didn't stick this on? C'mon, answer me!"

"Yeah, I did!" she cackled, almost jumping up and down, "I did, I did—but I didn't mean no harm. Honest, mister, I—"

"When'd you do it?"

"The last time, when you made me and the girl bring her in here. Up to then I kept rubbing her face with alcohol each time he brought her back to the door, but it didn't seem to help her any. I knew I should of gone out and reported it to Pasternack, but he—that feller you know—begged me not to. He begged me to give them a break and not get them ruled out. He said it didn't matter if she acted all limp that way, that she was just dazed. And anyway, there wasn't so much difference between her and the rest any more, they were all acting dopy like that. Then after you told me to bring her in the last time, I stuck my hand down the back of her dress and I felt something hard and round, like a carbuncle or berl, so I put a little gauze application over it. And then me and her decided, as long as the contest was over anyway, we better go out and tell you—"

"Yeah," he scoffed, "and I s'pose if I hadn't shown up she'd still be dancing around out there, until the place needed disinfecting! When was the first time you noticed anything the matter with her?"

She babbled: "About two thirty, three o'clock. They were all in here—the place was still crowded—and someone knocked on the door. He was standing out there with her in his arms and he passed her to me and whispered, 'Look after her, will you?' That's when he begged me not to tell anyone. He said he'd—" She stopped.

"Go on!" snapped Smitty.

"He said he'd cut me in on the thousand if they won it. Then when the whistle blew and they all went out again, he was standing there waiting to take her back in his arms—and off he goes with her. They all had to be helped out by that time, anyway, so nobody noticed anything wrong. After that, the same thing happened each time—until you came. But I didn't dream she was dead." She crossed herself. "If I'da thought that, you couldn't have got me to touch her for love nor money—"

"I've got my doubts," Smitty told her, "about the money part of that, anyway. Outside—and consider yourself a material witness."

If the old crone was to be believed, it had happened outside on the dance floor under the bright arclights, and not in here. He was pretty sure it had, at that. Monahan wouldn't have dared try to force his way in here. The screaming of the other occupants would have blown the roof off. Secondly, the very fact that the floor had been more crowded at that time than later, had helped cover it up. They'd probably quarreled when she tried to quit. He'd whipped out the pencil and struck her while she clung to him. She'd either fallen and killed herself on it, and he'd picked her up again immediately before anyone noticed, or else the Falvey woman had handled her carelessly in the washroom and the impaled pencil had reached her heart.

Smitty decided he wanted to know if any of the feminine entries had been seen to fall to the floor at any time during the evening. Pasternack had been in his office from ten on, first giving out publicity items and then taking a nap, so Smitty put him back on the shelf. Moe, however, came across beautifully.

"Did I see anyone fall?" he echoed shrilly. "Who didn't! Such a commotion you never saw in your life. About half-past two. Right when we were on the air, too."

"Go on, this is getting good. What'd he do, pick her right up again?"

"Pick her up! She wouldn't get up. You couldn't go near her! She just sat there swearing and screaming and throwing things. I thought we'd have to send for the police. Finally they sneaked up behind her and hauled her off on her fanny to the bleachers and disqualified her—"

"Wa-a-ait a minute," gasped Smitty. "Who you talking about?"

Moe looked surprised. "That Standish dame, who else? You saw her, the one with the bum pin. That was when she sprained it and couldn't dance any more. She wouldn't go home. She hung around saying she was framed and gypped and we couldn't get rid of her—"

"Wrong number," said Smitty disgustedly. "Back where you came from." And to the cop: "Now we'll get down to brass tacks. Let's have a crack at Monahan—"

He was thumbing his notebook with studied absorption when the fellow was shoved in the door. "Be right with you," he said offhandedly, tapping his pockets, "soon as I jot down—Lend me your pencil a minute, will you?"

"I—I had one, but I lost it," said Monahan dully.

"How come?" asked Smitty quietly.

"Fell out of my pocket, I guess. The clip was broken."

"This it?"

The fellow's eyes grew big, while it almost touched their lashes, twirling from left to right and right to left. "Yeah, but what's the matter with it, what's it got on it?"

"You asking me that?" leered Smitty. "Come on, show me
how you did it!"

Monahan cowered back against the wall, looked from the
body on the floor to the pencil, and back again. "Oh no," he
moaned, "no. Is that what happened to her? I didn't even
know—"

"Guys as innocent as you rub me the wrong way," said Smitty.
He reached for him, hauled him out into the center of the room,
and then sent him flying back again. His head bonged the door
and the cop looked in inquiringly. "No, I didn't knock," said
Smitty, "that was just his dome." He sprayed a little of the
alcohol into Monahan's stunned face and hauled him forward
again. "The first peep out of you was, 'I killed her.' Then you
keeled over. Later on you kept saying 'I'm to blame, I'm to
blame.' Why try to back out now?"

"But I didn't mean I did anything to her," wailed Monahan,
"I thought I killed her by dancing too much. She was all right
when I helped her in here about two. Then when I came back
for her, the old dame whispered she couldn't wake her up. She
said maybe the motion of dancing would bring her to. She said,
'You want that thousand dollars, don't you? Here, hold her up,
no one'll be any the wiser.' And I listened to her like a fool and
faked it from then on."

Smitty sent him hurling again. "Oh, so now it's supposed to
have happened in here—with your pencil, no less! Quit trying
to pass the buck!"

The cop, who didn't seem to be very bright, again opened the
door, and Monahan came sprawling out at his feet. "Geez, what
a hard head he must have," he remarked.

"Go over and start up that phonograph over there," ordered
Smitty. "We're going to have a little demonstration—of how he
did it. If banging his conk against the door won't bring back his
memory, maybe dancing with her will do it." He hoisted Monahan upright by the scruff of the neck. "Which pocket was the
pencil in?"

The man motioned toward his breast. Smitty dropped it in point-first. The cop fitted the needle into the groove and threw the switch. A blare came from the amplifier. "Pick her up and hold her," grated Smitty.

An animal-like moan was the only answer he got. The man tried to back away. The cop threw him forward again. "So you won't dance, eh?"

"I won't dance," gasped Monahan.

When they helped him up from the floor, he would dance.

"You held her like that dead, for two solid hours," Smitty reminded him. "Why mind an extra five minutes or so?"

The moving scarecrow crouched down beside the other inert scarecrow on the floor. Slowly his arms went around her. The two scarecrows rose to their feet, tottered drunkenly together, then moved out of the doorway into the open in time to the music. The cop began to perspire.

Smitty said: "Any time you're willing to admit you done it, you can quit."

"God forgive you for this!" said a tomb-like voice.

"Take out the pencil," said Smitty, "without letting go of her —like you did the first time."

"This is the first time," said that hollow voice. "The time before—it dropped out." His right hand slipped slowly away from the corpse's back, dipped into his pocket.

The others had come out of Pasternack's office, drawn by the sound of the macabre music, and stood huddled together, horror and unbelief written all over their weary faces. A corner of the bleachers hid both Smitty and the cop from them; all they could see was that grisly couple moving slowly out into the center of the big floor, alone under the funeral heliotrope arc light. Monahan's hand suddenly went up, with something gleaming in it; stabbed down again and was hidden against his partner's back. There was an unearthly howl and the girl with the turned ankle fell flat on her face amidst the onlookers.

Smitty signaled the cop; the music suddenly broke off. Monahan and his partner had come to a halt again and stood there like they had when the contest first ended, upright, tent-shaped, feet far apart, heads locked together. One pair of eyes was as glazed as the other now.

"All right break, break!" said Smitty.

Monahan was clinging to her with a silent, terrible intensity as though he could no longer let go.

The Standish girl had sat up, but promptly covered her eyes with both hands and was shaking all over as if she had a chill.

"I want that girl in here," said Smitty. "And you, Moe. And the old lady."

He closed the door on the three of them. "Let's see that book of entries again."

Moe handed it over jumpily.

"Sylvia Standish, eh?" The girl nodded, still sucking in her breath from the fright she'd had.

"Toodles McGuire was Rose Lamont—now what's your real name?" He thumbed at the old woman. "What are you two to each other?"

The girl looked away. "She's my mother, if you gotta know," she said.

"Might as well admit it, it's easy enough to check up on," he agreed. "I had a hunch there was a tie-up like that in it somewhere. You were too ready to help her carry the body in here the first time." He turned to the cringing Moe. "I understood you to say she carried on like nobody's never-mind when she was ruled out, had to be hauled off the floor by main force and wouldn't go home. Was she just a bum loser, or what was her grievance?"

"She claimed it was done purposely," said Moe. "Me, I got my doubts. It was like this. That girl the feller killed, she had on a string of glass beads, see? So the string broke and they rolled all over the floor under everybody's feet. So this one, she slipped on 'em, fell and turned her ankle and couldn't dance no more.

Then she starts hollering blue murder." He shrugged. "What should we do, call off the contest because she couldn't dance no more?"

"She did it purposely," broke in the girl hotly, "so she could hook the award herself! She knew I had a better chance than anyone else—"

"I suppose it was while you were sitting there on the floor you picked up the pencil Monahan had dropped," Smitty said casually.

"I did like hell! It fell out in the bleachers when he came over to apolo—" She stopped abruptly. "I don't know what pencil you're talking about."

"Don't worry about a little slip-up like that," Smitty told her. "You're down for it anyway—and have been ever since you folded up out there just now. You're not telling me anything I don't know already."

"Anyone woulda keeled over; I thought I was seeing her ghost—"

"That ain't what told me. It was seeing him pretend to do it that told me he never did it. It wasn't done outside at all, in spite of what your old lady tried to hand me. Know why? The pencil didn't go through her dress. There's no hole in the back of her dress. Therefore she had her dress off and was cooling off when it happened. Therefore it was done here in the restroom. For Monahan to do it outside he would have had to hitch her whole dress up almost over her head in front of everybody—and maybe that wouldn't have been noticed!

"He never came in here after her; your own mother would have been the first one to squawk for help. You did, though. She stayed a moment after the others. You came in the minute they cleared out and stuck her with it. She fell on it and killed herself. Then your old lady tried to cover you by putting a pad on the wound and giving Monahan the idea she was stupefied from fatigue. When he began to notice the coldness, if he did, he thought it was from the alcohol-rubs she was getting every rest-period. I guess he isn't very bright anyway—a guy like that,

that dances for his coffee-and. He didn't have any motive. He wouldn't have done it even if she wanted to quit, he'd have let her. He was too penitent later on when he thought he'd tired her to death. But you had all the motive I need—those broken beads. Getting even for what you thought she did. Have I left anything out?"

"Yeah," she said curtly, "look up my sleeve and tell me if my hat's on straight!"

On the way out to the Black Maria that had backed up to the entrance, with the two Falvey women, Pasternack, Moe, and the other four dancers marching single file ahead of him, Smitty called to the cop: "Where's Monahan? Bring him along!"

The cop came up mopping his brow. "I finally pried him loose," he said, "when they came to take her away, but I can't get him to stop laughing. He's been laughing ever since. I think he's lost his mind. Makes your blood run cold. Look at that!"

Monahan was standing there, propped against the wall, a lone figure under the arclight, his arms still extended in the half-embrace in which he had held his partner for nine days and nights, while peal after peal of macabre mirth came from him, shaking him from head to foot.

Horace McCoy's first novel, the classic *They Shoot Horses, Don't They?*, which used the dance marathon as a symbol for capitalism, was published in 1935. Woolrich apparently read and was much impressed by the book, judging from his use of its central symbol for his own purposes later that same year. The crux of his story, of course, is that the cop Smitty knew in advance that Monahan was innocent, yet proceeded, *for absolutely no reason*, to drive the man insane before he arrested the real killer. Those who have fought against the sickness of the Sixties or against that of the Thirties should find the point of this story equally meaningful to the torments of both decades.

One Night in Barcelona

In the Spanish hotel Maxwell Jones was still sleeping as evening drew on. His face was merged in the shadow where the pillows met the wall. His hands were hidden in white kid gloves. He always slept with white kid gloves on his hands; he always had, ever since he'd first fronted a band.

"For my sax solos, you know. It keeps them soft and flexible," he'd once explained to the boys in the outfit.

They'd laughed about it a lot behind his back, Stateside, when they were traveling buses and getting five hundred a stand. They'd stopped laughing now that they were the sensation of places like Brussels, Nice—and this one, Barcelona—and getting three thousand a week.

Six was the hour his day began. Six in the evening. As the lights began to twinkle outside in the Plaza de Catalunya, as the summit of the mountain Tibidabo, in the distance, darkened to rose-mauve in the afterglow of a gone sun.

Nunez, his valet, entered the room where Jones was sleeping, bent over him and prodded him on the shoulder.

"Senor," he said. "Senor Maxi."

"Fade it," Jones mumbled blurredly. "Two's my point." He opened his eyes. "I was cleaning up, anyway," he told the valet. "That's as good a time as any to quit a game." He put on a dressing-gown Nunez was holding out for him. It had a little silver saxophone embroidered on its breast.

"Whenever you're ready," Nunez ventured, "your bath is drawn."

Jones flung the dressing-gown on the floor and kicked it out of the way.

"I'll use bay rum," he decreed. "It saves time."

A waiter came in next grimacing, cringing, and clasping a bill of fare between both hands as if it were a breviary.

"The senor permits?" he faltered.

"Well, it's about time!" Jones snarled, turning his head and pulling out the wing-tie Nunez was in the act of doing up. "Maybe you think I can live on treble notes all night long?"

He took a pencil from the tremulous waiter and gashed a number of items down the line in rapid succession. "This, and this, and this!" he ordered. "And I want it up here inside of five minutes, get me?"

"Yes, senor. How many places does the senor want laid out?"

"Count 'em out there as you leave," said Jones gruffly. "They're all there, the sponges. They wouldn't miss a free feed."

"Yes sen—"

"Say senor once more," Jones shouted, "and I'll throw something at you!"

The waiter got out fast.

When three short tables had been brought into the outside room, placed end to end to make one long narrow one, and covered over with linen, dishes, glassware, and long thin loaves of Spanish bread Jones entered from the bedroom like a lord, dinner-jacket skintight across his broad shoulders, white handkerchief arrow-heading up out of his breast-pocket, white kid gloves on his hands once more. He ate in them, too.

"Evening, everybody," he said with an air of feudal hospitality.

They all sat down at the table. That was what they had been waiting for, some of them for two hours.

There were eight of them present tonight, not counting Jones. Bill Nichols (trumpet) and girl, Buzz Davis (drums) and girl, "Hot-shot" Henderson (bass trombone) and Roy Daniels (piano), and two unattached girls, that were nobody's girls, but just there for the food. They'd been coming around for about two weeks now.

With the fish course, a messenger entered the room carrying a small cardboard box.

"For the Senor Maxi," he announced, "from an admirer."

Jones opened it and looked inside. There was a single giant-sized white carnation, its stem carefully wrapped in silver paper, a pin for eventual use affixed to it. Also a note on orchid paper.

Jones gave this last to Nunez to read aloud, written Spanish being over his head.

Everyone turned around in their chairs to listen, as though a public speech were being made. Nunez cleared his throat and began to read: " 'I will be there again tonight, just as I am every night. You will see me but you will not know me. But if you will wear my flower in your coat, and if you will play *Symphonic* for me, you will make me supremely happy.

"(Signed) 'An aficionada who has not the courage to come closer.' "

"Every night regular, for three weeks now," Bill Nichols kidded. "Her old man must be in the florist business."

"Maybe he runs a funeral parlor," Davis suggested.

Toward the end of the meal, which was signalized by the pouring of boiling-hot coffee into large glasses partly filled with sugar, Nunez, who had been over at the partly open door, conferring with someone unseen on the outside of it, came back to Jones and leaning across his shoulder, whispered:

"There's a man outside wants to see you, senor."

"That's nothing new," Jones answered patronizingly. "There's always someone wanting to see me, in this town. Ask him what he wants."

"I already asked, and he wouldn't tell me, senor." Nunez shrugged. "He's from your own country."

Jones was suddenly wary. He shook his head.

"Tell him no. Not tonight—"

He stopped and looked. The ineffectively closed door had slowly swung back again and the man was in anyway. The chattering died down, and the others all turned and stared, taken back by this unmistakable piece of lèse-majesté.

He had on a dark-gray suit that could have stood a little pressing. There was a wrinkled topcoat slung over his arm. He carried a well-worn hat, brim slanted down in front. His eyes were blue, his skin-color was on the ruddy side, and his hair was cut down to bristles and sandy-light in shade.

"Close that door and keep—" Jones started to order Nunez, displeased.

But the man did it himself, from the inside now, and then came on slowly. He stopped about four or five feet from Jones' chair.

"You're Maxwell Jones," he said.

"Do I know you?" Jones answered.

"You start tonight."

"And maybe I finish tonight, too."

"I wouldn't count on that. I'd like a little talk with you."

Jones picked up his coffee-glass, put it to his lips and put it down again, without drinking anything.

Then he touched his napkin to the place the glass had touched.

"I'm eating, can't you see that?" But he said it a little thinly.

The man didn't answer; he just stood there waiting.

It was in English so the girls were cut off from the sense of it. But they must have gotten something of its tense, hushed import. None of them moved or spoke. All watched Jones and the stranger.

The man tired of waiting. He broke the silence. "Do you want it in front of all your friends, or do you want it just between the two of us? You can have it either way." He shifted his topcoat a little higher on his arm.

Jones rose at last.

"Okay," he said grudgingly. "Come inside."

"Let's do that," the man agreed ironically, and followed him into the bedroom and closed the door.

Jones seated himself on a chair, nervously turning a cigarette around and around in his fingers. The intruder stood there looking down at him. His topcoat had been flung across the top of the dresser, and his hands were sandwiched into the back pockets of his trousers. One of them, on the right, had a peculiar shape through the cloth, like a wedge, ending in a stubby rounded coil of metal. He just kept them there like that, while he talked.

"You're Maxwell Jones, and you're thirty-two."

"And you?" said Jones, with a rapidly evaporating arrogance that was escaping from him like steam and leaving him more wilted by the minute. "Or isn't this an introduction, maybe?"

"You don't need my name," the man said with a half-smile.

"One, four, oh, two, one, two. It's on here." He took something out of his pocket, the left one, and held it for Jones to see, then put it back.

Jones dropped his cigarette, picked it up, then threw it away for good.

"You're from a little place outside of Nashville called Liberty." The man gave that half-smile again. "Most people never heard of it, but you and I have, haven't we?"

"I've never been there in my life," Jones said haughtily.

"They think you have, and, friend, I just work for them."

"Who's *they?*" Jones asked. His eyes darted too wide of their mark, then came back center to the other man again.

"Now who do you suppose?" the man said ironically. "Sheriff Carney, the constabulary, just about the whole community, I reckon."

Jones moistened his lips. "What—what for?"

"They want to talk to you."

"What about?"

"This and that. About Amy Dwyer, the sheriff's daughter. About Mark Claybourne, son of the councilman. I guess you know." He elevated himself a little on the balls of his feet, sank down again on his heels. "They were both murdered, at the same time and place. I guess you know all that. Pretty grim stuff.

"They left a powerful lot of mourners. Influential mourners. Sheriff Carney. Amy was the apple of his eye. Greg Dwyer, her husband. Mark's wife who's the daughter of another member of the town council. Those three families, between them, just about own the community.

"It was more than a double killing, really. It was a triple one. Doc Stevens had promised Carney a grandchild—his first. All those people, not just two, were killed in one way or another. Mark's wife is as good as lying in the grave with him; she's just a ghost that goes walking around in a woman's dress.

"Greg Dwyer has to be picked up and carried home most every night from the tavern; and you can tell which way they took him by the alcohol smelling up the air. All those people paying up, for just a moment's heat run wild." He looked at Jones bitterly.

Jones' face was the color of wet cement. He stood up, shaking all over. He clenched a fist and pounded it against his forehead.

"I didn't do it," he said hollowly. He pounded again, and then a third time. "I didn't do it."

The other man spread his hand open.

"Tell them," he said coldly. "That's all you've got to do. I don't care whether you did or not, I just work for them."

Jones sat down again, his arms loose now, like ropes dangling toward the floor.

"I wasn't even there. I've never been in the place. I was born in Chicago—"

The man didn't consult anything. Any memorandum or anything.

"Sure. At Twenty-three-eleven Paige Street, in the back room on the fifth floor. At eleven at night, March eighteenth, Nineteen-Fifteen. Certificate issued by Doctor Sam Rollini—"

"Cut it out," Jones panted.

"The double murder in Liberty was committed by an Eddie Jones. And the baby born in Chicago was baptized Edward Jones. But there was a middle initial: M. The mother's name had been Edith Maxwell." The man grinned bleakly. "What did you do with the 'Ed'? Drop it in the middle of the ocean on your way over?"

"There's a hundred thousand Joneses," Jones said desperately.

The other man shook his head smilingly. "Not over here. Then why didn't you stay where there *are* a hundred thousand other Joneses? You would have been safer. That was a fool play on your part." He chuckled grimly. "And up in lights, yet, blazing away into the night. *Maxi Jones, King of the Saxophones.*" He shook his head again, marveling at it. "You were doing all right over here, weren't you?"

Jones began wringing his hands nervously. A faraway, wistful look came into his eyes, as if he were contemplating something that was already over, beyond recall.

"We packed 'em in in Paris," he faltered, as if he were pleading some sort of a case.

"You'll pack them in back there, too," the man promised.

"We were the biggest thing that hit the town since Josephine Baker brought over the Charleston."

"You'll be the biggest thing to hit Tennessee since the Darrow Case."

"We were held over six weeks in Cannes."

"You'll be held over about three weeks back home. That's about the usual time it takes them to get ready after sentence has been passed."

Jones' head went down; the other man could only see the top of it for a minute.

The man hoisted an elbow and looked at his watch. "Okay. Start packing."

Jones' head came up again, with a sort of final defiance.

"This is Spanish soil. You can't touch me."

The man tapped his own chest. "I've got an extradition warrant in here that says yes. I've got these—" He took out a pair of handcuffs, twirled them once, put them away again "—that say sure thing. And I've got this—" He showed him a gun for a minute, put that away again too "—that says 'You bet your sweet life.' So let's get started."

Jones stood up slowly.

"Where will the—the arraignment be held? Nashville?"

The other man shook his head. "Liberty. It's got to be held in the county in which the crime took place."

Jones tottered, and acted as though he were going to fall for a minute. He took hold of the back of the chair and held onto that.

"You're not taking me back to be tried for my life. You're taking me back to certain death. I'm dead already, standing here in front of you. There won't even be any trial; there won't be time for it to get started. I'll be torn to pieces first."

The other man eyed him without blinking. "They're dead, too, both of them," he said. "Everyone has to die sometime."

"But not at thirty-two, with flaming gasoline poured over you."

"They won't do that," the other man said. Not very strenuously.

"Are you from there?" was all Jones answered.

"I happen to be from upper New York State, myself. But that doesn't matter."

"I thought so," was all Jones said. He went over to the floor-to-ceiling windows and stood looking out.

The other man watched him.

"Don't go out on the balcony," he said. "This is three floors up." He stayed where he was. "Say good-by to it." He gave Jones time. Finally he said: "Ready now?"

Jones turned around.

"All right, I'm ready," he said. "I guess I always knew the number would end like this. Well, I'm over my stage-fright now. I'm all set. You won't have any trouble with me. Only—" He glanced around once more, longingly, at the powdery, lighted scene down below, outside the windows.

"Only what?" said the other man.

"Only, when a man's in the death-pen, they give him one last meal."

"You just got through. What was that, in there?"

"Give me one more night. Just one more night here in Barcelona."

"That's what you're going to have. The ship doesn't leave until tomorrow after sundown. The planes are booked solid, so I've got to take you back the slow way."

"I don't mean that," Jones said. "Let me play one last date at the club. Let me stand up there and say good-by with my fingers on the sax-keys. Let me see the crowds and the lights, and hear 'em howl for more. It's going to be awfully dark and quiet where you're putting me. Just a plain pine box without room to turn over in. Let me have just one more night, a farewell round."

"Do you think I'm crazy? And what am I supposed to be doing? Sitting here in the hotel room waiting for you with a lamp burning in the window?"

"I didn't mean alone. I meant in your custody. You'll be right with me. I won't be out of your sight. You've got the cuff-links, you've got the gat. What chance are you taking?"

"None," the man said flatly. "Because I won't be doing it."

"Not even if I gave you my word?"

"What is this? I'll give you mine instead. A short 'No.' How's that?"

"That's that, I guess," Jones admitted mournfully.

"What're you so leary about, anyway? You'll get a fair trial."

"Take a good look at me, mister, and then say that."

The man took the look, but he didn't say it.

"Yeah," Jones agreed softly, at the unspoken admission.

The man got a little sore.

"Ah, don't look at me like that!" he said. "That's the way they always look at you, all of them! It reminds me of a—" He didn't finish it.

"What?" Jones prompted.

"None of your business!" The man scowled. But then he went ahead and finished it anyway. "Of a dog I picked up in the street one day, right after it had been run over. I had to use my gun. Just before I did, it rolled its eyes up at me and gave me that same kind of look."

"They like to live, too," Jones agreed. "All of us do. Only, the dogs get off lucky. Other dogs don't set fire to them."

"Why do you keep harping on that?" the man said.

"Because *they* were roasted to death in a cabin, Claybourne and Amy Dwyer. And because Sheriff Carney swore that if he ever got his hands on the man that did it, he'd barbecue him alive."

"Then you *were* there in the town," the man said quickly. "To know that and to hear it. That was just an outburst of grief. Carney didn't really mean it."

"It was an unspoken promise, a pledge, that every man in the town will help him keep when the day comes," Jones said. "I can tell you're not from down around there, or you'd understand."

The man didn't say anything. He kept staring at the band leader with an odd intensity.

Jones nodded.

"Yes, I was there in the town when it happened," he said. "And I'm ready to take it; I made up my mind over there by the window a few minutes ago. I'm ready to die. I'm willing to go back with you without lifting a finger. But that isn't what I asked you for before. I only wanted one last night, just because it *is* so certain. And you won't give it to me—"

He must have seen something in the other's face.

"Well, if you won't give it to me of your own accord, how about letting me try to win it from you? How about giving me a chance, a sporting chance? I'll give odds. If you win, I'll go out of here without another word. If I win, just one more night for a finale, six hours more until the club closes down at four?"

He took out a pair of dice. Clicked and cast them. Bent and picked them up without seeing what they'd made.

"What do you think this is?" the detective said. "Rolling them to see who buys the drinks at a bar?"

"Be a sport," Jones said in a strangely husky, throbbing voice. "I'm your prisoner anyway. This doesn't alter the main idea. Hold out your hand."

The detective didn't move but Jones reached for his hand and put the dice in his palm.

"Are they straight?" the detective asked drily.

"They're straight," Jones said. "I make three thousand a week here, American. When you're in that bracket, it's the fun you want out of them, not the money. If they were loaded, I couldn't get any fun out of them."

"I see what you mean," the detective said.

"Go ahead," Jones said. "I'll take the highest odds you can stack against me. So high they're impossible to beat. *One throw*. One throw apiece."

The detective was still fiddling with them.

"Those odds aren't so steep," he said drily. "Suppose I pitch a three or four? You've got eight chances against one to better it."

"You didn't get me. Not like in the game. One throw, I said. And I have to make your point. Repeat it in my own throw."

"You can't do it," the detective said firmly. He was beginning to vibrate the dice a little in his palm. "It can't be done. You know that yourself. Why do you want to make it so tough for yourself?"

"Because I'm a fatalist," Jones answered. "And I want to find out if I'm meant to have this one last night or not. This is my way of pinning fate down and finding out the answer."

"Now I know they're spiked," the detective said skeptically.

"There's the phone. Call down and order another pair."

The detective went over to it, put his hand on it, watched Jones.

Then he came away again. "Now I know they're on the up," he said.

"Throw," Jones pleaded. "I can't stand much more of it." He wiped off his forehead.

"I haven't made any agreement," the detective warned him. "I haven't made my bargain with you." But he was starting to beat them up, first slowly, then faster and hotter. "This is between you and fate, strictly."

"I know," Jones said. "But I'm beginning to know you."

The detective suddenly let go of the dice with a jerk, and they landed. They turned up a two.

Jones didn't move, didn't even go over to where he could read them.

"What was it?" he asked from where he was.

The detective told him, picked them up. "That's a bad point," he said grimly. "I don't think 'fate' and you have much chance. That's the toughest point of the lot. If it had been an eight, for instance, you could have made it with maybe two fours, six and two, five and three—"

"I know how the combinations run," Jones answered quietly. "But maybe it's just as well. Now I'll find out for sure whether fate wants me to have this one last night or not. Now there'll be no mistake about it."

The detective handed him the dice. But then Jones just stood there holding them, for such a long time that finally the detective suggested: "Now you've lost your nerve. Now you want to call it off."

Jones shook his head slowly. "You don't call fate off like that. What is to be, is to be. I'm just wondering which answer's waiting for me, that's all."

He started to pump his hand. Then he opened it toward the floor, and the cubes flew out, and hit. The detective, watching him, saw him keep his eyes closed as he did so.

He opened his eyes, and without moving, said: "Read them for me."

The detective went over and got down, knuckling one hand to the floor. He stayed that way a minute, much longer than he needed to just read them. Then he gathered them together and got up. He still didn't say anything.

"Why is your face so white and strange-looking?" Jones said.

"I'd like to keep these," the detective said. "Do you mind?" He went ahead and put them in his pocket without waiting for the owner's permission.

"What was it?" Jones asked.

The detective took a deep breath. "It was a two," he said, his voice a trifle bated.

Jones sank down suddenly in the chair, as though his legs had collapsed.

"I sure was meant to have that night," he said, staring sight-lessly before him.

The detective took out a handkerchief and patted it across his upper lip. "I never saw anything like that," he admitted.

Jones looked up at him finally, focusing his gaze from far away.

"How about it?" he said.

The detective kept him waiting. He took out the manacles, and weighed them in the center of his hand, and threw them up, and caught them. Then he put them away again. He took out a .38, and checked it, and let Jones see that it was loaded. He let it lie flat in his hand for a moment, and gave it an emphatic smack with his other palm.

"You don't get a second break," he said. "Is that understood? You don't get any warning to halt and come back. You just get all six of these slugs at once, straight through the back. You're in my custody, and I have the legal right to do that to you. I wouldn't even be questioned for it.

"So be careful how you bend to get a drink of water from a cooler. And be careful how you move your hands, even if it's just to take up the saxophone. And be careful where you stand, when you're around me. I may not like it, but you'll be dead before you find it out. If you want it that way, you can have it. You don't get a second break."

He put the gun away.

"But you do get a first. You get your one last night in Barcelona."

Jones exhaled slowly. "You can tell you're not from—down around there," was all he said.

After a moment or two he got up from the chair.

"It's not taking on death that's tough, it's leaving off life. I better change my collar. It got all wilted since we came in here." He opened a cigarette case, looked in it. "I guess there's enough here to hold me until morning. After that—" He made a gesture of throwing it away.

"What's your name?" he added, evening the wings of his tie. "Do you mind?"

"Not at all," the detective answered. "Freshman. Kendall Freshman."

Jones nodded his head toward the closed door. "Do *they* have to know? The other fellows?"

"Not particularly. I'm not a press agent, I'm just a dick."

Jones poured a jigger of brandy, shot it through his teeth. Then he squared his shoulders, turned to face the door. "I'm ready. Let's go. Just one more night of being king."

Freshman tapped his pocket. "Remember, one false move, and the king is dead."

✤

There was a round of introductory handshaking in the outside room, sponsored by Jones.

"Meet my friend Mr. Freshman. He's sticking with me from now on."

No one asked any questions; it seemed as if, in their business, they were used to people drifting in, from nowhere; drifting on again, to nowhere.

Each man's world was his own. They let him be.

Jones broke it up. "Come on, let's travel. It's almost club-time."

They got rid of the girls by the simple expedient of dropping them then and there. Henderson gave his street pick-up a fare-well pat on the flank in parting, but the rest didn't even bid theirs that much of a good-by.

There was a concerted scramble for the stray cigarettes left behind, and the half-emptied bottles of wine, and even the unfinished portions of food (to be jealously wrapped and taken home to their families) on the part of the female detachment, almost before the door had closed behind their recent hosts. But the hosts seemed to take it all for granted, paid no attention. The squealing and heated imprecations carried all the way down the hall to where they stood grouped, waiting for the wirework lift to come up for them.

Jones and his escort stood very close together, a little to the rear. The others were in front of them.

"What time do you open?" Freshman asked.

"We don't go on till eleven. A tango band warms it up for us until then. Nothing much doing any earlier. They eat late here in Spain, you know."

They trooped into the shaky lift. Jones and Freshman stood with their feet touching, toe to toe and heel to heel, the left against the right. Freshman had his hand back somewhere, to the rear of him.

They emerged onto the crowded Plaza de Catalunya, with lights spotted all over it, like a huge pinball machine with the glass left off it. They hollered and they cat-called, and Henderson even blew a couple of wild notes on his instrument, and then they finally got a cab. Something that looked as though it had been through the Civil War. The Spanish one. And probably had.

They all piled into it together, stepping on each other's feet, and drove down the Rambla to its lower end.

Where it narrowed, a vivid scarlet neon-sign flashed on and off against the night sky, proclaiming: *Club New York*, and underneath in slightly smaller but no less fiery lettering: *El Hot Jazz, Orquestra Americana, Maxwell Jones, Rey de los Saxofonos*, each on a separate line.

"Billing," commented Freshman, as it suddenly turned the inside of the cab brick-red when they got near. "That's what tipped you off to me," he said to Jones after the others had cleared out ahead of them. "I was just passing through here. I wasn't even stopping over. I already had my plane ticket to Madrid in my pocket when that thing hit me in the eye through the cab window."

"I knew it was risky," Jones admitted, regarding it hypnotically. He gave a deep sigh. "But it was worth it."

Freshman looked at him curiously. "Does it do what they say to you, to see your own name up in lights like that? I'm just a dick, I wouldn't know."

"It does what they say to you. That's your pay-check. That's your bread and butter and wine."

They went in, cased instruments in hand. Single file except at the end, then Jones and Freshman side by side, elbow to elbow. The only difference being their strides; counterpoint, and not in step, otherwise, it would have been almost a lateral lock-step.

A long-drawn, shuddering sigh of ecstasy went up all over the room.

"Oooooh, Maxi."

"You're doing all right for yourself," Freshman remarked. "No wonder you wanted one last night. Funny world."

"Ain't it, though? On one side of the water, a bum. On the other side, a king. Same man."

They went into the dressing-room and sat around smoking. It wasn't meant for seven, but they all got in somehow. The ones who couldn't find anything to sit on, sat on what they had already, spreading handkerchiefs or newspaper-sheets between them and the floor.

Freshman stood up against the door, its seam running down his spine. He and Jones had broken contact for the first time since leaving the hotel-bedroom, but there was only one door.

Nobody asked Freshman anything further. They already seemed to take him for granted by this time. Just one more moocher who had attached himself to the outfit's leader; only this time a transatlantic one. Maybe cashing in on some past favor, back home in the lean days.

A knock hit Freshman in the kidneys, and a voice said through him, with a curiously ventriloquist-like effect:

"Listo para el senor Maxi."

They filed out. Again Jones and Freshman were last, again they were side by side.

"How are you going to fix this?" the detective asked.

"You want to stay in the wings? I'll be in full view of you there."

"But the rest of the room won't."

"You want to come right up onto the stand with us? Sit in the back line in an empty chair?"

"No, thanks. I don't play anything," Freshman said drily. "Push a table right up against it, front and center. I'll be sitting right under you while you lead. And when you knock off, no wings, you come and sit with me."

Then he added: "I never take it out of my pocket, you know. I shoot right through it."

He showed him two small darned patches, where there had been round holes made in the weave. About like moth-holes, but not made by moths.

"I believe you," Jones said wryly, "without that."

They passed the tango band going off, and looks without any lost love in them were exchanged by the rival musicians.

They filed up a short flight of slatted steps, and came out onto the stand and in full view of the night club. The pinkish light bothered Freshman's eyes for a second or two, until he got them gauged to it. Chairs were scraped around and put in place, and stands shifted over to match them. The tango band sat in different format.

Jones was bending down over the rim talking to the head-waiter. Somebody applauded, and he broke off to bow an acknowledgement, then went ahead. The headwaiter nodded, glanced at Freshman, shrugged. He went off.

Two waiters came over carrying a spindly table between them. They shoved it up against the pit of the bandstand. It was isolated; there was nothing but dancing-space all around it. It got the full benefit of the copper-colored spot sighted at the dance floor and stand. Then they dragged over a couple of chairs.

"There you are," Jones said. "That what you wanted?"

Freshman didn't answer. He vaulted down over the low edge
of the stand, right where he was, instead of going down the
ladder at the side and coming around front again.

He sat down on one of the two chairs. That way he was
looking straight forward at the band. And its leader. That way
the glare was behind him, and in their faces. That way the
dancers were behind him, wouldn't distract him by their constant movement.

He could feel people looking at him from all sides for a minute or two, but it soon wore off. They must have thought he was
some particularly close friend of Jones, to demand and get such
special privileges.

A waiter tried to put a cloth down, but Freshman wouldn't
let him.

"Leave it plain," he said gruffly. "Cloths can be jerked off and
then thrown over you, tangling you up."

The waiter tried to put down a glass ashtray, and he wouldn't
let him do that either. After an ashtray gets full, its contents can
be suddenly thrown in your eyes, blinding you.

"Does the senor want anything at all?" the waiter demanded
affrontedly.

"Just keep back and give me lots of room," Freshman said. "I
want to watch the music." That was the right word, too; he
wanted to see, not hear.

They had spread themselves all around now and were in their
places. They were making noises like crickets; squeaky, metallic
crickets.

Jones tapped his stick twice, spread his arms.

"Number Fifteen on the books," he said.

A rocket-bomb went off and people were dancing all around
on three sides of Freshman. He went ahead looking steadily at
Jones. There wasn't much to see, from the back like that.

Jones must have had an expensive barber. The back of his
neck, where the hair tapered off, was a beautiful job. None of
these straight lines running across. His coat rippled a little

across his back, with the play of his shoulders, which kept time to the beat. One leg kept jittering up and down, too. That was about all there was to see.

They played three numbers through, without a break.

Then the music stopped as though a switch had been thrown, and the stillness was deafening.

"Take five," Jones said to his musicians.

He came down the way Freshman had, vaulting over the edge, and sat down at the table with him.

He was panting a little, Freshman noticed, although he'd been standing still in one place; so all that shaking must have been work, too.

He was a band leader to the bitter end.

"How'd it sound?" he asked Freshman.

"Screwy," the latter said. "It hits the ceiling first, and then comes straight down from there."

"That's because you're under the edge of the stand."

"And that's where I'm staying," Freshman let him know.

Jones' eyes kept roving questioningly over the three sides of the room behind Freshman, going from table to table, lingering a moment, then going on again.

"What're you looking for, a raiding party to rescue you?" Freshman asked.

"No, that ain't it." Jones smiled bleakly. "I got this." He took the message that had come with the lapel-flower out of his pocket and showed it to him. "We're going to be shipmates for the next ten days so you may as well know about it."

Freshman read it, didn't say anything.

"She keeps teasing me. I know she's been here every night. I know she's in the room right now, somewhere over there, looking straight at me. The hell of it is, which one is she? If she doesn't tip me off tonight, she's going to be one night too late."

His men were starting to straggle out onto the stand again. He stood up unhurriedly.

"Well, happy half-notes," he said. "Be with you."

He was lithe and agile. He got up the way he'd come down; with the help of one hand and a catlike swing of the legs.

The musical thunderstorm broke again. The flattened-out dancing shadows wheeled slowly across the surface of Freshman's table. He sat and watched the rippling of Jones' back muscles under the cloth of his coat.

They seemed to play sets of three each time, and then rest. He came back again. He took a cigarette out of an expensive gold case and thumbed an expensive gold lighter to it. Then as an after-thought, he offered one to Freshman.

He began talking about it, suddenly. The other thing.

"I didn't do it, you know," he blurted out. He looked down at the table, as though he could see the whole thing reflected on there.

"I'd say that, too," Freshman said tonelessly.

"You'd say that, too. Only, they'd give you a chance to prove it. They won't do the same for me."

Freshman didn't dispute that, somehow. "I want you to know about it," Jones insisted.

"I don't have to know," Freshman parried. "I'm not a priest. I'm wearing a tie."

Jones brought his fist down on the table.

"I *have* to tell somebody about it! It's been shut up in me too long. And this is my night for spilling it."

Freshman sighed with a sort of wearied patience.

"Go ahead," he said, "I'm listening."

"I was the driver for the Carneys; the old man, the sheriff, and his son-in-law, Greg Dwyer. I guess you know that. I was the family chauffeur. They had a Packard job, old as Methuselah, but it still ran. Then they had a little Ford coupe. She used to drive that, Miss Amy. Young Mrs. Dwyer. It was her own. A present from her father. I still see it all in my nightmares. Peagreen.

"She'd go out in it in the afternoons, alone. Just for a drive, maybe. It must have been just for a drive. Always out in the country, not toward the village, like for shopping or anything. She'd come back in a couple of hours. About the time I'd go in and pick up the two menfolk."

His musicians were coming back onto the stand.

He turned his head abruptly, called: "Buzz, lead the next three for me will you? Twenty, Six, and Nine. I'm telling my life-story to this man."

"Wait'll Eight-oh-two hears about this," somebody said and grinned cheerfully.

Jones went ahead telling it to Freshman.

"First she'd just go once a week. Then afterwards, two or three times. Then pretty nearly every day. She'd always take a book with her. I guess she'd stop and read it in the car. Or maybe get out and sit in the shade of a tree. She was a slow reader, though. The jacket on the book was always the same color.

"There was an old backwoods woman did the washing for them. Took it home and brought it back. I met her once at the gate, coming in. She told me she'd spotted the pea-green coupe standing still off the road, in a grove of trees, miles out. She told me there wasn't anybody in it.

"She asked me what I supposed Miss Amy went all the way out there alone like that for. She told me she thought she spotted another car, a tan roadster, also empty, on the opposite side of the road. But this was a considerable distance below, not anywhere near the first car. And she sort of looked at me—you know how these old women do.

"I told her she ought to learn minding her own business. I told her she better keep that big mouth of hers closed.

"Maybe she did. Maybe it was somebody else's mouth. Maybe nobody's mouth at all. Sometimes things are just in the air, and they're catching from one person to another, like headcolds.

"I thought Greg Dwyer acted kind of strange, pretty soon

after that. His face was kind of white and set, like there was
something troubling him. Something private, between himself
and his conscience.

"Then the very next time she'd gone off on one of her lonesome rides, all of a sudden there he was back at the gate, in the
middle of the afternoon, without any warning. I wasn't supposed to pick him and the sheriff up until evening.

"He didn't ask for her; he didn't ask any questions. He didn't
even come into the house. I think I was the only one who saw
him. The others were all round in back. He just stayed there by
the gate. He beckoned, and I dropped the garden hose and
went over to him. He said he felt like taking a little drive and
told me to get the car out.

"I brought it around and he got in. Next to me, in front.

" 'Not that way,' he said when I started off. 'Out into the
country.'

"I backed and turned, and headed the other way. We went
for miles. Way, way out. Farther out, I think, than I'd ever been
before. Suddenly he said, 'Stop here!' "

Maxi Jones paused and drew a folded handkerchief out of his
pocket and carefully mopped his brow.

"I didn't see anything to stop for," he went on. "Nothing at
all. On one side there was a wooded patch. And on the other
a big open meadow, sloping downward from the road.

"He got out and he said, 'Wait for me,' and he went off. In
among the trees.

"I watched him. That's when I first saw it. By looking after
him, where he was going. A little fleck of pea-green visible
through the trees. The car must have turned off the road further back, where there was an opening, and skirted the far side
of the trees to where it was now, and then stopped.

"It couldn't have driven straight through from the place
where we were parked. There wasn't enough space between
the trees. You couldn't have seen it from the road in a thousand

years, unless you were looking for it.

"He took about ten minutes. Then he came back, stood beside the car and rested his hand on the door-top and he didn't say anything. It wasn't up to me to say anything, so I just waited for him.

"Finally he said, 'I nearly stepped on a rattlesnake in there just now. Ed, you got that gun with you?'

"They'd given me a gun. It went with the job. A hitch-hiker had robbed and murdered somebody on one of the roads about a year before, and it dated from then. As Sheriff, Carney had turned one of his over to me at that time, to keep with me in the car, and arranged it so that I was licensed to do so. It was mine, and yet it wasn't. It was on loan to me, you might say, but only so long as I was their driver. It wasn't my physical property. I was just the custodian.

" 'Give it to me,' he said. 'I'd like to go back in there and see if I can hit it.'

" 'Be easier to club it with a piece of deadwood, wouldn't it?' I suggested.

" 'Come on, let's have it,' he said, in a tone that meant he didn't want any argument about it.

"I took it out of the side pocket of the car and handed it to him. He put it in his pocket, and then he seemed to forget all about it. He didn't even go back the way he had come. He strolled straight down the road instead.

"I started to turn my engine over, to pace him slowly along, so he could get back in again whenever he took a notion to.

"He turned his head sharply, and said, 'Kill that. Stay where you are.' That was the last thing he ever said to me.

"He turned off the road, but this time on the other side, the meadow side, and went down the slope and across the big yellow-green open patch, diagonally, working his way toward a disused cabin that sat way over in the far corner of it.

"He kept getting smaller and smaller as he went. The cabin was facing the other way, toward a footpath that straggled off the road and went past it, and he came up to it from the rear. He went around two corners of it, to get to the front, and then I couldn't see him any more.

"The air was quiet and sleepy, like it is out there in the country. Then all of a sudden I heard two cracks, way off in the distance. Widely spaced. One, count ten, and then another. They carried slowly, like they do when the air is hot and hazy. They made a very small, lonely sound, no bigger than the snapping of a twig. It took me a minute to realize it must have been that gun I gave him.

"I said to myself, he must have got two rattlesnakes, not just one. Or else he fired twice at the same one. But why'd he go over that way, when the place he saw the first one was on the opposite side?

"But I knew I was lying to myself, just trying to keep my courage up by talking to myself. Something was starting to scare me stiff, while I sat there, and I knew it wasn't rattlesnakes; I was afraid to admit to myself what I thought it might be."

Jones took a long breath and shivered. It was a minute or two before he resumed:

"I sat there and I waited, and perspiration came out on my face. I couldn't take my eyes off that spot, where the cabin was located. It seemed to quiver in the heat-haze sent up by the meadow, the way an image does far off in the distance. Wisps of white steam began to trickle out of its seams here and there.

"I knew I was seeing things. I rubbed my eyes hard and stared for all I was worth. That only made the white tendrils come out more places. They were coming out all over the cabin.

"They darkened to dirty gray, then joined together in one big blur with orange teeth tearing at it. The next thing I knew the cabin was on fire. It had no windows, but the fire oozed out anyway, right through the clapboards, like orange water spilling out.

"Then all of a sudden I thought I heard a man screaming. Not a woman. It was a man's voice. I'm sure of it.

"I jumped out of the car, then stopped where I was, shaking all over. I didn't know what to do, whether to run down that way, or stay right where I was.

"Suddenly a tan roadster came bolting out from somewhere around the other side of the cabin, and went heaving along the dirt trail, and clawing at it, to get back up onto the road. I recognized it. It was Mark Claybourne's roadster.

"The smoke from the cabin was climbing up high now, like a big swirling mass of black ostrich feathers. You couldn't tell it was a man screaming any more. It was more like an animal. Like a horse I once heard locked in a burning barn.

"Then it stopped. I was glad it stopped; I couldn't have stood another second of it. The black smoke took a corkscrew twist in itself, and went up higher still. But no more screams came.

"The roadster had turned my way and was bearing down on me. It stopped short with a swipe of its rear wheels, when I almost thought it was getting ready to crash into my car head-on, and Greg Dwyer got out. He was alone in it. The gun I'd given him was in his hand.

"He'd stopped the roadster about twenty yards away. He came on the rest of the way on foot. Walking slowly, the way he'd gone into the trees, the way he'd gone down across the meadow. Slowly, but with a sort of springy knee-action, like when you're slightly crouched.

"All of a sudden I saw his face. I knew then. I don't know how I knew. I just knew. He was looking straight at me, with a terrible sort of directness. His stare was *aiming* at me. *Concentrated* on me. Not on the burning barn back there, not even on the car beside me, as if to make sure of getting away in it fast. His look was *nailing down* my face, like a target. Trying to hold it fast until he got to where I was. Or like a hunter, trying to creep up on something that he's caught sleeping on its feet.

"I knew then.

"I jumped back in, like a flash. I flattened the starter and shot

toward him. There was no time to turn the big job around. I
crouched down low in the seat. He jumped aside, just inches
from the front fender. Then he fired at me twice. And both
times he missed. I think he was too close to hit me. There is such
a thing you know. One bullet went out the other side of the car.
The other tore through the roof.

"I grazed the tan roadster by the thickness of a coat of paint,
but I managed to get safely by it. I kept going. I looked back and
I saw him jump into the tan roadster again, and drive off the
other way. Away from me. He didn't try to come after me. He
didn't have to. That would take care of itself. He went the other
way, like a man going to raise the alarm.

"I kept going. I'd gotten it. I'd gotten it just in the nick of
time.

"I knew what those first two shots in the cabin were for, now.
I knew what the shots at me on the road were for, too. His good
name was involved. The good name of the two most important
families in the town. Caesar's wife must be above suspicion you
know. What if this member of the clan or that one guessed the
truth later? No outsider ever would; they'd hang together.
What was a hired chauffeur's life compared to the honor of
Sheriff Carney and Town Councilman Asa Claybourne and
Town Councilman Netcher, whose daughter was young Claybourne's wife?

"I knew by heart what the story would be before I ever read
a word of it in the papers, and when I first saw it in print days
later and miles away, there it was just as I'd known it would be,
word for word. Miss Amy had gone out alone into the country
to read just once too often. I'd followed her in the Packard when
nobody was around, forced her into the cabin at gun-point."

For a moment Jones paused, looked intently at the detective,
then resumed his story.

"Claybourne had happened to pass by that way in his roadster. He was the hero of the piece. (You see, his family had a

good name to uphold too; they pulled plenty of weight in their own right.) He'd glimpsed the pea-green coupe standing there, and the Packard not far off, both empty. He hadn't thought anything of that, thought Miss Amy's husband must have joined her in the second car.

"But when he reached town he ran into Greg Dwyer himself, already uneasy and asking if he'd seen her. Claybourne told him what he had seen. Now thoroughly alarmed, the two of them had turned around and gone back together. They got out and separated. Dwyer went one way, looking for her, Claybourne the other.

"It was Claybourne who reached the cabin, unarmed, and trying to save her as any man would have, paid for it with his own life. The two of them were cremated alive; the murderer's bullets had only crippled them. The coroner's inquest established that fact. Dwyer was luckier. The two shots fired at him, when he tried to intercept the fleeing fiend, both went wild. But he'd gotten a good look at him. He'd seen who it was.

"I kept going. I crossed the State line before I ran out of gas. Then I ditched the Packard near some railroad tracks. They pointed north, that was all I cared about. I followed them on foot a while, and then I hopped a freight when it slowed for a crossing.

"*Wanted, Dead or Alive,* that's how the official wording goes. They had me either way. I knew I didn't have a chance. Dead I couldn't talk. And alive all the talking I could do would be to scream myself to death in some other blazing shack they'd take me to and lock me in. *Persons unknown,* in the dead of night. It was just a matter of time; then, or a little later. Well, I settled for a little later, and the world's been very good to me on the time I borrowed.

"And this is the little later now; tonight, in a big Spanish city, miles from there, years from then. But this is it just the same."

He looked at Freshman and smiled wryly: "Long speech, huh? Lots of breath wasted."

Freshman shook his head slowly, as if he couldn't explain it himself.

"You know, it's funny—but I believe you. It wasn't the words you used. I could almost see it reflected all over again in your eyes while you told it; the horror and the fear came back again. It's easy to lie with the mouth, but it's awfully hard to lie with the eyes."

"Thanks, anyway," Jones said indifferently. Then he added, "I kind of like you. Too bad we couldn't have met otherwise."

"I kind of like you, too," Freshman admitted. "It won't get you anything but I do. I like you better than any guy I was ever sent out to bring back to justice."

Jones said, "And there's no liquor on the table either."

With a blare of trumpets *Crazy Rhythm* burned out its brakes and squealed to a stop, like something coming around a fast curve. Jones returned to the table again.

"How's your fan mail coming?" Freshman asked drily.

Jones chuckled. "This showed up in the last delivery. She paid off—the one I was telling you about." He took out a sheaf of request-notes, all received during his last three-bagger, extracted one of them from the rest, and deftly palmed it across the table to Freshman, keeping it hidden under his hand. "Don't let her see me showing it to you."

Then he added:

"You better reread it to me. I don't trust the waiter, and there was a drum solo going on while he was trying to tell it to me in my ear."

It was in Spanish, meaning he would have had to get it second hand in any case. The note read:

If you should like to know me better, as I would like to know you, perhaps you will happen to pass through Valencia Street tonight on your way home. And if you do, perhaps you will happen to stop for a minute outside of Number 126. Just for a minute, to light a cigarette. And if you do, perhaps you will happen to find the key to Apartment 44, if you look around. Perhaps, who knows?

But if you are afraid, or if your heart is elsewhere, then do not pass through Valencia Street tonight on your way home.

One Who Has Watched
You From Afar

Jones nodded. "Yeah, that's what the waiter said."

Freshman passed the note back to him without comment.

Jones refolded it, placed it in his pocket.

"I suppose that's out?" he said, very casually.

"Did you ever hear of three on a blind date?" Freshman replied. "And brother, you're not going anywhere alone tonight."

Jones nodded, as though that was the answer he'd expected.

"What's the legal method in Tennessee, chair or rope?" he asked after a while, as though they'd changed subjects in the meantime. "I don't mean what am *I* going to get, I mean what have they got down on paper, that you're supposed to get, if you had lived that long?"

Freshman took a long time. When he finally answered, that wasn't the question he answered at all.

"Tell her okay," he said. "I'll walk over there with you."

Jones crooked his finger and a waiter sidled over.

"Tell whoever gave you that note—"

The waiter said, "Oh, the lady's gone long ago. She told me to wait half an hour after she left before giving it to you. She also made me promise not to tell you what she looked like, in case you asked. She gave me twenty pesetas not to. But if you really want to know, and if I put my mind to it real hard, I think I would be able to—" He kept looking down at Jones' hand, as if expecting another twenty pesetas to show up in it.

Instead, Jones laid it arrestingly on his arm, shut him up.

"Don't try too hard," he said. "I like it better this way." And to Freshman, when the waiter had gone off again, "It's a fare-well performance. It's a one-night stand if there ever was one. And that's how one-night stands should be; no names, and not even any faces."

✤

A human being dies just once. A night club dies each night. And it's just as brutal to watch.

Freshman watched the place die.

The crowd thinned first; that was its life-blood draining away. Each time the band played there were fewer on the floor. Until there were just three couples left. And then two. And then none. Nobody wanted to be the last couple on the floor; it was supposed to be bad luck.

The pink spot went out. That died and was gone. Then some-body pulled a switch and a whole circuit of marginal lights went out while shadows took over where they'd been. That was blindness setting in.

A new kind of music replaced the old. Pails clanked and brushes rasped, and all of a sudden there were a new set of dancers moving slowly around the floor; old and ragged and down on their hands and knees. Yesterday's dancers, coming back like ghosts, to a place where they'd once worn bright colors and paint and been straight and young; just like today's would come back on some tomorrow.

One of them picked up a bit of ribbon-bow someone had dropped, and looked at it a minute, then tucked it away in her rags.

All the tables were jammed together now, and up-ended back-to-back. The legs of the upper layer stuck stiffly up in the air. That was rigor mortis developing.

Jones said good-by to his men. They didn't know it was good-by; they thought it was just good night. He gave Freshman the wink, to let him understand what he was doing.

Jones had posted himself beside the exit where they'd have

to pass him on the way through to the street, and said good-by to them one by one as they came by.

And each one, misunderstanding, just said good night and thought he'd see Jones again tomorrow.

"Take it easy, Bill." And he put his hand on his shoulder a minute, pushed down hard. "Keep blowing 'em hot and fast, now."

" 'Night."

"Buzz, take care of this for me, will you?" He handed him his gold cigarette-case.

"What's the idea?"

"I don't want to carry it around where I'm going. You can give it back to me next time you see me."

One of them called back from the street entrance:

"You coming?"

"Don't wait for me," Jones answered, and the walls made it echo like a death knell.

He turned to Freshman.

"And that's the end of my fellows and me."

Freshman scrutinized him, closely.

"You wanted it that way. You didn't want 'em told."

"I still want it that way." Jones looked around at the night club's remains, cold in death.

"Let's get out of here," he said distastefully, "before they bury us with it."

It was the deadest hour of the night. It would be light in an hour, but in the meantime the darkness seemed to have redoubled itself, as if realizing it had a deadline to work against.

The towns of Spain never sleep altogether, but Barcelona was as close to a complete lull right now as it ever got, twenty-four hours around the clock.

You could hear a taxi-horn chirp three blocks away. You could hear a straggler trying to whistle up somebody all the way down at the next corner.

The stars were out in full array; cruel, glinting Spanish stars, with something fierce and revengeful in their brightness.

"Do you want to take a cab there?" Freshman asked him.

Jones tilted his face.

"Let's walk it. The air smells good."

"And any time you can say that in Spain, you better say it," his custodian grunted. "It ain't often."

It was in the residential sector up past the Rambla—"uptown" you might have called it, at least away from the city's heart; concrete apartment houses with funny rounded edges, and private homes nestled in their own shrubbery behind high iron railings.

There wasn't a sound here. Not a car on the streets.

"How we doing?" Freshman asked at last.

They stopped by a light, and Jones took out the note and consulted it for verification.

"One-twenty-six," he said.

There was a sudden metallic clash, knife-sharp, almost at their very feet. The sound made them both jump slightly. The complete silence had magnified it out of all proportion. They both started, looking around.

"There it is, over there." Jones went and picked it up, brought it back. A doorkey.

Freshman was looking up. "And this is the house. That window up there just closed. I saw it move."

It was a six-story flat, bone-white in the starlight, flush with the street; night-blind, not a light showing.

"Well—" Jones said dubiously. "Here goes!" He half turned to leave, as if he expected Freshman to wait out there on the sidewalk.

"Don't be in a hurry," Freshman let him know, turning with him. "I'm going in with you. I'll do my waiting upstairs, outside the flat door itself. There's such a thing as a back way out, you know."

"Help yourself," was all the bandsman said, noncommittally.

An iron-ribbed glass outer door opened at hand-pressure. An

inner, wooden door required the key. It opened easily. They went up a flight of tiled stairs, Freshman letting Jones take the lead. Night lights were burning on each of the successive floors they ascended to. They stopped at the fourth.

"There it is, up that way," Jones whispered. "Forty, forty-two, forty-four—"

"I'll take you right up to it," Freshman said adamantly.

"It's open," Jones said. "I can see the black running down the edge of it, from here."

"All right," Freshman said when they'd arrived in front of it. "I'll knock off here. You're on your own from here on in."

Jones just stood there. Then he looked down.

"My garter came undone."

"You're just stalling," Freshman said with a skeptical grimace. "Are you afraid to go in there?"

"No, I'm not. Look at it." He planted one foot against the wall, caught at a dangling strip of elastic, refastened it. "Been dragging half the way over here."

"Then why didn't you fix it before?"

"I was afraid to bend down too suddenly with you keeping your hand in your pocket."

"Maybe you were right," Freshman admitted. "Let's get it straight. I know there are things you could do. Take my advice, don't do them. The balconies in front. I can beat you down to the doorway from here, and I'll just shoot from there. Or if she has a gun in there, don't try to borrow it. I'm a professional. You're just an amateur. I'm telling you for your own good, Jones. The only way you'll leave is by this same door you're going in now."

Jones straightened the shoulders of his coat uncomfortably.

"I don't feel like a man going in to his last date. I can't get from one mood into the other. Maybe it's because you're with me."

"Come on back, then. No one's making you."

"I'd better go. This is the last one I'll ever have."

Freshman looked at his watch.

"Four forty-two on the nose," he said. "I'll give you until five. When you hear me rap on the door, come on out. If you don't, I'll come in and get you, handcuffs and all, right in front of her."

Jones straightened his tie. Then he reached for the doorknob, widened the already-open door, and stepped into the engulfing darkness beyond.

The door closed after him, this time fully.

There was nothing. Just blackness. It was like being executed already, and in the other world.

Then a soft voice said, "You?"

"Me," Jones answered.

A moment's wait. Then the voice came again.

"You took so long."

"Where is the light? I can't find it."

He felt in his pocket for his lighter, then remembered that he'd given it away.

She must have guessed his intention.

"No, don't. I don't want any."

"But I can't see my way."

"There is no further need to. Your way is ended. You are here. I have always dreamed of it this way, ever since I first saw you."

"But I can't see you."

"I have seen you. I know you well. I have seen you night after night. My heart doesn't need any lights."

"But what about me?"

"You have seen me, too. You have seen me many times and well. Are you afraid I am ugly? I assure you I'm not. Are you afraid I am old?"

"No," he said politely. "No."

"Then give me your word. No matches, no lighter, please. You will spoil the mood."

"All right, I promise," he said.

"Who is the other one, waiting outside?"

"Oh, you saw him? A friend."

"You did not trust me? You were afraid to come here alone?"

"I couldn't get rid of him. He—manages me. He's afraid to leave me out of his sight, day or night."

"Oh," she said. "An artist's representative. I understand. Come closer. Don't just stand there."

"But I'm afraid I'll stumble over something. I can't even see where I'm putting my foot."

"Just move slowly forward from the door. There is nothing between us. And you will finally come to me."

Bodiless hands found his in the dark. Ghost-hands, soft as silk, light as moths. They linked with his, then drew him gently forward.

And this, he thought, is my last night of freedom in this world.

✤

Freshman blew cigarette-smoke in the emptiness of the hall. He turned his head a little, and looked at the inscrutable door just behind his shoulder. Then he turned away again. He was feeling extremely tired of standing still in one place.

Finally he heard the street-door open, floors below. Someone started to come up the stairs. He'd been afraid of this all along.

"Now what do I do?" he wondered, uneasily.

He could pretend he was waiting to be let in; turn around and face the door expectantly.

Or he could pretend he was just leaving and make a false start toward the stairs as the intruder went by, then double back later to his present position.

In the end he did neither one. His profession emboldened him. It was his business to be standing stock-still in a strange hallway, in a strange house, in the middle of the night. He just stood there as he was, alongside the door, and put the burden of explanation on the other party.

It was a man. Middle-aged or better. He was not drunk, but there was wine on his breath, and his eyes were smoky from it.

He reached the landing and moved straight ahead. For a moment Freshman had an uneasy premonition he was making for that very same door. But he went on toward the foot of the next flight, and turned there, to go up.

He looked at Freshman as he went by.

"Evening," he muttered.

"Evening," Freshman answered, and looked him squarely in the eye.

The man glanced at him again, this time from a slightly higher level, as he started up the final flight. Then he nodded, in comradely understanding, as if he had solved it all to his own satisfaction.

"Afraid to go in and face her, eh? I used to be that way, too. Why don't you do like I do now? Why don't you take off your shoes first just outside the door? That way they never hear you. Otherwise, you'll stand out there in the hall all night."

He winked sagely, and he trudged on up out of sight.

I must remember that, thought Freshman. I may need it ten years from now.

He looked at his watch. Four forty-four and a half. . . .

In the room, darkness and two whispering voices.

"Where are you going?"

"I'm looking for a cigarette. I gave my case away. I have none with me."

"Reach behind you. There is a table. To your left. On it a box of them. Your fingers will find it."

"They have. I've got it."

Something loosely dangling, like a chain-pull, gave a smothered *plink*.

"Do not touch the lamp. You promised me."

"I won't. I didn't know there was one there."

"The box will play a tune, as the lid comes up. Do not be alarmed when you first hear it—"

She had spoken too late. A startling bell-like note had already sounded, and his fingers gave an involuntary jump away from it before he could control them. They struck pottery, there was an agitated swirl, and he could feel the lamp going over. He clawed at it, got only a handful of loose chain, and then that was snaked away from him.

There was a dull thud from the floor, without breakage, but followed by a blinding flash—or what seemed like one. It stayed on, however, in all its intensity, rocking a little, that was all. It glared upward through the upside-down shade, full into their faces, like a spotlight trained from the floor at their very feet.

Two livid satanic masks were the result, floating around without shoulders or bodies or background.

He could only see the one opposite him, not the one she saw.

There was dawning stupefaction on it.

It deepened instant by instant.

It became consternation.

It became unutterable horror.

She started to shake her head. She couldn't articulate. She could only shake wildly. As if in denial of this trick her eyes were playing upon her. He righted the lamp. The light broadened, naturalized, swam out about the room now as it should have.

He turned to see if that would moderate the stark terror that seemed to have engulfed her. It didn't. It augmented it, as if the more of him she could see, the greater became her unreasoning terror.

She gave a startled leap to her feet, as if the divan were afire. But it was *he* she was looking at. He remained with one knee crouched on it, half-sitting, half-standing.

She tried to scream. She couldn't articulate that either. He saw the cords of her neck swell out, then contract again. No sound came. Her larynx was paralyzed with horror.

She kept shaking her head, as if her only salvation, her very sanity, depended on denying what had taken place, and believing in her own denial.

She took a tottering step, as if to turn and flee. Instead, she clawed at the table the lamp had originally been on. A drawer leaped out from it, and her fingers groped inside. There was a flash as they knotted, swept high up over her head. The light exploded along a gleaming knife blade in her hand.

He was too transfixed to move in time; she would have surely had him.

The threatened blow never fell. Instead it crumpled, seemed to disintegrate into a swaying lurch that rocked her whole body. The knife fell, loosened from her fingers. Her hand dropped, limp, and clutched at her heart.

With the other she pointed, quivering, toward the opened drawer, as if asking him to help her. A bluish cast had overspread her lips.

She was trying to whisper something. "Heart-drops—quick!"

He turned and dredged a small vial from the drawer. Then before he could turn back and reach her with it, a swirl of violently agitated air rushed past him, as when something goes over.

When he turned back to her, the fall had already completed itself. She lay there still, one hand vaguely reaching toward her heart.

He picked her up and put her on the divan. He felt for her heartbeat.

He couldn't find it; it had expired.

Too panic-stricken to believe the evidence of his own senses, he snatched up the mirror-lined cigarette box, strewing its contents all over the floor. Then he held the inside of the lid to her lips. It was unadulterated horror. A miniature waltz started to play, there in front of her face. But the mirrored surface remained unclouded.

She was dead.

He whispered hoarsely aloud.

"She's dead. My God, she's dead!"

He didn't know what to do. He was so stunned at the sudden-

ness of it, its inexplicability, that he sat there numbed, beside
her, for a moment or two.

He picked up the knife after awhile, looked at it, dazed. Then
he looked over at the door.

He rose at last, started to go toward it, to open it, to call to
Freshman.

Then he stopped short, stood where he was, knife in hand.

He looked at it. Then he looked at the door. Then he turned
his head and glanced at her, where she lay in new death.

At last he went back to her.

He tested her one last time for signs of life. She was gone
irremediably. Nothing could ever bring her back again. He
picked up the heart-drops and put them into his own pocket.

Then he crouched over her as he had been before, one knee
resting on the divan, half-sitting, half-standing. He raised the
knife high overhead.

After a moment he shut his eyes, and the knife in his hand
drove downward and he felt something soft and thick stop it,
at the hilt.

He left it in her, and got up from there without looking. He
went toward the door. This time he didn't stop. He didn't walk
in a very straight line; he swayed, as though he were a little
unbalanced himself.

He swung the door back. All the way back, flat against the
wall, so there was a good unobstructed view of the room.

Freshman was standing there, a little to one side. The detective's head started to swing around toward him. He didn't wait
for it to finish.

"I've just killed her, Freshman," he said in a strangely steady
voice. "You'd better come in here."

This time it was Jones doing the hanging around waiting
outside the door. For just a moment or two, perhaps, but waiting alone, unguarded, just the same. Standing straight and stiff
as a cigar-store Indian, his back to the room, the way Freshman

had been before. He could hear Freshman moving around inside. He didn't look in to watch what he was doing. He kept his head turned the other way.

Freshman finished at last. He came out and carefully closed the door after him.

"I notice you didn't stir, did you?" he commented. "You had plenty of chance to make a break for it."

"Are you kidding?" Jones answered. "You could have dropped me with a shot straight down the stair-well from up here."

"Are you sure that's the only reason you stayed put?" Freshman asked drily. "Come on, let's go," he said.

They went down the stairs together and out into the street. They walked a preliminary block or so, until Freshman could flag a cab. Then they both got in. Not a word was said by either of them.

"Downtown," was all Freshman said to the driver.

That could mean either the main police headquarters or Jones' rooms at the Victoria, to wait for the following evening and the boat for New York. Either one was downtown from Valencia Street.

Jones didn't ask him which one it was going to be. Freshman didn't tell him. Spanish custody, or American. Leniency or lynch-law.

Jones kept telling off each intersection as they crossed it. You could tell he was doing that by the way his head gave a little side-turn each time. He was breathing kind of fast, though he was only sitting still in a taxi. His forehead glistened a little each time a streetlight washed over it. Finally he turned in desperation and stared into Freshman's face.

"What are you going to do about it?" he said hoarsely. "Why didn't you report it in from there?"

Freshman didn't answer. He kept looking straight ahead, as if he were made of stone.

"I'll tell them, if you don't!" Jones panted. "I'll holler it from the cab window."

"Now I've heard everything," Freshman murmured.

They hit the Plaza de Catalunya, the big light-frosted amphitheatre. And there the two eventual directions split. Until then they'd been identical, you couldn't tell one from the other. But now the giveaway had to come. The hotel was just offside, a few doors to the left. Headquarters was further down the Rambla.

The driver slowed and glanced around at Freshman.

"Which way now, senor?" Almost as though he knew of the decision that had to be made, but he couldn't have. It was just that this was a traffic hub, a wheel from which spokes shot out all over town.

"Para un momento," Freshman said.

They came to a dead halt.

The meter went pounding on. So did Jones' heart.

"Two murders now, one here, one back home," Freshman said, as though he were talking for his own benefit.

He'd taken out the pair of dice Jones had given him earlier in the evening, was tossing them up and down in his hand, knocking them together. The left, not the gun hand. "But they don't stack up alike, do they?"

When Jones moistened his lips and tried to say something, Freshman cut him short with a chop of his hand.

"Save your breath, I'm way ahead of you. You don't have to give it to me. I'll give it to *you*. This is a Latin country. They're lenient toward crimes of passion. Anything with a woman in it, and love, and jealousy. On the books, you could get death. But you won't. You're popular here—almost an idol. And the public influences judges and juries. Because judges and juries *are* part of the public, themselves.

"You'd get twenty years; maybe even only ten. With time off, with the public rooting for you, you could be out in five. With the bankroll waiting, to take up where you left off. And even if you got the rope here, that would still be a lot better than the lynching you're afraid you'll get back there.

"Those odds aren't bad. You don't have to be much of a gambler to take them. You're betting on almost a sure thing."

"Isn't there one thing you're overlooking?" Jones panted. "I didn't do the other one. I did do this."

"I'm not overlooking anything," Freshman let him know harshly. "Not a single damn thing, from beginning to end! You're the one overlooking something. And that's that possession is nine-tenths of the law. I've got you and they haven't."

Jones shut up, and his head canted down upon his chest, in admission of defeat.

Freshman gave a flick of his wrist, and the dice shot out of his hand and hit the asphalt outside the window. And bounced, and rolled, and finally lay still.

"Call that shot," he ordered.

"Two," Jones answered wanly, without lifting his head.

A big gasoline tank-truck rumbled by, and they vanished, kicked out of the way like gravel.

"Only God will ever know if you called it right or not," Freshman mused.

He leaned forward and banged the glass with his knuckles.

"Straight on down," he said. "To the Barcelona General Police Headquarters. I want to turn this man in."

Jones gave a sigh so deep that it was almost like three years of accumulated fear and misery rising up and drifting out of him, leaving him for good.

Going up the steps Freshman stopped and shoved his hand at him.

"Just a minute. Give me the heart-drops. I'll carry them from now on. The first thing they'll do is search you." He dropped the vial into his own coat pocket.

They went inside. He twisted Jones' arm around behind his back, held it gripped that way from then on.

They saw the man they were supposed to see, the higher-up.

Freshman knew how to work it. He showed his credentials.

An effusive Spanish greeting, complete with genuflections, was elicited.

"Ah, a fellow professional. At your service, Senor Freshman. What can I do for you?"

Freshman read from the jottings he'd made back there. "In the Apartment Forty-four in the house at One-twenty-six Valencia Street, there is a woman lying dead with a knife in her heart. The divorcee Blanca Fuentes, former wife of an industrialist, age twenty-seven, no living relatives. Better send somebody over there.

"This man has already admitted to me he did it. He gave himself up to me at the door. They were alone together in the room. Although I have a warrant for his extradition, he belongs to you."

"You will have to waive that, senor. He cannot leave Spanish soil now." He raised his finger. "Officers!"

Two policemen sprang forward. Jones changed hands.

They started to drag him out of the room between them. He dragged very easily, almost gracefully, muscles all relaxed.

Then suddenly he thought of something, balked. "Just one word more," he begged. "Just let me have one word more with him."

They brought him back beside Freshman again.

"I just thought of something," he said in English. "How did —how did you know I was carrying those heart-drops away with me in my pocket? I took them out of the drawer before I let you into the room."

"You damn fool," Freshman slurred, so low no one else in the room could have caught it even if it hadn't been in English. "What makes you think I wasn't down on one knee at the keyhole the whole time, from first to last?"

"Thanks," Jones breathed gratefully as they led him away to be booked for murder. You could hardly hear it. He said it more with his eyes and the expression on his face than with his voice.

Freshman came down the steps of the police station again a few minutes later, alone.

He reached in his pocket for a cigarette, and found the little vial of heart-drops. He switched his arm carelessly sideward, straight across his own body, and chucked it away.

In the hotel rooms late the next day Nunez was packing up Jones' belongings, under the watchful scrutiny of Freshman. The valet kept shaking his head mournfully from time to time.

"I miss him," he murmured. "This was the time I always woke him up. He always woke up with a grouch. I miss that, too." He sighed deeply. "I used to swipe little things from him while he lay sleeping. Cigarettes, change from his pockets. I'd gladly put them back again, if I could only have him sleeping there again."

Outside, the lights began to twinkle in the Plaza de Catalunya, the little side streets off the Rambla vanished one by one in a night-blue blanket, the guardian mountain Tibidabo stood out against the western glow. But the bed was empty. A pair of fresh white-kid gloves lay on it, ready for use.

Freshman went over to the door between the two rooms, looked out. They were all waiting in the outside room, the same as every other night, hanging around expecting to be fed.

"Blow," he said curtly. "No supper tonight. The party's over."

They filed out, singly and in twos. Trumpet, and girl. Drums, and girl. Bass trombone and piano. And two girls that were nobody's girls, but just there for the food.

They didn't resent the brush-off. They all looked sort of sad. The last one to go turned, in the doorway, and raised her arm and gave Freshman a sort of half-hearted wave of farewell.

"If you should ever see him again, wherever he is, tell him good luck from Rosario."

Freshman raised his own arm and gave her a solemn wave back.

The door closed. The party was over. The music was through.

He went back to the inside room and resumed his inventory. Somebody knocked.

"See who that is," he told the valet.

Nunez came back, his face chalky, his jaw hanging slack.

"What's the matter? You look like you've seen a ghost."

"I—I have just received a message from one," Nunez faltered. "She must be one!" He crossed himself.

Freshman took the box from him, examined the giant white carnation. He tore open the enclosed note and read it:

But if you will wear my flower in your coat, and if you will play *Symphonie* for me, you will make me supremely happy.

An aficionada who has not the courage to come closer.

"Every night, for three weeks now," the terrified Nunez quavered. "It must be flowers from the dead!"

Freshman sat down suddenly on a chair. He stayed there for several moments without saying anything. Then he got up again as suddenly and bolted out.

"I've got things to do!" he exclaimed. "I'll be back. Don't touch anything."

He returned an hour later. Nunez was still hanging around, too unnerved by the shock he had received to loot the place and clear out, as he would have done under ordinary circumstances. He smelled strongly of Jones' brandy, but he was cold sober none the less.

"It's all right," Freshman said. "I went down to headquarters and compared the two notes for handwriting. Then I went to the Club New York and cross-questioned the waiter. After that I went to a couple of other addresses, and talked to a couple of other people."

"She—she is alive, senor?"

"If you mean the woman who's been sending Jones these carnations every night for three weeks, she sure is. And she's going to be sitting there tonight in the club big as life and wondering what became of him."

"Then why are they still holding him? Why don't they let him go?"

"Because the woman who invited him to Apartment Forty-four, One-twenty-six Valencia Street, is just as surely dead. She's lying in the morgue right now. I just saw her with my own two eyes."

Nunez shuddered, his eyes rolling in his head.

"These are two different women, amigo," Freshman explained. "That's the waiter's dumbness, and my own carelessness in not comparing the two notes while he still had them both on him, and this damn Spanish indoor sport of sending mash-notes around night clubs by the dozen. The note wasn't meant for him; it was meant for somebody else. Two different people, carrying on a quiet little flirtation of their own from table to table, for some weeks past."

Freshman frowned thoughtfully. "I think what must have happened is, her admirer was sitting between her and Jones, and the waiter carried it to the wrong man. Instead of waiting to see that it had arrived safely, she grew timid and hurried away. Then the party it was intended for, also got up and left, thinking he'd been turned down.

"I don't blame the waiter too much. He's supposed to take orders for drinks, not play the part of Cupid."

Nunez carefully folded a hand-painted French necktie. He signed ponderously.

"But why did my patron kill her? That part is what mystifies me. It was not like him. I know him, I worked for him too long. He has a heart of gold. He would not hurt anyone. He would give the shirt off his back—"

"That part isn't going to make much sense to you," Freshman admitted. "You see, he was already wanted for something like this back in his own country. And if he *had* to stand trial for murder, he wanted it to be here in Spain, and not—"

He didn't finish it. He saw masked men, a burning barn, the screams of a roasting human being.

"I still don't understand," Nunez said helplessly. "Why commit a crime just because you want to be tried for it in some particular place? All you have to do is not commit it in the first place, then you wouldn't have to be tried for it any place at all."

"I knew *you* wouldn't understand," Freshman said, closing the last valise. "He does, though. And *I* do." And then he added softly, "And I guess that's just something between the two of us."

Maxi Jones, of course, is black. Probably the magazine editors decided that the interracial socializing in the story made it imprudent for his blackness to be stated explicitly, but the fact breathes through every pore of the story, which is a milestone in the treatment of black experience in crime fiction. Woolrich treated black themes quite frequently—indeed two of his *Argosy* novellas, "Holocaust" (12/12/36) and "Black Cargo" (7/31/37), deal specifically with black revolution—and in many of his best-known works he created fully human black characters, like the hotel maid in *The Bride Wore Black* and Sam in "Rear Window," decades before the Virgil Tibbs approach became fashionable. But for me, "One Night in Barcelona" is Woolrich's finest effort in this direction, and should have been collected in a volume long ago. The story's implied judgment that there is more justice for a black man in Franco's Spain than in the United States will not be lost on black readers today. Interesting sidelight: a bandleader named Max Jones is also the protagonist of Woolrich's last and worst novel, *Death Is My Dancing Partner* (1959), but this Jones is white and bears no relation to the Jones of the earlier story.

IV

IN THE TWILIGHT

The Penny-a-Worder

The desk clerk received a call early that afternoon, asking if there was a "nice, quiet" room available for about six o'clock that evening. The call was evidently from a business office, for the caller was a young woman who, it developed, wished the intended reservation made in a man's name, whether her employer or one of the firm's clients she did not specify. Told there was a room available, she requested, "Well, will you please hold it for Mr. Edgar Danville Moody, for about six o'clock?" And twice more she reiterated her emphasis on the noiselessness. "It's got to be quiet, though. Make sure it's quiet. He mustn't be disturbed while he's in it."

The desk man assured her with a touch of dryness, "We run a quiet hotel altogether."

"Good," she said warmly. "Because we don't want him to be distracted. It's important that he have complete privacy."

"We can promise that," said the desk clerk.

"Thank you," said the young woman briskly.

"Thank you," answered the desk man.

The designated registrant arrived considerably after six, but not late enough for the reservation to have been voided. He was young—if not under thirty in actuality, still well under it in appearance. He had tried to camouflage his youthful appearance by coaxing a very slim, sandy mustache out along his upper lip. It failed completely in its desired effect. It was like a make-believe mustache ochred on a child's face.

He was a tall lean young man. His attire was eye-catching—it stopped just short of being theatrically flamboyant. Or, depending on the viewer's own taste, just crossed the line. The night being chilly for this early in the season, he was enveloped in a coat of fuzzy sand-colored texture, known generically as camel's-hair, with a belt gathered whiplash-tight around its middle. On the other hand, chilly or not, he had no hat whatever.

His necktie was patterned in regimental stripes, but they were perhaps the wrong regiments, selected from opposing armies. He carried a pipe clenched between his teeth, but with the bowl empty and turned down. A wide band of silver encircled the stem. His shoes were piebald affairs, with saddles of mahogany hue and the remainder almost yellow. They had no eyelets or laces, but were made like moccasins, to be thrust on the foot whole; a fringed leather tongue hung down on the outer side of each vamp.

He was liberally burdened with belongings, but none of these was a conventional, clothes-carrying piece of luggage. Under one arm he held tucked a large flat square, wrapped in brown paper, string-tied, and suggesting a picture-canvas. In that same hand he carried a large wrapped parcel, also brown-paper-bound; in the other a cased portable typewriter. From one pocket of the coat protruded rakishly a long oblong, once again brown-paper-wrapped.

Although he was alone, and not unduly noisy either in his movements or his speech, his arrival had about it an aura of flurry and to-do, as if something of vast consequence were taking place. This, of course, might have derived from the unsubdued nature of his clothing. In later life he was not going to be the kind of man who is ever retiring or inconspicuous.

He disencumbered himself of all his paraphernalia by dropping some onto the floor and some onto the desk top, and inquired, "Is there a room waiting for Edgar Danville Moody?"

"Yes, sir, there certainly is," said the clerk cordially.

"Good and quiet, now?" he warned intently.

"You won't hear a pin drop," promised the clerk.

The guest signed the registration card with a flourish.

"Are you going to be with us long, Mr. Moody?" the clerk asked.

"It better not be too long," was the enigmatic answer, "or I'm in trouble."

"Take the gentleman up, Joe," hosted the clerk, motioning to a bellboy.

Joe began collecting the articles one by one.

"Wait a minute, not Gertie!" he was suddenly instructed.

Joe looked around, first on one side, then on the other. There was no one else standing there. "Gertie?" he said blankly.

Young Mr. Moody picked up the portable typewriter, patted the lid affectionately. "This is Gertie," he enlightened him. "I'm superstitious. I don't let anyone but me carry her when we're out on a job together."

They entered the elevator together, Moody carrying Gertie.

Joe held his peace for the first two floors, but beyond that he was incapable of remaining silent. "I never heard of a typewriter called Gertie," he remarked mildly, turning his head from the controls. "I've worn out six," Moody proclaimed proudly. "Gertie's my seventh." He gave the lid a little love-pat. "I call them alphabetically. My first was Alice."

Joe was vastly interested. "How could you wear out six, like that? Mr. Elliot's had the same one in his office for years now, ever since I first came to work here, and he hasn't wore his out yet."

"Who's he?" said Moody.

"The hotel accountant."

"Aw-w-w," said Moody with vast disdain. "No wonder. He just writes figures. I'm a *writer.*"

Joe was all but mesmerized. He'd liked the young fellow at sight, but now he was hypnotically fascinated. "Gee, are you a writer?" he said, almost breathlessly. "I always wanted to be a writer myself."

Moody was too interested in his own being a writer to acknowledge the other's wish to be one too.

"You write under your own name?" hinted Joe, unable to take his eyes off the new guest.

"Pretty much so." He enlarged on the reply. "Dan Moody. Ever read me?"

Joe was too innately naive to prevaricate plausibly. He scratched the back of his head. "Let me see now," he said. "I'm trying to think."

Moody's face dropped, almost into a sulk. However in a moment it had cleared again. "I guess you don't get much time to read, anyway, on a job like this," he explained to the satisfaction of the two of them.

"No, I don't, but I'd sure like to read something of yours," said Joe fervently. "Especially now that I know you." He wrenched at the lever, and the car began to reverse. It had gone up three floors too high, so intense had been his absorption.

Joe showed him into Room 923 and disposed of his encumbrances. Then he lingered there, unable to tear himself away. Nor did this have anything to do with the delay in his receiving a tip; for once, and in complete sincerity, Joe had forgotten all about there being such a thing.

Moody shed his tent-like topcoat, cast it onto a chair with a billowing overhead fling like a person about to immerse in a bath. Then he began to burst open brown paper with explosive sounds all over the room.

From the flat square came an equally flat, equally square cardboard mat, blank on the reverse side, protected by tissues on the front. Moody peeled these off to reveal a startling composition in vivid oil-paints. Its main factors were a plump-breasted girl in a disheveled, lavender-colored dress desperately fleeing from a pursuer, the look on whose face promised her additional dishevelment.

Joe became goggle eyed, and remained so. Presently he took a step nearer, remaining transfixed. Moody stood the cardboard mat on the floor, against a chair.

"You do that?" Joe breathed in awe.

"No, the artist. It's next month's cover. I have to do a story to match up with it."

Joe said, puzzled, "I thought they did it the other way around. Wrote the story first, and then illustri-ated it."

"That's the usual procedure," Moody said, professionally glib. "They pick a feature story each month, and put that one on the cover. This time they had a little trouble. The fellow that was supposed to do the feature didn't come through on time, got sick or something. So the artist had to start off first, without waiting for him. Now there's no time left, so I have to rustle up a story to fit the cover."

"Gee," said Joe. "Going to be hard, isn't it?"

"Once you get started, it goes by itself. It's just getting started that's hard."

From the bulkier parcel had come, in the interim, two sizable slabs wrapped alike in dark-blue paper. He tore one open to extract a ream of white first-sheets, the other to extract a ream of manila second-sheets.

"I'm going to use this table here," he decided, and planted one stack on one corner of it, the second stack on the opposite corner. Between the two he placed Gertie the typewriter, in a sort of position of honor.

Also from the same parcel had come a pair of soft house-slippers, crushed together toe-to-heel and heel-to-toe. He dropped them under the table. "I can't write with my shoes on," he explained to his new disciple. "Nor with the neck of my shirt buttoned," he added, parting that and flinging his tie onto a chair.

From the slender pocket-slanted oblong, last of the wrapped shapes, came a carton of cigarettes. The pipe, evidently reserved for non-occupational hours, he promptly discarded.

"Now, is there an ashtray?" he queried, like a commander surveying an intended field of action.

Joe darted in and out of several corners of the room. "Gee, no, the last people must have swiped it," he said. "Wait a minute, I'll go get—"

"Never mind, I'll use this instead," decided Moody, bringing over a metal wastebasket. "The amount of ashes I make when I'm working, a tray wouldn't be big enough to hold it all anyway."

The phone gave a very short ring, querulously interrogative. Moody picked it up, then relayed to Joe, "The man downstairs wants to know what's holding you, why you don't come down."

Joe gave a start, then came down to his everyday employment level from the rarefied heights of artistic creation he had been floating about in. He couldn't bear to turn his back, he started going backward to the door instead. "Is there anything else—?" he asked regretfully.

Moody passed a crumpled bill over to him. "Bring me back a—let's see, this is a cover story—you better make it an even dozen bottles of beer. It relaxes me when I'm working. Light, not dark."

"Right away, Mr. Moody," said Joe eagerly, beating a hasty retreat.

While he was gone, Moody made his penultimate preparations: sitting down to remove his shoes and put on the slippers, bringing within range and adjusting the focus of a shaded floor lamp, shifting the horrendous work of art back against the baseboard of the opposite wall so that it faced him squarely just over the table.

Then he went and asked for a number on the phone, without having to look it up.

A young woman answered, "Peerless, good evening."

He said, "Mr. Tartell please."

Another young woman said, "Mr. Tartell's office."

He said, "Hello, Cora. This is Dan Moody. I'm up here and I'm all set. Did Mr. Tartell go home yet?"

"He left half an hour ago," she said. "He left his home number with me, told me to give it to you; he wants you to call him in case you run into any difficulties, have any problems with it. But not later than eleven—they go to bed early out there in East Orange."

"I won't have any trouble," he said self-assuredly. "How long have I been doing this?"

"But this is a cover story. He's very worried. We have to go to the printer by nine tomorrow—we can't hold him up any longer."

"I'll make it, I'll make it," he said. "It'll be on his desk waiting for him at eight thirty on the dot."

"Oh, and I have good news for you. He's not only giving you Bill Hammond's rate on this one—two cents a word—but he told me to tell you that if you do a good job, he'll see to it that you get that extra additional bonus over and above the word count itself that you were hinting about when he first called you today."

"Swell!" he exclaimed gratefully.

A note of maternal instruction crept into her voice. "Now get down to work and show him what you can do. He really thinks a lot of you, Dan. I'm not supposed to say this. And try to have it down here before he comes in tomorrow. I hate to see him worry so. When he worries, I'm miserable along with him. Good luck." And she hung up.

Joe came back with the beer, six bottles in each of two paper sacks.

"Put them on the floor alongside the table, where I can just reach down," instructed Moody.

"He bawled the heck out of me downstairs, but I don't care, it was worth it. Here's a bottle opener the delicatessen people gave me."

"That about kills what I gave you." Moody calculated, fishing into his pocket. "Here's—"

"No," protested Joe sincerely, with a dissuading gesture. "I don't want to take any tip from *you,* Mr. Moody. You're different from other people that come in here. You're a Writer, and I always wanted to be a writer myself. But if I could ever get to read a story of yours—" he added wistfully.

Moody promptly rummaged in the remnants of the brown paper, came up with a magazine which had been entombed there. "Here—here's last month's," he said. "I was taking it home with me, but I can get another at the office."

Its title was *Startling Stories!*—complete with exclamation point. Joe wiped his fingertips reverently against his uniform before touching it, as though afraid of defiling it.

Moody opened it for him, offered it to him that way. "Here I am, here," he said. "Second story. Next month I'm going to be the lead story, going to open the book on account of doing the cover story." He harked back to his humble beginnings for an indulgent moment. "When I first began, I used to be all the way in the back of the book. You know, where the muscle-building ads are."

" 'Killing Time, by Dan Moody,' " Joe mouthed softly, like someone pronouncing a litany.

"They always change your titles on them, I don't know why," Moody complained fretfully. "My own title for that one was 'Out of the Mouths of Guns.' Don't you think that's better?"

"Wouldje—?" Joe was fumbling with a pencil, half afraid to offer it.

Moody took the pencil from Joe's fingers, wrote on the margin alongside the story title: "The best of luck to you, Joe—Dan Moody," Joe the while supporting the magazine from underneath with the flaps of both hands, like an acolyte making an offering at some altar.

"Gee," Joe breathed, "I'm going to keep this forever. I'm going to paste transparent paper over it, so it won't get rubbed off, where you wrote."

"I would have done it in ink for you," Moody said benevolently, "only the pulp paper won't take it—it soaks it up like a blotter."

The phone gave another of its irritable, foreshortened blats.

Joe jumped guiltily, hastily backed toward the door. "I better get back on duty, or he'll be raising cain down there." He half closed the door, reopened it to add, "If there's anything you want, Mr. Moody, just call down for me. I'll drop anything I'm doing and beat it right up here."

"Thanks, I will, Joe," Moody promised, with the warm, comfortable smile of someone whose ego has just been talcumed and cuddled in cotton-wool.

"And good luck to you on the story. I'll be rooting for you!"

"Thanks again, Joe."

Joe closed the door deferentially, holding the knob to the end, so that it should make a minimum of noise and not disturb the mystic creative process about to begin inside.

Before it did, however, Moody went to the phone and asked for a nearby Long Island number. A soprano that sounded like a schoolgirl's got on.

"It's me, honeybunch," Moody said.

The voice had been breathless already, so it couldn't get any more breathless; what it did do was not get any less breathless. "What happened? Ooh, hurry up, tell me! I can't wait. Did you get the assignment on the cover story?"

"Yes, I got it! I'm in the hotel room right now, and they're paying all the charges. And listen to this: I'm getting double word-rate, two cents—"

A squeal of sheer joy answered him.

"And wait a minute, you didn't let me finish. If he likes the job, I'm even getting an extra additional bonus on top of all that. Now what do you have to say to that?"

The squeals became multiple this time—a series of them instead of just one. When they subsided, he heard her almost gasp: "Oh, I'm so proud of you!"

"Is Sonny-bun awake yet?"

"Yes. I knew you'd want to say good night to him, so I kept him up. Wait a minute, I'll go and get him."

The voice faded, then came back again. However, it seemed to be as unaccompanied as before. "Say something to Daddy. Daddy's right here. Daddy wants to hear you say something to him."

Silence.

"Hello, Sonny-bun. How's my little Snooky?" Moody coaxed.

More silence.

The soprano almost sang, "Daddy's going to do a big important job. Aren't you going to wish him luck?"

There was a suspenseful pause, then a startled cluck like that of a little barnyard fowl, "Lock!"

The squeals of delight this time came from both ends of the line, and in both timbres, soprano and tenor. "He wished me luck! Did you hear that? He wished me luck! That's a good omen. Now it's bound to be a lulu of a story!"

The soprano voice was too taken up distributing smothered kisses over what seemed to be a considerable surface-area to be able to answer.

"Well," he said, "guess I better get down to business. I'll be home before noon—I'll take the ten forty-five, after I turn the story in at Tartell's office."

The parting became breathless, flurried, and tripartite.

"Do a bang-up job now"/"I'll make it a smasheroo"/
"Remember, Sonny-bun and I are rooting for you"/"Miss me"/
"And you miss us, too"/ *"Smack, smack"/ "Smack, smack,
smack"/ "Gluck!"*

He hung up smiling, sighed deeply to express his utter satisfaction with his domestic lot. Then he turned away, lathered his
hands briskly, and rolled up his shirt sleeves.

The preliminaries were out of the way, the creative process
was about to begin. The creative process, that mystic life force,
that splurge out of which has come the Venus de Milo, the Mona
Lisa, the Fantasie Impromptu, the Bayeux tapestries, Romeo
and Juliet, the windows of Chartres Cathedral, Paradise Lost—
and a pulp murder story by Dan Moody. The process is the same
in all; if the results are a little uneven, that doesn't invalidate
the basic similarity of origin.

He sat down before Gertie and, noting that the oval of light
from the lamp fell on the machine, to the neglect of the poly-
chrome cardboard mat which slanted in comparative shade
against the wall, he adjusted the pliable lamp-socket so that the
luminous egg was cast almost completely on the drawing instead, with the typewriter now in the shadow. Actually he
didn't need the light on his typewriter. He never looked at the
keys when he wrote, nor at the sheet of paper in the machine.
He was an expert typist, and if in the hectic pace of his fingering
he sometimes struck the wrong letter, they took care of that
down at the office, Tartell had special proofreaders for that.
That wasn't Moody's job—he was the creator, he couldn't be
bothered with picayune details like a few typographic errors.
By the same token, he never went back over what he had
written to reread it; he couldn't afford to, not at one cent a word
(his regular rate) and at the pressure under which he worked.
Besides, it was his experience that it always came out best the
first time; if you went back and reread and fiddled around with
it, you only spoiled it.

He palmed a sheet of white paper off the top of the stack and inserted it smoothly into the roller—an automatic movement to him. Ordinarily he made a sandwich of sheets—a white on top, a carbon in the middle, and a yellow at the bottom; that was in case the story should go astray in the mail, or be mislaid at the magazine office before the cashier had issued a check for it. But it was totally unnecessary in this case; he was delivering the story personally to Tartell's desk, it was a rush order, and it was to be sent to press immediately. Several extra moments would be wasted between manuscript pages if he took the time to make up "sandwiches," and besides, those yellow second-sheets cost forty-five cents a ream at Goldsmith's (fifty-five elsewhere). You had to watch your costs in this line of work.

He lit a cigarette, the first of the many that were inevitably to follow, that always accompanied the writing of every story —the cigarette-to-begin-on. He blew a blue pinwheel of smoke, craned his neck slightly, and stared hard at the master plan before him, standing there against the wall. And now for the first line. That was always the gimmick in every one of his stories. Until he had it, he couldn't get into it; but once he had it, the story started to unravel by itself—it was easy going after that, clear sailing. It was like plucking the edge of the gauze up from an enormous criss-crossed bandage.

The first line, the first line—

He stared intently, almost hypnotically.

Better begin with the girl—she was very prominent on the cover, and then bring the hero in later. Let's see, she was wearing a violet evening dress—

The little lady in the violet evening dress came hurrying terrifiedly down the street, looking back in terror. Behind her

His hands poised avariciously, then drew back again. No, wait a minute, she wouldn't be wearing an evening dress on the street, violet or any other color. Well, she'd have to change into it later in the story, that was all. In a 20,000-word novelette there would be plenty of room for her to change into an evening dress. Just a single line would do it, anywhere along.

She went home and changed her dress, and then came back again.

Now, let's try it again—

The beautiful red-head came hurrying down the street, looking back in terror. Behind her

Again he got stuck. Yes, but who was after her, and what had she done for them to be after her for? That was the problem.

I started in too soon, he decided. I getter go back to where she does something that gets somebody after her. Then the chase can come in after that.

The cigarette was at an end, without having ignited anything other than itself. He started another one.

Now, let's see. What would a beautiful, innocent, *good* girl do that would be likely to get somebody after her? She had to be good—Tartell was very strict about that. "I don't want any lady-bums in my stories. If you have to introduce a lady-bum into one of my stories, see that you kill her off as soon as you can. And whatever you do, don't let her get next to the hero too much. Keep her away from the hero. If he falls for her, he's a sap. And if he doesn't fall for her, he's too much of a goody-goody. Keep her in the background—just let her open the door in a négligée when the big-shot gangster drops in for a visit. And close the door again—fast!"

He swirled a hand around in his hair, in a massage-like motion, dropped it to the table, pummeled the edge of the table with it twice, the way a person does when he's trying to start a balky drawer open. Let's see, let's see . . . She could find out something that she's not supposed to, and then *they* find out that she has found out, and they start after her to shut her up —good enough, that's it! Now *how* did she find it out? She could go to a beauty parlor, and overhear in the next booth—no, beauty parlors were too feminine; Tartell wouldn't allow one of them in his stories. Besides, Moody had never been in one, wouldn't have known how to describe it on the inside. She could be in a phone booth and through the partition— No, he'd

used that gambit in the July issue—in *Death Drops a Slug*.
A little lubrication was indicated here—something to help make the wheels go around, soften up the kinks. Absently, he picked up the bottle opener that Joe had left for him, reached down to the floor, brought up a bottle and uncapped it, still with that same one hand, using the edge of the table for leverage. He poured a very little into the tumbler, and did no more than chastely moisten his lips with it.

Now. She could get a package at her house, and it was meant for someone else, and—

He had that peculiar instinctive feeling that comes when someone is looking at you intently, steadfastly. He shook it off with a slight quirk of his head. It remained in abeyance for a moment or two, then slowly settled on him again.

The story thread suddenly dropped in a hopeless snarl, just as he was about to get it through the needle's eye of the first line.

He turned his head, to dissipate the feeling by glancing in the direction from which it seemed to assail him. And then he saw it. A pigeon was standing utterly motionless on the ledge just outside the pane of the window. Its head was cocked inquiringly, it was turned profileward toward him, and it was staring in at him with just the one eye. But the eye was almost leaning over toward the glass, it was so intent—less than an inch or two away from it.

As he stared back, the eye solemnly blinked. Just once, otherwise giving no indication of life.

He ignored it and turned back to his task.

There's a ring at the bell, she goes to the door, and a man hands her a package—

His eyes crept uncontrollably over to their extreme outer corners, as if trying to take a peek without his knowledge. He brought them back with a reprimanding knitting of the brows. But almost at once they started over that way again. Just knowing the pigeon was standing out there seemed to attract his eyes almost magnetically.

He turned his head toward it again. This time he gave it a heavy baleful scowl. "Get off of there," he mouthed at it. "Go somewhere else." He spoke by lip motion alone, because the glass between prevented hearing.

It blinked. More slowly than the first time, if a pigeon's blink can be measured. Scorn, contempt seemed to be expressed by the deliberateness of its blink.

Never slow to be affronted, he kindled at once. He swung his arm violently around toward it, in a complete half circle of riddance. Its wing feathers erupted a little, subsided again, as if the faintest of breezes had caressed them. Then with stately pomp it waddled around in a half circle, brought the other side of its head around toward the glass, and stared at him with the eye on that side.

Heatedly, he jumped from his chair, strode to the window, and flung it up. "I told you to get off of there!" he said threateningly. He gave the air immediately over the surface of the ledge a thrashing swipe with his arm.

It eluded the gesture with no more difficulty than a child jumping rope. Only, instead of coming down again as the rope passed underneath, it stayed up! It made a little looping journey with scarcely stirring wings, and as soon as his arm was drawn in again, it descended almost to the precise spot where it had stood before.

Once more they repeated this passage between them, with identical results. The pigeon expended far less energy coasting around at a safe height than he did flinging his arm hectically about, and he realized that a law of diminishing returns would soon set in on this point. Moreover, he over-aimed the second time and crashed the back of his hand into the stone coping alongside the window, so that he had to suck at his knuckles and breathe on them to alleviate the sting.

He had never hated a bird so before. In fact, he had never hated a bird before.

He slammed the window down furiously. Thereupon, as though it realized it had that much more advance warning against possible armstrikes, the pigeon began to strut from one side to the other of the window ledge. Like a picket, enjoining him from working. Each time he made a turn, it cocked that beady eye at him.

He picked up the metal wastebasket and tested it in his hand for solidity. Then he put it down again, regretfully. He'd need it during the course of the story; he couldn't just drop the cigarette butts on the floor, he'd be kept too busy stamping them out to avoid starting a fire. And even if the basket knocked the damned bird off the ledge, it would probably go over with it.

He picked up the phone, demanded the desk clerk so that he could vent his indignation on something human.

"Do I have to have pigeons on my window sill?" he shouted accusingly. "Why didn't you tell me there were going to be pigeons on my window sill?"

The clerk was more than taken aback; he was stunned by the onslaught. "I—ah—ah—never had a complaint like this before," he finally managed to stammer.

"Well, you've got one now!" Moody let him know with firm disapproval.

"Yes, sir, but—but what's it doing?" the clerk floundered. "Is it making any noise?"

"It doesn't have to," Moody flared. "I just don't want it there!"

There was a momentary pause, during which it was to be surmised the clerk was baffled, scrubbing the side of his jaw, or perhaps his temple or forehead. Then he came back again, completely at a loss. "I'm sorry, sir—but I don't see what you expect *me* to do about it. You're up there with it, and I'm down here. Haven't—haven't you tried chasing it?"

"Haven't I tried?" choked Moody exasperatedly. "That's all I've been doing! It free-wheels out and around and comes right back again!"

"Well, about the only thing I can suggest," the clerk said helplessly, "is to send up a boy with a mop or broom, and have him stand there by the window and—"

"I can't work with a bellboy in here doing sentinel duty with a mop or broom slung over his shoulder!" Moody exploded. "That'd be worse than the pigeon!"

The clerk breathed deeply, with bottomless patience. "Well, I'm sorry, sir, but—"

Moody got it out first. " 'I don't see what I can do about it.' 'I don't see what I can do about it'!" he mimicked ferociously. "Thanks! You've been a big help," he said with ponderous sarcasm. "I don't know what I would have done without you!"— and hung up.

He looked around at it, a resigned expression in his eyes that those energetic, enthusiastic irises seldom showed.

The pigeon had its neck craned at an acute angle, almost down to the stone sill, but still looking in at him from that oblique perspective, as if to say, "Was that about me? Did it have to do with me?"

He went over and jerked the window up. That didn't even make it stir any more.

He turned and went back to his writing chair. He addressed the pigeon coldly from there. Aloud, but coldly, and with the condescension of the superior forms of life toward the inferior ones. "Look. You want to come in? Is that what it's all about? You're dying to come in? You won't be happy till you do come in? Then for the love of Mike come in and get it over with, and let me get back to work! There's a nice comfortable chair, there's a nice plumpy sofa, there's a nice wide bed-rail for a perch. The whole room is yours. Come in and have yourself a ball!"

Its head came up, from that sneaky way of regarding him

under-wing. It contemplated the invitation. Then its twig-like
little vermilion legs dipped and it threw him a derogatory
chuck of the head, as if to say "That for you and your room!"
—and unexpectedly took off, this time in a straight, unerring
line of final departure.

His feet detonated in such a burst of choleric anger that the
chair went over. He snatched up the wastebasket, rushed to the
window, and swung it violently—without any hope, of course,
of overtaking his already vanished target.

"Dirty damn squab!" he railed bitterly. "Come back here and
I'll—! Doing that to me, after I'm just about to get rolling! I hope
you run into a high-tension wire headfirst. I hope you run into
a hawk—"

His anger, however, settled as rapidly as a spent Seidlitz powder. He closed the window without violence. A smothered
chuckle had already begun to sound in him on his way back to
the chair, and he was grinning sheepishly as he reached it.

"Feuding with a pigeon yet," he murmured deprecatingly to
himself. "I'd better get a grip on myself."

Another cigarette, two good hearty gulps of beer, and now,
let's see—where was I? The opening line. He stared up at the
ceiling.

His fingers spread, poised, and then suddenly began to splatter all over the dark keyboard like heavy drops of rain.

*"For me?" the young woman said, staring unbelievably at the
shifty-eyed man holding the package.*

"You're

One hand paused, then two of its fingers snapped, demanding
inspiration. "Got to get a name for her," he muttered. He stared
fruitlessly at the ceiling for a moment, then glanced over at the
window. The hand resumed.

"You're Pearl Dove, ain't ya?"

"Why, yes, but I wasn't expecting anything."

("Not too much dialogue," Tartell always cautioned. "Get
them moving, get them doing something. Dialogue leaves big

blanks on the pages, and the reader doesn't get as much reading
for his money.")

*He thrust it at her, turned and disappeared as suddenly as he
appeared*

Two "appeareds" in one line—too many. He triphammered
the x-key eight times.

*and disappeared as suddenly as he had showed up. She tried to
call him back but he was no longer in sight. Somewhere out in
the night the whine of an expensive car taking off came to her
ears*

He frowned, closed his eyes briefly, then began typing automatically again.

She looked at the package she had been left holding

He never bothered to consult what he had written so far—
such fussy niceties were for smooth-paper writers and poets. In
stories like the one he was writing, it was almost impossible to
break the thread of the action, anyway. Just so long as he kept
going, that was all that mattered. If there was an occasional gap,
Tartell's proofreaders would knit it together with a couple of
words.

He drained the beer in the glass, refilled it, gazed dreamily
at the ceiling. The wide, blank expanse of the ceiling gave his
characters more room to move around in as his mind's eye
conjured them up.

"She has a boy friend who's on the Homicide Squad," he
murmured confidentially. "Not really a boy friend, just sort of
a brotherly protector." ("Don't give 'em sweethearts," was Tartell's constant admonishment, "just give 'em pals. You might
want to kill the girl off, and if she's already his sweetheart you
can't very well do that, or he loses face with the readers.") "She
calls him up to tell him she has received a mysterious package.
He tells her not to open it, he'll be right over—" The rest was
mechanical fingerwork. Fast and furious. The keys dipped and
rose like a canopy of leaves shot through by an autumn wind.

The page jumped up out of the roller by itself, and he knew

he'd struck off the last line there was room for. He pitched it aside to the floor without even glancing at it, slipped in a new sheet, all in one accustomed, fluid motion. Then, with the same almost unconscious ease, he reached down for a new bottle, uncapped it, and poured until a cream puff of a head burgeoned at the top of it.

They were at the business of opening the package now. He stalled for two lines, to give himself time to improvise what was going to be inside the package, which he hadn't had an opportunity to do until now—

He stared down at it. Then his eyes narrowed and he nodded grimly.

"What do you make of it?" she breathed, clutching her throat.

Then he was smack up against it, and the improvisation had to be here and now. The keys coasted to a reluctant but full stop. There was almost smoke coming from them by now, or else it was from his ever-present cigarette riding the edge of the table, drifting the long way around by way of the machine.

There were always certain staples that were good for the contents of mysterious packages. Opium pellets—but that meant bringing in a Chinese villain, and the menace on the cover drawing certainly wasn't Chinese—

He got up abruptly, swung his chair out away from the table, and shifted it farther over, directly under the phantom tableau on the ceiling that had come to a halt simultaneously with the keys—the way the figures on a motion picture screen freeze into immobility when something goes wrong with the projector.

He got up on the chair seat with both feet, craned his neck, peered intently and with complete sincerity. He was only about two feet away from the visualization on the ceiling. His little bit of fetishism, or idiosyncrasy, had worked for him before in similar stoppages, and it did now. He could *see* the inside of the package, he could see—

He jumped lithely down again, looped the chair back into place, speared avidly at the keys.

Uncut diamonds!

"Aren't they beautiful?" she said, clutching her pulsing throat.

(Well, if there were too many clutches in there, Tartell's hirelings could take one or two of them out. It was always hard to know what to have your female characters do with their hands. Clutching the throat and holding the heart were his own favorite standbys. The male characters could always be fingering a gun or swinging a punch at someone, but it wasn't refined for women to do that in *Startling Stories!*)

"Beautiful but hot," he growled.

Her eyes widened. "How do you know?"

"They're the Espinoza consignment, they've been missing for a week." He unlimbered his gun. "This spells trouble for someone."

That was enough dialogue for a few pages—he had to get into some fast, red-hot action.

There weren't any more hitches now. The story flowed like a torrent. The margin bell chimed almost staccato, the roller turned with almost piston-like continuity, the pages sprang up almost like blobs of batter from a pancake skillet. The beer kept rising in the glass and, contradictorily, steadily falling lower. The cigarettes gave up their ghosts, long thin gray ghosts, in a good cause; the mortality rate was terrible.

His train of thought, the story's lifeline, beer-lubricated but no whit impeded, flashed and sputtered and coursed ahead like lightning in a topaz mist, and the loose fingers and hiccuping keys followed as fast as they could. Only once more, just before the end, was there a near hitch, and that wasn't in the sense of a stoppage of thought, but rather of an error in memory—what he mistakenly took to be a duplication. The line:

Hands clutching her throat, Pearl tore down the street in her violet evening dress streamed off the keys, and he came to a lumbering, uneasy halt.

Wait a minute, I had that in in the beginning. She can't keep running down the street all the time in a violet evening dress; the readers'll get fed up. How'd she get into a violet evening dress anyway? A minute ago the guy *tore her white blouse and revealed her quivering white shoulder.*

He half turned in the chair (and none too steadily), about to essay the almost hopeless task of winnowing through the blanket of white pages that lay all around him on the floor, and then recollection came to his aid in the nick of time.

I remember now! I moved the beginning around to the middle, and began with the package at the door instead. (It seemed like a long, long time ago, even to him, that the package had arrived at the door; weeks and weeks ago; another story ago.) This is the first time she's run down the street in a violet evening dress, she hasn't done it before. Okay, let her run.

However, logically enough, in order to get her into it in the first place, he x-ed out the line anyway, and put in for groundwork:

"If it hadn't been for your quick thinking, that guy would have got me sure. I'm taking you to dinner tonight, and that's an order."

"I'll run home and change. I've got a new dress I'm dying to break in."

And that took care of that.

Ten minutes later (according to story time, not his), due to the unfortunate contretemps of having arrived at the wrong café at the wrong time, the line reappeared, now legitimatized, and she was duly *tearing down the street, screaming, clutching her throat with her violet evening dress.* (The "with" he had intended for an "in.") The line had even gained something by waiting. This time she was screaming as well, which she hadn't been doing the first time.

And then finally, somewhere in the malt-drenched mists ahead, maybe an hour or maybe two hours, maybe a dozen cigarettes or maybe a pack and a half, maybe two bottles of beer or maybe four, a page popped up out of the roller onto which he had just ground the words *The End*, and the story was done.

He blew out a deep breath, a vacuum-cleaner-deep breath. He let his head go over and rest for a few moments against the edge of the table. Then he got up from the chair, very un-steadily, and wavered over toward the bed, treading on the litter of fallen pages. But he had his shoes off, so that didn't hurt them much.

He didn't hear the springs creak as he flattened out. His ears were already asleep . . .

Sometime in the early morning, the very early early-morning (just like at home), that six-year-old of the neighbors started with that velocipede of his, racing it up and down in front of the house and trilling the bell incessantly. He stirred and mumbled disconsolately to his wife, "Can't you call out the window and make that brat stay in front of his own house with that damn contraption?"

Moody struggled up tormentedly on one elbow, and at that point the kid characteristically went back into the house for good, and the ringing stopped. But when Moody opened his blurred eyes, he wasn't sitting up at home at all; he was in a hotel room.

"Take your time," a voice said sarcastically. "I've got all day."

Moody swiveled his head, stunned, and Joe was holding the room door open to permit Tartell, his magazine editor, to glare in at him. Tartell was short, but impressive. He was of a great age, as Moody's measurements of time went, a redwood-tree age, around forty-five or forty-eight or somewhere up there. And right now Tartell wasn't in good humor.

"Twice the printers have called," he barked, "asking if they get that story today or not!"

Moody's body gave a convulsive jerk and his heels braked against the floor. "Gee, is it that late—?"

"No, not at all!" Tartell shouted. "The magazine can come out anytime! Don't let a little thing like that worry you! If Cora hadn't had the presence of mind to call me at my house before I left for the office, I wouldn't have stopped by here like this, and we'd all be waiting around another hour down at the office. Now where is it? Let me have it. I'll take it down with me."

Moody gestured helplessly toward the floor, which looked as though a political rally, with pamphlets, had taken place on it the night before.

"Very systematic," Tartell commented acridly. He surged forward into the room, doubling over into a sort of cushiony right-angle as he did so, and began to zigzag, picking up papers without let-up, like a diligent, near-sighted park attendant spearing leaves at close range. "This is fine right after a heavy breakfast," he added. "The best thing I could do!"

Joe looked pained, but on Moody's behalf, not Tartell's. "I'll help you, sir," he offered placatingly, and started bobbing in turn.

Tartell stopped suddenly, and without rising, seemed to be trying to read, from the unconventional position of looking straight down from up above. "They're blank," he accused. "Where does it begin?"

"Turn them over," Moody said, wearied with so much fussiness. "They must have fallen on their faces."

"They're that way on both sides, Mr. Moody," Joe faltered.

"What've you been doing?" Tartell demanded wrathfully. "Wait a minute—!" His head came up to full height, he swerved, went over to Gertie, and examined the unlidded machine closely.

Then he brought both fists up in the air, each still clutching pinwheels of the sterile pages, and pounded them down with maniacal fury on both ends of the writing table. The noise of the concussion was only less than the noise of his unbridled voice.

"You damn-fool idiot!" he roared insanely, looking up at the ceiling as if in quest of aid with which to curb his assault-tempted emotions. "You've been pounding thin air all night! You've been beating the hell out of blank paper! *You forgot to put a ribbon in your typewriter!*"

Joe, looking beyond Tartell, took a quick step forward, arms raised in support of somebody or something.

Tartell slashed his hand at him forbiddingly, keeping him where he was. "Don't catch him, let him land," he ordered, wormwood-bitter. "Maybe a good clunk against the floor will knock some sense into his stupid—talented—head."

The pulp writers had to produce millions of words under intense pressure in order to fill the dozens of lurid-covered mystery magazines that flourished from the late Twenties to the late Forties. Frank Gruber's *The Pulp Jungle* (Sherbourne Press, 1967) is the best reportage on how that fantastic tribe lived and worked, but the best fiction on the subject is "The Penny-a-Worder," which is not only a vivid and knowing (and funny) evocation of the pulp writers' milieu but also a beautiful specimen of late Woolrich, with a worthless pulp novella becoming symbol for any possible human achievement, and its fate standing for every achievement's frustration.

The Number's Up

It was a sort of car that seemed to have a faculty for motion
with an absolute lack of any accompanying sound whatsoever.
This was probably illusory; it must have been, internal combustion engines being what they are, tires being what they are,
brakes and gears being what they are, even raspy street-surfac-
ing being what it is. Yet the illusion outside the hotel entrance
was a complete one. Just as there are silencers that, when affixed
to automatic hand-weapons, deaden their reports, so it was as
if this whole massive car body were encased in something of
that sort. For, first, there was nothing out there, nothing in sight
there. Then, as though the street-bed were water and this bulky

432

black shape were a grotesque gondola, it came floating up out of the darkness from nowhere. And then suddenly, still with no sound whatsoever, there it was at a halt, in position.

It was like a ghost-car in every attribute but the visual one. In its trancelike approach and halt, in its lightlessness, in its enshrouded interior, which made it impossible to determine (at least without lowering one's head directly outside the windows and peering in at nose-tip range) if it were even occupied at all, and if so by whom and by how many.

You could visualize it scuttling fleetly along some overshadowed country lane at dead of night, lightless, inscrutable, unidentifiable, to halt perhaps beside some inky grove of trees, linger there awhile undetected, then glide on again, its unaccountable errand accomplished without witness, without aftermath. A goblin-car that in an earlier age would have fed folklore and rural legend. Or, in the city, you could visualize it sliding stealthily along some warehouse-blacked back alley, curving and squirming in its terrible silence, then, as it neared the mouth and would have emerged, creeping to a stop and lying there in wait, unguessed in the gloom. Lying there in wait for long hours, like some huge metal-cased predatory animal, waiting to pounce on its prey.

Sudden, sharp yellow spurts of fangs, and then to whirl and slink back into anonymity the way it came, leaving the carcass of its prey huddled there and dead.

Who was there to know? Who was there to tell?

And even now, before this particular hotel entrance. It was already in position, it had already stopped.

Then nothing happened.

Ordinarily, when cars stop someone gets out. That is what they have stopped for. In this case it just stood there, as though there were no one in it and had been no one in it all along.

Then the pale, blurry shape of a human hand, as when seen through thick dark glass, appeared inside the window and descended slowly to the bottom, like a pale-colored mussel foundering in a murky tank of water. And with it went the invisible line of a shade. The hand stopped a little above the lower rim and faded from sight again. The shade-line remained where it had been left.

The watch had begun. The death-watch.

In a little while a young man came walking along the street, untroubled of gait, unaware of it. The particular hotel that the ghost-car had made its rendezvous had a seamy glass canopy jutting out over the sidewalk with open bulbs set around the inside of it. But they only shone inward because its outer rim was opaque. Thus, as the young man stepped from the darkness of the street's back reaches under this pane of light it was as though a curtain had been jerked up in front of his face, and he was suddenly revealed from head to foot as in a spotlight.

In the car the darkness found breath and whispered, "That him?"

And the darkness whispered back to the darkness, "Yeah, same type build. Same light hair. Wears gray a lot. And this is the hotel that was fingered."

Then the darkness quickly stirred, but the other darkness quelled it, hissing: "Wait, he wants the girl too. The girl too, he said. Let him get up there to her first."

The young man had turned off and gone inside. The four glass leaves of the revolving door blurred and made him disappear.

For a moment more the evil darkness held its collective breath. Then, no longer in a whisper but sharp as the edge of a stiletto, "Now. Go in and get the number of the room. Do it smart."

The man behind the desk looked up from his racing form, and there was a jaunty young man wearing a snap-brim felt hat leaning there on one elbow. How long he'd been there it was impossible to determine. He might have just come. He might have been there three or four minutes already. Ghost-cars, ghost-arrivals, ghost-departures.

"Do something for you?" said the man behind the desk.

The leaner on his elbow nodded his head languidly, but didn't say.

"What?"

The leaner considered his bent-back fingernails, blew on them and rubbed them against his coat-lapel a little. "Guy that just came in. Got any idea what his room number would be?"

"Is he expecting—"

"No." He opened his hand and a compressed five-dollar bill dribbled out onto the desk and slowly began to expand. "He dropped this in front of the door just now. I seen him do it. Thought he might want it back."

"You taking it up to him?"

"No. You take care of it for me. I ain't particular." The elbow-leaner was fiddling with one of his cuff links now.

A conniving look appeared on the clerk's yeast-pasty face. He said, through immobile lips that made the words sound furtive, "I'll take it up to One-one-six for you in a little while."

"Try Streakaway in the third race tomorrow."

The five-dollar bill was gone now.

So was the jaunty young man in the snap-brim felt hat.

He knocked because they only had one key between them. The tarnished numerals 116 slanted inward as she opened the door for him. They kissed first, and then she said, "Oh God, I've been so frightened, waiting all alone here like this. I thought you'd never come back!"

She had sleek bobbed hair with a part on the side, and was wearing a waistless dress that came to her knees. The waist was down at the bottom.

"Everything's taken care of," he said soothingly. "The reservation's made—"

"You don't think anything will happen tonight, do you?" she faltered. "You don't think anything will happen tonight?"

"Nothing will happen. Don't be afraid. I'm right here with you."

"We should have gone home to my mother. I would have felt safer there. When something like this comes along, a woman wants another woman to cling to, one of her own kind. A man can't understand that."

"Don't be afraid," was all he kept saying. "Don't be afraid."

The knock on the door was craftily casual. It wasn't too loud, it wasn't too long, it wasn't too rapid. It was just like any knock on the door should be.

Their embrace split open down the middle, and they both turned their heads to look that way.

"Wonder who that is," he said matter-of-factly.

"I can't imagine," she said placidly.

He went over to the door and opened it, and suddenly two men were in the room and the door was closed again. All without noise.

"Come on, Jack," one said. "Nice and easy now."

"Nice and easy now," the other said.

"You must have the wrong party."

"No, we haven't got the wrong party. We made sure of that."

"Made sure of that," the other one said.

"Well I don't know you. I never saw you before in my life."

"Same goes for us. We never saw you before neither. But we know someone that *does* know you."

"Who?"

"We'll tell you downstairs. Come on now. Take your hat. Looks better that way."

The girl's head kept turning from one to the other, like a frightened spectator watching a ball pass to and fro at a deadly tennis match that is not being played for sport.

"You're frightening my wife. Won't you tell us what you—"

"His wife. Did you get that? 'The-lay-of-the-land,' they used to call her, and now this guy claims she's his wife. As that Guinan dame is always saying, 'Hello, sucker!' "

The girl quickly held the man back, her man. "Don't. I don't like their looks. Please, for my sake, don't."

"You got good sense, wife," one of them told her.

"Look, if it's money you want—we don't have much, but—here. Now please go and leave us alone."

One of them chopped the extended hand down viciously, and the bills sprayed like an exploded bouquet. His voice thickened to a muddy growl. "Come a-a-an," he said threateningly. "Outside." He backed a forearm up over his own shoulder in menace. "Walk," he said. "Don'tcha hear good?"

"Hear good?" said the other.

"This says you do." And there was a gun. Not much of it showing, just a sliver of the harmless end, peering above the lip of his pocket. But with one finger hooked down below in position.

"Don't scream," the other one warned the girl lonelessly. "Don't scream, or you'll wish you hadn't."

She shuddered like someone dancing. "I won't."

"Now come on," the first one said to the man. "You're going to walk with me, like this. Up against me, real close and chummy. Buddy-buddies."

They went out two by two. Slopping fondly against each other, from shoulder down to hip, like a quartet of drunks coming out of a speak at seven in the morning.

"Where you taking us?" he said in the elevator, going down.

"Just for a little ride." The expression had no sinister meaning yet in 1929. It meant only what it seemed to say.

"But why at this hour?"

"Don't talk."

As they made the brief passage from elevator to street, with a minimum of conspicuousness, the desk man carefully avoided looking up. He was busy, extremely busy, looking down into his racing form at that moment.

They walked her around to the outside of the car and put her in from there, next to a man who was already at the wheel. Him they put in from the near side, and then each one got in on opposite sides of him and pinned him down between them on the back seat. It was all done with almost fluid-drive sleekness, not a hitch, not a catch, not a break in its flow.

And suddenly, like in a dream, the street outside that particular hotel entrance was empty again, as empty as it had been earlier that night. The car was gone. It had departed as soundlessly, as ghostlike, as it had first appeared. A true phantom of the night.

But it had been there. It had brought three people and taken five away. That much was no illusion.

The ride had begun.

The theatre and club spectaculars seemed to stick up into the sky at all sorts of crazy angles, probably because most of them were planted diagonally on rooftops. *Follow Thru, Whoopee, Show Boat,* El Fay Club, Club Richman, Texas Guinan's. It gave the town the appearance of standing on its ear.

The car slid through rows of brownstones (each one housing a speakeasy on its lower floors) over as far as Eleventh, which had no traffic lights yet. Its only traffic was an occasional milk or railroad-yards freight truck, since no highway connected with it, and it came to a dead end at Seventy-second without even a ramp to its name. They ran down it the other way, to Canal Street and the two-year-old Holland Tunnel, engineering marvel of the decade.

The girl spoke suddenly, as they glided past endless strings of stalled New York Central freight cars. "Don't. Please don't. Please leave me alone."

"What's he doing to you?" came quickly from the back seat.

The man at the wheel answered for her. "Just straightening her skirt a little."

The other two laughed. But it wasn't even bawdy laughter. It was too cold and cruel for that.

When they reached the tunnel-mouth, the driver slowed. As he rolled the window down to pay the toll, she suddenly stripped off her wrist watch and flung it so that it struck the tunnel cop flat on the chest.

He caught it easily with one hand, so that it didn't even have a chance to fall. "Hey, what's that for?" he asked, but laughing good-naturedly.

"My girl friend here just now said she don't want to know the time any more from now on, and I guess that's her way of proving it."

The girl writhed a little, as though her arm were caught in a vise behind her back, but said nothing.

The cop pitched the watch lightly back into the car. "Just coming home from a party, folks?"

"No, we're going to one."

"Have fun."

"That's what we intend."

As they picked up speed, and the white tiles flashed blindingly by, the driver gave her a savage backhand swipe with his knuckles across her mouth.

She cried out piercingly, but it was lost in the roar of the onrushing tunnel. The man who called himself her husband made some sort of spasmodic move on the back seat, but the two guns pressing into his intestines from opposite sides almost met inside him, they dug in so far.

They came out into the open, and it was the grimy backwaters of Jersey City now. Tall factory stacks, and fires burning, and spreads of stagnant stinking water.

On and on the ride went. On and on and on.

They turned north soon and left the big city and all its little satellites behind them, and after a while even the rusty glow on the horizon died down and was gone. Then trees began, and little lumpy hills, and there was nothing but the darkness and the night and the fear.

"Don," she shuddered, and suddenly flung one hand up over her shoulder and back, trying to find his.

"Please let me hold her hand," he begged. "She's frightened."

"Let 'em hold hands," one of them snickered.

They held onto each other like that, in a hand-link of fear, two against the night.

"Don, she called me," he said. "Didn't you hear her? Don, that's my name. Don Ackerman."

"Yeah, and I'm Ricardo Cortez," countered one of them, with the flipness so characteristic of the period that it even came into play on a death ride.

On went the ride.

At one point his control slipped away from him for a minute. "God," he burst out, "how far are you taking us?"

"Don't be in a hurry to get there," the one on his left advised him dryly. "I wouldn't, if I was you."

And then again, a little later, "Won't you tell me the name of the fellow you think I am? Can't I convince you—"

"What's the matter, you don't know your own name?"

"Well, what've I done?"

"We don't know from nothing. You were just marked lousy, that's all. We only carry out the orders."

"Yes, but what orders?" he exclaimed in his innocence.

And the answer, grim, foreboding, was: "Oh, broth-urr!"

Then without any warning the car stopped. They were there. "The ride's over," someone said. "End of the ride."

For a moment nobody got out. They just sat there. The driver cut the ignition, and after that there was silence. Complete, uncanny silence, more frightening than the most threatening noise or violence could have been. Night silence. A silence that had death in it.

Then one of them opened the door, got out and started to walk slowly away from the car, through ankle-high grass that hissed and spit as he toiled through it. The others just stayed where they were.

There was some sort of an old dilapidated farm building with a slanted roof in the middle distance. It was obviously abandoned, because its windows were black glassless gaps. Behind it was a smaller shanty looking like a tool shed or lean-to, so close to collapse it was almost down flat. He didn't approach either one of them, he went around to the rear in a big wide circle.

They sat in silence, the four of them that were left. One of them was smoking a cigarette. But that didn't make any noise, just a red blink whenever he drew on it.

Finally the driver reached out and tapped the button. A single, lonely, guttural horn-blat sounded. Briefer than a question mark in the air, staccato as the span of a second split in two, yet unfolding into a streamer of meaning through the night air: Come on, what's taking you so long, we're getting tired of waiting.

The walker-in-the-grass came back to the car again.

"Yeah, it's there," he said briefly.

"He told us it would be," was the sardonic answer. "Didn't you believe him?"

There was a general stir of activity as the other two got out, each with a prisoner.

"All right, you and me go this way," the one with the girl said.

"No! Don!" she started to scream harrowingly. "Don-n-n-n!"

His smile was thin as a knife-cut across his face. "Don'll be taken care. Don't worry about Don."

He grasped her brutally by the upper arms, tightened his hold to a crushing vise and drew his lips back whitely, as though the constrictive force came from them and not his hands. He thrust her drunkenly lurching form from side to side before him. Her hair swayed and danced with the struggle, as though it were something alive in its own right. The darkness swallowed them soon enough, but not the sounds they made.

Now Don began to shout himself, frightened, crazed, straining forward like a thing possessed. "Let her go! Let her go! Oh, if there's a God above, why doesn't He look down and stop this!" His voice was willowy with too much vibrancy. The movements of weeping appeared upon his face, the distortion without the delivery. Skin-weeping, without tears.

When the man who had been with her came back he was

brushing twigs and leaves off his clothing, almost casually.

"Where is she?" they asked him.

"Where I left her." Then he added, "Wanna take a look?"

"I think I will take a look," the other assented, grinning with suggestive meaning.

But he turned up again almost at once, and his manner had changed. He acted disgruntled, like someone who's been given a false scent and gone on a fool's errand.

"Where is she now?"

"Still there."

"What's up?"

He said something low-voiced that the man she'd called Don wasn't able to catch. His fright-soaked senses let it float past on the tide of terror submerging him.

"A kid!" the other one brayed outright in his surprise. His face flicked around for an instant toward the prisoner, then back again. "Say, maybe he *was* telling the truth. Maybe she *was* his—"

"Couldn't you tell?" the third man demanded of the girl's original escort, a trace of contempt in his voice.

"Whaddya expect me to do, feel her pulse in the dark?"

"She gone or ain't she?" he wanted to know bluntly, unmoved by any thought of sparing the prisoner's sensibilities.

"Sure. What do I know about those things? I only know her eyes are wide open and she ain't looking."

The man who was being held thrashed rabidly until he almost seemed to oscillate like the bent wing of an electric fan when its spin is dwindling. "Let me go to her! Let me go to her!"

"Pipe down, Jack," one of them admonished, giving him a perfunctory slantwise clip along the jawline, but without any real heave behind it. "Nothing there to go to any more."

He threw his head back, stared unseeingly straight up overhead, and from the furrowed scalp, the ridged pate that his face had thus become, emitted a full-fledged scream, high-pitched as a woman's, unreasoning as a crushed animal's.

Then his hands rose, fingers hooked wide, and scissored in from opposite sides, clawing at his own cheeks, digging into them, as if trying to tear them off, pull them out by their very ligaments.

"No!" he shrieked, then "No!" he cried, then "No!" he moaned, on a descending tonal scale.

They had taken their hands off him, knowing he was no longer capable of much movement.

His head fell forward again, like something trying to loosen itself from his shoulders, and now he blindly, snufflingly faced the ground as if he were looking closely for something he'd dropped there. His feet carried him around in an intoxicated, reeling little half-circle, and he collapsed breast-first against the fender of the car, head burrowed down against its hood, clasped hands clamped tight across the back of it as if to keep his skull from exploding. His legs, stretched inertly outward along the ground behind him, twitched spasmodically now and then, as if trying to draw themselves in after the rest of him, and always slipped back again each time.

In his travail, words of pain filtered through, suffocated by the pressure of the car-hood against his nose and mouth.

"Mine! She was mine! Mine! Mine!" Over and endlessly over again. "My girl. She was my girl. It was going to be my little baby. I was waiting for it to be my little baby. All my hopes and dreams are gone. . . . Oh, I want to leave this rotten world! I want to get out of this rotten world!"

"You will. You're gonna." The eyes that looked down upon him held no pity, no softness, no feeling at all. They were eyes of stone.

"I don't care what you do to me now," he said. "I want to die."

"That's good," they told him. "We'll oblige."

"Kill me quick," he said. "The quicker the better."

"You're going to get it how we want it, not how you want it."

He wouldn't walk, or couldn't. Probably couldn't—emotional shock. Each took him by a shoulder, and his legs dragged along behind him out at full length, giving little jerks and bumps when they hit stones and other obstacles.

They brought him to the edge of a squared-off pit in the ground and let him fall flat on his face and lie there a minute. A dried-out-well shaft.

"You start the digging, Playback." It was the first time a name had been exchanged between any of them.

"Yeah, I always get the hard work."

Playback brought a shovel from the toppled-down tool shed, marked off an oblong of surface soil and started to break it up into clods ready for throwing down into the well-shaft.

The other man was saying to the third one: "These pocket-flashes ain't going to be enough to see all the way down there. How about one of the heads from the car?"

"Whaddya have to have light for, anyway?"

"You want to see him die, doncha? That's half the kick. Another thing, there might be space left between those chunks the air could get to him through."

"I have some extension wiring I can rig it up on."

"I don't care what you do now," the man on the ground droned. "I want to die."

"Always get the hard work," said Playback.

The detached headlight was set up on the lip of the well-shaft. The man who had brought it returned to the car to control it from the dashboard.

"Why don't you hurry?" said the man on the ground. "For God's sake, why don't you hurry? Why can't I die, when I want to so badly?"

The one nearest aimed a kick at him along the ground. "You will," he promised.

The headlight was deflected downward into the aperture.

"Give her the juice," the one beside it called back guardedly in the direction of the car.

A ghostly pallor came up from below, making the darkness aboveground seem even more impenetrable. Their faces, how-

ever, were now bathed in the reflection, like hideous devil-
masks with slits for eyes and mouths.

The other one came back from the car.

"There's got to be a lot more fill than that," the one standing
beside Playback criticized dissatisfiedly, measuring the results
of his efforts.

"I always get the hard work."

The other one grabbed the shovel from him and went at it in
his place. "If there's one thing that gets my goat," he muttered
disgustedly, "it's to have a guy along on a thing like this that's
always bellyaching, the way you do. Just one guy like that is
enough to spoil everyone else's good time."

The man on the ground had grasped hold of a small rock lying
near him. He closed his hand around it, swung his arm up and
tried to smash it into his own skull.

The nearest one of the three saw it just in time and aimed a
swift kick that averted it. The rock bounced out and the hand
fell down limp. It lay there, oddly twisted inside out, as though
the wrist had been broken.

After that there was silence for a while, only the sound of the
shovel biting into the earth and the hissing splatter of the loose
dirt.

They stood him up, his back to the well.

In the dark, desperate sky, just above the scalloped line the
treetops made, three stars formed a pleading little constella-
tion. No one looked at them, no one cared. This was the time
for death, not the time for mercy.

The last thing he said was, "Helen, sweetheart. Wait for me.
I'm coming to you." The last thing in the whole world.

Then they pushed him down. Took their hands off him,
rather, and he went down by himself, for he couldn't stand up
any more.

He went over backward, and in, and down. The sound of the
hit was't too much. It was soggy at the bottom yet, from the
long-ago water. Probably he didn't feel it too much. He was all

limp from lack of wanting to live, anyway.

He lay there nestled up, like in a foursquare clayey coffin.

He stirred a little, sighed a little, like someone trying to get comfortable in bed.

Playback tipped the shovel over, and a drench of earthgranules spewed down on top of him.

One bent leg got covered up. But his face still breasted the terrestrial wave, like a motionless swimmer caught in the upturn stroke of the Australian crawl and held fast that way, face over shoulder.

Playback brought another shovelful, and the face was gone.

One hand crept through, tentatively, like something feeling its way in the dark.

Playback brought another shovelful and erased the hand.

Three fingers wormed through this time, like a staggered insect that has been stepped on. They only made it as far as the second joint.

"If he said he wants to die, then why does he keep trying to break through to the surface and breathe for?" Playback asked, engrossed.

"That's nature," the one beside him answered learnedly. "His mind wants to die, but his body don't know any better, it wants to live no matter what he says to it."

The stirring fill had fallen motionless at last.

"It's got him, he's quit now," he decided after a further moment or two of judicious observation. "Throw her in on top of him, fill it up the rest of the way, and let's get out of here. I haven't had so much fresh air since—"

A girl opened the door first, looked cautiously up and down the deserted hotel corridor. Then she hitched her head at someone behind her, picked up a small valise from the floor and came on outside.

She was a blonde, good-looking and mean-looking, both at the same time.

"C'mon," she said huskily. "Let's go while the going's good."

A man came out after her. His eyes were the eyes of a poker player. A poker player in a game where the pot is life and death. He had a certain build, a certain way of walking. He was in gray.

He closed the door after him with practiced stealth. Then he stopped and raised his hand to the outside of it.

The girl looked around at him impatiently. "Can that, will you?" she snapped. "This is no time to play games. Every time you go in or out you take time off and fool with that."

"I'm a gambler, remember?"

"You're a gambler is right," she agreed tartly. "That's why the heat's on you right now. You should pay up your losses—"

"I'm superstitious. This little number's been awful good to me. All my big wins come from something with a six in it."

On the 9 at the end of 119 the bottom rivet was gone; only the top one remained. He swung it around loosely upward, made it into a 6 and patted it affectionately. "Keep on bringing me good luck like you always have," he told it softly.

"Didn't you hear me ask for 116 when we first holed up here?" he added. "Only somebody else was already in it. . . ."

The brutal senselessness of the human condition was always a central theme of Woolrich's work, but toward the end of his life it came close to becoming the only theme, as in this story of a man who dies for no reason at all. Woolrich used the loose hotel-room number device in the much earlier "Wake Up with Death" (*Detective Fiction Weekly*, 6/5/37), but only as a neat twist of plot; in this later story he integrates the concept into the theme as well.

Too Nice a Day to Die

Then she went back to where the cushions were, and quite simply and unstudiedly she lay down there, resting the back of her head on them.

There were no symptoms yet. To take her mind off it, she pulled a cigarette out of the package and lit it. Then, as was invariably the case whenever she smoked one, she took no more than two or three slow, thoughtful draws before putting it down on the ashtray and not going back to it again.

She thought of home. "Back home" she always called it whenever she thought of it. But there was no one there to go back to any more. Her mother had died since she'd left. Her father and she had never been very close. He had a housekeeper now, she understood. In any case, she had an idea he much preferred the unfettered company of his cronies to having her back with him again. Her sister was married and had a houseful of kids (three by actual count, but they seemed to fill the place to spilling over point). Her brother was doing his military hitch in West Germany, and he wasn't much more than a kid anyway.

No, there was no one for her to go to, anywhere.

It was beginning now. This was it. She wasn't drowsy yet, but she had entered that lulled state just preceding drowsiness. There was a slight hum in her ears, as if a tiny mosquito were jazzing around outside her head. It was too much effort to go ahead thinking things out any longer. She wouldn't beg the masked faces in the crowd for a friendly look any more. She wouldn't hope for the slot in the letterbox to show white any more. She wouldn't wish for the telephone to ring any more. Let the world have its wakefulness—she'd have her sleep. She turned her face to one side, pressed her cheek against the cushions. Her eyes drooped closed. She reached for the soaked cloth, to put it across them, so that they would stay that way.

Then she heard the bell ringing. First she thought it was part of the symptoms. It was like a railroad-crossing signal-bell, far down a distant track, warning when a train is coming. She contorted her body to try to get away from it, and found herself sitting up dazedly, propped backward on her hands. Consciousness peeled all the way back to its outermost limits like the tattered paper opening up on some circus-hoop that has just been jumped through.

It burst into sudden, crashing clarity then. It was right in the room with her. It was over there in the corner. It was the bell on the telephone.

She managed to get up onto her feet. The room swirled about her, then steadied itself. She felt like being sick for a moment. She wanted to breathe, even more than she did just to live, as though they were two separate processes and one could go on without the other. She threw the two windows open one after the other. The fresh air suddenly swept into her stagnant mind tingling like pine-needles in a stuffy place. She remembered to close off the key under the gas-burner in the kitchen-alcove.

It had never stopped ringing all this while. She stood by it, stood looking at it. Finally, to end the nerve-rack of waiting for it to stop by itself, she picked it up.

The voice was that of a woman. It was slightly accented, but more in sentence-arrangement than in actual pronunciation.

"Hello? It is Schultz' Delicatessen, yes?"

In a lifeless monotone Laurel Hammond repeated the question word for word, just changing it to the negative. "It is not Schultz' Delicatessen, no."

The voice, hard to convince, now repeated the repetition in turn. "It is not Schultz' Delicatessen?"

"I said no, it is not."

The voice made one last try, as if hoping persistence alone might yet result in righting the error. "This is not Exmount 3–8448?"

"This is Exmount 3–8844," Laurel said, with a touch of asperity now at being held there so long.

Unarguably refuted at last, the voice became properly contrite. "I must have put the finger in the slot the wrong way around. I'm sorry, I hope you weren't asleep."

"I wasn't, yet," Laurel said briefly. And even if I had been, she thought, it wouldn't have been the kind you could have awakened me from.

Still coughing a little, but more from previous reflex now than present impetus, she hung up.

It took a moment for it to sink in. Then she began to laugh. Quietly, simmeringly, at first. Saved by Schultz' Delicatessen. She wondered why there was something funny about it because of its being a delicatessen. If it had been a wrong-number on a personal call, or on a call to almost any other kind of establishment, there wouldn't have been anything funny in it. Why was

there something ludicrous about a delicatessen? She couldn't
have said. Something to do with the kind of food they sold,
probably. Comedy-food: bolognas and salamis and pigs'
knuckles.

She was laughing uncontrollably now, almost in fullblown
hysteria. Tottering with it, tears peering in her eyes; now holding her hand flat across her forehead, now over her ribs to
support the strain of the laughter. No joke had ever been so
funny before, no near-tragedy had ever ended in such hilarity.
She only stopped at last because of physical exhaustion, because
she was on the verge of prostration.

You couldn't go back and resume such a thing, not after that
kind of a farcical interruption. Your sense of fitness, your sense
of proportion, alone—any life, even the most deprecated one,
deserved more dignity than that in its finish. She turned on the
key under the burner again, but this time she lit a match to it.
She put on water, to make a cup of tea. (The old maid's solace,
she thought wryly: trade your hopes of escape for a cup of tea.)

I'll see it through for one more day, she said to herself. That
much I can stand. Just one more. Maybe something will happen,
that hasn't happened on all the empty, barren ones that went
before (but she knew it wouldn't). Maybe it will be different (but
she knew better). But if it isn't, then tomorrow night—she gave
a shrug, and the ghost of a retrospective smile flitted across her
face—and this time there'll be no Schultz' Delicatessen.

She spent the vestigial hours of the night huddled in a large
wing-chair, looking too small for it, her little harmonica-sized
transistor radio purring away at her elbow. She kept it on the
Paterson station, WPAT, which stayed on all night. There were
others that did too, but they were crawling with commercials,
this one wasn't. It kept murmuring the melodies of *Roberta* and
Can-Can and *My Fair Lady,* while the night went by and the
world, out there beyond its dial, went by with it. She dozed off
finally, her head lolling over like a little girl's propped-up asleep
in a grown-up's chair.

When the sun made her open her eyes at last, she gave a guilty start at first, thinking this was like other days and she had to be at the office. But it wasn't. It was the day of grace she'd given herself.

When she was good and ready, and not before, she called the office and told Hattie on the reception-desk: "Tell Mr. Barnes I won't be in today." It was after ten by this time.

Hattie was sympathetic at first. "Not feeling too good, nn?"

Laurel Hammond said, "As a matter of fact, I don't feel too bad. I feel better than yesterday." As a matter of fact, she did.

The girl on the reception-desk still tried to be loyal to a fellow-employe. "You want me to tell him you're not feeling good though, don't you?" she asked anxiously.

"No," said Laurel, "I don't. I don't care what you tell him."

The girl on the reception-desk stopped being sympathetic. She was up against something she couldn't grasp. She became offended. "Oh," she said, "just like that you take a day off?"

"Just like that I take a day off," Laurel said, and hung up.

A day off, a lifetime off, forever off, what difference did it make?

Shortly before noon, with a small-sized summer hat on her head and a lightweight summer dress buoyant around her, she closed the door behind her, put the key in her handbag, and stepped out to meet the new day. It was a fine day too, all yellow and blue. The sky was blue, the building-faces were yellow in the sunlight, and the shady sides of the streets were indigo by contrast. Even the cars going by seemed to sparkle, their windshields sending out blinding flashes as they caught the sun.

Where did you go on your last day in New York? That is, on your *last day* in New York? You didn't walk Fifth Avenue and window-shop, that was for sure. Window-shopping was a form of appraisal for the future, for a tomorrow when you might really buy. You didn't go to a show. A show was an appraisal of the past, other people's lives in the past, dramatized. A walk in the park? That would be pleasant, pastoral. The trees in leaf, the grass, the winding paths, the children playing. But somehow that wasn't for today either. Its very tranquility, its apartness, its *lostness* in the center of the buzzing, throbbing city, she had a feeling would make her feel even more apart, more lost,than she felt already, and she didn't want that. She wanted people around her; she was frightened of tonight.

She got on a bus finally, at random, and let it take her on its hairpin crosstown route, first west along Seventy-second, then east along Fifty-seventh. Then when it reached Fifth and doubled back north to start the whole thing over, she got off and strolled a few blocks down the other way until suddenly the fountain and flower-borders of Rockefeller Center opened out alongside her. She knew then that was where she had wanted to come all along, and wondered why she hadn't thought of it in the first place.

It was like a little oasis, a breathing-spell, in the rush of the city, and yet it was lively, it wasn't lonely in the way the park would have been. It was filled with a brightly dressed luncheon-break crowd, so thick they almost seemed to swarm like bees, and yet in spite of that it was restful, it was almost lulling.

She went back toward the private street that cuts across behind it, which for some highly technical reason is closed to traffic one day in each year in order to maintain its non-public status, and sat on the edge of the sunwarmed coping that runs around the sunken plaza, as dozens of others were doing. She'd come here once or twice in the winter to watch them ice-skate below, but now the ice was gone and they were lunching at tables down there, under vivid garden-umbrellas. Above, a long line of national flags stirred shyly in a breeze mellow as warm golden honey. She tried to make out what countries some of them belonged to, but she was sure of only two, the Union Jack and the Tricolor. The rest were strange to her, there were so many new countries in the world today.

And in every one of them perhaps, at this very moment, there was some girl like herself, contemplating doing what she was contemplating doing. In Paris, and in London, yes and even in Tokyo. Loneliness is all the same, the world over.

Her handbag was plastic, and not a very good plastic at that, apparently. The direct sunlight began to heat it up to a point where it became uncomfortable to keep her hand on it and she could even feel it against her thigh through the thin summer dress she had on. She put it down on the coping alongside of her. Or rather a little to the rear, since she was sitting slightly on the bias in order to be able to take in the scene below her. Then later, in unconsciously shifting still further around, she turned her back on it altogether, without noticing.

Some time after that she heard a curt shout of remonstrance somewhere behind her. She turned to look, as did everyone else. A man who up to that point seemed to have been striding along rather more rapidly than those around him now broke into a fleet run. A second man sprang up from where he'd been sitting on the coping, about three or four persons to the rear of her, and shot after him. In a moment, as people stopped and turned to look, the view became obstructed and they both disappeared from sight.

It was only then she discovered her handbag to be missing.

While she was standing there trying to decide what to do about it, they both came back toward her again. One of them, the one who had given chase, was holding her handbag under one arm and was holding the second man by the scruff of the coat-collar with the other. What made this more feasible than it might otherwise have been was that the captive was offering only a token resistance, handicapped perhaps by his own guilty conscience.

"Whattaya trying to do? Take your hands off. Who do you think *you* are?" he was jabbering with offended virtue as they came to a halt in front of Laurel.

"Is this yours?" the rescuer asked, showing her the handbag.

"Yes, it is," she said, taking it from him.

"You should be more careful," he said in protective reproof.

"Putting it down like that is an open invitation for someone to come along and make off with it."

The nimble-fingered one was quick to take the cue. "I thought somebody had lost it," he said artlessly. "I was on'y trying to find out who it belonged to, so I could give it back to them."

"Oh, sure," his apprehender said drily.

A policeman materialized, belying the traditional New York adage "They're never around when you want them." He was a young cop, and still had all his police training-school ideals intact, it appeared. Right was right and white was white, and there was nothing in-between. "Your name and address, please?" he said to Laurel, when he'd been told what had happened.

"Why?" she asked.

"You're going to press charges against him, aren't you?"

"No," she demurred. "I'm not."

His poised pencil flattened out in his hand. He looked at her, first with surprise then with stern disapproval. "He snatched your handbag, and yet you're not going to file a complaint?"

"No," she said quietly. "I'm not."

"You realize," he said severely, "you're only encouraging people like this. If he thinks he can get away with it, he'll only go back and do it some more. Before you know it, this city wouldn't be worth living in."

"You shouldn't be so good-natured, lady," another woman rebuked her from the crowd. "Believe me, if it was me, I'd teach him a lesson."

Yes, I guess you would, thought Laurel. But then, you have a whole lifetime ahead of you to show your rancor in. I haven't enough time left for that.

The prisoner had begun to fidget tentatively now that this unexpected reprieve had been granted him. "If the lady don't want to make a complaint, whaddye holding me for?" he complained querulously. "You got no grounds."

The quixotic young cop turned on him ferociously. "No? Then I'll find some, even if I have to make it loitering!"

"How could I be loitering when I was running full steam ah—" the culprit started to say, not illogically. Then he shut up abruptly, as if realizing this admission might not altogether help his case.

"Oh, won't somebody get me out of this, please!" she suddenly heard herself say, half in wearied sufferance, half in rebellious discontent. She didn't want to spend the little time there was left to spend standing in the center of a root-fast, cow-eyed crowd. Above all, she didn't want to spend it making arrangements to have some fellow-wayfarer held in a detention-cell overnight until he could be brought before a magistrate in the morning. She hadn't meant it for anyone to hear; she'd only meant it for herself. A plea to her own particular private fortunes of the day and of the moment.

But the man who had salvaged her handbag must have caught it and thought it was meant for him. He put a hand lightly under her elbow in guidance and opened a way for her through the ever-thickening crowd.

"Sure you won't change your mind, lady?" the cop called after her.

"I'm sure," she said without turning her head.

Once detached from the focus of attention, they continued to walk parallel to one another along the flower-studded, humanity-studded promenade or mall that led out to the Avenue. Past and past.

"You let him off lightly," he remarked. "Not even a lecture."

She nodded meditatively, without answering. It's so easy to be severe, she thought, when you're safe and intact and sure of yourself, as you probably are. But me, I feel sorry for the whole world and everyone in it, today, even that poor cuss back there.

"I remember, in Chicago once," he was saying, "I had my wallet lifted out of my back pocket right while I was standing in line outside the ticket-window in Union Station—"

They'd reached the Avenue. With one accord, without even a fractional hesitancy or break in stroll, they turned and continued on northward, back along the way she'd originally come. It was done as unself-consciously as though they'd known each other long and walked along here often. As naturally as though they had a common destination agreed upon beforehand.

She noticed it after a moment, but didn't do anything to disrupt it. On any other day, she realized, she would have been alerted, taut to separate herself from him. Not today. Until he said something, or did something, that was out of order—not today. It was better to walk with somebody, than to walk with nobody at all.

"—Things like that happen in all large cities, far more than they do in smaller places. I guess the huge crowds give them better cover."

"Aren't you from a large city yourself?"

"We like to think of ourselves as a medium-large city, but we're willing to admit we're no Chicago or New York. Indianapolis."

"Oh, where the speedway races are."

"Our only claim to fame," he said mournfully.

"I suppose you used to go to them regularly."

"I never missed a year until this year, and then I couldn't go because I was here. I saw it on t.v., but it wasn't the same. Like a midget-race around a twenty-one-inch oblong."

Suddenly and quite belatedly—for if she'd had any actual objections they would have manifested themselves long before now—he turned to ask: "I'm not bothering you by tagging along like this, am I? I never realized I was until this very—"

"That's quite all right," she said levelly. "It's not a pick-up. And if it were, I'd be the one who did the picking."

"Nothing of the sort," he asserted stoutly.

That was the conventional, the expected, answer, she recognized. But in this case it also happened to be true. A pick-up was a planned selection. This had been anything but that; unplanned, unsought-after, by both of them.

"Been here long?" she asked him, to get off the prickly topic.

"About six months now. I was transferred here to the Company's New York office."

She asked him a question out of her own melancholy experience. "Did you find it hard to adjust?"

"Very. I was king, back home. The only fellow in a houseful of women. I got the royal treatment. They spoiled me rotten."

That, she decided, was not apparent on the surface, at least.

"My mother spoiled me because I was the only son in a family of girls. (My eldest sister's married and lives in Japan.) My elder sister spoiled me because she looked on me as her kid brother, and the younger one looked up to me as her big brother. I couldn't lose."

"And what did you do to entitle you to all this?"

"Brought home money, and could always be depended on to fix the car or the t.v. without calling in costly repairmen, I suppose."

"That's fair enough value received," she laughed.

They'd reached Fifty-seventh Street. This time they did stop, but not to part, to decide what next to do, where next to go, together. They both seemed to have tacitly agreed to spend the balance of the afternoon together.

"Have lunch with me," he suggested. "I haven't had any yet, have you?"

"It's late; don't you have to go back to the office?"

"I have the day off. The Company's founder died, an old man of eighty. He hasn't been active in years, but out of respect to his memory all our offices everywhere were closed down for one day." He repeated his invitation.

"I'm not hungry," she said. "But I am thirsty, after that stroll in the sun. I'll take you up on an ice-cream soda."

They turned west for a short distance and stopped in at Hicks, at her suggestion. She waived a table, and they sat down at the counter.

"I stop in here every Christmas—or at least, the day before
—and buy myself a box of candy," she told him.

His brows rose slightly, but he didn't say anything.

"I have to," she added simply. "Nobody else does."

"Maybe next time around," he said very softly, "you won't
have to."

She had a chocolate malted and he a toasted-ham and coffee.

They walked on from there and entered the park at the Sixth
Avenue entrance, and drifted almost at a somnambulistic gait
along the slow curving walk that paces the main driveway
there, then finally straightens out and strikes directly up into
the heart of the park itself, toward the Mall and the lake and
the series of transverses.

Now they were becoming more personal. They spoke less of
outside things, of things around them and things on the surface
of their lives, and more of things lying below and within themselves. Not steadily, in a continuous stream, but by allowing
occasional insights to open up, like chinks in the armor that was
each one's privacy and apartness. Thus she learned many of the
things he liked, and a few he didn't, and he learned them too
about her. And surprisingly many of the things they liked were
the same, and not a few of the things they didn't, also.

We're remarkably compatible, the thought occurred to her.
Isn't it too bad we had to meet—so late.

It's not so late, she said to herself then, unless you will it to
be so. And a daring thought barely ventured to peer forth
around the corner of her mind, then quickly vanished again: it
needn't be late at all, it can be early, if you want it to be. Early
love, first love.

"What were you doing six months ago today, exactly to the
day?" she asked him suddenly.

"It's difficult to pin-point it that closely. Let's see, six months
ago I was still back in 'napolis. If it was a weekday, then I was
slaving over a hot draught-board until five; after five I was
driving back to the harem. If it was a Sunday I was probably out

driving in the crate with some seat-mate."

Anyone special? she wondered, but didn't say it.

"Why did you ask that?"

She upped a shoulder slightly. "I don't know."

She did, though. How different my life might have been, she couldn't help reflecting, if I'd met you—as you seem to be—six months ago instead of today.

"Do you get lonely at times, since you've come to New York?"

"Sure I do." Then he reiterated, "I sure do. Anyone would."

"It's easier for a man, though, isn't it?"

"No it isn't," he told her quietly. "Not really. Oh, I know, girls think that a man can go a lot of places they can't, by themselves. And he can. But what does he find when he goes to those places? Loud, laughing companionship for an hour—or for an evening. Did you ever know, you can be lonely with someone's loud laughter ringing right into your ear? Did you ever know?"

She had a complete picture, a vignette, of his life now, of that one aspect of it, without his having to say anything further.

"No," he said, "we're in the same boat, all of us."

They sat down on a bench overlooking the lake. They didn't talk any more for a while. After a time an indigent squirrel spotted them, made toward them by fits and starts, looked them over from a propitiatingly erect position, then scrambled up to the top-slat of the bench-back and ran nimbly across it. She could feel the fuzz of its tail brush lightly across the back of her neck. It stopped by his shoulder and sniffed at it inquiringly. "Sorry, son," he said to it. They both looked at it and smiled, then smiled to each other. Completely matter-of-fact, and far too venal to waste time allowing itself to be petted empty-handed, it dropped down to the ground again and went lumbering off bushy-tailed across the grass.

The irregular picket-fence of tall building-tops around them on three sides in the distance looked trim and spruce and spotless as new paint in the sunshine. Much better than when you were up close to them. It was a brave city, she decided, eyeing them. Brave in its other sense; not courageous, so much as outstanding, commanding. It was too nice a town to die in. Though it had no honeysuckle vines and no balconies and no guitars, it was meant for love. For living and for love, and the two were inseparable; one didn't come without the other.

By about four in the afternoon they were already using "Laurel" and "Duane" when they said things to each other. Sparingly at first, a little self-consciously. As though not wanting to abuse the privilege each one had granted to the other. The first time she heard him say it, a warm, sunny feeling ran through her, that she couldn't contradict or deny. It was like belonging to someone a little, belonging to someone at last. While at the same time you at last had someone who belonged a little to you.

There is no hard and fast line that can be drawn that says: up to here there was no love; from here on there is now love. Love is a gradual thing, it may take a moment, a month, or a year to come on, and in each two its gradations are different. With some it comes fast, with some it comes slowly. Sometimes one kindles from the other, sometimes both kindle spontaneously. And once in a tragic while one kindles only after the other has already dimmed and gone out, and has to burn forlornly alone.

By the time they left that consequential bench overlooking the tranquil little lake tucked away inside the park and started walking slowly onward in the general direction of her place, she was already well on the verge of being in love with him. And she sensed that he was too, with her. It couldn't be mistaken. There was a certain shyness now, like a catch, she heard somewhere behind his voice every time he spoke to her. The midway stage, the falter, between the assuredness of companionability and the assuredness of openly declared love. And when their hands accidentally brushed once or twice as they walked slowly side by side, he didn't have to turn his head to look at her, nor she to look at him, for them both to be aware of it. It was like a kiss of the hands, their first kiss. The heart knows these things. The heart is smart. Even the unpracticed heart.

They were beginning to be in love. The very air transmitted it, carried it to and fro from one to the other and back again. It had perhaps happened to them so quickly, she was ready to admit, because they both came to it fresh, wholehearted, without ever having known it before.

The June day was slowly ebbing away at last, in velvety beauty. The twin towers of the Majestic Apartments were two-toned now, coral where they faced the glowing river-sky, a sort of misty heliotrope where they faced the imminent starting-point of night. The first star was already in the sky. It was like a young couple's diamond engagement-ring. Very small, but bright and clear with promise and with hope.

New York. This was New York, on the evening of what was to have been the last day in the world—but wouldn't be now any more. It had been a lovely day, a nice day, too nice a day to die.

They emerged at the Seventy-second Street pedestrian outlet, and sauntered north along Central Park West for a few blocks, until they'd arrived opposite the side-street her apartment was on. There they waited for a light, and crossed over to the residential side of the great artery, on which the headlights of cars in the deepening dusk were like a continuous stream of tracer-bullets aimed at anyone with temerity enough to cross their trajectory. There they stopped and stood again, a little in from the corner—in what they both hoped was to be only a very temporary parting—for she had to cross once more, to the north side of the street, to reach her door.

For a moment he didn't seem to know what to say, and for a moment she couldn't help him. They both turned their heads and looked up one way together. Then they both turned the opposite way and looked that way together. Then they looked at each other and they both smiled. Then the muteness broke too suddenly, and they both spoke at once.

"Well, I guess this is where—"

"Well, I suppose this is where—"

Then they laughed and there was no more constraint.

She knew he was going to ask her to dinner—the first of all the many that they'd most likely share together—and he did. First she was going to agree with ready willingness, and then she remembered the things that were waiting upstairs. Waiting just as she'd left them, from last night. Waiting dark and brooding all through the sunny, glorious day—for tonight. The pillow on the floor, the cigarette-dish. The little bowl of water with the handkerchief still soaking in it, the blindfold that was to have shut out the sight of death. She shuddered to think of them now. But more than that, she didn't want them to still be there if she brought him up with her. She wanted to go up ahead and quickly disperse them, do away with them.

"Look, I'll tell you what," she said animatedly. "The next time —the very next—we'll go to a restaurant, if you want to. But tonight let's do this: let's eat in. It's a good night for cold-cuts." She knew he wouldn't misunderstand if she had him up so soon after meeting him; she already knew him well enough to know that. "I want you to go to Schultz' Delicatessen, and pick up whatever appeals to you—I'll leave that to you—and bring it up to the apartment. I'll make the coffee."

"Schultz'," he said dutifully. "Where is it?"

"I don't know," she admitted with a chuckle and a hand-spread. "But I know you can find it in the directory. I can give you the number. It's Exmount 3–8448. It's the same as my own number, just twisted around a little. Promise me you won't go anywhere else. Only Schultz'. I have a very special reason for it. I don't want to tell you what it is right tonight, but some day I will."

"I promise. Schultz' and nobody but Schultz'."

They separated. She started across the street on a long diagonal. She turned and called back: "Don't take too long."

"I won't," he answered.

Then she turned unexpectedly a second time.

"I forgot to give you the apartment-number. It's Three—"

It was a big black shape. It was less like a car than an animal leaping at its kill. It was feline in its stealth, and lupine in its ferocity, big malevolent eyes blindingly aglow. Whether its occupants were drunk, or crazed with their own speed, or fleeing from some misdeed, it gave her no warning. It came slashing around the corner like the curved swing of a scimitar.

She was caught dead-center in front of it. Had she been a little to one side, she might have leaped back toward her companion; a little to the other, she might have leaped forward to the safety of the empty roadway alongside it. She tried to, but at the same moment it swerved that way, also trying to avoid her, and they remained fixed dead-center to one another. Then there was no more time for a second try.

She didn't go down under it. It cast her aside in a long, low parabola. Then it slowed, then it stopped, with a crazy shriek that sounded like remorse. Too late.

She lay flat along the ground, but with her head propped up by the sharp-edged curbstone it had crashed against. The sound it had made striking was terminal. There could be no possibility of life after such an impact.

And it had been too nice a day to die.

During his last ten years Woolrich published an average of less than three stories a year, almost all of them shapeless, heavily introspective mood pieces, some of which worked, most of which didn't. This is one of the very best works of his last period—a haunting little piece of the world reminiscent of the refrain in Kurt Vonnegut, Jr.'s *Slaughterhouse-Five:* so it goes, so it goes.

Life Is Weird Sometimes

Have you ever seen a woman die? I hope you never have to, never do. I mean in violence, at your own hands. It isn't a good thing to see. When you see a man die, you see only yourself; not someone apart whom you once knelt to in your heart and offered up your love to. Revered and dwelt-on in your reveries. Or if not, some other man did.

She falls from higher than a man, from over the heads of men, whether they're lovers or husbands or brothers. And whether she was good or she was evil, whatever evil is, she falls with a flash and a fiery trace, like a disintegrating star plunging into the water. A man just falls like a clod; clay back to the clay he came from. That is why judiciaries and law-enforcers so seldom kill women by law, no matter what their crime.

And when it is done by one man alone, personally and individually acting as his own sentencer and his own executioner, as you do now, think how much more affecting and impact-bearing it is.

That face you see before you that has just finished dying will come back palely haunting into every night's sleep for the rest of your life, no matter how much she deserved it, no matter how tough your mind. You know it will, you know. That scene you saw before you that has just ended will come back meshed into every dream you ever dream again, so that you don't just kill her once, you kill her a thousand and one times, and she never stays quite dead. And all the brandy and all the barbiturates can't make it go away.

Those lips that pressed against yours like warm velvet and clung there in soft adhesion, look at them now, twisted into an ellipse, a crevice for a surprise that never finishes coming out. Those eyes that glittered with love and hate and laughter and hate and doubt and hate, and hate and hate and hate, they don't hate now any more. Those arms that gestured so gracefully in the light, and wound around you so importunately in the dark, paid out on the floor now limp and curlycued, like lengths of wide ribbon that have slipped off their spools. The polish on the fingertips of the one lying face-down looking strangely like five little red seeds burst out of some pod and lying there scattered. A polish that claimed proudly to be long-lasting. I know; I used to see the bottle. This will prove it now: it will outlast her.

The hair your hand strayed through over and over, and found so soft and responsive each time; lying there fanned out and flotsam like a mess of seaweed washed up on the shore.

The body that once was the goal, and the striving, and the will-o'-the-wisp of the act of love . . .

All of this now devastated, distorted, and in death.

No, it isn't good to see a woman . . .

I did a number of banal things that struck me strange, although I had never done this thing before and had no way of knowing whether they were banal or not, strangely out of key or not, or were to be expected to follow anything like that.

I smoothed down the sleeves of my shirt, first of all. They hadn't been rolled up, but I kept smoothing and straightening them down as though they had been. Then I shot my cuffs back into more conforming place, and felt for their fastenings. One had come open in the swift arm-play that had occurred, and I refastened it.

Then I looked at the watch on my wrist, not to tell the time, but to see if it had suffered any surface-harm. I prized it a great deal; some men do. It showed no signs of any harm, but to guard doubly against that, I stem-wound it briefly but briskly. You weren't supposed to have to, it was self-winding. But I figured the little added fillip would benefit it. I'd bought it in 1957 at Lambert Brothers for $150, and I'd never regretted it since.

Meanwhile she was dying there on the floor.

I went into the bathroom, and ran a little warm water, and washed off my hands. (Just like you do after you do almost anything.) Then I changed it to cold and smoothed a little of it on my hair. I don't like warm water on my hair, it opens the pores, I think you catch cold quicker that way.

I was going to use the john, but somehow it seemed indecent, disrespectful, I don't know how to say it. I didn't have to very badly anyway, so I didn't. It had only been a nervous reflex from the killing.

Then I dried off my hands on one of her towels, and came outside again.

By that time she had finished dying on the floor. She was dead now.

I bent down and put my hand to her forehead. It was the last time I ever touched her, out of all the many times I'd touched her before.

Put my hand to her forehead, and said out loud: "You can't think any more now in back of there, can you? It's quiet in back of there now, isn't it?"

What a mysterious thing that is, I thought. How it stops. And once it does, never comes on again.

When I came out into the outside room again, I saw her shoe still lying there, where it had come off in the course of our brief wrestle. It looked so pathetic there by itself without an owner, it looked so lonely, it looked so empty. Something made me pick it up and take it in to her. Like when someone's going away, you help them on with their coat, or their jackboots, or whatever it is they need for going away.

I didn't try to put it back on her, I just set it down there beside her close at hand. You're going to need this, I said to her in my mind. You're starting on a long walk. You're going to keep walking from now on, looking for your home.

I stopped and wondered for a minute if that was what happened to all of us when we crossed over. Just keep walking, keep on walking, with no ahead and no in-back-of; tramps, vagrants in eternity. With our last hope and horizon—death— already taken away.

In the Middle Ages they had lurid colors, a bright red hell, an azure heaven shot with gold stars. They knew where they were, at least. They could tell the difference. We, in the Twentieth, we just have the long walk, the long walk through the wispy backward-stringing mists of eternity, from nowhere to no- where, never getting there, until you're so tired you almost wish you were—alive again.

The gun I picked up and looked around with, not knowing what to do with it, and finally put it into my own pocket. I don't know why, don't know what made me. It had been hers in the first place. Just some kind of a tidying-up reflex, I guess. Don't leave things lying around. You learn that in your boyhood.

Then I opened the door and went out. And it was over.

Standing outside the reclosed door, I lowered my head thoughtfully for a moment and spit on the floor at my feet. Not the way you spit in anger or in insult, or even in disgust. But simply the way you would spit to rid your mouth of a bad aftertaste, to clear it out.

That television that I had noticed the first time, when I

crossed the hall on my way in, was still raging away from behind a door at the far end, set at right- (or left-) angles to all the rest of them, depending on which side they were on. No wonder the shot hadn't been heard around. It would have been drowned in the torrent of noise like a raindrop falling in an ocean.

The only thing I could figure was that whoever was in there with it had it turned or slanted in such a way that the full impact was away from them and toward the door and the hall beyond it, and they didn't realize what it was doing themselves. Some people are insensitive to television noise anyway; ask a cross-section of average neighbors, they'll always point one out.

It was belting the hall like a hurricane, only its waves were audial instead of wind and water. "What happened to me," it bragged at the top of its thundering tubes, "was a simple little pill called Compōz. Now I work relaxed and I sleep relaxed—"

And no one else does, I thought inattentively with a stray lobe of my mind.

I brought the car up to me—it was an automatic—and on the short, sleek glide down, a momentary impulse occurred to me to go up to Charlie when I got down below. He was the doorman. Go up to Charlie, hand him the gun, and say: "Better ring in to the police. I just killed her up there. I just killed twelve-ten."

But it had started to fade even before I got all the way down. Then when I got out and didn't see him around anywhere, that scotched it entirely. You don't hang around *waiting* to report you've killed someone. You do it with your throttle wide open or not at all.

Then when I emerged into the street, I saw where he was. He was one house length down, in front of the next building, helping some people get into a taxi *there*. It must have dropped a fare off there, and couldn't roll back to his stop-whistle because of the traffic coming on behind, so he and his party had had to go down there after it. They were bulky, and the furs on the women made them even bulkier, and they took a great deal of handling to shoe-horn in. His attention was fully occupied, and his back was to me.

He hadn't seen me going in either. Must have gone around the corner for a quick coffee break.

How strange, I thought, he didn't see me at either of the two points that count. But in between I bet he was killing time hanging around here in front of the entrance with nothing to do. That's the way those things go sometimes: try not to be seen, and everybody spots you; don't give a good damn whether or not you are, and everybody looks right through you just as though you weren't there.

I turned away from him and went on my way, up the street and about my business. The past was dead. The future was resignation, fatality, and could only end one way now. The present was numbness, that could feel nothing. Like Novocaine needled into your heart. What was there in all the dimensions of time for me?

I turned left at the first up-and-down transverse I came to, and went down it for a block, and stopped in for a drink at a place. I needed one bad, I was beginning to feel shaky inside now. I'd been in this place before. It was called Felix's (a close enough approximation, with a change of just one letter). It was three or four steps down, what you might call semi-below-sidewalk-level. It was kept in a state of chronic dimness, a sort of half-light. Some said so you couldn't see how cut and watered your drinks were.

It was just the place for me though. I didn't want a bright light shining on me. That would come quick enough, in some precinct back room.

My invisibility had run out though. I had no sooner sat down than, before my drink had even had time to get in front of me, a girl came over to me. From behind, naturally; that was the only way she could. She tapped me on the shoulder with two fingers.

I didn't know her, but she knew me, at second hand, it seemed. I leaned my ear toward her a little, so if she said anything I could hear what it was.

"Your friend wants to know why you don't recognize him any

more," was what she said, reproachfully. And with that prim propriety that sometimes comes with a certain amount of alcohol—and almost invariably when a feeling of social unsurety goes with it—she added, "You shouldn't be that way. He only wanted you to come over and join us."

"What friend? Where?" I said grudgingly.

She pointed with the hand that was holding the change left over from the record player she'd just been to, which impeded the accuracy of her point somewhat because she had to keep three fingers bunched over in order to hang onto the coins. "In the booth. Don't you see him?"

"How can I see anybody from here?" I asked her sullenly. "They're all wearing shadow masks halfway up their faces. All I can see is their foreheads." (The edge of the bar drew a line at about that height all around the room; the lights were below it, on the inside.)

"But he could see *you*," she challenged. "And so could I."

"Well, he's been in here longer than me. I only just now walked in through the door." I thought that would get rid of her and break it up. Instead it brought on a controversy.

She gave the sort of little-girl grimace that goes with the expression "Oo, what you just said," or "Oo, I'm going to tell on you." Rounded her mouth to a big O, and her eyes to match. Which sat strangely on her along with the come-on makeup and the Martinis or whatever they had been.

"You've been buzzing around up here for the better part of an hour. First you were sitting in one place, then in another, then you went over to the cigarette machine. Then you were gone for a while—I guess to the telephone or the men's room —and then you came back again. We had our eyes on you the whole time. Every time he hollered your name out, you'd look and then you'd look away again. So it wasn't that you didn't hear, it was you didn't want to h—"

"What is my name then, if he hollered it so many times?"

I nearly fell over. She gave me my name; both of them in fact. Not quite accurately, but close enough to do.

Still unconvinced, but willing to be, I went over with her to
take a look at him. He was in a sour mood by now over the
fancied slight. He wouldn't get up. He wouldn't smile. He
wouldn't shake hands. He was also more than a little smashed.
His head kept going around on his shoulders; the shoulders
didn't, just the head.

I didn't know him well at all, but I did know him. But this
wasn't the night nor the particular segment of it to become
enmeshed with stray one- or two-time acquaintances. All I
kept thinking, with inwardly raised eyes, was: Why did I
pick this particular place? There's a line of bars all along
this avenue. Why did I have to come in here and run into these
two?

"I appreciate this no end," he said sarcastically.

"You got your wires crossed," I told him briefly. "I just came
in."

"You tell him," he said to the girl.

"Look," she catalogued, "we saw everything you got on. Just
like you have it on you now."

("But not on me, on someone else," I put in.)

"This same light-gray shortie coat—" She plucked it with her
fingers.

("There's been a rash of them all over New York this season.")

"And a shave-head haircut?"

("Who hasn't one?")

"And even a shiny tie clip that flashed in my eyes from the
light every time you turned a certain way?"

("Everyone carries some kind of hardware across the front.")

"But *all three* of them match up," she expostulated. "You're
wearing them all."

"So was somebody else. Half an hour ago, or maybe twenty
minutes, sitting on the same stool I was, that's all. It was a
double-take." And I omitted to add: You're both blurry with
booze, anyway.

He turned to address the girl, as a way of showing me what
his feelings toward me were. "He's copping a plea. You think

you know a guy, and then you're not good enough for him."

"Your knowing me ended right now," I said tersely.

He pushed his underlip out in hostility. "Then stand away from my table. Don't crowd us like that."

He got up in his seat and gave me a stiff-arm back, hand against chest.

I shoved him in return, also hand against chest, and he sat down again.

This time he got up and came out and around from behind the table and swung a roundhouse at me. I can't remember whether it clipped or not. Probably not or I'd be able to.

I swung back at him and could feel it land, but he only gave a little. Maybe a step back with one foot.

His second swing, and the third of the whole capsule fight, and I went sprawling back on my shoulders across the floor. He was springier than he looked in his liquored condition.

The whole thing didn't take a half-minute, but already everyone in the place was around us in a tight little circle, the way they always are at such a time. The bartender came running out from behind, cautioning, "All right, all right," in an excited voice. All-right what he didn't specify.

He helped me up, and then continued the process by arming me all the way over to the door and just beyond it, before I knew what was happening. He didn't throw me out, simply sort of *urged* me out by one arm. There he let go my arm, told me, "Now go away from here. Go someplace else and do that." And closed the door in my face.

I guess I was the one selected to be evicted because the other fellow had had a girl with him, and from where the bartender stood it looked as if I had gone over and accosted them, said something out of the way to her. The pantomime of what he had witnessed alone would have been enough to suggest that to him, without the need of an accompanying sound track.

He had turned his back to me, and was walking away from the door, when I reopened it wide enough to insert my head, one foot and one shoulder past it, and to protest indignantly: "I still have a drink coming to me. I paid you for it, and I never got it. Now where is it?"

"You've had enough," he said arbitrarily and quite inaccurately. I hadn't had anything. "You're cut off."

And with that he came back toward me, and this time did push me, gave me a good hearty shove out through the partial aperture I had been standing in. So tempestuous a one in fact that I went all the way back and over, and again sprawled on my shoulder blades in a sort of arrested skid across the sidewalk.

This time he locked the door from the inside (evidently a temporary measure until I should go away) and pulled down a shade across the grimy glass portion of it in final dismissal.

It was the second time I'd been toppled in about three minutes and I blew a fuse.

I got up into a crouched-over position, like a runner on his mark just before the start of a race. I swung my head around, this way and that, looking for something to throw. There was a fire hydrant, but it was immovable. There was one of those Department of Sanitation wire-lattice litter baskets that stud the sidewalks of New York. I went over to that, still at a crouch, and looked in it for something heavy. All I could see from the top was layers of newspapers. So instead of throwing something from its contents, I threw the whole receptacle itself.

Lifted it clear, hoisted it overhead, took a few running steps with it, scraps of litter raining out of it, and let it fly.

The door responded with an ear-splitting bang like the backfire from a heavy truck's exhaust tube.

But it wasn't strong enough to break the glass, which was what I'd been trying for, or my throw wasn't strong enough, or there was a wire-mesh backing protecting the glass. It just fractured it and rolled off, leaving behind a star-shaped cicatrice that looked like it was made of powdered sugar.

The barman flew out and grabbed me. I never saw anyone come out of anywhere so fast. Everyone else came out too, and some stayed and some skipped out on their drinks.

A couple of patrol cars knifed up in pincers formation, one

with the traffic, one against the traffic, dome lights dead for surprise value, and caught me in between them.

The next thing I knew I was standing in front of a police sergeant's desk.

The barkeeper said his door pane was worth fifty-five dollars. I felt like saying his whole place wasn't worth fifty-five dollars, but I wasn't in a position to submit appraisals. The desk sergeant asked him if he would be willing to drop the complaint if I made good on the fifty-five dollars. He said he would. The desk sergeant asked me if I had fifty-five dollars. I checked myself out, and said I didn't have. The desk sergeant asked me if I could *get* fifty-five dollars. I said I'd try. The desk sergeant said I could use his phone.

I called up Stewart Sutphen, my lawyer. I knew it was no use calling his office at that hour of the night, so I called his home instead. He wasn't there either. He was up in the country somewhere. He was always up in the country somewhere whenever you tried to reach him, I reflected rather disgruntledly. He had been the last time too, I remembered. He was the out-of-town-ingest attorney I ever heard of. He'd once told me he liked to go over his briefs up where it was quiet and peaceful and there were no distractions, at one of these little country hotels or wayside stopping-off places. I often wondered if anyone went along to help him turn the pages, but that was a loaded question. And none of my business besides. He seemed to be happily enough married. I'd met his wife.

I left my name and where I was, and asked her to tell him to come down in the morning with the fifty-five dollars.

The fifty-five being in default, my pocket-fill was taken away from me, stacked into an oblong manila folder, the flap of this was wetly and sloppily licked by a police property clerk who seemed to be oversalivated, and it was then pummeled into adhesion, and held, to be returned to me on exit. My name and my other details were entered on the blotter, and I was booked and remanded into a cell to be held overnight on a D. and D. charge.

I'd never been in one of them before. Actually, it wasn't so bad. If you closed your eyes a minute and didn't stop to tell yourself what it was, it could have been any barren little room, except that the light was on the outside and never went off all night.

I was alone in it. There were two bunks in it, but the other one was fallow. D. and D., drunk and disorderly (conduct), must have been on the scarce side that night. There are runs on various types of charges at certain times, the cops will tell you that in their line of work. The blanket smelled of creosote, that's the part I remember most. I could hear somebody nearby snoring heavily, but I didn't mind that, it took a little of the aloneness away.

Even the breakfast wasn't too bad. No worse than you'd get in an average elbow-rest cafeteria. And of course, on the city. They passed it in about six, a little earlier than I usually had mine. Oatmeal, and white bread, and a thick mug of coffee. I skipped the first two, because I don't like soupy oatmeal and because I don't like cottony white bread, but I asked for a refill on the coffee and was given it not only willingly but even (I thought I detected) with a touch of fellow feeling by him outside there in the corridor. I guess I wasn't the usual type he got in there.

And meanwhile I kept thinking: Don't they know yet? Don't they know what I've done? Why is it taking them so long to find out? I thought they were so fast, so infallible.

Sutphen came around ten in the morning and paid out my damages, and in due course they unlocked me and indicated me out. On our way down the front steps of the detention house side by side, he shook his headful of tightly spun pepper-and-salt clinkers at me and gave me a mildly chiding: "A man your age. Breaking bar windows. Brawling. Trying to do, act like a perpetual juvenile?" Beyond that he had nothing else much to say. I suppose to him it was too trifling, and not a legal matter at all but one of loss of temper.

I didn't tell him either what I'd done. I don't know why; I

couldn't bring myself to. He was more the one to tell than the cops. My friend and lawyer in one. It would have given him a head start at least on figuring out what was best to do for me. But I was tired and beat. I hadn't closed my eyes all night in the detention cell. I knew once I told I wouldn't be left alone; I'd be dragged here and lugged there and hustled the next place. I wanted time to sleep on it and time to think it out and time to tighten my belt for what was coming to me.

He asked me if he could drop me off, in a perfunctory way. But I knew he was anxious to get back to his office routine and not play anyone's door-to-door driver. And I wanted to be alone too. I had a lot of thinking to catch up on. I didn't want anyone right on top of me for a while. So I told him no and I walked away from him down the street on my own and by my lonesome.

And thus the night finally came to its long-drawn-out end, the memorable unforgettable night that it had been.

I felt rotten, inside and out and all over. Like when you've had a tooth that hurts, and have had it taken out, and then the hole where it was hurts almost as bad as before. You can't tell the diff.

But the paradox of the whole thing was this: on the night that I committed a murder, I was only locked up on disorderly conduct charges.

As you will see in Section II of the bibliography that follows, one of the manuscripts Woolrich left unfinished at his death was a novel called *The Loser*. "Life Is Weird Sometimes" constitutes the first chapter of that novel, although it stands up well both as an independent story and as an excellent example of late Woolrich, with love, death, irony and bitterness intermingled in equal parts. The eventual fate of this story's protagonist may be learned from Woolrich's "The Release," in Robert L. Fish's MWA anthology *With Malice Toward All* (Dutton, 1968); for "The Release" is the last chapter of *The Loser*.

Cornell Woolrich:
A Checklist

by
HAROLD KNOTT
FRANCIS M. NEVINS, JR.
WILLIAM THAILING

INTRODUCTORY NOTE

This is, we hope, a comprehensive checklist of the writings of Cornell Woolrich. It has been close to twenty-five years in the making, and the labor involved (especially for Messrs. Knott and Thailing) has been of Herculean proportions. But we now believe we have tracked down everything that Woolrich wrote.

In Part I, Novels and Story Collections, each book by Woolrich is given a code designation consisting of (1) the initials of the book's byline (CW, WI or GH) and (2) the book's chronological number among the titles published under that byline. Thus *The Doom Stone* is CW 16—the sixteenth book published under

Woolrich's own name; *Six Nights of Mystery* is WI 13; *Fright* is GH 2.

In Part II, Woolrich's Unfinished Manuscripts, codes have proven unnecessary, and the reader should be pleased to find that this section resembles an essay more than a computer printout.

In Part III, Short Fiction, every Woolrich story or novelette is given a code designation consisting of (1) the name, initials, or first syllable of the magazine of original publication, and (2) the story's chronological number among the Woolrich tales published in that magazine. Thus "You Bet Your Life," the twenty-eighth story Woolrich published in *Detective Fiction Weekly*, is DFW 28; "I.O.U.," the seventh story he published in *Double Detective*, is Doub D 7. The short-fiction coding takes no account of the byline under which any story was published, for the various bylines have no functional significance in Woolrich's fiction, and stories originally published under one byline have frequently been reprinted under another. It should be noted that due to editors' vagaries there are many changes in the texts of Woolrich's stories from one printing to the next; most of the substantial revisions and abridgments are reflected herein. It should also be noted that *Mike Shayne's Mystery Magazine* and *Rex Stout's Mystery Magazine* (or *Monthly*), which reprinted several Woolrich tales apiece but never published any of his stories as originals, are respectively abbreviated MSMM and RSMM. Finally, all reprints of Woolrich stories in the magazine variously known as *Saint Detective Magazine, Saint Mystery Magazine*, and *Saint Magazine* are listed as being in SMM.

In Part III, the original title of each story is followed by the story's alternate titles and by data on its subsequent appearances in books of Woolrich's short fiction, anthologies, and other magazines. Only the more significant anthology and magazine reprintings are listed here, but all appearances in Woolrich's own books of short fiction are listed. Thus one can use this checklist to pursue any Woolrich story from its book appearance to its magazine and anthology appearances, or from its original magazine publication to its appearance in another magazine, an anthology, or a book of Woolrich's short fiction.

Part IV, Woolrich as Adapted, deals primarily with citation of and comment on the movie adaptations of Woolrich's work from 1929 to the present. Some incomplete notes on radio and television adaptations of Woolrich are also included.

We would like to thank the following gentlemen for their assistance at one stage or another of the work: Michael Avallone, William J. Clark, Frederic Dannay, Dan J. Marlowe, Frank D. McSherry, Jr., Norman Miller, Robert B. Miller, Jr., Hans Stefan Santesson, Philip Schwendeman, Charles Shibuk, and Donald A. Yates. Miss Pat Erhardt deserves special thanks for her help at every stage of the project.

In 1964 Anthony Boucher wrote of Woolrich's bibliography that it "is so inextricably confused that no one has ever mastered it (least of all himself)." We grieve that neither Boucher nor Woolrich lived to see the job of mastering it completed, and we wish our readers well in their explorations herein.

I. NOVELS AND STORY COLLECTIONS

A. As by Cornell Woolrich

1. *Cover Charge* (Boni & Liveright, 1926).
   NOTE: Woolrich later turned this novel into a three-act play of the same title, which was copyrighted in 1931 and renewed in 1959, but which seems never to have been performed.
2. *Children of the Ritz* (Boni & Liveright, 1927). Serialized as CH 3.
3. *Times Square* (Liveright, 1929). Serialized as LGS 1.
4. *A Young Man's Heart* (Mason, 1930).
5. *The Time of Her Life* (Liveright, 1931).
6. *Manhattan Love Song* (Godwin, 1932).
6½. *I Love You, Paris* (1933, unpublished).
   NOTE: In his manuscript autobiography, Woolrich relates how he came to write this last in his cycle of early romantic novels, and how he wound up throwing it in the garbage.

7. *The Bride Wore Black* (Simon & Schuster, 1940).

   NOTE: In this, his first and perhaps best-known mystery novel, Woolrich, like Hammett and Chandler and a host of others, drew on motifs he had previously used in shorter work. Thus, the famous balcony-murder scene is derived from AAF 1 ("I'm Dangerous Tonight") and the climax from BM 11 ("Borrowed Crime"). But in the novel, the earlier material is fused into a new and organic whole. The book has been frequently reprinted under its original title, and once (Pyramid Book #80, 1953) as *Beware the Lady*. The Collier paperback edition (#AS 606, 1964) contains an excellent introduction by Anthony Boucher.

8. *The Black Curtain* (Simon & Schuster, 1941). Expanded from DFW 30 and DD 15.

9. *Black Alibi* (Simon & Schuster, 1942). Expanded from SDM 1.

10. *The Black Angel* (Doubleday Doran, 1943). Expanded from DD 2 and BM 6.

    NOTE: The most recent paperback edition (Ace Book #06505, 1969) contains an afterword by Michael Avallone.

11. *The Black Path of Fear* (Doubleday Doran, 1944). Expanded from DFW 49.

12. *Rendezvous in Black* (Rinehart, 1948). Revision of CW 7.

13. *Savage Bride* (Gold Medal Book #136, 1950).

14. *Nightmare* (Dodd Mead, 1956). Contents: I'll Take You Home, Kathleen (DS 4); Screen Test (DD 1); Three O'Clock (DFW 36); Nightmare (A 20); I.O.U. (Doub D 7); Bequest (DT 2).

15. *Violence* (Dodd Mead, 1958). Contents: Don't Wait Up for Me Tonight (Story 2); Guillotine (BM 12); That New York Woman (DD 25); Murder, Obliquely (Shad 1); The Moon of Montezuma (F 1); The Corpse in the Statue of Liberty (DD 5).

16. *Hotel Room* (Random House, 1958). Contents: The Night of June 20, 1896 (new); The Night of April 6, 1917 (new); The Night of November 11, 1918 (new); The Night of February 17, 1924 (J 1); The Night of October 24, 1929 (new); The Night of . . . (new); The Night of September 30, 1957 (new).

17. *Death Is My Dancing Partner* (Pyramid Book #G374, 1959).

18. *Beyond the Night* (Avon Book #T354, 1959). Contents: The Moon of Montezuma (F 1); Somebody's Clothes—Somebody's Life (F-SF 1); The Lamp of Memory (A 13); My Lips Destroy (HS 1); The Number's Up (new); Music from the Dark (DM 1).

19. *The Doom Stone* (Avon Book #T408, 1960). Revision of A 16.
20. *The Ten Faces of Cornell Woolrich* (Simon & Schuster, 1965). Contents: One Drop of Blood (EQMM 4); Somebody on the Phone (DFW 26); Debt of Honor (Doub D 7); The Man Upstairs (MBM 2); The Most Exciting Show in Town (DFW 10); The Night Reveals (Story 1); Steps Going Up (BM 12); The Humming Bird Comes Home (PD 2); Adventures of a Fountain Pen (DS 6); I Won't Take a Minute (DFW 41).
    NOTE: This volume contains an introduction by Ellery Queen.
21. *The Dark Side of Love* (Walker, 1965). Contents: Je t'Aime (EQMM 6); The Clean Fight (new); The Idol with the Clay Bottom (new); The Poker-Player's Wife (SMM 1); Story To Be Whispered (SMM 2); Somebody Else's Life (F-SF 1); I'm Ashamed (new); Too Nice a Day to Die (B 1).
22. *Nightwebs* (Harper & Row, 1971). Contents: Graves for the Living (DM 2); The Red Tide (DS 5); The Corpse Next Door (DFW 20); You'll Never See Me Again (DS 3); Dusk to Dawn (BM 8); Murder at the Automat (DD 10); Death in the Air (DFW 17); Mamie 'n' Me (AAF 3); The Screaming Laugh (CD 1); One and a Half Murders (BBD 1); Dead on Her Feet (DD 7); One Night in Barcelona (MBM 6); The Penny-a-Worder (EQMM 1); The Number's Up (CW 18); Too Nice a Day to Die (B 1); Life Is Weird Sometimes (new).
    NOTE: This collection contains a long introduction by Francis M. Nevins, Jr., and a comprehensive bibliography of Woolrich's writings.

B. As by William Irish

1. *Phantom Lady* (Lippincott, 1942). Expanded from DFW 39; serialized as DFW 48.
2. *I Wouldn't Be in Your Shoes* (Lippincott, 1943). Contents: I Wouldn't Be in Your Shoes (DFW 32); Last Night (DS 5); Three O'Clock (DFW 36); Nightmare (A 20); Papa Benjamin (DM 1).
    NOTE: Almost all reprint editions of this collection are incomplete. Thus, only stories 1 and 2 from the first edition appear in *I Wouldn't Be in Your Shoes* (Mercury Mystery #82, c1945); only stories 3, 4 and 5 in *And So to Death* (Jonathan Press Mystery #J31, c1945); and only stories 4, 3 and 1 in *Nightmare* (Reader's Choice Library #12, c1950).

3. *Deadline at Dawn* (Lippincott, 1944). Expanded from DFW 45.
4. *After-Dinner Story* (Lippincott, 1944). Contents: After-Dinner Story (BM 9); The Night Reveals (Story 1); An Apple a Day (new); Marihuana (DFW 46); Rear Window (DD 23); Murder-Story (DFW 27).

   NOTE: This collection was reprinted both under its original title and as *Six Times Death* (Popular Library Book #137, c1947).
5. *If I Should Die Before I Wake* (Avon Murder Mystery Monthly #31, 1945). Contents: If I Should Die Before I Wake (DFW 24); I'll Never Play Detective Again (BM 3); Change of Murder (DFW 6); A Death Is Caused (DD 28); Two Murders, One Crime (BM 20); The Man Upstairs (MBM 2).
6. *The Dancing Detective* (Lippincott, 1946). Contents: The Dancing Detective (BM 10); Two Fellows in a Furnished Room (DFW 44); The Light in the Window (MBM 4); Silent As the Grave (MBM 3); The Detective's Dilemma (DFW 42); Fur Jacket (DD 31); Leg Man (DD 29); The Fingernail (DT 1).
7. *Borrowed Crime* (Avon Murder Mystery Monthly #42, 1946). Contents: Borrowed Crime (BM 11); The Cape Triangular (DFW 33); Detective William Brown (DFW 35); Chance (BM 19).
8. *Waltz into Darkness* (Lippincott, 1947).
9. *Dead Man Blues* (Lippincott, 1948). Contents: Guillotine (BM 12); The Earring (DFW 50); If the Dead Could Talk (BM 21); Fire Escape (MBM 5); Fountain Pen (DS 6); You Take Ballistics (Doub D 2); Funeral (A 9).

   NOTE: The third story from the original edition is omitted from the reprint *Dead Man Blues* (Mercury Mystery #135, c1950).
10. *I Married a Dead Man* (Lippincott, 1948). Expanded from TW 1.
11. *The Blue Ribbon* (Lippincott, 1949). Contents: The Blue Ribbon (new); The Dog with the Wooden Leg (DS 1); The Lie (DFW 29); Hot Towel (Doub D 4); Wardrobe Trunk (DFW 22); Wild Bill Hiccup (A 15); Subway (A 4); Husband (new).

    NOTE: The sixth and the last stories from the original edition are omitted from the reprint *Dilemma of the Dead Lady* (Graphic Book #20, 1950).
12. *Somebody on the Phone* (Lippincott, 1950). Contents: Johnny on the Spot (DFW 9); Somebody on the Phone (DFW 26); Collared (BM 14); The Night I Died (DFW 13); Momentum (DFW 43); Boy with Body (DD 6); Death Sits in the Dentist's Chair (DFW 1); The

Room with Something Wrong (DFW 34).

NOTE: The third and fourth stories from the original edition are omitted from the reprint *Deadly Night Call* (Graphic Book #31, 1951, and #81, 1954).

13. *Six Nights of Mystery* (Popular Library Book #258, 1950). Contents: One Night in New York (BM 6); One Night in Chicago (BM 14); One Night in Hollywood (BM 22); One Night in Montreal (A 2); One Night in Paris (A 3); One Night in Zacamoras (A 17).

14. *Strangler's Serenade* (Rinehart, 1951). Expanded from MBM 1.

15. *Eyes That Watch You* (Rinehart, 1952). Contents: Eyes That Watch You (DD 15); Stuck (DD 11); Charlie Won't Be Home Tonight (DD 14); Murder with a U (DD 19); All at Once, No Alice (A 18); Damned Clever, These Americans (A 10); Flat Tire (DD 12).

16. *Bluebeard's Seventh Wife* (Popular Library Book #473, 1952). Contents: Bluebeard's Seventh Wife (DFW 15); Morning After Murder (DFW 14); Silhouette (DFW 37); The Hat (DFW 38); Humming Bird Comes Home (PD 2); Through a Dead Man's Eye (BM 15).

17. *The Best of William Irish* (Lippincott, 1960).

NOTE: This attractive triple-decker, containing the complete texts of WI 1, WI 3, and WI 4, is the best introduction to Woolrich extant.

C. As by George Hopley

1. *Night Has a Thousand Eyes* (Farrar & Rinehart, 1945). Expanded from A 8.

2. *Fright* (Rinehart, 1950).

II. WOOLRICH'S UNFINISHED MANUSCRIPTS

At the time of his death, Woolrich was working on four projects: two novels, a book of short fiction, and his autobiography. That none of these were finished is a loss that every perceptive reader of Woolrich will feel in his bones.

A. *Into Yesterday.* This is my title for an untitled novel on which Woolrich apparently worked for a long time. Although pages 1–22 of the manuscript are missing, the major event in them is clear from the context: Madeline Chalmers, the protagonist, has accidentally killed a girl named Starr Bartlett. Guilt-obsessed, she steps into Starr's life, goes to Starr's home town, becomes acquainted with Starr's widowed mother, and learns that Starr's life had been mangled by two people: her estranged husband, Vick Herrick, and Vick's ex-wife, the singer Adelaide Nelson. Madeline returns to New York City, locates Adelaide, and insinuates herself into the singer's life with the intent of destroying her (a procedure not unlike that of Julie in *The Bride Wore Black*). But events take the reins out of Madeline's hands, and a homicide cop named John F. X. Smith comes very close to the truth about her. When the danger passes, she goes after Vick Herrick, and after several poignant blind-alley encounters reminiscent of *Deadline at Dawn*, she finds him. Again she begins to insinuate herself into her victim's life, but this time she finds herself, against her will, falling in love with her intended quarry, just as Starr had. The evocation of the last hours before she carries out her plan to kill him is one of the most haunting and terrifying things Woolrich wrote in the last twenty years of his life. The manuscript trails off before we learn what happened to Madeline and Vick, and by the cutoff point both they and the other tortured people in this novel have become so achingly real that the sense of loss is unimaginable.

B. *The Loser*. In pages 1–17 of this manuscript the narrator, Cleve Evans, kills an unnamed woman (the motive, as always in late Woolrich, has to do with the death of love), stops in at a bar afterward for a drink, and inadvertently winds up with a perfect alibi. This chapter appears in the present book under the title "Life Is Weird Sometimes." In pages 18–35 there is a flashback to the first meeting of Cleve Evans and Janet Bartlett, who at once begin to fall in love. At the end of the chapter Janet is about to tell Cleve some incident out of her past. Unfortunately Cleve already has a wife, a bitchy singer named Adelaide. In pages 38–56 Cleve returns to Adelaide's apartment, packs his things, and tells her he is in love with another woman. She refuses to give him up: he is her possession. He leaves her as she swears revenge on him and his new woman. Cleve and Janet motor to Mexico for divorce and remarriage, return to New York City to live, and are supremely happy. At the end of this chapter comes the first hint that their happiness is menaced.

Next comes a five-page fragment entitled "The Death of Love, The Love of Death," narrated in the third person, and describing a time when Adelaide was in love with her manager D'Angelo. How this was intended to fit in with the rest of the book is not clear.

The next 22 unnumbered pages are again narrated by Cleve. The police come to his and Janet's apartment to arrest Janet for Adelaide's murder. Cleve fights the detectives like a madman, swears that he, not she, killed Adelaide, and winds up in Bellevue.

Between this point and the final chapter, Cleve apparently went away and found some evidence that will enable his lawyer to get Janet's murder conviction reversed. At the beginning of the last chapter he returns to the city and the lawyer tells him that Janet committed suicide in her cell that morning. Cleve returns to the apartment they shared and jumps out the window.

Interestingly enough, the last chapter of *The Loser* was published shortly after Woolrich's death as an independent short story, "The Release," in Robert L. Fish (ed.), *With Malice Toward All* (Dutton, 1968). In the published version it is Cleve who has been in prison for murdering Adelaide. He returns to New York City after being pardoned and finds that Janet, unaware of the pardon, has killed herself that morning. The published version is more polished than either of the two variant manuscripts of the chapter.

C. *I Was Waiting for You: Tales of Love and Despair.* This is a collection of short fiction which Woolrich was trying to put together in his last years. The typed title page lists the following as the proposed contents: (1) "I Was Waiting for You"; (2) "New York Blues"; (3) *"Now I've Got You"*; (4) "Two Lives"; (5) "Old Husband, Young Wife"; (6) "Don't Let Men Hurt Her, Jimmy." At the bottom of the title page is the following quotation:

> But pass in silence the mute grave of two
> Who lived and died believing love was true.
> —*Edna St. Vincent Millay*

"I Was Waiting for You" is a long unfinished story, set during World War I and the Twenties, and dealing with a young man named Bruce Eadlin and a girl named Eva Brundage, who never meet but who in a kinder world would have met and loved. Separate sections relate the love and sexual problems of each. "New York Blues," which was completed and purchased by *Ellery Queen's Mystery Magazine* before Woolrich's death and published in its December 1970 issue, is an unbearably moving mood piece in which a man who has killed his wife sits in a hotel room and waits for the police to pick him up. *"Now I've*

Got You" was published in the May 1968 issue of *EQMM* as "For the Rest of Her Life." "Two Lives" is a mere fragment, dealing with the abduction of baby Christopher Kemp the day before Pearl Harbor. Since a similar fate befell Starr Bartlett's brother in *Into Yesterday*, I suspect that Woolrich incorporated his plan for this story into that unfinished novel. The final two titles, "Old Husband, Young Wife" and "Don't Let Men Hurt Her, Jimmy," appear to be no more than titles: Woolrich died before he could write the stories he intended to be called by those names.

D. *Blues of a Lifetime: Personal Stories.* This unfinished autobiography found among Woolrich's papers contains five sections in reasonably finished form. "The Poor Girl" deals with the author's love affair in his late teens with a lower-middle-class girl named Vera, and with Vera's unhappy end. In "Remington Portable NC69411" he recounts how he first began to write and comments extensively on what it means to be a writer. In "Even God Felt the Depression" he evokes the penniless year of 1933, tells how he wrote a novel he couldn't sell and wound up throwing it in the garbage, and discusses sex, religion, poverty, his mother, and other subjects. "President Eisenhower's Speech" provides much insight into Woolrich's life with his mother during their last years together, and describes a disastrous fire in Woolrich's apartment building in 1957. "The Maid Who Played the Races" is a quietly humorous little gem in which Woolrich tells how he was mistaken for a jockey one day in Seattle, and ended up having to sneak out of his hotel in the middle of the night.

It is rare indeed for the unfinished work of a mystery writer to be published after his death; but Woolrich was far more than a mystery writer, and the work he left behind is closer in quality to *The Last Tycoon* than it is to, say, *The Winter Murder Case.* We can but hope that some courageous and generous publisher will take a risk with these manuscripts, and give Woolrich's many readers the chance to share them.

III. SHORT FICTION

All-American Fiction

1.   11/37   I'm Dangerous Tonight.
            NOTE: The scene in which Sarah Travis pushes her

husband off the deck of the S.S. *Gascony* is the model for the famous balcony murder in CW 7 *(The Bride Wore Black)*.

2.   3,4/38 Jane Brown's Body. (F-SF 10/51.)
3.   5,6/38 Mamie 'n' Me. (CW 22.)

Argosy

1.   12/28/35 Hot Water. (EQMM 6/61.)
2.   1/25/36 The Crime on St. Catherine Street. (WI 13, as "One Night in Montreal"; EQMM 12/66, as "All It Takes Is Brains.")
3.   5/16/36 Underworld Trail. (WI 13, as "One Night in Paris.")
4.   8/22/36 You Pays Your Nickel. (WI 11, as "Subway"; *The Third Mystery Companion*, A. L. Furman, ed., 1945, as "The Phantom of the Subway"; Avon Detective Mysteries #1, March 1947.)
5.   9/ 5/36 Gun for a Gringo.
6.   11/ 7/36 Public Toothache Number One.
7.   12/12/36 Holocaust.
8.   2/27/37 Speak to Me of Death. (EQMM 3/49; Fantasy Fiction, 5/50; SMM 3/66. Story was expanded into GH 1.)
9.   6/19/37 Your Own Funeral. (WI 9, as "Funeral"; EQMM 2/48, *Ellery Queen's 1962 Anthology, Ellery Queen's Lethal Black Book*, 1965, as "That's Your Own Funeral.")
10.   7/ 3/37 Clever, These Americans. (WI 15, as "Damned Clever, These Americans.")
11.   7/31/37 Black Cargo.
12.   11/13/37 Oft in the Silly Night.
13.   12/18/37 Guns, Gentlemen. (CW 18, as "The Lamp of Memory"; *The Fourth Mystery Companion*, A. L. Furman, ed., 1946, as "Twice-Trod Path.")
14.   1/29/38 Death in the Yoshiwara. (Manhunt 1/53, as "The Hunted.")
15.   2/ 5/38 Wild Bill Hiccup. (WI 11; *The Armchair Companion*, A. L. Furman, ed., 1944; Avon Western Reader #3, 1947; SMM 11/63.)

16.   1/14/39   The Eye of Doom, Part 1. (Short Stories, 12/58, as "The Devil with the Sparkling Face." Verbatim reprint.)
16.   1/21/39   The Eye of Doom, Part 2. (SMM 7/62, as "Two Against the Terror," with ending slightly changed.)
16.   1/28/39   The Eye of Doom, Part 3.
16.   2/ 4/39   The Eye of Doom, Part 4.
                  NOTE: The first three installments of this serial, along with a completely new fourth part, were published in book form as CW 19 *(The Doom Stone)*. The new Part 4 was reprinted as an independent short story, titled "Tokyo 1941," in *The Award Espionage Reader*, Hans Stefan Santesson, ed., 1965.
17.   2/ 3/40   Senor Flatfoot. (WI 13, as "One Night in Zacamoras," with several sections completely rewritten but no significant plot changes.)
18.   3/ 2/40   All at Once, No Alice. (WI 15; EQMM 11/51; Verdict, 7/53; *Ellery Queen's 1966 Mid-Year Anthology.*)
19.   6/23/40   Cinderella and the Mob. (EQMM 7/53; Keyhole, 4/60; *Ellery Queen's 1963 Mid-Year Anthology.*)
20.   3/ 1/41   And So to Death. (WI 2, CW 14, RSMM 12/46, as "Nightmare.")

Baffling Detective Mysteries
1.   3/43   The Death Rose. (EQMM 9/59, as "Dead Roses.")

Bizarre
1.   1/66   Too Nice a Day to Die.
                  (This appearance almost simultaneous with the story's publication in CW 21; CW 22.)

Black Book Detective
1.   7/36   One and a Half Murders. (CW 22.)

Black Mask
1.   1/37   Shooting Going On. (SMM 10/58.)
2.   2/37   Murder on the Night Boat.
3.   5/37   I'll Never Play Detective Again. (WI 5; EQMM 7/63.)

4. 6/37 Mimic Murder. (SMM 7/58; *The Saint Mystery Library* #130, 1960.)

5. 9/37 Nelli from Zelli's.

6. 10/37 Face Work. (WI 13, as "One Night in New York"; EQMM 12/46, *Ellery Queen's 1968 Anthology*, as "Angel Face." Story was incorporated into CW 10.)

7. 11/37 Cab, Mister? (EQMM 9/50.)

8. 12/37 Dusk to Dawn. (CW 22.)

9. 1/38 After-Dinner Story. (WI 4; EQMM 9/43; *Ellery Queen's 1964 Anthology.*)

10. 2/38 Dime a Dance. (EQMM Fall 1941, under original title; WI 6, *Murder by Experts* [Queen, ed., 1947], *Fourteen Great Detective Stories* [Haycraft, ed., 1949], Mystery Digest 9/58, *Ellery Queen's 1968 Mid-Year Anthology*, as "The Dancing Detective.")

11. 7/39 Borrowed Crime. (WI 7. The climax of this story was revised and incorporated into the last chapters of CW 7.)

12. 8/39 Men Must Die. (WI 9, CW 15, as "Guillotine"; CW 20, EQMM 4/47, *Ellery Queen's 1969 Mid-Year Anthology*, as "Steps Going Up.")

13. 9/39 Crime by the Forelock.

14. 10/39 Collared. (WI 12, EQMM 7/49, *Ellery Queen's 1963 Anthology*, under original title; WI 13, as "One Night in Chicago.")

15. 12/39 Through a Dead Man's Eye. (WI 16; EQMM 3/51; *Ellery Queen's 1964 Mid-Year Anthology.*)

16. 4/40 Post Mortem. (*The Second Mystery Companion*, A. L. Furman, ed., 1944; RSMM 6/46.)

17. 10/40 C-Jag. (*The Pocket Mystery Reader*, Lee Wright, ed., 1942, as "Cocaine"; Mystery Digest, 12/58, as "Dream of Death"; EQMM 12/65, as "Just Enough to Cover a Thumbnail.")

18. 4/41 Cool, Calm and Detected. (EQMM 5/56, as "The Absent-Minded Murder.")

19. 5/42 Dormant Account. (EQMM 5/53, under original title; WI 7, as "Chance.")

20. 7/42 Three Kills for One. (Triple Detective, Autumn

1952, under original title; WI 5, as "Two Murders, One Crime"; EQMM 9/53, as "The Loophole.")

21.   2/43 If the Dead Could Talk. (WI 9; *The Mystery Companion*, A. L. Furman, ed., 1943; EQMM 7/46; SMM 4/64.)

22.   7/44 Picture Frame. (WI 13, as "One Night in Hollywood"; EQMM 6/54, as "Dead Shot.")

Breezy Stories

1.   4/35   Spanish and What Eyes.
2.   6/35   Don't Fool Me.
3.   8/35   Clip Joint. (College Life, Winter 1936.)
4.   10/35 No Kick Coming.
5.   11/35 Flower in His Buttonhole.
6.   12/35 Annabelle Gets Across.
7.   3/36   Pick Up the Pieces.
8.   4/36   The Clock at the Astor.
9.   7/36   His Name Is Jack.
10.   1/37   Jimmy Had a Nickel.
11.   5/37   Kidnapped.
12.   7/37   The Girl Next Door.
13.   10/37 I Knew Her When.
14.   1/39   The Invincibles.

Clues Detective

1.   11/38 The Screaming Laugh. (CW 22.)

College Humor

1.   9/26   Honey Child.
2.   1/27   Bread and Orchids.
3.   8/27   Children of the Ritz, Part 1.
3.   9/27   Children of the Ritz, Part 2.
3.   10/27 Children of the Ritz, Part 3.
3.   11/27 Children of the Ritz, Part 4.
             NOTE: This serial was published in book form as CW 2.
4.   8/28   Mother and Daughter.
5.   2/29   Bluebeard's Thirteenth Wife.

6.   6/29 We're Just a Lot of Smart Alecks.
7.   1/30 Gay Music.
8.   8/31 The Girl in the Moon.

College Life

1.   10/28 The Good Die Young.
2.   5, 6, 7/34 The Next Is On Me.

Detective Fiction Weekly

1.   8/ 4/34 Death Sits in the Dentist's Chair. (WI 12, under
                   original title; EQMM 6/58, as "Hurting Much?")
2.   8/18/34 Walls That Hear You.
3.   12/ 7/35 The Death of Me.
4.   12/14/35 The Showboat Murders.
5.   1/11/36 Cigarette. (MSMM 3/65.)
6.   1/25/36 Change of Murder. (WI 5; *Murder for the Millions*,
                   Frank Owen, ed., 1946; MSMM 12/62.)
7.   3/21/36 Blood in Your Eye.
8.   4/ 4/36 The Mystery of the Blue Spot.
9.   5/ 2/36 Johnny on the Spot. (WI 12; EQMM 11/48.)
10.   5/16/36 Double Feature. (CW 20, EQMM 9/55, as "The
                   Most Exciting Show in Town.")
11.   6/20/36 Nine Lives.
12.   7/ 4/36 Dilemma of the Dead Lady. (WI 11, as "Wardrobe
                   Trunk"; revised, EQMM 3/64, as "Working Is for
                   Fools.")
13.   8/ 8/36 The Night I Died. (Originally published as by
                   Anonymous.) (WI 12; EQMM 6/50; *Ellery Queen's
                   1965 Mid-Year Anthology*; *13 Ways to Dispose of
                   a Body*, Basil Davenport, ed., 1966.)
14.   8/15/36 Murder on My Mind. (WI 16, as "Morning After
                   Murder"; Five Detective Novels, Spring 1952, as
                   "The Morning After Murder.")
15.   8/22/36 Bluebeard's Seventh Wife. (WI 16.)
16.   9/26/36 Murder in the Middle of New York.
17.   10/10/36 Death in the Air. (CW 22.)
18.   11/14/36 Afternoon of a Phony.

19. 12/26/36 The Two Deaths of Barney Slabaugh. (Reprinted in same magazine, 3/51.)
20. `1/23/37 The Corpse Next Door. (CW 22.)
21. 2/27/37 Blue Is for Bravery. (EQMM 3/55, as "Invitation to Sudden Death.")
22. 3/27/37 Round Trip to the Cemetery.
23. 6/ 5/37 Wake Up with Death.
24. 7/ 3/37 If I Should Die Before I Wake. (WI 5; MSMM 12/64.)
25. 7/17/37 Vision of Murder.
26. 7/31/37 Somebody on the Phone. (WI 12; CW 20; EQMM 4/49; *These Will Chill You*, Lee Wright & Richard G. Sheehan, eds., 1967; *Ellery Queen's MiniMysteries*, Queen ed., 1969.)
27. 9/11/37 Murder Story (WI 4; EQMM 2/59, as "The Inside Story.")
28. 9/25/37 You Bet Your Life. (EQMM 3/58, as "Don't Bet on Murder.")
29. 10/ 9/37 The Lie. (WI 11.)
30. 12/ 4/37 The Gun But Not the Hand. (Incorporated into CW 8.)
31. 2/19/38 Endicott's Girl. (EQMM 2/58.)
32. 3/12/38 I Wouldn't Be in Your Shoes. (WI 2.)
33. 4/16/38 The Cape Triangular. (WI 7; EQMM 2/63.)
34. 6/ 4/38 Mystery in Room 913. (EQMM 12/49, under original title; WI 22, as "The Room with Something Wrong.")
35. 9/10/38 Detective William Brown. (WI 7.)
36. 10/ 1/38 Three O'Clock. (CW 14; WI 2; *And the Darkness Falls*, Boris Karloff, ed., 1946; The Avon Mystery Story Teller, 1946; Verdict, 9/53.)
37. 1/ 7/39 Silhouette. (WI 16.)
38. 2/18/39 The Counterfeit Hat. (WI 16, as "The Hat"; EQMM 10/61, as "The Singing Hat.")
39. 3/ 4/39 Those Who Kill. (Expanded into DFW 48 and ultimately into WI 1. Original short story reprinted, MSMM 4/66.)
40. 2/17/40 Death in Duplicate. (EQMM 9/56, as "The Ice Pick Murders.")

41. 6/22/40 Finger of Doom. (CW 20, as "I Won't Take a Minute"; *Great American Detective Stories*, Boucher ed., 1945, under same title; EQMM 1/57, as "Wait for Me Downstairs"; Mysterious Traveler, 3/52, as "I'll Just Be a Minute.")

42. 10/26/40 The Detective's Dilemma. (WI 6; SMM, Spring 1953.)

43. 12/14/40 Murder Always Gathers Momentum. (WI 12, EQMM 5/49, as "Momentum"; reprinted in original magazine, 4/51, as "Murder Is a Snowball"; SMM 7/54, as "Murder Gathers Momentum.")

44. 2/ 8/41 He Looked Like Murder. (WI 6, as "Two Fellows in a Furnished Room.")

45. 3/15/41 Of Time and Murder. (Expanded into WI 3. Original short story reprinted, EQMM 3/54, as "The Last Bus Home.")

46. 5/ 3/41 Marihuana. (WI 4; separate publication as Dell 10¢ Book #11, c1950.)

47. 6/14/41 The Fatal Footlights. (EQMM 6/55, as "Death at the Burlesque.")
            NOTE: The magazine's title was now changed to *Detective Fiction*.

48. 5/42 Phantom Alibi, Part 1.
48. 6/42 Phantom Alibi, Part 2.
            NOTE: The magazine's title was now changed to *Flynn's Detective*.

48. 7/42 Phantom Alibi, Part 3.
48. 8/42 Phantom Alibi, Part 4.
48. 9/42 Phantom Alibi, Part 5.
48. 10/42 Phantom Alibi, Part 6.
            NOTE: This serial was expanded from DFW 39, and was published in book form as WI 1 *(Phantom Lady)*.

49. 12/42 Havana Night. (Later expanded into CW 11.)
            NOTE: The magazine's title was now changed to *Flynn's Detective Fiction.*

50. 2/43 The Death Stone. (SMM 11/55, under original title;

WI 9, EQMM 2/46, *Ellery Queen's 1967 Anthology*, as "The Earring"; New Detective, 11/50, as "The Blood Stone.")

51. 4/43 The Death Diary. (MSMM 2/63.)
52. 8/43 Come Witness My Murder.

Detective Story

1. 2/39 The Dog with the Wooden Leg. (WI 11.)
2. 8/39 The Book That Squealed. (*The Fourth Mystery Companion*, A. L. Furman, ed., 1946, as "Library Book.")
3. 11/39 You'll Never See Me Again. (Detective Story Annual, 1941; Dell 10¢ Book #26, c1950; CW 22.)
4. 5/40 One Last Night. (CW 14, as "I'll Take You Home, Kathleen.")
5. 9/40 The Red Tide. (Revised, WI 2, as "Last Night"; revision reprinted, MSMM 12/58, as "Last Night a Man Died"; original version reprinted in CW 22.)
6. 4/45 Dipped in Blood. (WI 9, as "Fountain Pen"; CW 20, EQMM 10/64, as "Adventures of a Fountain Pen.")

Detective Tales

1. 7/41 The Customer's Always Right. (WI 6, EQMM 9/44, Encore 9/45, as "The Fingernail.")
2. 9/42 Implacable Bequest. (CW 14, as "Bequest.")

Dime Detective

1. 11/15/34 Preview of Death. (CW 14, SMM 7/67, as "Screen Test.")
2. 3/ 1/35 Murder in Wax. (Later incorporated into CW 10.)
3. 4/ 1/35 The Body Upstairs.
4. 5/ 1/35 Kiss of the Cobra.
5. 7/ 1/35 Red Liberty. (Revised, CW 15, as "The Corpse in the Statue of Liberty.")
6. 9/35 The Corpse and the Kid. (WI 12, as "Boy with Body"; EQMM 10/49, as "Blind Date.")
7. 12/35 Dead on Her Feet. (CW 22.)

8. 4/36 The Living Lie Down with the Dead. (EQMM 12/55, as "One Night to Be Dead Sure Of.")
9. 6/37 Blind Date with Death.
10. 8/37 Murder at the Automat. (CW 22.)
11. 10/37 Stuck with Murder. (WI 15, as "Stuck.")
12. 5/38 Short Order Kill. (WI 15, as "Flat Tire.")
13. 5/39 The Case of the Killer Diller.
14. 7/39 Charlie Won't Be Home Tonight. (WI 15; EQMM 9/51; *Ellery Queen's 1966 Anthology.*)
15. 9/39 The Case of the Talking Eyes. (WI 15, as "Eyes That Watch You"; EQMM 4/67, as "The Talking Eyes." Story incorporated into CW 8.)
16. 6/40 Meet Me by the Mannequin. (EQMM 2/55.)
17. 9/40 Flowers from the Dead. (SMM 4/62.)
18. 11/40 The Riddle of the Redeemed Dips.
19. 3/41 U, As in Murder. (WI 15, as "Murder with a U.")
20. 5/41 The Case of the Maladroit Manicurist.
21. 6/41 Crazy House.
22. 10/41 Murder at Mother's Knee. (EQMM 12/54, as "Something That Happened in Our House.")
23. 2/42 It Had to Be Murder. (SMM Winter 1953, under original title; WI 4, All Mystery 10–12/50, *A Treasury of Great Mysteries* [Haycraft & Beecroft, eds., 1957], EQMM 2/69, as "Rear Window.")
24. 9/42 Orphan Ice. (*Murder for the Millions,* Frank Owen, ed., 1946, as "The Orphan Diamond.")
25. 12/42 The Hopeless Defense of Mrs. Dellford. (Revised, Manhunt 1/58, as "The Town Says Murder"; same revision, CW 15, as "That New York Woman.")
26. 1/43 The Body in Grant's Tomb. (EQMM 12/48.)
27. 3/43 If the Shoe Fits.
28. 5/43 Mind Over Murder. (WI 5, as "A Death Is Caused.")
29. 8/43 Leg Man. (WI 6; EQMM 5/45; *Ellery Queen's 1967 Mid-Year Anthology.*)
30. 9/43 Death on Delivery.
31. 3/44 What the Well Dressed Corpse Will Wear. (WI 6, as

"Fur Jacket"; EQMM 3/45, as "The Mathematics of Murder"; *Murder for the Millions*, Frank Owen, ed., 1946, and RSMM 5/47, as "The Body of a Well-Dressed Woman.")

Dime Mystery

1. 7/35 Dark Melody of Madness. (WI 2, as "Papa Benjamin"; CW 18, as "Music from the Dark.")
2. 6/37 Graves for the Living. (CW 22.)

Double Detective

1. 11/37 Waltz.
2. 1/38 You Take Ballistics. (WI 9; EQMM 2/47; Verdict, 8/53.)
3. 2/38 Never Kick a Dick.
4. 3/38 Hot Towel. (WI 11.)
5. 8/38 The Woman's Touch.
6. 10/38 I Hereby Bequeath.
7. 11/38 I.O.U.—One Life. (CW 14, as "I.O.U."; CW 20, EQMM 10/54, as "Debt of Honor.")

Ellery Queen's Mystery Magazine

1. 9/58 The Penny-a-Worder. (CW 22, under original title; SMM 3/67, as "Pulp Writer.")
2. 3/59 Blonde Beauty Slain. (*Ellery Queen's 14th Mystery Annual*, 1959; *Twentieth Century Detective Stories*, Queen, ed., 1964.)
3. 1/62 Money Talks.
4. 4/62 One Drop of Blood. (CW 20; *Ellery Queen's Mystery Mix*, 1963; Bizarre, 10/65.)
5. 4/64 Steps . . . Coming Near. (SMM 7/65, as "The Jazz Record"; *Ellery Queen's 1969 Mid-Year Anthology*, As "Steps Coming Near.")
6. 6/64 When Love Turns. (CW 21, as "Je t'Aime.")
7. 12/64 Murder After Death.
8. 7/66 It Only Takes a Minute to Die. (*Ellery Queen's All-Star Lineup*, 1967.)

Liberty

1. 10/11/30 Soda Fountain Saga. (Abridged, SMM 3/60, as "Soda Fountain.")

Live Girl Stories

1. 11/28 Hollywood Bound, Part 1.
1. 12/28 Hollywood Bound, Part 2.
1. 1/29   Hollywood Bound, Part 3.
1. 2/29   Hollywood Bound, Part 4.
1. 3/29   Hollywood Bound, Part 5.
         NOTE: This serial was published in Book form as CW 3.

McClure's

1. 10/26 Dance It Off.
2. 8/27   The Gate Crasher.
3. 10/27 The Drugstore Cowboy.

Mystery Book Magazine

1. 8/45   Four Bars of Yankee Doodle. (Expanded into WI 14.)
2. 8/45   The Man Upstairs. (WI 5; CW 20; RSMM 2/46; *Murder for the Millions*, Frank Owen, ed., 1946.)
3. 11/45 Silent As the Grave. (Abridged, WI 6.)
4. 4/46   The Light in the Window. (WI 6.)
5. 3/47   The Boy Cried Murder. (SMM 9/54, under original title; WI 9, as "Fire Escape.")
6. Autumn/47 One Night in Barcelona. (CW 22.)
         NOTE: "Too Good for the Irish," an editorial column quoting from an autobiographical letter of Woolrich, appeared in the January 1947 issue of this magazine.

Pocket Detective

1.   1/37   The Heavy Sugar. (EQMM 12/50.)
2.   3/37   The Humming Bird Comes Home. (WI 16, CW 20, EQMM 3/50, under original title; SMM 2/64, *The Saint Magazine Reader* [Charteris & Santesson, ed., 1966], as "The Humming Bird.")
3.   4/37   Death in Round Three. (EQMM 7/51.)

Saint Mystery Magazine

1.   10/62   The Poker Player's Wife. (Revised, CW 21.)
2.   5/63   Story To Be Whispered. (CW 21, with a different ending.)
                 NOTE: The magazine's title was now changed to *Saint Magazine*.
3.   10/66   Mannequin.
4.   9/67   Intent to Kill.

Serenade

1.   3/34   Between the Acts.
2.   3/34   Insult. (Published under pseudonym of Ted Brooks.)
3.   6/34   The Very First Breakfast.

Shadow

1.   4, 5/47 Death Escapes the Eye. (Revised, CW 15, as "Murder, Obliquely.")
2.   12/47, 1/48 Death Between Dances.
                 NOTE: The February-March 1947 issue of this magazine contains a one-page autobiographical letter from Woolrich.

Smart Set

1.   9/28   Girls, We're Wise to You.
2.   11/28   Girls, I Know Your Line.
                 NOTE: These are articles, not stories.

Story

1.   4/36   The Night Reveals. (WI 4; CW 20; *Fear and Trem-
                bling, Hitchcock, ed., 1948; EQMM 8/48; *Story
                Jubilee*, Whit Burnett, ed., 1965; *Ellery Queen's
                1970 Mid-Year Anthology*.)
2.   10/37   Goodbye, New York. (*The Story Pocket Book* [Whit
                Burnett, ed., 1944], EQMM 3/53, *Ellery Queen's
                1969 Anthology*, under original title; CW 15, as
                "Don't Wait Up for Me Tonight.")

Strange Detective Mysteries

1.   7,8/39 The Street of Jungle Death. (Later expanded into
                CW 9.)

Sweetheart Stories

1.   8/38   Deserted, Part 1.
1.   9/38   Deserted, Part 2.
1.   10/38   Deserted, Part 3.
1.   11/38   Deserted, Part 4.

Ten Detective Aces

1.   9/37   Taxi Dance Murder.

Thrilling Mystery

1.   1/36   Baal's Daughter.

Today's Woman

1.   4/46   They Call Me Patrice. (Later expanded into WI 10.)

Stories Published Only in Book Form

1.   An Apple a Day. (In WI 4.)
2.   The Blue Ribbon. (In WI 11; reprinted in *World's
        Greatest Boxing Stories*, 1952.)
3.   Husband. (In WI 11.)

IV. WOOLRICH AS ADAPTED

A. Movies

The most complete essay in this area is Edward Connor, "Cornell Woolrich on the Screen," *Screen Facts*, Vol. I, No. 5 (1963). James Agee, the greatest film critic of the 1940's, comments penetratingly on several of these movies in *Agee on Film*, Vol. I (1958). Messrs. Nevins, Knott and Thailing disagree at times as to the films' quality with each other and with Connor and Agee, who also differ at times.

1. *Children of the Ritz* (First National, 1929). Directed by John Francis Dillon from a screenplay by Adelaide Heilbron based on CW 2. Players: Dorothy Mackail, Jack Mulhall. "The critics were not enthusiastic. Film Daily said: 'Not for an intelligent audience, but will please the flapper minds.'" Connor, p. 36.

2. *Manhattan Love Song* (Monogram, 1934). Directed by Leonard Fields from a screenplay by Fields and David Silverstein based on CW 6. Players: Robert Armstrong, Nydia Westman, Dixie Lee,

Helen Flint, Franklin Pangborn. "A labored comedy." Connor, p. 36. "It *is* a bit removed from the thing Woolrich actually wrote," Thailing remarks.

3. *Convicted* (Columbia, 1938). Directed by Leon Barsha from a screenplay by Edgar Edwards based on BM 6. Players: Rita Hayworth, Charles Quigley, Marc Lawrence. "The reviews were poor with many comments on the cheapness of production." Connor, p. 37.

4. *Street of Chance* (Paramount, 1942). Directed by Jack Hively from a screenplay by Garrett Fort based on CW 8 *(The Black Curtain)*. Players: Burgess Meredith, Claire Trevor, Louise Platt, Sheldon Leonard. "Of the Woolrich films I have seen, my favorite is *Street of Chance*," Knott writes. "It is one of the rare occasions, I think, when Hollywood made a movie that was better than the book." Thailing says: "I can't quite agree that *Street of Chance* was better than *The Black Curtain.*"

5. *The Leopard Man* (RKO, 1943). Directed by Jacques Tourneur from a screenplay by Ardel Wray based on CW 9 *(Black Alibi)*. Players: Dennis O'Keefe, Jean Brooks, Margo. "Of all Woolrich books brought to the screen *The Leopard Man* was truest to the spirit and content of the original." Connor, p. 38. Knott disagrees: "It had a badly mutilated ending, but the early scenes of terror, especially in the cemetery, were very well done."

6. *Phantom Lady* (Universal, 1944). Directed by Robert Siodmak from a screenplay by Bernard C. Schoenfeld based on WI 1. Players: Ella Raines, Franchot Tone, Thomas Gomez, Alan Curtis, Elisha Cook, Jr. "No great shakes as a movie." Connor, p. 40. Knott differs: "It was well done except for revealing the murderer too early." James Agee remarks: "Some of the dialogue . . . is like a nail on a slate; and the producer also permits a good deal of amateurish reading. Even the effects are not all they might be. . . . The late reels of the picture slacken, and the ending . . . is halfheartedly done. But . . . there is plenty in *Phantom Lady* to enjoy, and to be glad of." *Agee on Film*, Vol. I, pp. 77–78.

7. *Mark of the Whistler* (Columbia, 1944). Directed by William Castle from a screenplay by George Bricker based on BM 19. Players:

Richard Dix, Janis Carter, Paul Guilfoyle, Porter Hall. "High quality." Connor, p. 41.

8. *Deadline at Dawn* (RKO, 1946). Directed by Harold Clurman from a screenplay by Clifford Odets based on WI 3. Players: Bill Williams, Susan Hayward, Paul Lukas, Lola Lane. "At best *Deadline at Dawn* was only a fair picture." Connor, p. 41. Agee comments: "At its worst the picture is guilty of . . . pseudo-realism and pseudo-poetry about the lost little people of a big city. . . . But on the whole I think it is a likable movie. Odets . . . is obviously one of the very few genuine dramatic poets alive." *Agee on Film*, Vol. I, p. 197.

9. *The Black Angel* (Universal, 1946). Directed by Roy William Neill from a screenplay by Roy Chanslor based on CW 10. Players: June Vincent, Dan Duryea, Peter Lorre, Broderick Crawford, Wallace Ford. "As a movie *Black Angel* wasn't bad but the story it told was certainly not the one found in the book, and a very exciting and suspenseful tale got lost in the transfer." Connor, p. 42. Knott dissents: "The Woolrich mood came through perhaps best of any of the movies." Agee remarks: "Most of the people who wrote, directed, photographed, and played in this one have worked as if they believed that no job is so trivial but what it deserves the best you have. I particularly liked Dan Duryea's performance." *Agee on Film*, Vol. I, p. 217.

10. *The Chase* (United Artists, 1946). Directed by Arthur Ripley from a screenplay by Philip Yordan based on CW 11. players: Robert Cummings, Michele Morgan, Steve Cochran, Peter Lorre. Knott says: "It was about the most horribly mutilated picture I have ever seen from any book." Thailing agrees: "The worst mutilation of a Woolrich book was *The Chase* which some simple-minded baboon tried to make out of *The Black Path of Fear.*"

11. *Fall Guy* (Monogram, 1947). Directed by Reginald LeBorg from a screenplay by Jerry Warner based on BM 17. Players: Dennis O'Keefe, Robert Armstrong, Teala Loring, Elisha Cook, Jr.

12. *Fear in the Night* (Paramount, 1947). Written and directed by

Maxwell Shane, based on A 20. Players: Paul Kelly, DeForest Kelley, Ann Doran.

13. *The Guilty* (Monogram, 1947). Directed by John Reinhardt from a screenplay by Robert E. Presnell, Jr., based on DFW 44. Players: Bonita Granville, Don Castle, John Litel, Regis Toomey. "A superior mystery. . . . It stands high among films in which it is im possible to spot the killer before the surprise finale." Connor, p. 43.

14. *I Wouldn't Be in Your Shoes* (Monogram, 1948). Directed by William Nigh from a screenplay by Steve Fisher based on DFW 32. Players: Don Castle, Elyse Knox, Regis Toomey.

51. *Return of the Whistler* (Columbia, 1948). Directed by D. Ross Lederman from a screenplay by Edward Bock and Maurice Tombragel based on A 18 ("All at Once, No Alice"). Players: Michael Duane, Lenore Aubert, Richard Lane, James Cardwell, Anne Shoemaker. "A fair thriller." Connor, p. 43.

16. *Night Has a Thousand Eyes* (Paramount, 1948). Directed by John Farrow from a screenplay by Barre Lyndon and Jonathan Latimer based on GH 1. Players: Edward G. Robinson, Gail Russell, John Lund, Virginia Bruce, William Demarest. "A faithful reproduction of the novel," Knott writes. Nevins dissents: "It's a silly debasement of what may well be Woolrich's greatest novel. An excellent analysis of how and where the film goes off the tracks appears in Gordon Gow, *Suspense in the Cinema*, pp. 125–130 (1968)."

17. *The Window* (RKO, 1949). Directed by Ted Tetzlaff from a screenplay by Mel Dinelli based on MBM 5. Players: Bobby Driscoll, Arthur Kennedy, Barbara Hale, Paul Stewart. "A very well done picture," says Knott.

18. *No Man of Her Own* (Paramount, 1950). Directed by Mitchell Leisen from a screenplay by Sally Benson and Catherine Turney based on WI 10 *(I Married a Dead Man)*. Players: Barbara Stanwyck, Phyllis Thaxter, Richard Denning, John Lund, Lyle Bettger. "There was a strong smell of soap opera about the picture." Connor, p. 45.

19. *Rear Window* (Paramount, 1954). Directed by Alfred Hitchcock from a screenplay by John Michael Hayes based on DD 23. Players: James Stewart, Grace Kelly, Raymond Burr, Wendell Corey, Judith Evelyn, Thelma Ritter. "It was very well done as Hitchcock always is," Knott writes. For a detailed analysis of the film see Robin Wood, *Hitchcock's Films,* pp. 62–71 (1965). See also François Truffaut, *Hitchcock,* pp. 159–166 (1967).

20. *Nightmare* (United Artists, 1956). Written and directed by Maxwell Shane, based on A 20, which he had also adapted and directed in 1947 under the title *Fear in the Night.* Players: Edward G. Robinson, Kevin McCarthy. "It was adequate," Knott states.

21. *The Boy Cried Murder* (Universal International, 1966). Directed by George Breakston from a screenplay by Robin Estridge based on MBM 5. Players: Fraser MacIntosh, Veronica Hurst, Phil Brown, Beba Loncar, Tim Barrett. Thailing writes: "Although the film follows the story line pretty well, it somehow fails to capture Woolrich's moody atmosphere as neatly as the earlier version *The Window.*"

22. *La Mariée Était en Noir* (France, 1967). U.S. title: *The Bride Wore Black.* Directed by François Truffaut from a screenplay by Truffaut and Jean-Louis Richard based on CW 7. Players: Jeanne Moreau, Jean-Claude Brialy, Michel Bouquet, Charles Denner, Claude Rich, Daniel Boulanger, Michel Lonsdale. The great French director's simultaneous homage to Woolrich and to Hitchcock was acclaimed by the critics but failed thumpingly at the box-office. Both Knott and Thailing consider the film one of the two finest screen adaptations of Woolrich.

23. *La Sirène du Mississippi* (France, 1969). U.S. title: *Mississippi Mermaid.* Directed by François Truffaut from his own screenplay based on WI 8 *(Waltz into Darkness).* Players: Jean-Paul Belmondo, Catherine Deneuve, Michel Bouquet, Nelly Borgeaud, Marcel Berbert. Truffaut's second film based on Woolrich changes the time from 1880 to the present and the setting from New Orleans to an island in the Indian Ocean, but remains faithful to the broad outlines of Woolrich's novel, and even manages to make the main characters credible.

Appendix: Woolrich in Argentina

Mr. Norman Miller, a New York film historian, has uncovered three Argentinian films based on Woolrich.

1–A. *El Pendiente* (AAA, 1951). Directed by León Klimovsky from a screenplay by Ulyses Petit de Murat and Samuel Eichelbaum based on DFW 50. Players: Mirtha Legrand, José Cibrián, Francisco de Paula, Héctor Calcaño, Raúl del Valle.

2–A. *Si Muero Antes de Despertar* (San Miguel, 1952). Directed by Carlos Hugo Christensen from a screenplay by Alejandro Casona based on DFW 24 ("If I Should Die Before I Wake"). Players: Néstor Lavarce, Floren Delbene, Blanca del Prado, Homero Cárpena, María Angélica Troncoso.

3–A. *No Abras Nunca esa Puerta* (San Miguel, 1952). Directed by Carlos Hugo Christensen from a screenplay by Alejandro Casona based on DFW 26 and PD 2 ("Somebody on the Phone" and "Humming Bird Comes Home"). Players: Angel Magaña, Roberto Escalada, Renée Dumas, Norma Giménez, Nicolás Fregues.

B. Radio

Here is a representative sampling of Woolrich material as adapted (sometimes by Woolrich himself) for radio.

Last Night. Suspense, 6/15/43. Adapted by Woolrich from DS 5 ("The Red Tide"). For details see the afterword to "The Red Tide" in this volume. With Margo, Kent Smith.

The White Rose Murders. Suspense, 7/6/43. Adapted by Woolrich from BDM 1 ("The Death Rose"). With Maureen O'Hara.

The Singing Walls. Suspense, 9/2/43. From BM 17 ("C-Jag"). With Preston Foster.

Phantom Lady. Lux Radio Theatre, 3/27/44. From the film of the same title based on WI 1. With Brian Aherne, Ella Raines, Alan Curtis.

Post Mortem. Suspense, c1945. From BM 16. With Agnes Moorehead.

I Won't Be a Minute. Suspense, 12/6/45. From DFW 41.

The Black Path of Fear. Suspense, 3/7/46. From CW 11. With Cary Grant.

Deadline at Dawn. Lux Radio Theatre, 5/20/46. From the film of the same title based on WI 3. With Joan Blondell, Paul Lukas, Bill Williams.

Phantom Lady. Mystery Hour, 8/17/46. From WI 1 or the film taken therefrom. With Franchot Tone, Roger Pryor.

Nightmare. Mystery Theatre, 8/30/46. From A 20.

The Chase. This Is Hollywood, 11/9/46. From the film based on CW 11. With Michele Morgan, Robert Montgomery.

They Call Me Patrice. Suspense, 12/12/46. From TW 1, which was later expanded into WI 10 *(I Married a Dead Man)*. With Susan Peters.

The Bride Wore Black. Mystery Theatre, 2/7/47. From CW 7. With June Havoc.

A Death Is Caused. Mystery Playhouse, 1947. From DD 28.

Deadline at Dawn. Mystery Playhouse, 1948. From WI 3 or the film taken therefrom.

Nightmare. Suspense, 3/14/48. From A 20. With Eddie Bracken.

If the Dead Could Talk. Suspense, late 1948. From BM 21.

The Night Reveals. Suspense, early 1949. From Story 1. With Fredric March. Thailing says: "To my mind it is absolutely the greatest Cornell Woolrich story ever done for radio. . . . It has stood out sharply in my mind to this day."

Wardrobe Trunk. RCA Playhouse, 4/4/49. From DFW 12.

Murder Always Gathers Momentum. RCA Playhouse, 10/27/49. From DFW 43.

If I Should Die Before I Wake. Nightmare, 8/25/54. From DFW 24. With Peter Lorre as the child-murderer, a role strikingly similar to the one he played in Fritz Lang's great 1931 film, *M*.

C. Television

Again our checklist of television adaptations of Woolrich is selective and representative rather than exhaustive, but should provide some idea of his adaptability to the medium.

Revenge. Suspense, March 1949. From CW 11 *(The Black Path of Fear)*.

Three O'Clock. Robert Montgomery Presents, c1952. From DFW 36.

Lullaby. Mirror Theater, 10/3/53. From PD 2 ("Humming Bird Comes Home"). With Agnes Moorehead, Tom Drake.

Wait for Me Downstairs. Pepsi-Cola Playhouse, 10/9/53. From DFW 41. With John Hudson, Allene Roberts.

Summer Dance. Mirror Theater, 11/21/53. From Shad 2 ("Death Between Dances"). With Jane Greer, Barbara Bates.

You Take Ballistics. Program unknown, c1954. From Doub D 2.

The Chase. Lux Video Theater, 12/30/54. From the film of the same title, based on CW 11 *(The Black Path of Fear).* With Ruth Roman, Pat O'Brien, James Arness.

Debt of Honor. Stage 7, 2/20/55. From Doub D 7. With Edmond O'Brien.

Husband. Ford Theater, 10/13/55. From the story published originally in WI 11. With Barry Sullivan, Mala Powers, Jonathan Hale.

The Blue Ribbon. Ford Theater, 11/10/55. From the other story published originally in WI 11. With Scott Brady, Gene Barry, Marjorie Rambeau, Stanley Adams.

Once Upon a Nightmare. Fireside Theater, 1/3/56. From DD 22 ("Murder at Mother's Knee"). With Jane Wyman, David Kasday, Arthur Space, Vivi Janiss, Emile Meyer.

The Big Switch. Alfred Hitchcock Presents, 1/8/56. Directed by Don Weis from a teleplay by Richard Carr based on DFW 6 ("Change of Murder"). With George Mathews, Beverly Michaels, George E. Stone, Joseph Downing.

Sit Down with Death. Climax!, 4/26/56. Adapted by James P. Cavanagh from BM 9 ("After-Dinner Story"). With Ralph Bellamy, William Talman, John Williams, Vicki Cummings, Constance Ford.

Momentum. Alfred Hitchcock Presents, 6/24/56. From DFW 43. With Skip Homeier, Joanne Woodward, Ken Christy.

Rendezvous in Black. Playhouse 90, 10/25/56. From CW 12. With Franchot Tone, Laraine Day, Boris Karloff, Tom Drake, Viveca Lindfors, Elizabeth Patterson.

Four O'Clock. Suspicion, 9/30/57. Directed by Alfred Hitchcock from a teleplay by Francis Cockrell based on DFW 36. With E.G. Marshall, Nancy Kelly, Richard Long. This hour-length masterwork is the most faithful adaptation of Woolrich ever made, and

may well be the most suspenseful film in Hitchcock's entire
career.

Bluebeard's Seventh Wife. Schlitz Playhouse of Stars, 3/21/58. From
DFW 15. With Ralph Meeker, Phyllis Avery, Hugh Marlowe.

Post Mortem. Alfred Hitchcock Presents, 5/18/58. Directed by Arthur
Hiller from a teleplay by Robert C. Dennis based on BM 16. With
Joanna Moore, Fred Robbins, Steve Forrest, Roscoe Ates, James
Gregory.

Fire by Night. Moment of Fear, 7/22/60. Adapted by David Davidson
from Story 1 ("The Night Reveals"). With Mark Richman, Fay
Spain, Phyllis Hill, Frank Overton.

Papa Benjamin. Thriller, 3/21/61. Directed by Ted Post from a teleplay by John Kneubuhl based on DM 1. With John Ireland, Jeanne
Bal, Jester Hairston.

Late Date. Thriller, 4/4/61. Directed by Herschel Daugherty from a
teleplay by Donald S. Sanford based on DD 6 ("The Corpse and
the Kid"). With Larry Pennell, Edward C. Platt, Jody Fair, Chris
Seitz. Despite a censorial last-minute reversal of Woolrich's ironic
ending, this is one of the very best adaptations of Woolrich to film,
with a superb Jerry Goldsmith score.

Guillotine. Thriller, 9/25/61. Adapted by Charles Beaumont from BM
12 ("Men Must Die"). With Alejandro Rey, Robert Middleton,
Danielle de Metz. This film is second only to Hitchcock's *Four
O'Clock* in its faithfulness to Woolrich's story and mood and its
evocation of Woolrich's unbearable suspense.

The Black Curtain. Alfred Hitchcock Hour, 11/15/62. Directed by
Sydney Pollack from a teleplay by Joel Murcott based on CW ,8.
With Richard Basehart, Gail Kobe, Lola Albright, Lee Philips,
Harold J. Stone.

Jane Brown's Body. Journey to the Unknown, 10/2/68. Directed by
Alan Gibson from a teleplay by Anthony Skene based on AAF 2.
A rather foolish British attempt to translate Woolrich's horror
novelet of the late Thirties to mod London of the swinging Sixties.
The film-makers had the further uproarious idea of rewriting the
story into a weak imitation of Hitchcock's *Marnie.* This gem was
televised less than a week after Woolrich's burial.